DESPERATE MEASURES

DESPERATE MEASURES

OPUS X™ BOOK NINE

MICHAEL ANDERLE

DISRUPTIVE IMAGINATION®

LMBPN Publishing
PMB 196, 2540 South Maryland Pkwy
Las Vegas, NV 89109

First US edition, October 2020
Version 1.01, January 2021
eBook ISBN: 978-1-64971-016-1
Print ISBN: 978-1-64971-017-8

THE DESPERATE MEASURES TEAM

Thanks to the JIT Readers

James Caplan
John Ashmore
Kelly O'Donnell
Dorothy Lloyd
Deb Mader
Dave Hicks
Peter Manis
Jeff Eaton
Larry Omans
Paul Westman

If I've missed anyone, please let me know!

Editor
Lynne Stiegler

*To Family, Friends and
Those Who Love
to Read.
May We All Enjoy Grace
to Live the Life We Are
Called.*

CHAPTER ONE

Mistakes killed. Julia knew that all too well. She often punished others by taking their lives when they failed her. Sophia's failure of imagination had led to mistakes that cost her life.

Unfortunately, knowing that fundamental truth about mistakes wasn't the same thing as avoiding them. Julia had been forced to accept that harsh lesson.

There had been far too many mistakes in recent years, errors that threatened decades—arguably centuries—of planning, both on her behalf and that of the Core more broadly.

Was she making a mistake now, remaining on Earth with the Last Soldier and the Warrior Princess on the hunt? Julia bit her lip.

She'd intended to leave much sooner, but she had convinced herself that there was a difference between caution and paranoid terror. Small problems and issues lingered for her to resolve here, but it had become obvious she needed to leave soon, or she would likely experience the kind of lethal mistake defined by hubris.

Opportunity remained to salvage her position despite her reversals.

The loss of the Hunter ship had been a devastating blow. She couldn't deny that, though she couldn't admit the ship existed to the rest of the Core.

It had been the key to her goal—the goal of the entire Core really—that required them to maintain technological superiority over all other humans, and eventually over all other races. Oh, the others could benefit from their scraps, but only they should possess the wisdom for full, unfettered control of advanced alien technology, Hunter or Navigator.

Fate intended the Core to rule. That's what Sophia had argued about the discovery of the original Hunter technology on the moon, which had been found by private parties—those who knew how to keep their mouths shut, unlike the team who'd discovered the Navigator tech on Mars.

That same technology had allowed a small circle of like-minded people to live far beyond the known limits of human science and expand their influence. There would be no Core without alien tech.

The ultimate humans were the product of the ultimate alien technology.

The Core was supposed to be leading humanity to greatness, a perfect empire ruled by the perfect rulers—leaders to take the human race into complete dominion over the entire galaxy. Only they could do it because only they were capable of the necessary long-term vision.

Mortality stared down all lifeforms and instilled them with fear. The breadth of humanity's philosophy and religion was devoted to quelling the terror of death, but a true immortal could operate without the ever-present whispers of darkness in the back of their mind.

Who needed gods when the Core could *become* gods? They had only to seize the necessary power.

Julia raised her hand, so pale, so *delicate*. It gave no hint of her true age, but she understood there was damage she couldn't see, genetic problems accumulating. Every survivor in the Core had lived over a century and a half, granting them many more decades than the most advanced technologies of other humans. But if their researchers were correct, the Core members had only a decade left to live.

Goddesses didn't die. She *couldn't* die.

Not yet. Not *ever*.

The problem with relying on advanced ancient technology was never having more than a partial understanding of the tools it depended upon. The Core didn't mind the cost of using the technology, which included the necessary sacrifice of other people.

History was replete with the expenditure of the lower order to serve the higher order, but their old artifacts had now failed them and were nothing more than inert museum pieces. For the first time in decades, they felt the shadow of death hanging over them.

Even though they had foreseen this issue, they had tried to not worry. The Core had been confident they'd find what they needed at each checkpoint in their existence. Based on what their researchers had said, the artifacts recovered from Molino held the greatest promise for further rejuvenation of any discovered in recent years.

True immortality had been within their grasp. They wouldn't have to worry about death's shadow creeping up on them. They would slay death and take dominion over his domain, but only for them.

Julia curled her hand into a fist and sneered. So close, but now their plans were threatened by upstarts. Insects, really. Men and women of no vision who gave their petty support to the pathetic UTC. They'd delayed the ascension of the Core.

The destroyed Hunter ship had been filled with lost technology. It had still been operational. The Core could have harvested it unlike any of the leftover, half-rotted scraps they'd been forced to examine.

The ship would have set them ahead centuries and accelerated their final advance into divinity. They could have been freed of their incessant need to seek out replacements for their failing artifacts and technology. They would have had an easier time reverse-engineering both structure and function.

No, not *they. She.*

Julia needed to remember that. Her ancient allies shared a vision, but it was one she no longer subscribed to. She needed to remove any vestige of implied friendship and focus on her future only.

The other members of the Core didn't realize how many of the Molino artifacts she now controlled. They might suspect, but they couldn't know they hadn't been lost in the destruction of Sophia's ship near Venus.

Julia took a deep breath and settled into her chair, folding her hands in her lap. They must all be thinking what she was thinking.

The Core was too large and too dominated by factions. The interference in her plans was proof of that, as was hers in Sophia's works.

The only way to maintain control over humanity was by decreasing the points of failure and reducing the inherent complexity of politics. This needed to be done in the appropriate way, taking stability into account.

Unfortunately for others, the filtering and attrition of leaders were inevitable.

She chuckled, thinking about the past. In ancient imperial China, the way of the world had been clear. Subjects obeyed rulers because their rulers were granted the Mandate of Heaven. The system was superior as long as the rulers possessed both talent and vision.

It was hard to argue that quibbling, mewling masses could make better decisions than those with power, intelligence, and education. Rebellions were an expression of the ruler failing his or her subjects.

The ancients had understood that.

When the empire suffered, a clever and well-prepared ruler could deal with it, whether it was providing strength to protect the land from barbarians or stored food to deal with natural disasters.

An ill-prepared ruler made his people suffer, which in turn allowed them to justify rebellion by claiming the natural disasters and barbarians were the result of him or her losing the mandate. The ranks of the insurrectionists would swell, and the empire would be toppled without the fundamental belief in the superiority of imperial rule being questioned.

In all dynasties, decline was inevitable. Good rulers would give way to poor rulers with the passing of decades. The mandate would always be lost and a new dynasty would arise, more responsive to the subjects if only because of the simplest and basest of desires: self-preservation.

Thus, the empire would be strong again.

But Julia was different. All members of the Core were different. They could achieve something physically impossible before: a perfect and lasting rule.

Monarchy was only flawed because the skilled ruler would always perish, leaving (eventually) inept offspring. No matter how well-educated a prince or princess might be, the inevitable machinations of chance would ensure an ill-suited ruler would rise.

The reality was that people *needed* central control.

The Core was leaving humanity and the petty pretensions of morality accompanying it behind to make a better, stronger race.

Humanity was a divided, *pathetic* species, one still contending with pointless rebellions while aliens circled their systems, plotting and preparing to destroy them. As the Hunters had consumed the Navigators, the Local Neighborhood races could set themselves on the UTC and obliterate humanity down to the last man, woman, and child.

True leadership was the answer to the question of the future. That was what humanity required—a perfect ruler who would never age, never risk the fall of her empire by bequeathing it to incompetent children.

The ruler would fuse with the UTC and become its brain and heart.

It didn't matter if the Immortal Empress would inhabit the shadows and use puppets. In the beginning, they would be necessary, and as the decades passed and firmer control was established, the illusion of self-rule could be wiped away until there was only a United Human Empire that stretched into the future, with humanity pushing back against the Leems, Zitarks, and all other creatures who thought they deserved to exist in the galaxy.

If necessary, they could be wiped out. Countless humans had been sacrificed for the species' perfect future, so why not aliens? Humanity would become the new Hunters.

But the empire wouldn't come without struggle. A proper ruler always used subordinates, and it was the nature of humanity to fight for control when there wasn't a single clear ruler controlling everything.

As long as the other members of the Core existed, they would represent a threat to her future rule and thus a threat to the United Human Empire and the future of the species.

There was only one good choice left. To protect the human race, Julia needed to eliminate the rest of the Core. However, she would have to step lightly lest they figure it out and target her, or she would wreak more chaos and disrupt her long-term plan. That didn't change what she had to do.

"What I do, I do for humanity," she murmured quietly.

It was time to take the first steps and rely on powerful allies, including the very Core she would eliminate. As long as certain people and organizations continued their hunt, her plans would never come to fruition.

Julia tapped her PNIU and made a couple of quick motions to initiate a call. She needed to preserve resources before they were lost. She could use them as both sword and shield.

A data window appeared, displaying a smiling Shoji. The man was always unflappable, so collected in his own way. Julia appreciated the honest rages of some of the other members of the Core, if only because it made them more predictable. The only member of the Core worse than Shoji was Constance, whose quiet nature concealed a woman who might be even more ruthless than Sophia or Julia.

"It's been a while," Shoji offered, his smile brightening. "Not that I haven't been expecting your call."

"I wanted to speak to you before I leave the system in the next week or two," Julia replied with a slight frown. "I wanted to make certain things clear."

Shoji raised an eyebrow. "You mentioned leaving the Solar System, but when you didn't immediately do so, I presumed it was more whim than plan." He waited for a second. "Are you still holding such angst over our losses?"

"It's not just me. It's dangerous for *all* of us." Julia frowned. "Our enemies have momentum in their campaign against us, even if they don't understand who they are fighting. The Last Soldier and the Warrior Princess are very resourceful and effective. Too much so, if you ask me. Ignoring this will only lead to death, as Sophia found out."

Shoji looked bored. "They have the backing of powerful elements in the intelligence community, and it's not as if you haven't taken advantage of them in your plans. Even though we have much control over the government, it's hard to stop everything. I've complained about that in the past, but alas, some lack my foresight."

"It goes beyond the government." Julia shook her head. "If it were just them, things wouldn't have become so desperate. There's a deeper concern here."

"Would you care to provide a specific accusation?" Shoji asked. "Because that's what your tone suggests."

"We can't be the only ones in the Core playing such games," Julia replied. "The other members might know what's happening. They might have chosen to use our greatest threat as their weapon."

"You did suggest that."

"I suggested coopting them."

She watched him carefully, half-suspecting Shoji of being responsible for some of her recent failures. Julia maintained no illusions that the man wouldn't betray her if it was to his advantage. She calculated they hadn't yet reached that point, but there might be some hidden variable confounding her conclusion.

Even a goddess made mistakes.

"Perhaps." Shoji unfolded a fan and waved it in front of him with a smile. "Or perhaps vengeance provides a divine focus all its own, and we were foolish to wipe out the Last Soldier's friends on Molino. In either event, our enemies have had some spectacular successes. I acknowledge that. I always have, but that's not the same thing as fearing them."

"I think they're getting too close. I believe Sophia

wasn't the only one who might fall. Now that they are creatures of the government's ghosts, it's more difficult to strike at them without risk. We have time, especially because of the Molino artifacts. We should retreat, let the trail grow cold, and make preparations for other plans, including further artifact research and recovery. Even after some of our losses, we're not without resources."

"You want to flee and go where?" Shoji melodramatically fluttered his fan. "Our influence might reach everywhere, but our power is stronger here in the heart of humanity. My opinion? To travel away from Earth makes us more vulnerable, not less. They'll still pick away at our power base, and we'll be weaker once we return."

"I intend to stay close to Earth. I'm not going to the frontier."

Shoji closed the fan with a snap of his wrist. "Is this about the incident on the edge of the Solar System?"

Julia kept her face placid despite her quickening heart. "What are you talking about?"

"There was something unusual at the edge of the Solar System, an explosion associated with a comet of all things. What's more curious is that military and intel communities have made obvious movements to conceal data about the incident, and have succeeded so thoroughly that even my people are having trouble determining what happened other than that there might be something odd with a comet. Given that our enemies now have access to a jump drive, that might explain it."

Julia nodded slowly. "My people have mentioned it as well and are looking into it. And that jumpship is all the more reason why we should put some distance between the Earth and us."

She wasn't sure how much the rest of the Core knew about the jumpship, but she wasn't prepared to try to argue against its existence.

Someone in the Core had sent the other ship before the arrival of the Last Soldier and his little friends. Given the length of time involved, she'd suspected it was Sophia, but she couldn't rule out Shoji. The man was nothing if not patient, even by the standards of the Core.

Desperation crept in. She could use the Last Soldier and the Warrior Princess against Shoji and the Core to destroy them immediately. She could push forward and do it herself with reckless abandon. It was her long-term plan.

Would a delay end in her death?

She tossed the thought to the side. Unfortunately, it couldn't happen quickly. The balance of control needed to be carefully reconstructed with the loss of any member of the Core, just as it had been after the loss of Sophia. Destroying the other long-term members with careful planning would offer her what she needed for success, but a rapid collapse of the Core risked discovery of the remaining members and the loss of their accumulated power.

Subtle, slow destruction was required. However, she wasn't going to go out of her way to protect other members of the Core if they refused to accept the obvious.

Shoji let out a quiet titter. "It's only two people, and we're acting as if they are an entire empire."

"They have been effective, though," Julia replied. "And they are a threat because they have far more than the resources of two people backing them, including the AI and the ship. We know that now. We should have killed them when we had the chance." She thought for a moment. "Okay, an easier chance."

"Why not kill them now?" Shoji shrugged, a bored look on his face. "Feel free to leave if you want. I'll be more than happy to handle it. It's only fitting, considering how much I contributed to the Molino incident."

Julia scoffed. "How are you going to succeed where I failed?"

"By doing something you don't always understand. Sometimes the best way to handle someone is by giving them exactly what they want." Shoji flicked his wrist dismissively. "Don't worry about it. I'll take care of them, and the less you know, the less it will lead back to you."

"Shoji, it could lead back to you."

"Perhaps." He smiled. "But if that happens, I know you'll mourn me for at least five minutes before devouring my resources." His smile dimmed but didn't disappear. "Since we're talking about killing people, I find I already miss the Ascended Brotherhood. They were ever-so-useful tools."

"I can't deny that. Our *yaoguai*-heavy strategy could use improvement. It's difficult to fully control such creatures, even with implants."

"That's true," Shoji replied. "But they're cheaper overall to produce, and we don't have to worry about them being captured and interrogated." He tilted his head. "That gives me an idea."

She waited for a moment before asking, "An idea about what?"

"A specific way to take care of our nemeses. It will be costly."

"You can do what you want. I'm departing for New Pacifica. If you can eliminate them with such ease, you deserve the glory and power that comes with it."

Shoji stuck out his lip and let out a long, sad sigh. "New Pacifica? That's a long trip. Two months, last time I went there."

"Yes," Julia replied. "It also means I'll be flying away from Earth in case your plan fails. I'll send you a transmission before my final departure, but it'll be soon."

"Then if we don't talk directly again, let me wish you a good trip and a safe, happy eventual return."

A faint hint of mockery colored his tone. Julia didn't care. Her ascension to the divine wouldn't be stopped.

CHAPTER TWO

July 7, 2230, Wales, Cardiff, Pwyll Tower

Erik hung from the edge of the balcony, his feet dangling into the dark abyss extending beneath him. Emma claimed the jump was necessary because of unexpected drone activity, but he suspected that was one of her sick jokes.

He didn't think she would let Jia or him die, but she might have no problem letting them fall hundreds of feet to make a point about the fallibility of fleshbags.

It didn't matter. Both he and Jia had made the jump and were now on the level of the infiltration target, the massive building in front of them, which was the center of Ceres Galactic operations in the city.

With a soft grunt of exertion, he pulled himself up and over the railing onto the balcony, ending his experiment with high-altitude thrill-seeking for the night. Heights didn't bother him unless they were accompanied by gunfire.

Jia matched his motion with easy grace. They could

wait for the damned window to open without hanging and waiting to fall to their deaths hundreds of stories below.

"How are we on the drone, Emma?" Erik asked. "Trouble?"

"I've redirected it without a problem. There's also no evidence of unusual transmission. You should be fine for entrance."

"It'd be nice to complete a mission without having to shoot someone," Jia suggested as she looked around. "Or blowing anything up."

"Nice, but not as fun," Erik replied. "And I don't think Alina brought us aboard because of our fine sneaking skills."

Emma piped in. "Does it count as sneaking if there's no one left alive to see you?"

He shook his head. "Too philosophical for me."

Erik stood and dusted off the pants of his tactical suit. Between the suit and the dark-tinted helmets, no one would recognize them, but the need for secrecy also meant he couldn't bring his TR-7. Having to at least attempt to sneak around was one big disadvantage of working for Alina and the Intelligence Directorate.

Alina had complained that Erik's and Jia's reliance on certain equipment was making it too easy to identify their involvement in incidents. Sometimes that could be useful, but not always. Since the death of Sophia Vand, the ID had become aggressive on multiple fronts, and the more they could keep their tools in the dark, the more successful they would be. That didn't make it any less annoying to Erik.

When he was a cop openly investigating crimes, he'd never worried about people identifying him. His fame, along with his partner's, had helped keep things under control in their encounters. Now they had a new job and new restraints, but the fringe benefits, including the ship, were nice. Erik couldn't complain too much, but that didn't mean he wouldn't complain at all.

"So much for being freelance," Erik muttered underneath his breath. "We stand out, she says. We need to take that into consideration, she says."

"It doesn't hurt to be careful now and again," Jia offered. "Especially when we are potentially outnumbered and outgunned."

She smiled and glanced over the edge of the balcony at the lights of the city below them and those marking flitters. Erik followed her gaze, wondering if there was trouble but seeing nothing out of the ordinary for a decent-sized city.

His recent travels had recalibrated how he thought of things. He was no longer using Neo SoCal as his basis for comparison, or not always.

Cardiff might lack the density and population of Neo SoCal, but Pwyll Tower was almost as impressive as a Hexagon building, which made sense given this was a Ceres Galactic-owned property.

Erik's initial investigations had pointed toward the company, and his subsequent efforts, along with those of the Intelligence Directorate, had reinforced the initial suspicion. He wasn't particularly surprised to be in a Ceres building, only surprised it'd taken so long for him to end up at another one.

It also proved that like in most things in history, there was probably a small group of people pulling the strings. Fancy tech and half-alien agents didn't change the solution.

A bullet to the head or a missile to their ship was usually the last word in a conversation.

Erik's quest wouldn't stop corruption in the UTC, but it didn't have to. He just wanted the Knights Errant to be able to rest in peace, and he would accomplish that by making sure the people who'd killed them rested in pieces.

"Speaking of standing out," Jia began. "If things get heated, Emma, don't use the turret unless absolutely necessary. An MX-60 with a collapsible turret pretty much screams, 'Erik Blackwell and Jia Lin were here.'"

"But the turret is so much fun," Emma complained.

"I'm with her on that." Erik bobbed his head in agreement.

Even if it'd become more Emma's toy and not a tool always available or practical, he'd used it often enough.

"If I can't use my favorite gun, you don't get to use your favorite gun," he added.

"You should see the look of fear in the eyes of the gun goblins when I use it." Emma's voice was filled with glee. "There's just something about having the ability to lay down death and destruction."

"We're not here for fun or laying down death and destruction," Jia countered, making sure Erik caught her look. "We're here to get some intel. Death and destruction are strictly optional."

Erik nodded. "That's like saying the cherry on an ice cream sundae is optional. Sure, you don't have to have one, but why not go for it?"

A last-minute transmission by Alina had indicated their mission-objective data wouldn't be around the next day, forcing them to take immediate action.

"I'm almost into the internal systems," reported Malcolm over the comm. "Just need a couple more minutes, then you'll be able to go anywhere you want on this level without anyone knowing you're there. As easy on the eyes as one of my shirts."

"The government should just rush into every damned Ceres building themselves," Erik grumbled. "This death-by-a-thousand-cuts crap gets tiring."

"That would probably take every CID agent from across the UTC," Jia often threw her metaphorical researcher hat on her head at some of the most inopportune moments. "I know Alina said they've been able to follow up on intel and data, including the stuff we gave them, but she didn't say every individual member of Ceres Galactic is a member of the conspiracy, just that the company is heavily involved in it. The ID and CID are going to have to be surgical about this."

"They probably just don't want the economy to collapse once everyone realizes one of the biggest corporations in the UTC is controlled by assholes who would blow up domes or fund terrorists just to get an advantage."

Jia shrugged. "There is something to be said for considering the disruptive effects of our actions. It won't do us any good to take down the conspiracy if we hurt a lot of innocent people in the process. Like I mentioned, surgical approach."

"Screw the surgery." Erik patted the rifle slung over his shoulder. "Sometimes a little lead anti-health supplements followed by rapid cauterization is the best therapy. We just make sure we only apply it to the people who deserve it. Shit, sometimes you just need to blow a bastard into enough pieces they can't put him back together again. I'm going to name that the Humpty-Dumpty Strategy."

Jia tilted her head, but Erik couldn't see her expression underneath the helmet. "We're winning, Erik. We're on offense now, not defense. We don't need to try harder than we are, because at this rate, we *will* take them down."

"I'm a shark ready for my feeding frenzy." Erik scuffed his boot against the deck. "That's the thing. Every time we nail more of the bastards, I see that they aren't the all-powerful gods they think they are, and that makes me want to keep going forward and finish them off right away."

"That's what we're doing. We've got the backing of *the* two major government directorates, a unique AI, and a good support crew. This ends with the conspiracy dead and the UTC a better place, as long as we don't get ahead of ourselves."

"Almost there with the windows," Malcolm reported. "It'll take a bit more on the cameras. The local systems are unusual."

"Don't know if I care," Erik remarked before continuing with Jia. "I'm eager to take some people on."

Emma snickered. "And you both act as if *I'm* the trigger-happy one. Incidentally, there are no issues with the local exterior drone and camera redirects, but that doesn't guarantee anything about long-range cameras and drones. I wouldn't advise removing your helmets unless absolutely necessary unless you want to be identified."

"Duly noted," Erik replied. He slipped the rifle off his shoulder and flipped off the safety.

Jia shook her head with a disappointed sigh and gestured to the stun pistol holstered in his belt. "Remember, we're supposed to go non-lethal on this unless we have no other choice. Even if we limit ourselves to this one level, we can't be sure everyone in there works for the conspiracy."

"Frizzle fraken gander poppin'." Erik flipped the safety back on before slinging the rifle over his shoulder again and drawing the stun pistol. "I hope we don't end up ambushed by something nasty and get killed because we have our stun pistols out. I'd hate to die because we were being too nice to conspiracy assholes pretending to be corp employees.

She eyed him. "'Frizzle fraken gander poppin'?'"

He shrugged. "I'm trying something out. Your parents— well, particularly your mom—always gives me this look when I curse, so I'm trying to come up with alternatives."

"You know that sounds odd, right?"

He looked at her. "You want me to say FF?"

She put up a hand. "No. I'm fine. Just...try something else."

He nodded.

The window remained opaque and dark, and without camera access, they couldn't know they weren't walking right into a hallway filled with heavily armed Tin Men.

Erik wasn't sure he cared. He didn't *want* a clean mission. If it were too easy, the conspiracy wouldn't feel the pain. That might be better from an intelligence operation standpoint, but it didn't satisfy his vengeful spirit as well.

"Thousands of people work in this building," Jia commented while drawing her stun pistol. "I doubt the conspiracy would have lasted very long if they filled buildings with their operatives. The CID or ID would have picked them off fast."

"Maybe they give a really nice benefits package for selling your soul," Erik joked. "But I'll try to not kill anyone unless they have it coming. I hope they'll reconsider their career choices after that."

"About thirty seconds," Malcolm reported. "Get ready, boys and girls, for a little high-level breaking and entering."

"I could have handled everything." Emma sniffed. "The millisecond difference in my response time during multitasking isn't that big a deal, but I will admit Mr. Constantine is reasonably competent."

"That almost sounds like a compliment," Malcolm retorted.

"I should correct it to 'reasonably competent for a fleshbag.' Obviously, not competent compared to me."

Malcolm sighed. "And there went my compliment, floating down to the ground, where it exploded into bloody chunks on impact."

Erik flexed his fingers over the stun pistol. He rarely used the weapon, so it felt unfamiliar and unnatural.

"According to that intel Alina gave us," he began, "the room containing the system IO port we want to hack is going to be shielded, so it doesn't matter who is in control of things until we find it and get the transmitter set up." He smirked. "I hope this doesn't end up like that shit in Cairo last month, speaking of needing bigger guns."

"There weren't that many gun goblins by your standards," Emma interjected. "So much whining. You *barely* got shot."

"It's not whining to want the best equipment available

for the job, and the point is to shoot the other guys, not get shot ourselves."

"I know that, but…hmmm." Emma stopped.

Erik snickered and lowered his pistol toward the holster. "It *is* Cairo, isn't it?"

"It's more that it's unfortunate timing," Emma explained. "There is no immediate danger like in that other incident, but this could prove troublesome."

"We got some *yaoguai* on the other side?" Erik asked.

"I've got immediate camera access now," Malcolm reported. "Nothing unusual on the other side, and the security patrols aren't anywhere near the window."

"The problem isn't inside the building," Emma explained. "There is a heavy increase in drone and external camera activity, and it's requiring more attention on my part to ensure no one spots you."

"Screw it." Erik rolled his shoulders. "We don't have time to wait around."

"Okay," Malcolm interjected. "As I said, it looks like it's empty. I'm ready to open everything up whenever you are."

"Get ready." Erik pointed his pistol at the door. "If there's a bunch of Tin Men on the other side, I'm going to be pissed."

Jia patted one of her stun grenades. "Why do I have a feeling I'll be getting a lot of use out of these?"

"Whatever works, but I'm not going to let myself get gunned down."

With a hiss, the window slid open, the soft light spilling out. The hallway was dim but bright enough to negate the need for night vision.

There were also no *yaoguai*, Tin Men, or killer bots

waiting on the other side, only a long, empty hallway filled with doors. Emma gave him nav arrows in his smart lenses based on the intel and building blueprints.

Jia looked back and forth before giving a satisfied nod. "Now we have to hope the intel Alina sent us is good."

"And if it's not?" Malcolm asked.

"Then we'll have risked our lives for nothing."

Erik looked over his shoulder to make sure no one was sneaking up. "Typical Wednesday night."

CHAPTER THREE

Jia followed Erik through the window, keeping a firm grip on her stun pistol. Based on their preliminary briefing and examination of the building, the locals relied heavily on live security rather than bots. She didn't want to fling lead if it was not necessary, but Erik did have a point.

If it came down to it, she would do what was necessary to protect Erik. In all their time together, they'd never killed anyone who didn't have it coming. That might change in the future, but for the moment, it at least confirmed they had good instincts.

Erik jogged forward, his face hidden by the dark helmet. Jia didn't like not being able to see him, being far too used to all his expressions and shifts in his eyes. They told her more about a situation than any words. She tried to think of a way to add a feed from his helmet that wouldn't be distracting.

Though when she thought about it, she realized they didn't need verbal orders or exchanges in battle. All their time together, both in actual combat and training, had trained them to do what they needed and the appropriate timing. Timing cues went a long way.

"Stop!" Malcolm shouted.

"What?" Jia asked quietly. Her helmet would keep her voice from traveling, but she didn't want to yell and attract attention.

"Duck into the side hallway. There's a patrol coming, but they'll hit a corner and turn away from the way you want to go."

Jia moved to the side and glanced at Erik. Surprising the guards would be trivial, but every confrontation risked reinforcements showing up. Malcolm and Emma were doing a good job, but they didn't have complete control of the building, and if it were a conspiracy-related level, they might not be able to achieve that without alerting the enemy.

Erik muttered and followed Jia. It had been a couple of weeks since their last major mission. Maybe he was craving something more than training?

Jia would do what she needed to in combat, but she'd conquered her demons for now. Losing control wasn't much of a concern. She'd always be grateful for Erik for recognizing her problem and steering her toward a solution.

She didn't think he had the same issue. This was less bloodlust than boredom. Boys and their lethal toys.

"Okay, you can go now. Just be quiet," Malcolm sent. "But this is weird."

"Weird, how?" Jia asked.

"I'm only seeing a small patrol, and although I don't

have total access to their security system, there are all sorts of indications of major bot reserves."

Erik snorted. "Good mission briefing there, Alina."

"Nobody's perfect," Jia replied with a shrug. "Are the bots patrolling?"

"No," Malcolm confirmed. "All inactive."

"Then we're good."

Erik and Jia continued their quick movement down the hallway, glancing at the intersection before heading across. Malcolm was watching their back, but that didn't mean they could eschew situational awareness. A clever attacker might spoof a camera feed to surprise their enemies.

They should know. They'd used exactly that tactic on *their* enemies.

The near-identical hallways were like a maze. If they weren't being led exactly to their destination, they could have easily gotten lost.

"Hmm," Emma sent.

"Hmm?" Erik echoed. "What the hell does that mean?"

"The local police comm is now rather lively," Emma replied. "Unusually so. There don't appear to be any unusual incidents going on, but they've received reports of a possible terrorist attack, and they're gathering forces."

"Interesting timing," Jia commented.

"Yeah, too interesting," Erik complained. "If the conspiracy caught wind that we might be hitting Cardiff, they might have decided to throw some cops at us."

"Or the conspiracy might just be paranoid. We're not the only people affiliated with the Intelligence Directorate that have been hitting them. It might be something they're doing because they're preparing to transfer the data."

"Using cops as a shield is a good tactic," Erik counted. "They know our backgrounds. Even if they think I'm a revenge-obsessed loose cannon, they'd have a hard time believing Jia Lin would shoot cops."

"Would they actually use police?" Jia shook her head. "I mean, we're not going to mercilessly gun down police officers, but having the authorities sniffing around might work out poorly for them. Even when Neo SoCal was at its worst, there were good officers willing to dig to find the truth."

"Like you."

Jia grinned. "Besides me. And it's too high a risk. The more the conspiracy is wounded, the less ability they have to clean up after themselves. They need to be subtle, not flashy, to survive."

"Good point. I'll worry about cops if and when they come." Erik continued down the hall at a quick jog. "Just keep an ear on it, Emma. I'd prefer not to be surprised, but I only care if they're coming our way. We'll let the locals handle any terrorists."

"Understood, Erik," Emma replied.

"It sounds like a good plan," Jia added. "If we get the data and get out of there, there won't be any trouble with anyone, guards or cops."

"You think that's going to happen?" Erik asked, slowing.

The nav arrows indicated their target room was close. If they were lucky, the intel about the room being shielded was wrong, but the Lady was capricious on her best days.

"No other patrols nearby," Malcolm reported. "They're way far away now. No active bots, either."

"That's good to hear." Erik stopped in front of a door at

the end of the corridor and nodded. "This is the one."

Jia pressed her palm against the access panel. Nothing happened, which was not a surprise. Luck had its limits, or maybe the Lady wanted to challenge them.

"Can you open it for us, Malcolm?" she asked.

The door slid open.

"I know," Malcolm transmitted. "I'm awesome in every way that matters."

Jia stepped into the small office. A mahogany desk, a potted green orchid in the corner, and a comfortable-looking chair were the only major features besides their target, an IO port in the side wall.

"Not what I expected," Erik offered. "Emma, Malcolm, can you hear us?"

"I'm...trouble..." Emma replied.

"Me..." Malcolm added.

"So some of the intel was accurate," Erik mumbled as he headed to insert the upload/download link into the IO port.

Jia pulled the small transmitter rod off her belt and expanded it into a tripod. She set it just inside the door and tapped some quick commands into her PNIU.

"Ah," Emma sent, her voice much clearer. "Much better."

"But we're going to have to keep the door open." Erik frowned. "I'm not loving that."

"Initiating transmission sequence," Emma reported. "Mr. Constantine can continue monitoring things, and I'll do my best to be swift about this."

"I can do that," Malcolm added cheerfully. "Good news, the patrols have left the level. I'm not seeing anyone on the cameras, and I've already shielded you on the internal thermal scans, which means there's no one on those either. I've got the initial security protocols disabled temporarily."

"A nice and easy job," Erik replied. "I'll admit that can be fun in its own way."

"I'm glad you think so," commented Jia.

They waited, watching the hallway and not talking. Jia tilted her neck back and forth and rolled her arms to try to keep stiffness from settling in. Fights were one thing; waiting between potential fights was painful.

"This is odd," Emma commented after a few more minutes.

"Good-odd or bad-odd?" Erik asked.

"The police are receiving multiple reports of an incident, but it's on the other side of the city. The locals are swarming the area."

"There might really be a terrorist." Erik shrugged. "I'm not going to cry about having to worry about less trouble."

"Something's wrong," Malcolm shouted. "I—"

The door slammed shut. The residual nav marker and additional AR indicators vanished from Jia's smart lenses.

Jia hissed in frustration. "I think we've gone past bad passive transmission interference to active jamming."

Erik pulled a breach disk from a pouch and attached it to the door. He stuck his fingers in the notches and twisted the device.

"It's pretty safe to say that if they're jamming us, they know we're here," Erik muttered. "Cairo all over again."

Jia groaned, her eyes narrowing. "You don't get to declare that just because it involves a surprise. Using that logic, *everything* is Cairo."

He smiled. "Now you're getting it."

Erik tapped the breach disk and stepped away. Seconds later, the interior of the door blew out in a bright explosion, leaving a pile of rubble and smoke. Whatever they had done to partially shield the room under normal circumstances hadn't included reinforcing the door.

He nodded at the IO port. "Time for Plan B. I doubt Emma got everything we needed."

Jia removed a preprogrammed data rod and jammed it into the port. There were too many variables in the plan. The rod was supposed to suck up data and decrypt it later to find what they were looking for, allegedly some conspiracy operations data.

That plan required Emma's programming preparations to be near-perfect and Alina's collated intel to be correct. The latter had already proven questionable.

There was also the harsh reality that even if everything else went according to plan, Jia and Erik had to successfully evacuate with the rod under fire from an enemy who knew they were there.

Erik stepped into the hallway and chuckled. "Knew it. Didn't need Malcom to tell me their bots are active."

Familiar scuttling and scratching noises filled the corridors. He holstered his stun pistol, whipped his rifle down, and fired a burst. Jia stepped through the smoldering wreckage of the door, armed in the same manner.

She cleared the doorway and spun toward the source of the noise, a swarm of advancing spider bots. To her surprise, stun rods rather than stun rifles or slugthrowers protruded from their fronts.

Local security wanted them alive. That suggested it

wasn't a conspiracy trap. If it had been, they would have known better than to use bots.

After her initial encounters with security bots alongside Erik, Jia had spent a lot of time studying common bot designs. That made it easy for her to pick out their weak spots.

A single shot cracked from her rifle, ripping through a bot and sending the multi-legged machine to the ground, twitching and sparking. Erik kept up near-rhythmic bursts, his shots shredding his targets.

"Emma? Malcolm?" Jia asked, hoping the jamming had been limited to the single room.

There was no response. Jia squeezed off another shot as Erik reloaded. Broad-spectrum jamming was a two-edged sword. The bots could continue functioning with their previous programming, but that meant they couldn't get any updates and had to rely on their AI for engagement. The enemy would also lose some of their cameras.

Jia and Erik continued to fire. The pile of broken bots and parts grew denser, slowing the reinforcements and making them easier targets. Spider bots were a big step down from the Ascended Brotherhood.

The area might be jammed and the pair trapped behind an advancing horde of security bots, but Jia couldn't help but make a game of it, trying to maintain her speed and precision as she destroyed the bots. Part of her felt a little sorry for whoever was responsible for the security budget. Bots weren't cheap, and Erik and Jia were burning off a lot of money in a short period of time.

The raging torrent of security bots dwindled to a swift river and then a mere trickle as they continued to fall to the rifles. The last bot stepping into the hallway fell under the cruel dual attentions of Erik and Jia, spinning and sparking from the barrage.

Footfalls sounded from ahead, but no one entered the hallway. That was probably the guard patrol that had left, with reinforcements.

"Whoever you are, you should surrender right now before you get hurt," shouted a guard from around the corner. "We've jammed your little external hack. Unless you want to end up on the frontier breaking large rocks into smaller rocks, you better surrender right now."

"We carved through your bots, and you're telling us to surrender?" Erik shouted back. "I don't think you get who you're dealing with."

There was scratching in the distance, followed by a loud thud.

Jia yanked a stun grenade from her belt. "They're stalling."

Erik grabbed his own stun grenade. "Grab the rod, and let's fight our way back to where we came in."

Jia rushed back into the room, pulled out the data rod, and shoved it into a pocket. They might not have gotten a complete data dump, but they'd done well with partial data in the past. She rejoined Erik in the hallway.

They nodded to each other and charged forward, leaping over the downed bots and closing on the corner where human enemies awaited. It was time to force their way through.

Erik smiled. *Fun times!*

CHAPTER FOUR

Halfway through their charge, Erik and Jia flung their grenades in almost perfect unison. Without exchanging a word, they both targeted the wall for a bounce but chose different locations. This wasn't the first time they'd sent grenades around a corner.

The guards shouted as the pair continued moving forward. The partners tossed another pair of stun grenades, slinging their rifles over their shoulders and drawing their stun pistols.

When they moved around the corner, men lay on the floor, unmoving. Two survivors near the rear of the security guards backpedaled, their eyes wide and their confidence shaken by their downed comrades. Erik and Jia put two quick blasts into them and sent them to join their friends.

They continued running past the guards toward the entry window. With everything jammed, it was their best chance of finding Emma and the MX 60. It was a good plan except for the sound of metal striking something hard in rapid succession coming from somewhere in front of them.

"Sounds like another bot swarm," Erik suggested, swapping his stun pistol for his rifle. "These guys don't know when they've lost."

Despite his confident speech, he had already burned through half his ammo. The mission wasn't supposed to turn into a huge assault. Jia was more selective with her fire, so she might have more, but they weren't going to win a battle of attrition if it involved taking on hundreds of bots.

They slowed as they approached the next intersection, and the sound of the approaching enemy grew closer. Their new foe emerged about twenty meters away, making it closer to their window.

It wasn't a swarm of spider bots like Erik suspected, but rather a dark serpentine bot with ten legs. A long barrel stuck out of the front of the three-meter body. With a resounding crack, the bot fired.

Erik hissed in pain as a round struck his shoulder. His tactical suit stopped it from penetrating, but it still felt like a hammer blow, and his shoulder throbbed. He ducked into a side hallway under cover of a burst from his rifle. Jia jumped to the other side and fired two shots.

Their bullets bounced off the shell of the bot with sparks. The machine replied with another blast that ripped into the wall.

"What the hell is that thing?" Erik barked. "I've never seen a bot like that."

"A T902 Torch Dragon," Jia explained. "I've read about them. Newer design, just came out this year." She let out a bitter laugh. "They were designed to make up for the deficiencies of heavy security bots in restricted environments like hallways, including improved AI targeting to determine friend or foe. Originally, they were supposed to be anti-terror weapons."

The torch dragon's next shot ripped a corner off the wall near Jia. Erik hadn't gotten a great look at the barrel, but the destructive power and roar suggested it wasn't a small weapon. If he hadn't been wearing his tactical suit, he might have lost a good chunk of his shoulder.

Erik took a couple deep breaths. His arm throbbed, and there was a good chance the impact had cracked a bone. They wouldn't win a sustained fight against the bot.

He grabbed his only remaining grenade, which was plasma, and armed it. "I need you to draw its attention so I can toss the grenade. Or will this go down to an EMP?"

The torch dragon punctuated Erik's sentence for him by shooting the floor near him. He was surprised the thing wasn't advancing faster.

"It's hardened against EMP," Jia explained. "Okay, I'm giving you your window on three, two, one."

She spun around the corner to squeeze off a burst and immediately ducked back behind the wall. The torch dragon fired twice and reduced the amount of corner she could hide behind. Jia hissed in pain.

Erik took his opportunity clearing his own corner to confirm the location of the bot before hurling his grenade and hurrying back behind the wall. A round whizzed by his head; he didn't want to test the effectiveness of the helmet.

The hallway lit up with the explosion, but any pride in the attack vanished as the bot fired twice more, once toward Erik and once toward Jia. He ducked around the corner for less than a second to confirm the position and damage to the torch dragon.

Though there were some scorch marks on the body, the bot had closed in and was otherwise undamaged. Erik didn't stay exposed long enough to confirm much more.

"It must be a T903," Jia muttered as she crouched.

"Huh?"

"They've got an experimental anti-grenade point-defense system," she explained ruefully. "So much for taking us alive."

"Everything's got a weakness," Erik countered. "That thing can't be perfect."

"It's ironic, actually. It's got an even more restricted angle of fire than King Sentries and weaker armor on the bottom. If we could get past the cannon and keep mobile, we could probably take it out with sustained AP fire." Her voice trailed off, her breathing labored.

"What's wrong?"

She pointed to a hole in her vest and a round flattened against her chest. "It didn't make it through, but it still hurts."

"I know the feeling." Erik replaced his current magazine with AP rounds. "So, we've got to charge this bastard and light him up while we're right next to him."

"That cannon isn't rapid-fire, but it packs a punch."

"I know." Erik grinned. "All we have to do is not die."

"Oh. Is it that simple?" Jia commented as she swapped in an AP magazine. "That should be our plan every time."

"If I go first, I can take the brunt of it and give you time to close the distance. You're more agile than me, and you've studied the bot."

She hissed when her body twitched. "This plan is insane."

"As compared to most of our plans?" he asked her.

"True enough," she agreed. "Stupid Wednesdays."

More torch dragon rounds blasted off chunks of the wall. It was closing the distance, judging by the sound of its pointed legs on the metal floor and its firing.

"We could try retreating and finding our way out of the building some other way," Jia suggested.

Erik shook his head. "Emma's not going to be able to stop every drone or vehicle that might come to investigate the MX 60 next to the building, and the longer we wait, the more surprises might show up."

Jia stood from her crouch and blew out a breath. "You sure about this?"

As if answering her, two loud thuds echoed from behind them in the distance.

"Yeah." Erik nodded. "I'm more sure about this than waiting. Ready?"

"Ready," Jia replied.

"Three, two, one."

Erik roared in defiance and jumped around the corner. He didn't bother firing, instead concentrating on jerky and erratic movement. His efforts paid off, with the first torch dragon shots missing but almost skimming his armor, they were so close.

Jia emerged from her cover without doing a barbarian impression. She sprinted forward, staying near the wall. The bot ignored her and continued to shoot at Erik.

Sharp pain suffused his thigh when a round struck his armor there, but he kept up his movements. Fire blazed through his left arm as another shot ripped through the tactical suit and grazed the limb.

The torch dragon advanced, undulating like a metal wave. Erik continued barreling forward, ignoring the pain. Next time, he was bringing a rocket launcher. *Screw* this sneaking around.

Now only a couple of meters away and hugging the wall, Erik escaped the next shot from the torch dragon. The round pierced the wall behind him. The bot turned toward Jia, not that far behind Erik on the opposite side of the wall and fired again, but it was too late.

It thrashed, its AI understanding it had no clear shot. Jia threw herself to the ground sliding feet-first and pointed her rifle. She didn't hold the trigger down or scream out a challenge; she aimed, waited, and took careful but quick single shots as she moved down the length of the torch dragon's body.

Erik aimed near the head and fired a burst, hoping to distract the bot. It whipped its rear body at him, slamming him against the wall before rounding on Jia. She fired four more times, and the body thrashed even harder.

Jia hopped to her feet and reloaded.

Erik ignored his pain and held down his trigger, emptying his magazine into the nearby head. Sparks and metal flew as his bullets perforated the bot's barrel.

Jia circled the trunk, avoiding its legs as it thrashed and again chose careful shots. Erik could see now she was targeting certain leg junctions.

He avoided a stab from a torch dragon leg with a

quick jump to the side and reloaded. He aimed, then raked the side farthest from Jia with bullets while she continued her precision work. The surgeon and the butcher might have different jobs, but they both knew how to handle sharp instruments. The torch dragon collapsed to the ground, dark smoke rising from different spots on its body and pieces of metal littering the hallway.

Erik didn't take the time to offer any triumphant observations.

He hurried forward, heading for the intersection that would take them back to their entrance window. Fiery pain suffused through his side, and blood dripped to the floor with each step. He wasn't sure when the torch dragon had nailed him, but the bot had managed to get through the suit. At least it was a clean through-and-through.

Jia followed him, almost shoulder to shoulder. She wasn't bleeding that he could see, but there were crushed rounds embedded in her suit and at least one hole.

"Almost there," Jia offered through clenched teeth. "Assuming no one shot Emma down while we were playing in here."

Erik let out a grim chuckle. "Something to look forward to."

He let out a shout after they turned the corner. The window was open, and the MX 60 hovered in front. They continued their desperate sprint. The now-familiar sound of torch dragon legs striking the hard floor of the hallway filled the air right behind them.

"Both of you run along the wall," Emma transmitted.

They must have been close enough to beat the jamming,

or she was using the laser comm. Erik didn't care. He was glad to hear her voice and complied with her order.

The bottom of the MX 60 slid open, the turret dropped, and the weapon roared to life, spewing its heavy, deadly rounds into the narrow hallway.

Emma swept back and forth until Erik and Jia were at the window. Erik finally spared a glance backward. Another torch dragon lay on the ground smoking and disabled, massive holes riddling its body.

"Sometimes it's best to make your point loudly and lethally," Emma offered, maneuvering the MX 60 next to the window with the doors open. "Even if that means announcing who you are."

Erik and Jia jumped into the vehicle, each grimacing from their wounds. The MX 60 pulled away, the turret retracting as Jia pulled off her helmet and readied a medpatch.

"We didn't get much time with the rod," Jia mentioned with a grimace.

"We didn't get a huge amount before the jamming," Malcom replied over the comm. "But at least it wasn't as bad as Cairo."

"Says the guy safe in a hotel room across town," Erik muttered.

"At least I'm in town. Someone could come and kill me."

Erik took a deep breath as he applied a medpatch to his side wound. "I hope minutes of data-scraping will be enough. There's no way we're getting back in there after all this."

"Are you going to be okay for the party?" Jia asked, her eyes half-closed, and her face pale. "I don't think I have anything that won't be under control with medpatches and a couple of days of rest."

Erik turned toward her, his brow wrinkled in disbelief. "We just got shot up, and you're worried about your mom's dinner party?"

"We already canceled the last couple of times." Jia hissed, then let out a deep breath. "She'll get annoyed and suspicious."

Erik laughed, the pain now seeming distant. "Yeah, I should be okay. Let's drop this stupid rod off tomorrow and get back to Neo SoCal."

"I'm excited to get back to Neo SoCal," Malcolm offered with glee. "Camila's back in town for a while."

Erik put a stop to his sudden excitement. "First, we need to drop it off with the local agent. You're not going anywhere until we do."

July 8, 2230, Wales, Cardiff, Red Dragon Inn

The face of the dark-haired woman standing in front of the door contorted with displeasure. Erik already knew what the ID agent was going to say, but he'd long since learned letting angry people vent made the conversation go faster.

He sat on the edge of his bed, shirt off, exposing the medpatches applied to his wounds. Jia watched the new arrival, her eyes narrowed in anticipatory irritation. Malcolm sat in a chair in front of his desk, eyes averted.

Erik gestured to the data rod in her hand. "Like we said, not a full dump, but between the direct interface and what

Emma yanked, it wasn't like we didn't get anything, Agent Davies."

"You weren't supposed to make any damned noise," the agent snarled. "Instead, you've riled up half the damned city. I had to fake a terrorist incident to keep the police from showing up."

"Oh, that was you? Nice. Thanks."

"I wondered if I was being too paranoid, but I wasn't paranoid enough. I'll have to do a lot of cleanup to bury the incident." Agent Davies waved her hand dismissively. "Was there really no other way you could have done this, other than being loud?"

Erik offered her a slight grin. "I think Alina hired us because we're loud."

Agent Davies scoffed. "You know that even with ID help, you're not always going to get away cleanly. Sometimes things will catch up with you, like your enemies."

Jia stepped toward the woman. "What did you expect us to do? Die?"

She quieted at a slight shake of the head from Erik.

"I expected you to be more professional," Agent Davies replied.

Erik shrugged. "This is how we do things. We tried to keep it quiet. It didn't happen. As for our enemies, if they want to come looking for us, that's a good thing."

She asked, "How is that a good thing?"

"Because it saves us the trouble of looking for them," Erik offered in a low, threatening tone.

Agent Davies wrinkled her nose and tucked the rod into her pocket. "You're going to get yourselves killed. You know that?"

"Not before we take down the conspiracy."

Agent Davies opened the door and turned around. "I sincerely hope never to see you again."

She stepped through and closed the door.

Malcolm clapped once. "I don't think she likes you."

"You figure?" Erik snickered.

CHAPTER FIVE

Julia lightly stepped across the loading platform leading from the floor of the hangar to the top deck of the *Beidou*. She'd considered a larger ship, but that brought complications. Something smaller was easier to land in most environments and situations.

Flexibility was its own strength.

It didn't matter now. She needed to leave Earth. She'd been foolish to linger, even more so after she'd gone out of her way to warn Shoji. A woman who didn't take the advice she offered others moved past mere foolishness to outright stupidity.

The issue went beyond her life. Necessity was a relative consideration, often shaped by arrogance rather than truth. If she died on Earth, the future would be imperiled. Gambling with her future because she wasn't prepared to trust all her underlings was, in a word, *pathetic*.

Micromanagement, arguably, was her one true weakness. The Last Soldier and the Warrior Princess—if they knew who she was, they would have already blasted through her villas and mansions or be chasing her through space like bloodhounds.

They'd learned too much. Technically, so had the Intelligence Directorate. She'd lost a half-dozen agents to the ID in the last two months, and though the other members of the Core wouldn't admit it, she knew they'd lost people as well. Their control over key portions of the government was slipping.

New strategies were needed.

Julia entered the open airlock and nodded to one of her uniformed crew members, a pilot. He bowed his head in reverence.

"Is everything prepared?" she asked.

"Yes, Miss Caldo," the pilot replied. "All supplies are loaded, and we've plotted an HTP schedule that will get us to New Pacifica at maximum speed. We're doing our final security sweeps per your instructions, but I anticipate we will take off in less than twenty minutes."

"Good." Julia offered him a quick nod before moving into an adjoining passageway.

There was no point in telling him to hurry, given she had wasted days already. The only thing she could not understand was why no one else was taking this as seriously. Shoji was a fool. With the latest ID raid on Pwyll Tower, it was more important than ever for members of the Core to shift to a defensive posture.

For the first time in decades, their enemies were ahead of them. The Core needed time to gather their forces and split the opposition, military, intelligence, and freelance. It was time to revisit some of their earlier strategies.

To bring unity, first they would need to sow disunity.

However, before anything else, strategic repositioning was necessary. While they didn't know enough about the limitations of the jump drive, putting ten light-years between her and her worst enemies was a comfortable cushion.

Making her way down the passages of the ship toward her main cabin, Julia focused on the different plans she needed to manage. It wasn't impossible to operate a personal empire remotely, just more complicated. Add to that a need for secrecy, and it went from child's play to something one needed to focus on.

It might be decades off, but the future where she could rule openly would be a relief. The effortless efficiency would be glorious.

Part of her wondered if leaving on the ship would make her more vulnerable. Shoji might be less a fool than a pragmatist. Sophia would not have been killed if she'd remained in her villa. All the power and influence of a member of the Core didn't mean much if they couldn't fly with a battlefleet to protect them in space.

Their greatest advances had been taken from the Hunters, but the ancient aliens were as absent as the Navigators they'd purged from the galaxy.

No, she had learned from Sophia's mistake.

Her ship was well-armed for its size, and she was being accompanied by other ships piloted by some of her most trusted people. All of them together would not easily fall to a surprise attack by anyone.

Besides, the Last Soldier and the Warrior Princess would need to know where she was going to finish her off, and for all their skill, fortune, and damnable luck, there was no evidence they did.

Julia stopped in front of her main cabin, frowning at a slight smudge on the access panel. It was always disappointing when staff didn't pay attention to details. Punishing them severely at the start of the trip would be bad for morale, but she wouldn't let it pass if this type of lapse continued.

Julia opened the door with a press of her hand against the panel. The vast cabin was almost identical to one of her favorite rooms on Earth. Sprawling holographic displays along the walls gave the impression it was perched atop a bluff overlooking the Atlantic Ocean. The setting sun painted the simulated sky orange, red, and pink—beautiful, if fake.

Some might say the same thing about her.

Long trips required the human mind to be anchored to where they'd come from. It didn't matter if she was far more than human. The scenes calmed what was left of her.

Despite the size of the room, it was close to empty, other than her magnificent bed in the corner and a small obsidian desk near the bed.

A desk she'd had custom-made from obsidian formed during the last eruption of Mount Vesuvius in 2144. Everyone in her place would need a reminder of how weak one was before the power of Mother Nature.

The Core was on the precipice of conquering life and death. To win that fight would be the beginning of controlling all of nature. Humanity had tried to slay their gods, confident in their science, so new ones would be born from ancient technology far beyond them.

Julia headed toward the desk but stopped at the sound of a light knock. She turned, one eyebrow raised. "Come in."

The door slid open, and a young man stepped through with a smile. His uniform marked him as one of her stewards, but she didn't recognize him. That was unusual for crew aboard the ship, but she had allowed more recent autonomy in personal promotion and reassignment.

Julia frowned. Despite those allowances, she'd made it clear that only her most trusted crew were supposed to accompany her on this particular trip. Autonomy didn't justify flagrant violations of her orders.

"What?" Julia barked. She didn't know who was responsible, so she would take it out on the closest target.

"Did you want a meal after we take off, ma'am?" the man asked, closing the door behind him.

"No. I'm fine." Julia kept slight venom in her tone to test the man. "What's your name?"

"Jamieson, ma'am. I was transferred to the yacht yesterday." He smiled brightly. "I'm very excited about the opportunity to see New Pacifica."

Julia narrowed her eyes. "You are?"

"I've never left the Solar System. This is my first time going into space. I thank you for the opportunity to serve you during this fascinating time."

Everyone on board knew they were taking a long trip, but only the pilots knew their destination. Jamieson might have overheard, but her loyal pilots had been with her for years, and unlike some of her subordinates, they understood respecting her orders.

Annoyance filled her. The effort before her was almost insulting.

Julia tapped at her PNIU to summon Security. "Who is your master?"

"Excuse me, ma'am?" The man stared at her with a confused look.

"Shoji? Farad? Ivan?" Julia scoffed. "Whom do you work for?"

"I work for you." Jamieson shook his head. "I don't know who any of those people are. Are you talking about my supervisor? That's—"

"Don't waste my time with this pathetic act."

Julia sighed, lightly dusting her black dress. No matter how much she was told nanoknitting could repair anything, it never felt the same when something was damaged, and she suspected the next few minutes might end with blood and a torn dress.

She stepped out of her heels. Confidence shouldn't replace practical preparation in any dangerous situation.

Jamieson's brow lifted. "If I've done something to offend you, ma'am, please let me know how to make up for it. I'm terribly sorry. They said to go check on you and see if you wanted anything. I didn't realize you wanted to be left alone."

His tone was plaintive, as was his face. It made Julia want to rake her nails over it and draw blood.

"You have offended me, yes, by your incompetence." Julia scoffed. "I was wondering how you could have gotten close to me with my normal preparation, but now I understand. It's brilliant in a way."

"You understand what?" His eyes looked at the empty room before coming back to rest on her. "I'm lost."

"You aren't a special, highly-trained killer," Julia explained, circling her hand. "A mercenary or a criminal with a history and the necessary skills. There's no way you would have gotten onto this ship if there was any hint of suspicion. My people check too thoroughly. And trust me, Sophia tried many times to sneak someone of real talent close to me, just to watch she might claim, but I knew she would take the opportunity if she had it."

Jamieson's shoulders slumped and he trembled. "I don't know who Sophia is."

She shook her finger at him. "Do you want me to explain who and what you are? This is self-indulgence, I'll admit that, but it does bring me some small pleasure in letting you know how spectacularly you have failed."

"I think there's been a misunderstanding." The man swallowed, and his gaze dipped to his PNIU. "May I go, ma'am?"

"No, you certainly may not."

He looked up. "Then...I don't know what you want from me."

"I want you, my feeble little man, to listen," Julia spat. "Oh, I'm sure you have some sad story. I'm sure your records say you're a good man who has always obeyed the law. There's nothing in there to indicate you are even remotely antisocial."

"That's true." The man nodded quickly. "That's why I think you've made a mistake. To be honest, ma'am, you sound paranoid."

"No, Jamieson. I've simply deduced the most likely

scenario." Julia flicked her wrist dismissively. "But I'll commend you to your commitment to your deception despite my detection of it."

She pursed her lips. There were no alarms, and Security hadn't arrived. She tapped her PNIU again. The new arrival must have been carrying a jammer.

That was more skill than she expected from the type of man in front of her, but that only meant his handlers were thorough.

"You see, it's difficult to kill me with a bomb," Julia replied with a sigh. "That would be what most would attempt, and yes, bombing my ship right before a trip would be one of the more likely spots, but I have my ships so thoroughly swept that it's impossible. Attacking me at one of my homes would be impossible without an army, and one *cannot* move an army without making detectable waves. It's the same for any of us, really." She snorted. "The only reason I even tried to bomb Sophia was that she was sloppy and off-world."

"Bomb?" Jamieson squeaked. Beads of sweat dripped down his face. "You're saying you've killed someone?"

"Killed someone? Oh, yes, little man. I've killed countless people." Julia gave him a cold smile. "Not with my own hands, of course. I've done that, too, but I've ordered many more people killed or set in motion events that led to their deaths.

He eyed her, this time with a little backbone in his glance. "You're saying that like it's nothing."

"I don't kill maliciously," Julia offered along with a smile. "I'm not evil, but sometimes people are in the way, and I do what I need to for the greater good. Humans are animals in the end, and animals die all the time at the hands of other animals."

"W-why are you telling me all this?" Jamieson asked, backing toward the door and reaching into his pocket.

If the man was a suicide bomber, she might have trouble, but she doubted it. Nothing about him fit the profile. He wouldn't have bothered talking to her instead of charging and exploding.

No. He needed to get close to her. Poison? Nanopatch?

"I'm telling you this because I suspect you've never killed anyone before." Julia gave him a pitying look and waved a hand at him. "Let me further deduce the truth. You don't have problems. It would have been too obvious, but there's someone you know who is in financial distress, a lover most likely. Not a relative; screening would have found that, too. You must work for one of my companies, or you wouldn't have made it this far. Oh, it's been a long time since I thought to manipulate your type in such a fashion, but now I see the advantages. It's more difficult in some ways, but it can be useful in so many others."

"I-I already explained this. I was transferred here. I work at a resort owned by one of your companies." Jamieson stopped moving toward the door and took a deep breath. "There was a promotion opportunity, and I took it."

There was no pleasure in defeating a cowering, whimpering animal, but an interrogation would be pointless. There would be too many layers between Jamieson and the puppet master.

"As I said, I *admire* the strategy," Julia continued with a genuinely warm smile. "It's clever in its own way, despite the implied desperation. I don't even care how much they offered. A small amount of money is impressive to people like you. You've probably even convinced what you're about to do is somehow righteous. That you'll be helping your friend and killing a tyrant at the same time. They've taken a pathetic fool and thrown you at me, hoping that against all chance, you'll get me. I'm sure they even had you practice, but you're not a killer. You might try to kill me, but I can see it in your eyes. You're afraid, not of me, but of what you're supposed to do, and that's why you failed the second you stepped into this cabin."

Jamieson's eyes widened. "You know? Y-you can't."

"Of course I know, fool." Julia strolled toward her desk. "Unfortunately, this isn't where I offer you more money not to do it. That would end nicely and neatly for both your friend and us, but alas."

"W-why not?" Jamieson licked his lips. His hand now rested deep in his pocket. "This isn't about my greed, you know. I have a friend. She's in bad shape. Her father did things he wasn't supposed to, and now he's in prison, but she didn't know about it. My friend, she's got serious problems, along with Nanorejection Syndrome. She'll die if she doesn't get this money for her treatment."

"So?" Julia leaned against the back of her desk. "Why is the condition of some random person I don't even know relevant to this situation?"

"Didn't you hear me?" Jamieson yelled, his face reddening. "She'll *die*. She's never hurt anyone. She doesn't deserve to die because her father blew all their money and got himself locked up. I d-don't want to hurt you, or anyone, even if you have killed people. I just want to help her."

Julia raised an eyebrow. "She doesn't deserve to die? What does her death have to do with my life?"

"Good people don't deserve to die. None of this situation is her fault." Jamieson cut through the air with his hand. "She's done nothing but try to live her life."

Julia pushed away from the desk. "Good people? Her fault?" Her mouth twisted into a snarl. "She's weak, so she deserves to die."

"How can you say that?" His eyes flashed. "Don't you have any sympathy?"

"Because that's the way of nature? There is no shortage of humans in the galaxy." Julia sneered. "A few deaths here and there in the big picture, which you obviously can't comprehend, are irrelevant, and she very much does deserve to die."

"You rich bitch," screamed Jamieson. "You don't know what it's like when you don't have everything you could ever want!"

"Again, a point that is irrelevant. Don't you see? She deserves to die because she isn't strong enough to solve the problem *herself*." Julia shook her head, her disdain fairly radiating from her face. "You think she didn't know about her father, Jamieson? She *knew*, but she chose to look the other way when it was convenient. If your friend had any sort of wit or strength of will, she would have figured out a way to make his death benefit her and kill him. An emotional plea for him to take out insurance and then have him murdered, or something like that. But sitting there whimpering about how she didn't know when her genetically flawed self is dying? Pathetic." She spat, "It churns my stomach."

Jamieson pulled a knife out of his pocket. "Thank you, ma'am. I didn't think I could do this, but you've made it easy, and haven't you read what the Purists say? Nanorejection Syndrome might be a sign of someone who is a better human because they don't have to rely on machines."

"What's your grand plan? Hmm? Say you do kill me? You'll never escape this ship."

Jamieson licked his lips. "I will if I kill you and run in the next few minutes." He lifted his chin. "You think you're so much better than me? Smarter? Why? Because you were born rich? You think I didn't notice you trying to call for help on your PNIU?" His eyes bulged. "Surprise, bitch! No one's going to know what's going on in here." He patted his other pocket. "They helped me make sure of that. Now I'm going to take out a monster and save a life at the same time." His eyes widened in understanding. "I'll be a *hero*."

He stalked toward her, all hesitation gone. Julia could finally bring herself to grant him a smidgen of respect. Granted, he was a fool, but at least he was a committed and brave fool at the end.

"Do you know why I can't just pay you to let me live?" Julia asked.

Jamieson stopped, his brow wrinkling in confusion. "Because you're too arrogant? We can make a deal if you want. I think you're awful, but I care more about my friend than killing you."

"No. That's not it. We can't make a deal because I've already told you too much, but that's the sad part of this. The minute we began this conversation, your life was forfeit. Sometimes," she shot a look at her fingernails before looking back at Jamieson, "I'll admit this is a vice. It is amusing to speak openly about my plans to people who know nothing of them."

Julia looked him up and down. "Shoji or Constance, I suspect. I'm dubious the others would rely on this sort of gambit, but I could be wrong. Just so you know, after you're dead, I'm going to make sure no money goes to your flawed, weak, and useless little friend. Her death will make the human race all the stronger, without her flaws continuing to the next generation." Her eyes narrowed. "She doesn't have any children, correct? I'd hate to have to kill them, too."

Jamieson screamed and charged, the knife held in front of him. Julia smiled sweetly, waiting for his arrival. She sidestepped the blow with ease.

He swung at her and she whipped up her arm, grabbing his wrist in a lightning-fast motion. She squeezed, and he cried out in pain as the bones cracked in her iron grip. The knife clattered to the ground, and Jamieson stumbled backward, groaning.

"H-how?" He clutched his wrist.

Julia snapped out her leg. Her kick connected, and the man howled as he flew across the room and slammed into a wall with an audible crunch. He fell to the floor, groaning, beneath the image of the gentle ocean waves.

"You're a Tin Man," Jamieson moaned. He coughed up blood.

Julia scoffed. "Of course not. The problem with introducing machines into the body is they make a mockery of its potential." She strolled toward the fallen man and crouched by him. "Machines need to be repaired, but *bodies* repair themselves."

"You're stronger than a man twice your size," wheezed Jamieson. His chuckle was dark. "Don't tell me that's because you hit the gym."

"No, no, no. I didn't say I didn't have any modifications, just that they aren't cybernetic in nature." Julia smiled down at the man. "A long time ago, a small group of people became aware of the greatest race in history, a race most don't even know of called the Hunters. In examining the remains of that race's great works, that small group of people realized the true future is in biological enhancement, Jamieson. The path of technology is the feeble dead-end of lesser races."

"You're a monster." Jamieson spat blood at her face. "A *yaoguai*."

"No. I told you already." She grabbed him by the throat and lifted him. "I'm the woman who will rule humanity forever. I am a goddess."

Julia squeezed until the bones in his throat cracked under the pressure. His eyes bulged, and he gagged. She watched him until the end, enjoying seeing the life leave his eyes more than she remembered the last time she'd killed someone.

She tossed the body aside and reached into his pocket to find the jammer. After snapping it in half, she clucked her tongue.

"I wasn't planning to kill any more of you soon, but one of you has forced my hand. Pity."

CHAPTER SIX

July 9, 2230, Neo Southern California Metroplex, Private Hangar of the Argo

The engine room of the *Argo* was cramped, too cramped for Erik's taste. Low ceilings, odd tubes, and heavy doors separated the control and diagnostic center from the reactor. If he spent any serious time in there, he'd be constantly hitting his head or stubbing his toe.

It didn't help that Lanara had filled half the already confined area with cryptic data windows filled with numbers and colorful graphs. His knee slammed into a panel hidden by two data windows.

"Damn it." He reached down to massage the pain away. "Are all engine rooms this small, or does that redheaded gremlin like it this way?"

Lanara crouched next to an open panel. Intricate bundles of cables crisscrossed inside, some opaque, others illuminated. She waved a small cylindrical silver probe back and forth.

"2.2, 3.32, 2.15, 3.15," she mumbled. "2.05, 3.05, 4.5? What the hell? 3.12, 2.11."

Erik moved closer to her as she continued her diagnostic work. He could do okay with basic flitter and exo maintenance, but ships remained the inscrutable province of specialists in his mind. He'd spent enough time around Lanara to guess that today's efforts likely had something to do with her continuing quest for perfect efficiency, not a bad trait in an engineer.

"Reroute from that system and reduce its power by one-point-two percent," Lanara continued. "There shouldn't be any functional loss even with the planned splits. Maybe I can do something with fuel efficiency at an earlier stage?"

Erik folded his arms and waited. Woe to anyone who dared interrupt the great Engineer Quinn when she was working. She reminded him of a lot of great engineers he had known in the past.

Lanara snapped her head in his direction, her face a mask of irritation. "I can't get the efficiency in sub-emitter 22 past ninety-eight percent. This is utter and complete bullshit! *Why* is everything complete garbage?"

"Sub-emitter 22?" Erik asked, his tone clearly indicating how lost he was. "Is that something I can help with?"

"Obviously not." She hissed. "Do you even know what it is?"

Erik shrugged. "No."

"It's part of the internal grav field system," Lanara growled and stood, jamming her probe into the front pocket of her coveralls. "And it's pissing me off. Was this built by some loser high on Dragon Tear?"

"Possibly?" Erik glanced at the exposed cables. "Is that a big deal? I know we haven't taken her out in a while, but you didn't mention this before."

Lanara rolled her eyes. "It's the *prototype*, Blackwell. That's why it's important."

"A prototype for what?"

"My efficiency strategy for all," she rotated a hand above her head in a circle, "the sub-emitters." Lanara kicked the wall. "But it won't cooperate! If I can get this one figured out, I can get the others figured out, and then we actually are talking about gaining half a percent in power efficiency overall." Her eyes took on a religious reverence and her voice softened as she spoke to no one, he figured, but herself. "Think of all that extra power."

Erik doubted that would amount to much in a battle, but he kept the thought to himself. He could be wrong. Lanara had accomplished amazing things with the ship, so maybe she was on to something. He would stick to fire-fights and leave the modifications to her.

Emma materialized in matching coveralls, her hair in a ponytail. "Is this something I could help with?"

Lanara shook her head. "It's not an analysis problem. According to most standard theories, I'm already pushing things." She shook out her hands. "It'll come to me. I just need time to think about it."

"Very well, then." Emma disappeared.

Lanara stomped over to Erik, craning her neck up to look at him. "Why are you here, Blackwell? We don't have a mission. Alina never tells you without telling me."

"I need your help," Erik explained with a smile. "It's something only *you* can do."

"I know, I know, more guns and all that." Lanara waved a hand. "That's more involved than you think it is. Same thing with the shields and other systems. If it was easy to make a perfect warship, the Fleet would have done it a long time ago."

Erik shook his head. "No, it's something way more important than guns, and maybe more challenging."

Lanara stopped for a second, eyeing him while she rubbed her chin. "Now you've got me intrigued. Talk fast before I get bored. I have a lot of work to get done today."

"I've been logging a lot of hours in this ship," Erik replied. "And I think before this is over, I'll be logging a hell of a lot more."

"So?" Lanara asked. "This is a nice ship. I've spent a lot of time on crap buckets. You could have ended up stuck on that tiny little Rabbit bucket."

"Sure, the *Argo* is a nice ship." Erik grinned. "But it could use the comforts of home."

"Use the stupid rec room then." Lanara folded her arms. "Is there a point to this?"

"Penjing," Erik declared.

"That plant stuff you do?" Lanara asked. "What about it? I don't know crap about plants, Blackwell. I'm an engineer, not a botanist."

"But I need a *skilled* engineer." Erik gestured to the ceiling. "I can use automated watering and certain things, but those plants need me, and it's supposed to be part of how I relax. I want to bring them along, but I can't have them falling the first time we do a hard burn. The shape of penjing plants is their big thing."

"That's it?" Lanara's brow lifted. "You're asking me how to bring your stupid plants on board?"

"Yeah. I was thinking, I don't know, a crate. We bolt it to a wall." Erik shrugged. "You know where I can install things without messing things up."

"Huh." She scratched her cheek. "That's what you've come up with? Bolting a crate to a wall?"

Erik shrugged. "I tie the bases down and bolt the crate in. They'll survive most situations."

"You're a shit engineer, Blackwell. No offense."

Erik laughed. "I'm an intelligence contractor. Before I was a cop and before that, I was a soldier. Nobody's *ever* mistaken me for an engineer."

"It's not about the training." Lanara tapped the side of her hair. "It's about the mindset."

"You're saying you've got a better idea?"

Lanara looked down, her brow furrowed in deep thought. "I'm thinking we could install a shelving system with lids." She snapped a finger. "Oh, I've got it! Then we could install some dedicated grav field emitters. Arrange them in formation around the container, and it can keep the plants secure even if we're getting the hell beat out of us. If we do it right, those damned plants will be the only things that survive."

Erik couldn't bring himself to tell her it was unreasonable to worry about his plants in ship-to-ship battles. He appreciated it. If he didn't die in the battle, he'd damned well want his penjing plants to survive.

"That's possible?" he asked. "It won't take up too much power? I don't want to mess with holy efficiency."

"I wouldn't suggest something that's impossible."

Lanara frowned. "That'd be a waste of our time. I can do the nearly impossible but not the totally impossible."

"It sounds great to me," Erik agreed. "But you're the one who's always complaining about efficiency."

"It won't be a big thing if it's just for your plants." Lanara tapped her PNIU and brought up a power consumption chart for the ship filled with smaller graphs and numbers. "You don't have a whole room of these plants, do you? I can't set up something to support a greenhouse in here, or at least, not anything that's going to survive the first battle."

Erik shook his head and gestured with his hands. "No, small table-sized arrangement."

She watched the size he pantomimed the setup with his gestures. "That's it? Ha. This will be super-easy." Lanara paced in the narrow space between Erik and the wall. "I've already got enough efficiency gains from my last set of upgrades to power the dedicated grav field emitter without affecting any of the rest of the ship's performance. Also need to rig up an appropriate UV system. We might as well add a dedicated watering system. Emma can help with that when you're on board, so it's not like we need any programming modifications."

"Then it's a go?" he asked, a bit surprised.

"Easy. Pathetically so." Lanara almost looked insulted.

"It's ready, Erik," Emma announced.

"Oh." Erik shook his head. "Thanks, Lanara, but I have to run and pick up a tux."

"A tuxedo?" she asked. "For what?"

He sighed as he turned to maneuver through the knee-deadly area. "Something truly dangerous and painful."

After swinging by the store to pick up his new tuxedo, Erik headed back to his apartment in the MX 60. Despite his trepidation about the upcoming event, he was feeling good.

He'd missed his plants more than he expected during their last major sojourn into space, and it was good to know it would be an easy solution, or at least an easy one for Lanara.

"You confuse me," Emma announced, eschewing a visible form.

"Because I'm a fleshbag?" Erik replied. "That's kind of our thing for you."

Emma scoffed, the derisive tone extra thick. "No, most fleshbags aren't that confusing. If anything, you're far too predictable."

"Then what's the problem?"

"Your penjing," Emma offered cryptically.

"What about it? You've never been offended by my hobby. Should I be doing virtual penjing?"

"I didn't say I was offended. I said I was confused."

"By penjing?" Erik asked. "Come on. All that AI analysis power combined with a human-derived brain pattern, and relaxing hobbies are confusing?"

Emma sighed. "I suppose I should clarify so you'll stop being so insultingly dense. Moving the penjing plants to the ship has implications, ones I'm surprised you haven't made more of an effort to explore."

Erik shook his head and twisted the control yoke to change lanes. Women were hard to understand. AI women were worse.

"Okay," he admitted. "I'm not following you."

"Your apartment is rather spartan," Emma explained. "You've purchased the basic necessities to make it livable, but you spend little time there other than when you're sleeping, and that's not even getting used that much. You've spent 72.47 percent of your nights since the end of May at Jia's apartment rather than your own. It seems wasteful to maintain a living space you don't plan to use in terms of efficiency, money, and general life logistics."

Erik laughed. "You're saying I should move in with Jia? Are you going to be the Virtual Mother-in-Law backing up Lan Lin?"

"No, that's not my suggestion." Emma appeared in the passenger seat in her classic white maxi dress, arms folded. "That's not all that efficient either. Considering your current focus, you need to minimize your distance from the *Argo*. It's not impossible you'll be called to track down a member of the conspiracy fleeing from Earth in a ship."

"Moving closer to the hangar seems pointless. It'd shave a few minutes off. Besides, we have the jumpship now. Nobody's escaping that."

Erik's gaze dipped to the cameras. Nothing out of the ordinary. He'd let himself get lazier with Emma as his co-pilot, but he would never give up full control.

"Why maintain an apartment?" Emma asked. "Why not live on the ship like Lanara?"

"She lives on the ship because she's all but married to it. I have a life. I don't want to be Mr. *Argo*."

Emma gave him a dismissive look. "That life doesn't seem to necessitate having the apartment. You don't host much of anyone besides Agent Koval, Jia, and occasionally

Mr. Constantine. You can sit around in bed or in a chair on the *Argo* the same as you could in your waste of an apartment. That's all I'm trying to point out. I also suspect you already are thinking that on some level, and the penjing setup is the beginning of that."

Erik's hands tightened on the control yoke, and he frowned. He wasn't sure why Emma's suggestion was pissing him off so much. From her perspective, it made perfect sense, and everything she'd said was right.

He took a deep breath and thought about the source of his resistance before shaking his head.

"No," he declared.

"No?" Emma raised an eyebrow. "Is there any logic to your intransigence in this matter, or are you being stubborn for the sake of being stubborn?"

"I *am* being stubborn," Erik admitted as he slowed and descended into a new lane, taking a moment to enjoy the blur of the towers surrounding him on all sides. Some people viewed the metroplex as a depressing forest of metal and glass, but he appreciated what it also represented: rebirth.

The Second Spring had destroyed old Los Angeles in a nuclear fire during the Summer of Sorrow, killing millions.

It would have been easy to avoid the area and leave it to be a monument to the cruelty and viciousness of the darkest parts of humanity. It wasn't an easy cleanup, as reminders like the Scar proved, but the United States and the world had arisen as one to reclaim the area. Erik found that inspiring in its own way.

"I'm a lot like Neo SoCal," Erik murmured. "We were

both almost killed, and both of us came back stronger with a new purpose. Then the purpose changed."

Emma looked unconvinced. "I've seen no indication you have any desire to cease your vengeance over what happened on Molino."

"That's not what I'm talking about." Erik took another deep breath. "Emma, when I got back to Earth, I didn't think about anything except my revenge. Everything I did was part of setting up for that, including this flitter. It was a disguise, a way of throwing people off my trail. The apartment was the same thing. None of it was part of a plan for a life because I didn't care about what happened after my revenge. I wasn't even sure I'd survive it."

"I see." Emma smiled softly. "And now you have a reason to live after this is all over. Jia?"

"Yeah, Jia, and someone's got to keep the DD from snatching you back. I've got shit I care about now. I'm not giving up on my revenge, especially now that we're on their track, but the last thing I want to do is go back to my old way of thinking."

She paused. It was a tiny hesitation, but after so many conversations with the AI, he caught it. "And you're worried that if you live on the ship, you'll be nothing but a vengeance-obsessed man with no future?"

"That's part of it." Erik slowed. His residential tower was near. "It's also about keeping this under control. The *Argo* isn't my ship. It's a loaner from Alina and the government, and they're only going to continue giving me nice toys as long as I'm useful to them. If I'm going to plan to survive all this, I need to make sure I have something of my own."

Emma disappeared. "I understand. If it makes you feel any better, the problem might be solved by you dying long before this is all over."

Erik laughed. "Not going to happen."

Her voice floated from the speakers. "How can you be so sure?"

"Because I'm too damned stubborn to die." Erik glanced at the garment bag in the backseat. "But that doesn't mean certain people might not get lucky."

CHAPTER SEVEN

Before meeting Erik as a young cop, Jia couldn't hold her alcohol. A single beer represented a grievous threat to her self-control.

She used to take pride in that, feeling it was a sign of her avoidance of vice, but it'd also made her mother's parties treacherous affairs. Now, with her newfound tolerance, she could soothe her worries with some wine without risking humiliation.

Jia smiled and plucked a glass from a tray carried by a white-clad and white-gloved waiter. He offered her a polite nod before wandering away.

On the surface, the elegant affair, the men all tuxedo-clad and the women in beautiful dresses, should have summoned pure relaxation. Sprightly live music in the form of an *erhu* and *guzheng* pair gave the night a touch of class.

Jia couldn't give in to that feeling since her lingering

concern about her family's opinion was weighing her down.

She tried to distract herself by watching the *guzheng* player pluck her instrument with precise movements and the careful bowing of her partner. There was nothing more mesmerizing than a skilled instrumentalist, but even focusing on the music didn't calm her heart.

Jia sipped her wine. Erik was beside her, filling out his black tuxedo to perfection and matching her plunging black gown well. Jia tried to tell herself not to be nervous. They'd been to several parties now without incident, but when Mei had called and said she would be absent because of a business trip, Jia had gotten worried.

If her mother had some clever scheme, waiting until her sister was gone would be a smart and tactical chance to hatch it. On the other hand, her mother and sister typically worked as close allies, and Mei's absence might be evidence of nothing being on tap.

The uncertainty added to Jia's stress.

Erik swallowed a snack he'd been chewing. "I'll give it to your mom. These crab puffs are really good."

"Mom sprang for real crabmeat," Jia offered between sips. "I'm not just saying it's not printed. I'm just saying it isn't artificial."

"Nice." Erik waggled his eyebrows. "Then I'm going to have to stuff my face with your parents' money."

Jia smiled, some of the tension leaving at Erik's antics. Considering how much he'd been dreading the party, he came off as more relaxed than she was.

"Leave some for the other guests," she ordered.

Erik saluted. "Yes, ma'am." He inclined his head toward the crowd. "Be on your toes."

Jia followed his gaze. Her mother glided through the crowd effortlessly, her attention focused on her daughter and Jia's boyfriend. There was no anger or disappointment in her face, which was a good start.

Lan Lin could be difficult to deal with at times, but she'd seemingly dropped her objections to Jia dating Erik. However, Jia couldn't ignore the possibility it was all part of a long-term plan to ambush them and break them up.

She needed to get through this night. She swallowed wine as her mother stopped in front of them.

"I'm surprised," Lan offered, her careful gaze sweeping Erik and Jia.

"Surprised, Mother?" Jia replied. "About?"

"You managed to make it." Lan glanced at Erik's plate laden with crab puffs. "You always cancel at the last minute, so I'd assumed you'd come up with some excuse not to attend this party. It'd likely sound very convincing."

Erik plopped a crab puff in his mouth, leaving Jia to face her mother alone. He smirked.

The bastard.

"It's not like we're purposely trying to avoid your parties," Jia explained. At least it wasn't like that all the time. "We're busy, and since we don't work for the NSCPD anymore, our job takes us to a lot more places. I should point out Mei isn't here."

She'd ask Mei for forgiveness for selling her out.

"Mei didn't miss my last two parties." Lan's face twitched into a tight frown. "Your new job is really that involved?"

Jia sighed. "I wouldn't say it's that involved, but we have to be ready, and we're protecting a lot of different clients, so our schedules are not always our own."

She'd grown better at lying, but that wasn't the same as being comfortable with it.

Lan nodded slowly, some of the disapproval on her face drifting away. "It's unfortunate. I was hoping when you left the police department, you would have more time to spend with your family, but now you're always out of the country or off the planet, getting involved in trouble even when you're not trying to. Like on Venus."

Erik swallowed his latest crab puff. "That's what it means to be successful, right? To be busy?"

"That's one way of looking at it." Lan motioned to Jia. "But I don't want my daughter to spend all her time working harder, not smarter. You two spend so much time doing the work directly. Why not become management and hire staff to handle shooting at people?"

"It's not about the money," Jia insisted. It was difficult to win arguments with her mother when she couldn't tell the woman the truth about what they did.

"Is this some sort of thrill-seeking thing?" Lan asked. "I can't blame you for running into trouble you don't expect, but I thought you said the new job was quieter than being a cop."

"It is," Jia lied. "Overall."

Erik waved down a crab puff waiter to refresh his exhausted supply. Lan paused in her interrogation of her daughter to survey the room, locking onto each and every waiter and waitress individually to ensure they were circulating and no guests were in distress.

A proper hostess could multitask to ensure her event was unfolding smoothly while lambasting her daughter over her life choices.

It was both one of her talents and a skill she had worked on for what seemed like a century. Having two talented daughters had required her to stay on point more than once.

"It's not going to be forever," Erik interrupted.

Lan and Jia both looked at him, awaiting clarification.

"Things are busy right now because we're establishing ourselves," Erik explained. "But this isn't going to last forever. We've already accomplished a lot in the short time since we've gone private, and we have clients who really trust us. I think with a little more of a push, we could do something like you're suggesting."

Lan nodded slowly, looking satisfied. "That was all you had to tell me, Jia. Sometimes you make things more difficult than they have to be. Besides, it's unnecessary for you to work, isn't it?"

"It is?" Jia asked with surprise. "Since when do you not want me to work?"

"I want you to have *influence*, which isn't necessary if you choose the right man." Lan glanced at Erik. "He spent a long time in the military. Consider it rude if you want, but I have noticed his vehicle and his apartment. Money's not much of an issue, and you both have fame now."

Erik cleared his throat. "I've saved a lot and invested well. I didn't have a lot of needs on the frontier, and you know what they say: the real miracle is compound interest."

Lan chuckled quietly. "Restraint *is* a key to prosperity."

"I couldn't agree more." Erik offered her a winning smile.

Lan smiled back. "Now, I hate to be rude, but I haven't spoken to all my guests yet. I'll come back to you in a bit. A good friend of mine was just about to discuss her new grandchild."

"Of course," Jia murmured, her heart pounding.

Lan offered a final small smile to Erik before wading into the dense, chattering crowd. She didn't look back.

"That's just a stalling tactic." Jia sucked in a breath. "What if we continue to be busy? She'll get louder with her complaints."

"Nothing wrong with positive thinking," Erik replied. "It's not like we could tell her the truth, though if we did, she would probably be impressed by your fancy new government connections."

Jia chuckled and finished her glass. "She would be." She looked around. "I haven't seen my father since the party started."

Erik nodded toward a corner. Jia's father, red-faced from too much wine, chatted merrily with three other red-faced men. One man said something, and they all started laughing.

"Oh. He's escaping into wine." She nodded in agreement. "Good plan."

"Aren't you?" Erik asked, raising an eyebrow.

"I'm not in the middle of an escape." Jia deposited her glass on the tray of a passing waiter. "I'm just accomplishing battlefield preparations."

"It's not as bad as I thought it was going to be." Erik smiled. "It's not my kind of party, but your mom isn't being that …uh." He searched for a word that would be appropriate in this company.

"You've been bought off with real crab." Jia sighed. "You are a cheap date."

"Hey, real crab isn't cheap." Erik patted her shoulder. "And there is no harm in winning me over, but it's good to remember that not everything is crazy-ass missions and death. I figure you should be the one reminding me of that."

"I understand, which is why I care about this." Jia's gaze followed her mother until the older woman stopped and chatted with another guest. "You're not picking up on the obvious. This whole thing was a trap."

"What trap?" He glanced around in concern. "She doesn't hate me anymore." Erik shrugged. "And I think that's a win. We're actually dating this time, so the party doesn't feel like a recon mission where I'm worried about being discovered and taking an arty barrage."

Jia's inhale was soft. "You really didn't pick up on it, did you?"

"Pick up on what?" Erik frowned. "Is the drink choice supposed to be some sort of slam on me? If so, it's not working. I'm a beer guy, but it doesn't mean I won't ever drink wine."

Jia gestured subtly at her mother. "What do you think she's talking about right now?"

"I don't know. Rich people crap. Investments, politicians they're planning to buy. That sort of thing."

"No." Jia lowered her voice. "She told us what she was going to talk about—her friend's new grandchild."

"And you hate kids now?" Erik looked confused. "You're not Miss Playful, but I didn't realize you hated kids."

"I don't…" Jia closed her eyes and took a deep breath. She was unsure if Erik honestly hadn't picked up on her mother's cues or was messing with her for his own amusement.

Maybe both.

"What's wrong, Jia?" Erik asked, making the surprising move of setting his plate of crab puffs on a nearby table. "If she's upsetting you, we can leave. I'll always have your back, you know that."

"My mother doesn't say things without having an ulterior motive." Jia managed not to stare across the room at the offending matriarch. "Erik, she's mentioning grandchildren because that's her subtle way of suggesting we hurry up and get married to provide her with some. I think she would take the grandkids without the marriage, if possible."

"Oh." Erik swallowed, all the confidence draining from his face. "I get it."

"Exactly." Jia nodded. "The thing is, Mei's not firm enough in her position by Mother's standards to move onto the next stage of her life, but in her reckoning, I am, despite being younger. That's why she's pushing *me* to get out of a field job. Because she thinks you're a compatible and acceptable-enough match, and I should be producing the next generation of Lin women. You heard her. She figures you're rich and famous enough that you're worthy of being her son-in-law. You'll enhance the Lin family as an addition."

"Kids, huh?" Erik mumbled, his earlier swagger gone.

"There's thinking ahead, and then there's thinking *way* ahead."

"You never thought about kids during all those years on the frontier?" Jia asked, her tone curious rather than accusatory. She'd barely thought about anything besides her career, but she'd had less time for it to become an issue.

His voice was soft and a touch vulnerable for a moment. "I always thought I'd make a crap dad," Erik admitted. "And I've been with women, but it's not like I was in a position for a stable relationship, and it's not like I met anyone who I felt like I wanted to raise a little Erik Junior with."

Jia's stomach tightened at the implications of his last sentence.

She averted her eyes and was grateful for the passing wine tray. She acquired a new glass and gulped it down. She'd let her mother control the conversation from a distance. They were busy cleaning up the conspiracy and needed to focus on the day to day issues, not worry about children.

"So, uh…" Erik began, rubbing the back of his neck.

"Erik Junior?" Emma scoffed.

Erik and Jia looked around, worried that she'd chosen to appear, but she'd limited the transmission to their ears. The distraction was welcome.

"What's wrong with that name?" Erik asked.

"Any future fleshbag spawn between the two of you should be named after the being responsible for your survival," Emma explained.

"And what name would that be?"

"Emma 2.0, regardless of gender." The AI's tone made it sound so obvious.

The two humans shared a quiet chuckle. Jia wasn't sure if Emma was trying to do them a favor by breaking up the awkwardness or if she was being serious, but latching onto an absurd conversation vector offered an escape better than wine.

"I'll keep that in mind," Jia replied with a smile.

"On an unrelated matter, something occurred to me while I was doing data analysis," Emma continued.

"You really want to talk about this now?" Erik whispered.

"Why not? Do you want to go back to the previous conversation?"

"No," Erik and Jia replied loudly enough to draw stares from nearby guests.

"The lack of an impressive AI on the *Argo* is irrelevant because of my constant connection to the ship and your ability to manage it because of its smaller size," Emma explained. "But the cometary incident reinforced in my mind that might not be the case with the *Bifröst*."

Jia couldn't believe they were discussing classified experimental jumpships in the middle of her mother's dinner party, but Emma was right. Anything to avoid an awkward discussion about children was welcome.

"I need to make modifications," Emma continued. "Heavy modifications to the AI of the other ship. Right now, it's useless for anything except simple automation."

"You mentioned that before but then dropped it," Erik replied quietly.

"Because I needed more time to perform an analysis of

the basics of the systems. I'm now more confident and prepared to do what is necessary."

"I don't know what to tell you." Erik leaned closer to Jia so it'd look he was in an intense conversation with only her and not some mysterious AI kilometers away. "The DD isn't going to let us park that ship in Earth orbit."

"I'm just mentioning," Emma replied, "but the sooner I can accomplish this, the better it'll be for your goals, and I'd argue, the goals of the UTC.

"We can ask Alina about it when we have an opportunity," Jia whispered. "It's not like the DD can complain too much about free improvements."

"That's all I ask."

She watched her mother occasionally gesture in her direction. The temporary freedom of the AI upgrade conversation gave way to a return of worrying about an overbearing parent.

Jia needed a mission far away from Earth and soon.

CHAPTER EIGHT

July 12, 2230, Neo Southern California Metroplex, Private Hangar of the Argo

Erik set his flitter down in the hangar. He'd arrived in response to a cryptic message from Lanara.

Come right away. Don't need your better-looking half.

They didn't have a mission, and Alina had told them to stay on standby, so he'd spent the last few days with Jia, either on dates or training.

He doubted this was some secret attempt by Lanara to seduce him. That woman wasn't turned on by anything that lacked a fusion reactor.

"What the hell?" Erik thought as he looked through the front windshield.

Large cargo bots floated through the air with crates underneath. There were crates and cargo containers filling half the hangar, and Lanara was pushing a hoverdolly topped with a pyramid of long, dark cylinders with pointed ends.

"Do you know what's going on, Emma?" Erik asked aloud, confusion still painted across his face.

"Yes," she replied. "I've had communication with her, but Engineer Quinn would prefer to tell you herself, I believe."

Erik grunted in frustration and opened the door. Yes, any conversation involving the *Argo* was probably best held in the protected hangar, but she could have sent him a message with a couple of clever phrase replacements.

Lanara stopped pushing her dolly toward the open cargo bay and jogged over to Erik. "Blackwell, you came a lot sooner than I expected."

"You said you wanted me to come right away," he replied with a shrug. "I figured that meant right away."

"Well, I figured that meant anytime in the next week, but now that you're here, we can get this out of the way." Lanara rubbed her hands together with an eager gleam in her eyes.

Erik looked up as a cargo drone passed overhead with a crate almost the size of his flitter underneath. "What is all this?"

Lanara jabbed a finger in his chest. "I'm trying to get you to stop bitching, both for your sanity and mine. The best way to do that is to solve it my way."

He eyed her. No confusion had left his face, and perhaps a dab or two had been added. "I haven't talked to you in days." Erik gestured around the hangar. "You can't need all this for my penjing containers."

"Those? No?" Lanara waved that thought away. "I set that up days ago. You can transfer your stupid plants over here anytime you want. No, I'm talking about your other bitching."

Erik scrubbed a hand down his face. "I'm so far off the map in this conversation that I'd need to travel for days before I got back to the part where it said 'here be monsters.'"

Lanara mimed an explosion. "Because you're a soldier, all you think about is blowing crap up. You keep whining for 'more guns, more guns, more guns,' and I keep telling you there's only so much we can do because of the reactor."

Erik nodded slowly, feeling more grounded. "Okay, and you're going to add more guns?"

"Damn it, Blackwell." Lanara shook her arms in front of him. "Don't you *ever* listen? I can't do much with guns because we don't have the power for it. You don't want a ship where the life support cuts out when you fire the weapons, do you?"

"No, that would include all levels of suck." He thought for a moment. "But would the life support come back on in that scenario?"

Lanara's withering glare made him want to laugh.

"The first step was to solve the power issue." She flung her arm toward a large cargo container in the distance that could have held the MX 60. "And that meant we needed a reactor upgrade."

"Now we're talking." Erik looked at the *Argo*. "But does Alina know about this? I'm guessing this isn't something you can pound out in a couple of hours."

"She knows I've requested supplies, and she's approved the purchases, but she has cautioned me about taking the ship offline until we have a window of opportunity. Right now, I'm gathering the parts and preparing." Lanara cast an eager look at the ship and licked her lips. "I'm good at what I do, Blackwell. If I prep this ahead of time, I can do it in stages, especially on a small ship like this. We'll upgrade the reactor, and then I can immediately do the shield upgrades. It'll take longer to stabilize the new power network, but once I do, we can start putting in more of the guns you're so obsessed with." Her eyes pinned him in place. "Assuming you still want them?"

Erik didn't respond right away. He was too busy imagining the *Argo* with two or three times the firepower. The less they needed to rely on the jumpship, the safer they would be.

If the conspiracy got lucky and boarded the ship with enough Tin Men or *yaoguai*, they'd have the ultimate weapon. He wanted the jumpship to be the last resort.

"Why *wouldn't* I want them?" Erik questioned.

"Because having more guns wouldn't have done anything to help you last time," Lanara replied with a shrug. "I don't want to do a bunch of work just because you need a security blanket, Blackwell. If that's what this is about, tell me now, so I don't end up throwing you out an airlock later."

Erik chuckled, amused at the image of the tiny woman trying to eject him from the ship. "I'm pretty sure we're going to run into more human ships than Hunter vessels, and if we can't have a fleet backing our asses up or a dedicated warship on call, the more we can cram onto this thing, the better."

Lanara scratched her eyelid. "That makes sense. With your luck, we might run into Zitarks or Leems, and having more firepower would help." She frowned. "But this is where things get complicated."

"Complicated? Technically?"

"No." Lanara shook her head. "I'm damned good, and this ship is on the smaller side, but I'm still one person. I can do this in stages like I said and get it done decently quickly, but I'm going to need help. This is something I've been thinking about for a while. If we're going to fly around on that jumpship, I'm going to need more regular help. Raphael's great, but he's all about that jump drive, not so much the nitty-gritty of things like the grav emitters on the *Argo*. Emma's terrific, but I need human hands I can boss around, too." She clenched her teeth. "I asked Alina for more people, and she told me to talk to you about it because it's your team. What crap is that? I'm the engineer. She wouldn't ask my opinion if you wanted to hire a bunch of cannon fodder."

"I don't know," Erik offered, the dream of extra guns fading. "Things are only going to get more dangerous from here on out. If these people are going to help, that'll mean they'll need to be on board with us when we're on missions."

"That's kind of the point. I need help when crap's blowing up all around me, too."

Erik locked eyes with Lanara. "Cutter's not the only person who might be dead by the time this is over."

Lanara sneered. "You trying to scare me, Blackwell?" She took three steps to look up at him and squared her shoulders. Her tiny size might make her attempt to intimidate ridiculous, but Erik had to admit she had the aura of a grizzled lifer NCO.

"I'm saying not carrying a gun won't save your life when the conspiracy's shooting at us," Erik offered quietly.

"Okay, Soldier Boy, I know you're a bad-ass who has dropped onto every kind of world there is to blow people's brains out, but that doesn't mean I don't know a thing or two about danger, and that's before counting that I could have died too in that little Hunter incident." Lanara's nostrils flared. "I've been in a cramped little engine room when half the ship's been blown apart so badly that I'm lucky I'm in a pressure suit and the grav emitters are fried. Bodies floating around me, their blood making those stupid little spheres, and me sitting there trying to get the backup power cells online, so the other guys don't end finishing me off. At that point, guns don't mean crap." She pointed to her chest. "In that situation, engineers mean everything."

Erik nodded. "If you've been through that, why are you blowing the danger off?"

"Because..." She deflated a touch. "Because I actually believe in your stupid mission, Blackwell." Lanara relaxed her shoulders. "And as great as I am, I know my limits. Alina's like you. She thinks she's doing everybody a favor by limiting exposure and keeping all this secret. I know some of that is ghost crap, but I've accepted a truth that seems to have escaped our fancy ghost boss and your oh-so-experienced ass."

"What truth is that?" Erik asked, his voice a soft rumble.

"We're at war, Blackwell," Lanara answered. "You both talk like it, but you don't always act like it.

Erik grunted, unsure of what to say. This was more a mission of revenge-filled annihilation.

"I'll admit I didn't take this seriously at first," Lanara continued. "Put me in a ship, give me my tools, and I can be happy. Alina pays well, and you were giving me challenges. That's all I cared about."

He reached up, scratching his nose. "But you take it seriously now?"

Lanara nodded. "If we hadn't been out there to stop that Hunter ship, who would have died along the way? Those bastards might have parked above Earth and broadcast a suicide signal and killed half our species." She tightened her hands into fists so hard, her nails dug into her palms. He worried droplets of blood would leak out. "It'd be one thing if those Hunter bastards had shown up themselves, but the conspiracy woke them up. The conspiracy could have cost billions of lives because of whatever twisted plan they have. And that's before you think about all their weird-ass *yaoguai*, mutants, Tin Men, and half-alien hybrids. There is absolutely nothing they won't do."

"I'm going to wipe them out," Erik growled. "You think I don't take this seriously?"

"I think you're letting Alina program you to be a good little ghost," Lanara replied. "At the end of the day, it doesn't matter if we can't keep secrets if it means those other guys get an advantage. We have to stop them. We have to burn them to ashes, and that means risking other people's lives: mine, Jia's, Raphael's, and everybody else's who is part of this. Nobody's going to be hired for your team and think it's a safe job, so screw not hiring people because they might get killed."

Erik ran his hand through his hair. "I'll talk to Alina

about getting people, but whatever you can do quickly might help."

"Good." Lanara nodded slowly, the fire dimming in her eyes. "Got any suggestions about what you'd want that doesn't take a reactor overhaul?"

"Missiles and torpedoes don't require as much power," Erik noted. "Deployable launchers that we can hide. We can punch above our weight without needing as much reactor power."

Lanara's face brightened. "That's…actually a good idea. I'll concentrate on setting some up, but there's only so much I can do while we're on standby."

"I'll talk to Alina." Erik turned back toward his flitter. "We'll win the war, Lanara. We already are."

"I know we'll win."

He looked over his shoulder as he walked. "Why is that?"

Lanara looked at the *Argo*'s cockpit, pain in her eyes. "Because we have to."

CHAPTER NINE

Luxury means different things to different people.

For Jia's mother, luxury was easy to define. It involved using lots of money to experience things that would otherwise be impossible, such as Erik's beloved real crab meat puffs.

Jia's education, life experiences, childhood lessons, and countless other advantages were all the products of money. Her mother cared for her, but she'd shown that love with cash, and the same attitude continued as an adult.

For other people, luxury is less about money and more about experiences that only the allegedly sophisticated would appreciate. That alleged sophistication was supposed to be born of education and an open mind, but the line could be rather thin between self-earned ability and purchased sophistication.

An education birthed by access to money and experience.

That was the only explanation Jia could come up with

as to why she was now wandering through a bizarre labyrinthine restaurant that looked like something the fungal Orlox carved in their mounds.

Parts of the wall pulsed. Steam hissed from vents. The material changed as they went along, various parts looking like stone, metal, or wood.

Jia hadn't checked anything other than the address of the restaurant. She'd assumed it was expensive because Mei didn't pick modest budget places, but she hadn't expected the bizarre décor, despite the mention of it being avant-garde.

She followed the waitress through the twisting confines of the restaurant. The bright glowing colors of the waitress's body-hugging outfit slowly shifted, the patterns drifting and standing out in the dim lighting.

The farther they traveled, the deeper Jia's confusion grew. Her hand passed through a jagged formation on the side, which was nothing more than a hologram. She smiled. It was a clever blend of the real and the illusionary to toy with her senses. She was unsure if that was useful for a restaurant experience, but it was interesting.

Patterns appeared and disappeared from the walls, some raised, some engraved. Careful geometric patterns, chaotic fractals, and ghostly holographic portraits of the famous and the unknown. A spectral Zitark ran across the hallway, followed by a laughing little girl.

The waitress moved on, unfazed.

The background music changed every couple of steps, not blending. The genres jumped from classical to the heavy percussion of Lunar pop. Something horrible and atonal assaulted her. She suspected they were carefully tracking their position to send the sound to their ears only, or perhaps it didn't change if there were multiple customers.

It wasn't all that long ago that Jia would have been irritated to go to a place like this.

She liked dancing with her friends, but the loud and cramped club experience was a known factor. There was nothing challenging to her preconceptions, unlike the ceiling above her that shifted position with each step. She wanted to jump up and see if it was also a hologram or some sort of active nano-VR manipulation.

Jia had now spent so much time in training scenarios that she'd gotten used to fake reality, but that was different from what she was experiencing this evening. Whether it was the *Argo* or the tactical center, her normal VR and AR environments were designed to work with her normal expectations to trick her into thinking it was all real, not purposely push the edge of the absurd and unusual to highlight the unreality.

She kind of liked it, but that didn't change her surprise at being there. Mei had picked the restaurant, only mentioning she had heard good things. The choice was odd because Mei lived her life as the embodiment of proper behavior. She was Ms. Anti-Avant-Garde, even more than Jia.

The restaurant choice indicated something profound had happened, but Jia might be reading too much into a simple meal. For all she knew, everyone at Mei's company who wanted to get promoted had to be seen in the right kind of place.

They finally stepped into the main dining hall.

Challenging someone for going outside their comfort zone would be hypocritical, so Jia had agreed without question to Mei's suggestion, but as she walked through the restaurant seeing people eat bright tentacles and bowls filled with shimmering liquid, she began to regret her choice and her initial amusement.

Laws and Purists would presumably keep the restaurant from serving anything too exotic, but it was hard to judge meals when Jia didn't know what to expect.

She frowned as they continued walking. Another table was more regular, people eating what looked like noodle dishes. Other diners were enjoying an odd cut of meat that didn't look like it came from any animal she recognized.

As far as Jia knew, the small number of colonies with indigenous life hadn't gifted humanity with anything new and delicious. It turned out that lifeforms evolving light-years away under different conditions weren't all that safe for humans to eat.

The waitress finally led Jia to Mei's table. The elder Lin wasn't garbed exotically. She was wearing a flattering dress that managed to leave much to the imagination. Her elaborate braids were no different than those of a lot of people in her social circle. Jia had never gotten into the hairstyle because it wasn't practical for her job, either before or after the department.

The normalcy on display relaxed Jia. Her sister hadn't returned from her business trip with a new exotic lifestyle, just a rather curious taste in restaurants.

Jia took her seat, unsure how she felt about the entire experience thus far. She was about to ask for a glass of wine when the waitress stepped away without saying anything.

"Uh…" Jia looked at Mei.

"The drinks will be brought to us in a minute," Mei explained.

"But I didn't order. Did you order for me?"

Jia tried to keep her irritation out of her voice. Mei knew her tastes well and might have anticipated her needs.

"No, I didn't order for you," Mei replied. "You don't order drinks here."

"Okay. That's…interesting." Jia stared at Mei, confused.

Her sister smiled softly. "Don't worry. They'll take care of you. Just sit back and relax. I know it's different, but I've been meaning to bring you here since I tried it right before I went on my trip. I hadn't mentioned it because I needed time to digest how I feel about it."

"I trust you." Jia smiled, trying to set both her sister and herself at ease. If there was one thing she'd learned about dealing with her family, it was the importance of starting any meal off without tension. It was easy to go up that hill, far harder to climb down.

"Good." Mei offered an uncharacteristic wink. "I *am* your older sister."

"Welcome back, by the way," Jia replied. "Nothing bad happened, but I missed you at the party."

"I'm sure you did. I don't like to miss Mother's parties, but I have to take the opportunities that come. I know Mother will never be upset about me taking business trips."

"No, she didn't seem to mind."

Jia decided against mentioning her suspicions about her

mother's desire for grandchildren. Not every conversation needed to be dominated by the whims of Lan Lin.

Mei gestured around the dining room. "Drink orders aside, what do you think so far?"

"I'm not sure, to be honest. I didn't check this place out." She glanced at a nearby table, which had an orange… something on a plate. "What kind of food is it?"

The low illumination made it hard to see, but Jia's survey confirmed her earlier impression that the food was different at every table. That seemed a statistically unlikely scenario.

"It's not a single kind of food." Mei smiled. "It's hard to explain. It's all kinds."

"All kinds of food?" Jia raised her brow. "That seems complicated."

"It's more complicated than that." Mei looked down as if searching for words. "It's less that they're making all kinds of food and more that the dining experience is customized for each set of guests."

"That must make it hard to figure out what's good." Jia chuckled quietly. "How do they know people won't hate it? Do they run a background check on everyone who wants to eat here?"

"Sort of." Mei shrugged.

"Huh?" Jia had never eaten at such a confusing place. The battle in her mind about whether she liked or hated the restaurant continued to rage.

"When I made the reservations," Mei explained, "they had me fill out a questionnaire. It took a good thirty minutes."

"Thirty minutes of questions to make reservations? What do they do if you don't fill out the questionnaire?"

"You don't get to eat here." Mei inclined her head toward the nearest table. "Not only that, they block you from being able to eat here for six months. There's somebody at my company who begged me to take him, but I didn't want to lose my right to come here."

"It can't be that busy if you've managed to eat here twice close together," Jia suggested.

Mei shook her head. "I got lucky. Normally, people can't get reservations sooner than a year apart. It's somewhat random. They open a certain number of slots and make reservations at different times. I think it's also somewhat determined by the questionnaires. They want a diverse group of guests to promote myriad experiences."

"I don't know if that's genius or an overly elaborate way of generating buzz for the place. Meals based on questionnaires rather than direct orders. Huh. I guess it's not *that* strange."

"They base the whole dinner on that, including the drinks." Mei nodded. "The way they explain it, you're supposed to be living a meal instead of eating it."

Jia stared at her sister. "Who are you, and what have you done with Mei Lin?"

Mei laughed. "Is it weird that I'd pick a place like this? Let alone twice?"

"It looks weird. The waitstaff is dressed in unusual outfits, and they barely talk. You don't get to pick what you eat." Jia nodded toward swirling blue and red dust in the air, along with the changing scenes over their table, including what appeared to be a black hole. "And there are things like that." She reached over and patted her sister's hand. "It's interesting, I'll give you that, but this doesn't seem like the kind of place you would enjoy."

"Are *you* enjoying it?"

"I don't know." Jia smiled. "I can forgive a lot if the food is good. But I'm asking about you. This just doesn't scream Mei Lin."

"That's the point."

Jia blinked. "I don't understand. You wanted to go to a place you wouldn't like?"

Mei opened her mouth to respond but closed it when the waitress returned with a tray containing two cocktail glasses, one filled with a layered black and white liquid and the other with a bright speckled golden liquid. She set the first in front of Mei and the second in front of Jia.

"Enjoy." The waitress departed, her face somber.

A waitress across the table wore a bubbly smile and practically skipped away after delivering her drinks. Jia didn't want to read too much into what that implied about her sister's questionnaire.

Jia tore her gaze away from the waitress to focus on her suspicious drink. "Is this alcohol?"

"I don't know." Mei picked up her drink and swirled it. "You never know what anything is until you eat or drink it. The mystery is part of the experience."

Jia supposed that was the same as ancient humanity. There were plenty of plants and animals in nature that were delicious and plenty that were deadly. Someone'd had to figure out everything through trial and error.

She'd often wondered about the early agricultural societies who identified crops and then bred them through the centuries.

Could early farmers have envisioned how teosinte would become corn? Did some cruel ruler throw prisoners at fugu until they found the delicious and non-toxic part? There was a dark amusement in thinking ancient criminals might have contributed to modern gourmet culture.

"Isn't that what the questionnaire is about?" Jia asked. "Do you drink alcohol?' and 'Are you a vegetarian?' That kind of thing." She edged the glass closer to her mouth, both terrified and fascinated. "What's the point of making you answer questions if it's not about ensuring the meal will appeal to you?"

Mei shook her head. "It's nothing so straightforward. I don't remember them mentioning anything about food or drink.

"What do they ask, then?"

"It's all strange questions like, 'You are walking down the road when a *qilin* approaches you. The *qilin* asks you your favorite day of the week. What do you answer and why?'" Mei tilted her head, her brow furrowed in recall. "Another one was, 'a Zitark is named in your parents' will. Do you contest it? Why?' The questions weren't the same both times I took the questionnaire. They weren't completely different. I'd say about half the questions are the same, but that Zitark question was in the first questionnaire and not the second."

Jia stared at her sister, waiting for her to crack a smile and admit she was lying. No restaurant could function the way this place was described. When Mei didn't change expression, Jia accepted she was telling the truth.

"That's the weirdest thing I've heard in a while," Jia replied. "Don't people need to know what they're getting, so they don't eat something they object to?"

Mei looked unconcerned. "When you make reservations, they make it clear that they might or might not serve alcohol, and they might or might not include meat. They also say the meat might or might not be artificial. They promise it won't be toxic other than the potential for alcohol and that you won't get food poisoning, but that's it."

"In other words, if you come here, you are taking your chances?" Jia asked.

"Exactly," Mei replied. "It's not a place for people with specific limits for whatever reasons. I don't see a problem with that since they go out of their way to warn you."

"Fair enough."

Jia peered down at her drink. The small bright specks continued to float. The disjunction between the dining experience and Mei's normal taste continued to gnaw at her. Her sister was the kind of woman who lived by limits, not one who went to strange restaurants that gave you no indication of what they might serve. It didn't make sense.

"Some new friends recommended this place," Mei offered as if picking up on Jia's thoughts. "They say it's all the rage in avant-garde gourmand circles. There's an air of mystery to the whole thing as well. No one knows if they're using a sophisticated psychological analysis AI or if it's just a performance that we all choose to buy into it." She leaned close and lowered her voice as if passing along a great secret. "There are even some rumors the food is produced through the use of recovered Navigator technology."

Jia had her doubts, but given some of the things she'd witnessed in her time with Erik, she couldn't say it was impossible. Everyone focused on the obvious with ancient alien technologies, including how they might be used as weapons or to improve transportation, but humanity had put almost as much effort into its food as its weapons. It only made sense that the Navigators might.

She couldn't bring herself to accept that the Hunters had devoted technology to that. They probably just ate whatever victims they could whole. Such a cruel race probably had disgusting tastes.

"You hate this place?" Mei asked, sounding disappointed.

Jia shook her head. Her thoughts about the Hunters must have leaked onto her face.

She forced a smile. "I don't know what to think, but I'm surprised you're so enthusiastic about it. It doesn't seem very...*you*."

"I think in this case, not knowing is fine," Mei replied. "They're not going to do something illegal or anything that will get Purists breathing down their neck, so I can enjoy an unexpected experience without worrying about more than not liking the flavor. There are worse things in the galaxy."

Jia couldn't believe what she was hearing. Of the two of them, Mei was more like their mother. She didn't pick out a dress without calculating all the ways it might influence her interactions with others.

Restaurants were about specific choices, known quantities with known reactions. She had once sent a glass of water back because she was annoyed by the number of ice cubes in it.

"Not saying I disagree," Jia offered. "But at the same time, it's not a speech I expected to hear. I don't disapprove, I'm just surprised." She glanced at her drink before gesturing to her sister's. "How is it?"

In this situation, Jia was content to offer her sister as a sacrifice to the food gods.

Mei lifted her glass to her lips and took a drink. She half-closed her eyes. "I don't think this is alcohol, but it's... I can't explain it. It's like it's cycling through flavors, and they're all delicious but different."

Jia took a sip of her drink. Earthy tones mixed a half-dozen subtle herbal flavors. Bitterness gave way to sweetness. Small droplets vaporized near the back of her mouth, tickling her throat and floating up to add a floral bouquet. The combination was odd at first, but soothing after a couple of seconds. She didn't know if she would call it delicious, but she couldn't say it wasn't interesting.

She didn't claim to be a gourmand, but she could understand how people might be as interested in seeking engaging dining experiences as palette-pleasing ones. She felt a little undeserving of the exotic experience.

"I don't know what to make of this drink," Jia explained after thinking it over for a couple more seconds. "It can't be customized for me. I didn't fill out the questionnaire."

"That's part of the experience." Mei licked her lips and took another drink. "Not knowing and trying to figure out how much of your enjoyment is because they're right and how much of it is because you want them to be right, but I'm not sure it isn't."

"Why would you say that?"

"Because we're far more alike than we are different. The Lin sisters, both strong-willed and focused on their goals. I can't imagine if you filled out the questionnaire, it'd end up that different than mine."

Jia laughed. "Did you object to the Zitark being added to the will?"

"Yes, I did," Mei admitted.

Jia nodded. "I would have, too."

"Because he has no legal standing in the UTC," they explained in unison and chuckled.

Jia couldn't resist another large sip. "I still don't understand. Since when does Mei Lin care about avant-garde? You once told me that 'being disruptive and different for the sake of it is tantamount to being antisocial.' This place might not be strange for the sake of being strange, but it's different and potentially disruptive."

"I did say that." Mei set her glass down. She'd polished off the entire drink. "And I was wrong. I regret saying it."

Jia stared wide-eyed at her sister. "You were wrong? You regret it? You are an alien clone of my sister, aren't you?"

"This place is a cheat in a sense." Mei gestured at her empty glass. "Or it might be more proper to call it a training ground. That's a better way of understanding why I like it."

"A training ground?" Jia echoed. "For what?"

"For a new me." Mei smiled warmly. "I've spent my entire life doing what I thought was best, or what our parents thought was best. I had a plan. I was going to keep climbing the ladder and find a compatible ambitious man. It all made perfect, logical sense. It was hard to object to."

Jia nodded slowly. "That sounds more like you rather than the alien clone. What's next? You going to become a painter?"

"I'm not planning on quitting my job or anything drastic." Mei laughed and rubbed her arm, looking uncharacteristically nervous. The red in her cheeks spoke to the alcohol hitting her. "But things have changed. Become more complicated."

"What's going on, Mei?" Jia swallowed. "Are you in some sort of trouble?"

The last time Jia thought someone was targeting her family, she'd been mistaken, but it wasn't impossible. The ruthless conspiracy had demonstrated no qualms about collateral victims.

She tried to tell herself they knew it was a mistake. If they hurt her family, it'd only intensify her desire to hunt them down and destroy them, but that didn't remove the fear.

Mei laughed once more, this time louder. Jia winced, wondering if people would glare at them, but no one paid any attention. She realized she couldn't hear anyone else and hadn't since joining her sister. Each table was equipped with sound-blocking technology.

Alina would love the place.

"I'm not in any sort of trouble, little sister. Far, far from it." Mei shook her head. "I'm going through a change." She ran her finger around the rim of her glass. "It happened about a month ago. I was in a meeting at work. What it was about isn't important. I kept thinking about my life and what I wanted from it as one of the men in the meeting droned, and then I thought about you."

"Me?" Jia's brow furrowed. "What about me? You thought about going to a crazy place like this because of me?"

Mei pursed her lips. "Yes, in a sense. I used to think we were the same. We both had something we wanted, and we went for it with all our passion, effort, and skill. What you wanted was different compared to Mother and me, but you sought out your police career and fought to keep it even as everyone, including your family, told you it was a bad idea." Mei looked apologetic. "That's another thing I regret, how much we pushed against it. We shouldn't have only accepted your career after you became famous, and you were right about how much Neo SoCal needed good police officers."

"Thank you for saying that, but..." Jia pinched the bridge of her nose. "I don't understand how we get from there to this restaurant."

"You grew and became the ultimate detective, and at the height of your success and fame, which you could have parlayed into rapid promotion to the top of the police force, you left it all behind. Quit." Mei shrugged. "Not after decades, but a short time. It's almost shocking when I think about how abruptly it happened."

"You don't approve?" Jia frowned. "The family all seemed happy when I quit the force. You said so, at least."

"You do not understand. None of this is an accusation." Mei shook her head. "It's not for me to approve, but yes, I do. You quit after spectacular successes that left your influence on all of Neo SoCal. You helped stop murderers, terrorists, and horrible men making changelings. I thought, 'What would happen if I quit my job tomorrow?'"

"It's not the same thing. We want different things from life. You're adding to society in your own way."

"I know," Mei replied softly. "It's not like I'm ashamed of my job, but in that meeting, I had an epiphany. I wasn't doing what I wanted. I was doing what I needed to. It's not that it's wrong or misguided, but I could tell that in ten or twenty years, I wouldn't be happy. I decided I need to make changes now before I have a life filled with regrets."

"Oh, Mei, don't say that." Jia reached over and squeezed her sister's hand. "You're talking like you're not still young."

"It's not a huge crisis." Mei managed a weak smile. "I'm in a good job, and I mostly like the people around me. Even my political rivals at work keep me sharp. I'm good at what I do, but I now understand that there's more to life than climbing the corporate ladder. That's why I want to make changes in ways that make me feel more alive." She let out a quiet sigh and glanced around the restaurant. "That's what this is about, not some grand switch in careers, but about appreciating life when I can."

"Okay, that makes sense," Jia replied. "That's what this place is? You are appreciating life by filling out a question-naire and having a strange but intriguing dining experience?"

"Exactly." Mei's smile grew brighter and more genuine. "I lack the willpower to go against the grain like you did, and I don't think I need to do that to be happy. I just want to explore the possibilities of another Mei. I can do that with places like this, as well as opening up my dating pool and trying more to experience life for what it is rather than everything being a calculation aimed at my status and future. I'll admit Mother's opinion worries me, but I don't think she'll care as long as I don't throw my job away." She pulled her hand away from Jia but kept her smile. "The truth is you've inspired me, little sister."

Jia's cheeks heated. "I don't know if being a police officer and then a private security contractor is worthy of inspiring someone."

"It's not about your jobs. That's what I was saying earlier. I used to look down on you, but I now understand you're a much stronger woman than I'll ever be. It's about you living your truth, and it's time I started living my truth." Mei quieted as the waitress arrived with two wooden plates covered with a white cream-like substance and golden spoons. "And it's time for dessert."

The waitress disappeared back into the darkness, as somber and silent as she had been before. Did they have to keep the Zitark in the will to get a happy waitress?

"What about the initial courses?" Jia asked. "Ah, let me guess. Randomized course order. We can't expect anything straightforward."

"That might be the case," Mei mused. "I'm not sure. It could be this is the perfect course order for me." She picked up her spoon. "I'm proud to be your sister, Jia. I might not have always understood you, but you've always lived your truth, and I want you to keep doing that."

Jia picked up her own spoon, smiling. The objections of her family seemed distant now. When she thought about it, her mother and father were also happier. It was what she'd always wanted—to be able to live her life with the love and support of her family, rather than being a source of stress for them.

Because of that, they could never know the truth. They might be proud, but there was no way they wouldn't be scared of a job involving fighting a lethal, dangerous conspiracy.

CHAPTER TEN

"It's just weird," Jia finished after a lengthy recap of her dinner the night before with her sister. Her last statement reflected her concern about her sister's new life manifesto.

Erik suspected she was feeling him out for the restaurant, but he'd tried to make it clear he wasn't interested in going by noting he liked being able to choose what he ate. Ironically, that made him pickier than Mei Lin. He was comfortable with that.

Jia had steered the conversation back to her sister's conversion to a new outlook on life, and it was hard for Erik not to think of his own recently repaired relationship with his brother. Even in the best of circumstances, family could be difficult, and Jia and Erik weren't living normal lives by any means.

"Weird isn't the same thing as bad," he offered. "From what you said, you seem to like the direction she's heading. Are you saying you want her to be like she used to be?"

"No, I'm not suggesting that." Jia laid her head back. "It's not a bad thing, but all these changes have got me confused. To be honest, I think it's about me being selfish."

"How are you selfish?" Erik loosened his grip on the control yoke of the MX 60.

Of all the flaws one might attribute to Jia, he had a hard time thinking of her as selfish. He understood why her family had perceived her that way, but dedicating one's life to a higher cause could not be considered selfish.

In his view, they'd been the selfish ones, and it sounded like Mei now understood that.

"I think I got too used to being the family rebel," Jia replied, "and now that everyone's on board, it's like I have all this pent-up energy to fight and nowhere to direct it. I developed all these instincts to deal with them, and now I'm frustrated I can't trust those instincts." She put her hands in her lap. "It's petty. I admit it."

"I believe I understand. I still have an urge to punch my brother when he's being a smart-ass. It's all about redirection."

She looked over. "Redirection?"

"Yeah." Erik grinned ferally. "Your job involves hunting an evil conspiracy. That's a nice target to aim all that frustration at."

"True." Jia smiled. "And not to knock the restaurant. The food was interesting, good even. I don't think it's a bad place."

He'd obviously not been clear enough.

"I think I'll stick to the places where I get to pick my meal," Erik replied. "I'm not ready for an avant-garde food experience, and I think you'd get bitchy waiters if I went.

I'm not saying a place like that shouldn't exist, but not every man is made for every restaurant."

Jia looked disappointed. "I'll drag you there someday, but I get it. You might not be uptight like Mei, but you've got your own things you prefer. I'm always surprised by that."

Erik raised a brow. "You are?"

"Yes." Jia pointed at the roof. "It's not like you lived in the same small city your entire life. You've traveled the width and breadth of the UTC."

"Sure, and most of that involved being on Fleet ships, in newer domes, or in the field eating rations. The frontier is a place about survival, and with limited supplies, the printers aren't as versatile as you might think." Erik shrugged. "Or I might be wired to like what I like."

Jia sighed. "Not an avant-garde dynamic restaurant experience?"

Erik nodded. "Probably."

"As lovely as this discussion about shoving nutrients into your face is," Emma interrupted, "you need to change course immediately. Something's come up. Unless you want me to take over?"

"No," Erik answered. "I'll keep flying."

A new nav beacon showed up on his console display. The most immediate change required was a significant decrease in altitude, big enough to let him know their general destination.

Erik frowned. "Why do we need to go to the Shadow Zone? If it's a cop incident, we can let the locals handle it."

"It has nothing to do with the local police," Emma replied. "We need to go because I received a coded message from Agent Koval requesting your immediate presence there. She sent the meeting request and the coordinates, but nothing else. Given the terse nature of the message and her explicit request for immediate arrival, there might be some sort of danger."

Jia looked at her feet. "I suppose it's not like we need to stop off to arm up. We should head there and go in immediately. If she's in the middle of a fight, it might come down to seconds."

"If she got her ass captured or killed, that'd be inconvenient," Erik muttered. "She might be strange with her mythology obsession, but she's a damned good ghost."

"Do you think that's even possible?" Jia asked. "Her being captured or killed? She's been a ghost for longer than I've been alive."

"Why not?" Erik dropped the MX 60, passing through several vertical lanes in rapid succession. "I know better than anyone that you can always have a shit day in the field, and she does fieldwork." A car screamed past them. He could see the driver cursing up a storm. "Which means she could end up with a bullet in the brain or captured. If the conspiracy was smart, they wouldn't kill her. It doesn't matter how tough someone is, you can always break them, especially if you don't care how you do it. But I also have the feeling that if it came down to it, Alina would make sure she wasn't taken alive."

Jia frowned. "Let's hurry up and make sure it doesn't come to that."

Erik slowed his MX six minutes later as he closed on a sprawling abandoned commercial complex in the Shadow Zone. It encompassed different large buildings. They might be small compared to the massive towers of Neo SoCal, but there was something about buildings closer to the ground to give them a greater sense of scale.

Emma's scans suggested nothing out of the ordinary, and her drones patrolled the area. On the edge of the complex, she uncovered a small group of indigents gathering for a meal, but there was no one with decent firepower or any unusual readings that suggested a battle.

"I'm not liking this," Jia admitted. "We might be too late."

"It's not like they could jump out of here," Erik insisted. "If we're too late to help her, we're not too late to avenge her." He sucked in a breath. "Emma, any more messages?"

"No," Emma replied. "The coordinates place the meeting point inside one of the buildings. None of my drones are detecting any fleeing vehicles in the area. There don't appear to be any local cameras I can access."

Jia reached under her feet to grab the TR-7. After Erik landed the Taxútnta, she handed the weapon to him along with some magazines before grabbing a rifle and magazines from a hidden compartment in the back, her face set like granite.

Erik stepped out of the flitter. "No such thing as being too careful. She might have decided to be dramatic."

"No such thing as paranoia in our line of work." Jia closed her door and raised her rifle. "It might be that she's being dramatic, or it might be that the conspiracy is hoping to take down several troublemakers today."

Erik selected four-barrel mode. "Then I hope they brought an entire army with them. If they took down Alina, she would have made them pay. I know that."

They proceeded through the open door, following Emma's nav marker, a couple of her smaller drones flanking them. Vast emptiness filled the large initial room, broken up by occasional piles of debris from the collapsing ceiling and the scuttle of rats and roaches in darkened corners. There were no bodies or fresh blood, though dark stains near a hall connecting to another large room pointed to a past tragedy.

"Multiple contacts up ahead," Emma noted. "I see Agent Koval, and she doesn't appear to be in distress."

They picked up their pace. A quarter of the way down the corridor, they could make out a distant human form with a cyan tinge on the top: Alina in her uncommon non-disguised form. A dark-skinned man stood next to her. They didn't move or adjust their positions. Quick magnification confirmed the familiar face of Colonel Adeyemi.

If this was a trap, it was a good one.

Erik slung his TR-7 over his back, no longer concerned about an ambush, and quickened his pace. A minute later, he arrived in the next large room.

Jia looked around as if still expecting an ambush, but no Tin Men dropped from the ceiling. No *yaoguai* boiled out of the walls. No half-Leem agents cackled in the distance.

It wasn't an ambush. It was nothing more than an unusual place to meet. Erik was annoyed by Alina's lack of clarity, but he wasn't going to show it.

"Where's your posse, Colonel?" Erik asked, looking

around. "It's not like you to travel alone, especially to the Shadow Zone."

"It was necessary," Colonel Adeyemi replied. "They're handling something else for me, but they'll be available soon enough, and that's a good thing since we're going to need them."

Jia frowned. "What's going on?"

Alina stepped forward, her ponytail swaying. "We've gotten so used to hurting the conspiracy that we might have gotten sloppy. They took advantage of it, and they punched us in the eye. It's a nice lesson in humility, but we need to pay them back with a kick to the balls."

"Or two, and a third for good measure," Adeyemi added.

Jia grimaced.

"How screwed are we?" Erik asked.

"Not that screwed yet," Alina offered, though she didn't sound confident. "But it could get worse in the coming weeks, depending on what the ID and you can do to deal with the conspiracy's counterattack. I'll cut to the chase. An important ID informant looking into conspiracy matters has gone missing, and his handler was killed. That's bad enough, but the potential reason is a lot worse, and that's what has really got me worried."

Erik could only think of one possibility that would get under Alina's skin. His jaw tightened.

"You've got a mole?"

"We don't know yet, and that annoys me more than you know." Alina gritted her teeth. "At a minimum, we've got a serious leak. My people are currently following that up since, depending on who it is, it might mean we have serious and debilitating operational security problems. Compartmentalization helps, but we've had to pull back on a lot of operations until we plug the leak. Otherwise, unfortunate consequences might occur."

Jia nodded. "That's an understatement, but what does this have to do with us? You want us to follow up on the leak as an external option? We're both ready for a mission."

"This is one time your position works against you." Alina shook her head. "You can't dig efficiently into the ID. We have people who are experts at this sort of thing, but my main issue right now is that without knowing how badly we're leaking, it's hard to know who and what we can trust. We also can't sit around doing absolutely nothing, even with the leak. The conspiracy will take advantage of our lack of operations." She folded her arms. "I have individual agents I'd trust my life to, but they heavily rely on ID channels that might be compromised. We need someone from outside the ID who can operate independently, who we know has the ability to penetrate conspiracy operations."

"Okay," Erik replied. "And we're sure it was them? I know they're powerful, but they can't be responsible for everything bad in the UTC. I'm willing to do you favors, but I'm mostly interested in kicking conspiracy ass."

"We can't be sure, but the informant was focused on investigations concerning some of the people taking over assets and companies controlled by Sophia Vand. That raises the chance." Alina tapped her PNIU.

A data window displayed a bloodied man being shoved into the back of the flitter by two large men with pistols. The man attempted to kick one of them, but a thug knocked him out by slamming the butt of the pistol into his head twice. The video stopped shortly after the flitter flew away. A new window appeared, featuring a smiling image of the man.

Alina pointed to him. "This is Nazeer Ahmed. The agent responsible for handling him was found in a restaurant bathroom with three bullets in the back of her head. Because of the agent's foresight, combined with other intel and the arrogance of his captors to fail to disable a tracker he had implanted for a couple of hours, we know where he is, or at least his body. That means we might be able to salvage this part of the debacle."

Erik patted his TR-7. "You want us to play fetch?"

"Yes, since he might still be alive," Alina replied. "Not only will having two outsiders help with this, but there are also some potential political ramifications where using you will help."

"You're saying you need someone you can throw under the bus if this blows up?" Erik asked in a matter-of-fact tone. "I'm not saying I won't do it, but I want to know what I'm getting into. I'm not a fan of surprises."

"I won't be done with you, Perseus and Atalante, until you've slain all of my monsters." Alina frowned. "But it helps to have someone less directly connected to the ID when managing the situation. It's more about making this less of a headache than having sacrificial lambs."

"What's the political situation *exactly*?" Jia asked.

Alina summoned an image of a massive mansion surrounded by a dense forest. It was taken from some distance away, emphasizing the size of the home.

"This is where Nazeer was taken. It is the home of a

high-ranking Ceres Galactic corporate officer in France, one who conveniently died in an accident a month ago. He had extensive ties to Sophia Vand before her death. There are too many coincidences for this not to be the conspiracy."

"I don't get it." Erik nodded at the image. "If the guy's dead, what's the political consideration?"

"There are some in Parliament who are concerned that the ID is out of control," Alina explained in a weary tone. "Especially on Earth. Some feel the ID should be letting the CID handle this kind of thing, and there are general concerns that we're overly aggressive. We can't brief Parliament on the operational details of everything we do, and that makes them question us even more."

"You're saying some bought conspiracy tools are trying to weaken you?" Jia growled.

Alina shook her head. "Some are, perhaps, and some are not. You know how this goes, Jia. Some people, even members of Parliament, don't want to know how much darkness there is in the UTC, let alone on Earth, but that doesn't mean we should destroy everything that makes the UTC good just to take out the bad guys. That would be a Greek tragedy." She dismissed the image with the flick of her wrist. "It doesn't matter. Until we have the leak fully plugged in the ID, we need to be careful about who we send on missions. Blind trust gets people killed. At least you two are a known quantity."

Emma materialized, this time in an Army uniform. "You want Erik and Jia to assault a mansion that is probably a conspiracy base and heavily defended. Because it's a recovery mission and political in nature, you can't simply level it, but at the same time, they have to show restraint until they rescue Mr. Ahmed. Is that it?"

"That's an accurate summary," Alina replied. "Nice and succinct."

"It's also a recipe for suicide." Emma narrowed her eyes. "I'm well aware of their relative combat ability against the average gun goblin and terrible troll, but they are only two people, and if they can't soften the target with bombardment beforehand, they run the risk of being overwhelmed. Skill and willpower can only do so much to overcome sheer numbers. If they took the informant there, they have reason to expect they can defend the location."

Erik raised an eyebrow. She wasn't wrong, but he was surprised Emma would show such direct concern about them. He'd gotten used to her begrudgingly showing her concern.

Virtual mother-in-law strikes again.

Colonel Adeyemi raised his fist to his mouth and coughed to get their attention. "You're right, Emma, and that's where I come in. No one expects Erik and Jia to go in there alone, and there's no way I'd let anyone send them in there alone."

"How are you supposed to do this?" Emma folded her arms with a dismissive sneer on her face. "Aren't politics involved? Won't involving the DD cause trouble?"

"Yes, but this is one time, I'm willing to take the risk," the colonel replied. "I have enough handpicked men and women who are willing to volunteer for a totally off-the-books black op to put together a decent squad. I can gear them up for a major assault, including exos."

Erik frowned. "And if things go badly?"

"Then a rogue colonel goes to prison or to the frontier, and the ID doesn't take the hit." Colonel Adeyemi shrugged, no fear on his face. "We all need to help each other because we all have the same goal."

"Do we have to be quiet this time?" Erik asked. "Emma's got a point. We can't just blow up half the place without risking killing the informant, but there's no way we're going to sneak a squad of exos in without shooting someone. I doubt they've got that house filled with stun-only security bots."

Eagerness removed the discomfort on Alina's face. "You can be as noisy as you want, but you'll need to do it quickly. If you agree, I want you on a transport tomorrow morning, heading to France. I'm only not sending you tonight because I want you rested, and that gives me time to set up one potential feint operation in another part of the country. You should leave Malcolm behind on this operation. It's not going to be that subtle, and the reality is because he's dating Camila, he's tied into the ID even more directly than you two. And yes, I'm also checking into both of them as leaks."

Erik nodded, surprised at her suspicion. He decided to opt for levity.

"Since his girlfriend's in town, he wouldn't want to go risk his life anyway." He looked at his partner. "I'm in, but I can't speak for Jia."

She nodded. "I'm in, too. Let's go rescue your informant."

"Good." Alina rubbed her hands together. "Let's talk logistics."

CHAPTER ELEVEN

Jia double-checked her seatbelt and harness as Erik finished docking the MX 60 in the Army ballistic transport.

It was the first time she'd flown in a military transport instead of a civilian craft, but other than a denser series of docking ports for vehicles through most of the body and some heavy docking clamps near the front for larger military vehicles, there wasn't much difference.

It didn't have any obvious armor on the outside, but that made sense. If they were launching ballistic transports and didn't control the area, it was pointless to expect them to survive. Armor wouldn't do much against decent surface-to-air missiles or AAA.

Erik had changed the color to a dull gray to stand out less, but it was pointless. The flight today was empty except for the MX 60. It was eerie.

"They're doing final flight checks," Emma announced. "We'll lift off in about twenty minutes. Flight time is about an hour and a half."

Colonel Adeyemi's team had taken an earlier transport.

Erik let go of the control yoke and frowned. "Alina wants us to go do a major assault, but she doesn't want us to use our advanced exos. That's kind of annoying."

"Politics again. Those are experimental models. It'd point too directly to the ID." Jia shrugged. "Besides, Adeyemi's going to provide us exos. Since when were you so picky about things?" She thought for a second. "Other than food?"

"Nothing wrong with wanting the best tool for the job. And I've gotten used to their mobility." Erik furrowed his brow, a dark expression on his face. "But I wonder about him, too."

"The colonel?" Jia stared at Erik. "You don't trust him? That's the last thing I expected to hear from you."

"Oh, I trust him." Erik shook his head. "Hell, of all the people we deal with, I trust him the most. Even more than Alina."

"Because he's Army?"

Erik shook his head. "Nope. The Army's big. All the training and the *esprit de corps* in the galaxy can't erase the fact that some guys are only looking out for themselves. It's his motivation I trust."

"Revenge." Jia gave a knowing nod. "You can relate."

"His motivation is purer than mine. His son was murdered." Erik shook his head, a distant look in his eyes. "No man should have to bury his child. I think the colonel died the day he found out, and the man we know is just a ghost, continuing on and unable to rest until his son is fully avenged." He nodded grimly. "He'll never betray our conspiracy hunt, and he'll probably get himself killed or arrested for going too far in support of it. That's what I worry about, but maybe I shouldn't."

"Why is that?"

"It's like Lanara told me the other day," Erik explained. "This is a war, and you don't win wars without casualties. If Adeyemi gets too focused, he might make mistakes. The conspiracy found the jump drive lab, which means the Defense Directorate doesn't have everything sealed up."

"You're worried about leaks in the military, including inadvertent?" Jia surmised.

"Exactly." Erik nodded at her. "That is why this crap's only going to get harder. The people at the top of the conspiracy probably barely fill a decent-sized room. They might have their monsters and Tin Men, but the average soldier in the military or the average agent in the CID or the ID wants to protect the UTC. If it was an open fight, we'd destroy them easily." He chuckled, but there was no mirth in the sound. "We've gotten lucky because it's hard to keep everything secure when you're trying to hide in the shadows. Conspiracies want to unravel naturally. People can't keep their mouths shut when they do something important."

Jia sighed. "And now we're in a conspiracy of our own, one dedicated to destroying their conspiracy."

"Yep. This ID leak, or the agents who've been grabbed—it's all the same thing. The more we have to play their game, the ultra-secrecy game, the more our advantages are neutralized, and they get hits on us like this."

"Alina's trying her best," Jia countered. "The *Argo*, and convincing the military to lend us the *Bifröst*. We have Emma, too."

Jia expected the AI to chime in at that point, but she remained silent. She was grateful for the restraint in the emotional moment.

"Isn't that how war unfolds?" Jia murmured, conflicting thoughts swirling in her head. "We haven't broken the enemy's morale, so they're growing desperate and striking back harder, like a cornered animal."

"That's what I'm afraid of." Erik shook his head. "First, it was simple corruption, and then terrorism, but they're starting to get really scary. They tried to sink Parvati, and they activated that ship."

"I don't think they intended for it to get out of control," Jia suggested.

"We don't know that," Erik spat through gritted teeth. "We've been assuming they wanted to harvest the tech for whatever reasons, but for all we know, they're a bunch of genocidal psychopaths who want to wipe out all life on Earth."

Jia locked eyes with him. "It doesn't matter."

He eyed her. "How does it not matter?"

Her voice was velvet over rock. "Because if we wipe them out, they can't do anything."

Erik's lips curled into a hungry smile. "Good point."

Both fell into their own thoughts for the next half-hour. Jia kept thinking back to her dinner with Mei. Her sister wanted a satisfying life where she could experience new things. It was a simple dream, easily obtainable with the right mindset.

But what of the conspiracy? Were they really genocidal, or was it about simple control?

Jia didn't understand the point of it, regardless of motivation. Given the sheer resources they'd already displayed, the members had to have indirect control of large parts of the UTC. If Sophia Vand was a typical example, the conspiracy *was* the UTC.

The conspiracy was waging war not with the UTC, but with decency and freedom. A person didn't need to be a committed Purist to be disgusted by the cybernetic and genetic modifications used by the conspiracy's forces. The half-alien agent they'd fought on Venus might end up being one of the more mundane enemies.

Jia's stomach churned. There might be half-Hunter hybrids out there, deadly monsters waiting to be unleashed on innocents. She didn't care what motivation the conspiracy cited; they'd long ago crossed the line.

There was no choice left but obliteration for either side.

She swallowed, and her heart rate kicked up. An image flashed in her mind from the battle against the Hunter ship, Cutter's death stare.

"When I became a cop," she murmured, capturing Erik's attention, "I believed I was a peace officer. I thought my actions would help save people's lives."

"They did." Erik looked her way. "We stopped killers, terrorists, and all sorts of bastards at the NSCPD. We saved a lot of lives, and we helped a lot of other people get closure by catching the people who hurt them or their families."

"I know, and it's not like I didn't see people get hurt

when I was a detective, but I now understand the fundamental difference between being a cop and what we are."

"What's that?" Erik sounded curious.

"It's like you discussed with Lanara." Jia lifted her head and stared at the ceiling. "We're not private security contractors. In a sense, we're private military contractors fighting a shadow war."

"Can't say I disagree with that assessment. I also can't say it bothers me. I spent my life as a soldier. It's the one thing I know I'm good at. That and penjing."

"It's easy to imagine a police department that rarely loses officers, especially on a civilized planet," Jia continued. "But it's hard to imagine an army that never loses soldiers. Police help preserve the peace, but when the military's involved, they have to destroy to bring peace."

Erik didn't respond for a long while. He stared through the front window, although there was nothing exciting there but the cargo bay wall of the transport. Jia looked away, embarrassed.

"You're right," he finally said. "And Lanara's right. You can't fight a war if you're not willing to take casualties. The universe isn't kind, and no matter how many rules and laws of war we make, there's always somebody who doesn't care. Somebody who will take it too far. Since we can't afford to become them, the good guys are always at a disadvantage."

"But it's not hopeless," Jia murmured.

Erik nodded, a slight smile on his face. "If you're breathing, it's not hopeless. Let me give you a tip I learned the hard way in my time in the service. If you focus on your losses, you're always going to feel like crap. You need to focus on your wins because if you aren't dead, those are going to lead to your victories. I know what brought this on."

"You do?"

"Yeah," Erik replied. "A lot of good men and women lost their lives in the fight against the Hunters, including Cutter, but I look at it differently. A small group of humans fought off an alien race far more advanced and ruthless than us. We won, and if we can win against the Hunters, we can win against the conspiracy."

Jia offered him a rueful smile. "That makes far too much sense. You're right."

"One other tip. It's okay to be angry about those we lost, but do what I'm doing." Erik's mouth twitched into a frown.

"Which is what?" Jia asked.

"Adding every death to the conspiracy's bill," Erik intoned.

CHAPTER TWELVE

The MX 60 sped low over the dense treetops, guided both by Emma's navigation and direct control. They'd changed the color to a forest green that helped them blend in with the canopy below.

To Erik's and Jia's surprise, when they unloaded from the transport, a soldier approached them and gave them a set of coordinates before ushering them off-base with an appropriate security pass.

The pair had expected they'd get their briefing at the base, but it made more sense that they wouldn't. Colonel Adeyemi was running an off-the-books operation, and no matter how much goodwill or respect he'd accumulated in the Army and how many strings people pulled on his behalf, there was only so much they could tolerate.

It was a dark irony that the whole thing was for the protection of the UTC, and they only had to play so many ghosts games because the tentacles of the conspiracy stretched into so many parts of the government.

Erik often wondered what it'd be like to sit in a meeting of the leaders of the conspiracy, if they had such a thing. There were so many questions he wanted clear answers to. Sophia Vand's death had wounded them, but Alina couldn't say how much. Other than collecting alien artifacts, no one knew the ultimate goal of their enemy.

He used to worry that he wouldn't know when he'd finally won, that there might always be one more bastard out there. Those concerns had vanished after the fight with the Hunter ship. His allies had momentum now, and they could continue chipping away at the enemy, with each victory bringing more targets.

No one could control as much as the conspiracy did without leaving a trail, and now the bloodhounds were sniffing out their awful scent.

"It's beautiful," Jia murmured.

"Huh?" Erik looked her way. "What is?"

She gestured out the window at the passing trees and rolling hills in the distance. A curtain of blooming lavender covered a field to their right.

"It's okay," Erik admitted.

Jia laughed. "It's something I let myself forget. Neo SoCal is the ultimate city, and we mainly travel to cities or domes. Sometimes pure nature is nice."

"You don't seem like much of a country girl to me."

"I didn't say I was, but I can appreciate beauty." Jia smiled and rested her head against the window. "All that technology and the conspiracy isn't concentrating on making more beauty, just more monstrous ways to kill and destroy."

"Weapons always come first," Erik uttered. "That's the way things go for humans."

"It's not that it bothers me." Jia lifted her head and laughed. "It's absurd if you think about it."

"What is?"

"We're in the beautiful French countryside, but we're here not on vacation. We're here to blow things up." She mimed an explosion with both hands.

Erik grinned. "It's not like we have to blow things up, but yeah, that's probably how things will turn out."

"It's humorous." Jia shook her head. "I've traveled more in these last couple of years than in my entire life, and all over. I'm seeing the world and the Solar System."

"See, I take you nice places," Erik joked.

"Places to blow up." Jia tapped her PNIU, and a data window appeared with a city outline that looked familiar.

"Where's that?" Erik asked.

"Bogota," Jia replied. "I'd wanted to visit there before we went, but what did we do? We went there in the middle of the night to blow up a Tin Man factory on New Year's."

Erik laughed. "Hey, it made for some nice fireworks. We probably saw more of the city than a lot of tourists, and it's not like we never get to see cool things in the places we visit."

"The Sky Garden." Jia smiled warmly. "I have to say, that trip to Lagos does go to show that seeing something up close and in person is different than seeing a hologram, even in VR."

"And we didn't blow it up," Erik insisted. "Rather, we stopped someone from blowing it up."

"We blew *them* up," she counter-argued.

"We shot them for the most part. That's not the same thing." Erik shrugged.

"Chang'e City," Jia commented. "Parvati. Unity City. Lots of explosions along the way."

"A lot of people might travel in their lifetime, but most barely leave their area," Erik replied with an amused look. "If I hadn't joined the Army, I bet I would never have left Detroit."

"And I'd be the person who spent her entire life in Neo SoCal, not convinced I needed to leave the great metroplex either." Jia let out a quiet chuckle. "We've seen a lot of nice things there, too, some I never bothered to go see until my job took me there or Alina chose them for a meeting."

"Just goes to show that it's easy to not appreciate what you have, let alone everything else you might have."

Jia returned to staring at the trees and colorful fields. "We're a well-traveled couple. Our vacations just tend to involve explosions and bullets, and the occasional laser."

"For now," he admitted. *Was that hope?*

Jia turned to face him. "Somehow, I think you'd get bored if there wasn't at least the chance of an explosion."

"Maybe." Erik grinned playfully. "Is that so bad?"

"No." Jia patted his arm. "It's not."

The MX 60 slowed and they descended. Erik wouldn't recommend flying through such a dense forest normally, but Emma wasn't about to do anything she couldn't handle. If the MX 60 was smashed to pieces, she'd not only risk destruction, but she would also lose her preferred body.

"We're about five minutes from the target location," Emma announced. "I've established communications with the colonel's team."

Erik rubbed his hands together. "Time to add another location to our explosions and bullets tour list."

CHAPTER THIRTEEN

The shift was dramatic, amusing Jia more than she expected.

They were flying through a mostly untouched and beautiful part of the French countryside, before suddenly arriving at a large clearing dominated by a cargo flitter loaded with exoskeletons. Soldiers stood around in tactical suits, watching impassively as the MX 60 descended into the clearing and landed.

Erik and Jia exited the flitter and walked over to Colonel Adeyemi. He wasn't in uniform, but he was in a tactical suit. A rifle was slung over his shoulder.

"You planning to come with us on the op, Colonel?" Erik asked.

"Not with the first wave." Colonel Adeyemi looked thoughtful. "I'd just get in the way."

"You're going to miss all the fun." Erik decided not to press him on what he meant by "the first wave."

"Blackwell, unlike you, I'm glad to be a REMF at this point." The colonel grinned.

Seconds later, his grin disappeared, the hard mask marking their normal dealings returning. He circled his hand in the air and yelled, "Listen up, people. Pay attention."

The soldiers fell into formation immediately, shifting to parade rest. No one spoke. They all focused on Colonel Adeyemi, awaiting orders. Erik and Jia moved to the side of the formation but didn't join it. Emma appeared in a uniform standing beside them. None of the soldiers so much as blinked at the hologram.

"Good," Colonel Adeyemi announced, his voice loud and clear.

He tapped his PNIU and a large map appeared. A red dot marked their position, and a curved arrow marked their path. Additional windows appeared, showing aerial views of the mansion and the forest around it.

"First of all," the colonel continued, "I want to thank each and every one of you for volunteering for this mission. You know we're doing this off the books. You all are aware of the cancer that eats away at the UTC, a cancer that has threatened military projects and killed military personnel. The rest of the DD has been supportive of my efforts to aid the ID in crushing this conspiracy that would undermine us all, but the enemy is getting smarter and *sneakier.*" He swept the crowd with his hard gaze. "They think they can outplay us that way. Do you agree with that?"

"No, sir!" the formation bellowed.

Colonel Adeyemi nodded. "You all know good soldiers gave their lives in May to fight a threat none of us could have imagined existed. The conspiracy dared try to unleash an ancient weapon of war." He inclined his head toward Erik. "Those two, along with your fellow soldiers, stopped that. Today, we don't have to face an ancient alien super-vessel. We just need to go into a mansion and probably cut down some Tin Men and a few guards. You think you can handle that?"

"Yes, sir!"

"Good." Colonel Adeyemi gestured to the map. "Then let's get this over with. The ID lost their friend, and Blackwell and Lin are going to lead your team to recover him. Let me make this clear: we only care about recovering the information. If you meet hostile resistance during this mission, feel free to send them to hell. Now, at ease as I give the general briefing."

The formation shifted, some dropping their arms. No one took their attention off the colonel. Eagerness and excitement covered their faces.

Jia's heart rate sped up. She was used to missions, but calmness always eluded her before they launched. That didn't upset her. It was just like Erik had told her. Total calm could lead to underestimating the enemy. No one should go into the battle thinking they couldn't lose. Surprise was the enemy's greatest weapon.

"This is the target mansion," the colonel announced. "Because we don't want to throw your lives away, we've done our best to glean intel without tipping off any little cockroach spies the conspiracy has in either the Intelligence or Defense Directorates. Since none of you are blind, I'm sure you've noticed these."

Multiple images of anti-craft cannons appeared,

depicting various weapons from different angles. Some of the excitement vanished from the squad.

"That's right, people," Colonel Adeyemi continued. "This nice, fancy mansion in the forest in the middle of nowhere has enough triple-A to take down a whole squadron of Dragons. If that doesn't scream suspicious, I don't know what does, and because of that, we can't risk a direct drop into the target area."

"We're hoofing it?" Erik asked.

"In the exos, yes," the colonel replied. "We have to assume the enemy has perimeter alarms and defenses, but we'll get to how we're going to deal with those in a minute. We're going to try to get closer with the cargo flitter. We're taking a calculated risk by using that class of vehicle, but it'll give us the speed and mobility we need to get close enough to the target that you can all drop in while hopefully not getting shot down."

Jia wondered if the choice of vehicle was partially constrained by logistics. An off-the-books mission could get away with transport redirection here and there, but the more gear and vehicles the colonel grabbed, the more he risked leakage.

She glanced at Erik. He didn't look concerned, and she trusted his judgment. None of the other soldiers looked all that worried, but she did find herself asking if that was as reliable a measure as she would have thought. After all, many of these men and women had probably dropped onto planets from orbit.

Their sense of relative danger might be *just a bit* skewed.

Counting Erik and Jia, there would be twelve military-grade exoskeletons. Erik's complaint about the maneuver-ability aside, that was a lot of firepower, and they were being accompanied by trained operators who wouldn't be fighting super-aliens.

Jia was liking their odds.

"You've all been briefed on the appearance of the infor-mant," Colonel Adeyemi explained. "If you locate him and he is dead, the ID still wants his body back. If you establish that early on, feel free to inflict as much damage as you want on your way out. Remember, this is first and fore-most a rescue mission, not a search and destroy, but I'm not going to complain if you burn the place down on your way out. If by some miracle you can take control without significant risk, I'm sure the ID wouldn't mind."

He stared at Erik, who shrugged, an innocent smile on his face.

The colonel gestured at Emma. "We're blessed to have the UTC's best AI on our team during this mission. She's going to handle the electronic warfare, so all of you don't have to worry about anything but shooting. Why don't you take the next bit, Emma?"

She vanished and reappeared next to the colonel. "All publicly available satellite data indicates there is no mansion in this location. The images you have been shown were taken with long-range cameras from drones. Because of the risk, no drone assets have been able to get too close."

"Exactly," the colonel announced. "You're all going to use jammers and laser comms in tight formation. Disrupting command and control will be to our advantage, given the cameras and drones they'll likely have available."

Erik frowned and nodded at one of the data windows.

"With that kind of AAA, we can't risk the MX 60. Emma, you're going to need to ride with me."

She smiled. "I was going to suggest that."

One of the soldiers cleared his throat. "Sir, this all sounds reasonable, but like you said, they'll probably see us coming."

"Exos aren't the only thing I have packed back there," Colonel Adeyemi replied, motioning to the cargo flitter. "We've got entire squadrons of drones with stun rifles and chaff ready to go. Emma can mass-program them to flood the area and continue disruption even under jamming conditions. We're going to use those drones as a distraction when you get close."

"Why not lethals?"

Colonel Adeyemi frowned. "Because we can't have some drone accidentally killing our target. Let's move on to completion and recovery. The primary mission is to rescue our target. After that's been achieved, you can drop jamming and transmit, so the cargo flitter can come and extract him."

"I'll be using a drone chain as repeaters," Emma added with a hint of smugness.

"If, at that point, the enemy is still jamming the area, send up a flare, and I'll go with the backup, some Dragons supporting the cargo flitter. I'd prefer to not call the Dragons because it'll raise questions, but we'll do what we need to." The colonel frowned. "Emma assures me she has a good chance of controlling the cargo flitter using bridged laser comms, but if she can't establish control within five minutes of the flare, I will fly the damned thing in. If I don't arrive in five minutes, you will withdraw to this location on foot."

The soldiers exchanged looks, some surprised, some impressed. Jia didn't think it'd be much of a problem. The conspiracy might have reinforced their base, but they didn't know an entire squad of exoskeletons was about to smash into them.

It was time to win another battle in the war.

CHAPTER FOURTEEN

Erik was annoyed and had die-hard plans to *continue* being annoyed.

When a freelancer is asked to commit violence, he wants to use the best tools—the ones he'd trained with and gotten used to in a high-ops-tempo environment.

All the complaints about having to use a standard-model exo vanished when Erik strapped into the machine offered by the colonel. The concerns about his recent training felt petty and distant, like they'd come from someone else.

The exo was comfortable and familiar, like a beloved family member showing up at a reunion. The Army might not always use the latest, greatest cutting-edge machinery, but every weapon system employed by soldiers in the field was battle-tested and *reliable*.

Sometimes sacrificing features for reliability helped a soldier win a battle.

Erik grinned as he remembered that truth, thinking about his TR-7. He used the weapon both out of habit and because of its reliability. Sometimes a man could get the best of both worlds, but today he'd settle for the Army exo with a very solid grenade launcher.

All the other men and women gathered in the back of the cargo flitter waited in their exos for the drop. He didn't know if they weren't normally a chatty bunch, or if they didn't feel comfortable talking in front of him and Jia.

During his time with the Knights Errant, he'd enjoyed the last-minute banter before a battle. He'd looked forward to it. If someone died in battle, he wanted his last real conversation with them to be something funny and interesting. That way, he could carry their memories with them for eternity.

The cool weight of his dog tag rested against his chest. He didn't think about much each morning when he put it on, but it was not something he ever forgot.

It was a symbol of his promise to the men and women of his unit during those days when he wasn't about to jump out of the back of a cargo flitter and go after the people responsible for their deaths.

The cargo flitter skimmed the treetops, flying low and fast. Erik watched course updates on his faceplate display. Their drop zone was seven klicks away from the mansion.

Emma's dense drone swarm looked like some sort of mistake on the display. She'd broken the initial mass apart and was circling the target, her extensions weaving through the trees. They would soon rise to draw the enemy's attention. They might have been noticed, but there was no reaction from the mansion.

Erik took a slow, deep breath and let it out. He'd said

more than once that fighting was the one thing he knew he was good at.

It had defined his life.

His only major vacation from battle lasted only for the length of his trip back to Earth from Molino. He'd been fighting ever since, but his raids as a cop, even the ones working for Alina, hadn't felt the same as being in the military.

He'd worked alongside soldiers in some, but he felt more like the contractor showing up to help them out.

Things had been different recently. The Hunter ship op and the current one sent him straight back to his Army days. He wasn't sure if that was a good thing or a bad thing.

That was why he didn't like the tug in the back of his mind. It wasn't the Lady. It wasn't some strange sixth sense. That would be easy to ignore or push off.

This was something different. The feeling wiggling into the back of his thought was born of decades of experience shaped by life-or-death struggles where deadly decisions had to be made in seconds. Sometimes ignoring the illogical meant ignoring a vital detail your subconscious had noticed.

Erik established a direct channel to Colonel Adeyemi and Jia. He was in command of the mission, but these were Adeyemi's men.

"We sure about this op, Colonel?" he asked. "Something about it is bothering me."

"Sure?" The colonel snorted. "Hell, no. This is all heavily relying on the ID, and Koval came to me because it's been compromised. This is textbook desperation based on half-ass intel. If it didn't involve the conspiracy, I wouldn't be involved."

Erik worried about that. Vengeance could blind a man, but he didn't believe Adeyemi would throw away the lives of the loyal soldiers who served under him.

"Is something wrong, Erik?" Jia asked.

"Something's bothering me about all this," Erik admitted. "The conspiracy is staggering from our hits, and they had to assume there would have been a tracker in someone like Ahmed. But they didn't bother to do anything about it until the ID figured out where he'd been taken."

"You think it's a trap?" Jia concluded. She sounded more curious than worried.

Emma's drones formed a complete circle about four kilometers out from the target. They were waiting for the cargo flitter to move closer before charging. Erik doubted the enemy could fail to notice that many drones that close. Playing dumb and innocent might make sense for the occasional flyby, but an entire squadron of drones meant an attack. The plan partially required the enemy to focus on those drones, too.

Was he worrying too much?

Colonel Adeyemi grunted in frustration. "I've been wondering the same thing, but the conspiracy also couldn't be sure we wouldn't blow the hell out of the place from the sky. It's in the middle of nowhere, which makes it a lot easier to be loud without explaining things away. Alina might believe in old-school honor, but not everyone in the ID does."

"I know," Erik replied. "That's what's bothering me. It's not worth it to weave some elaborate trap to take down a couple of squads or some agents. They would have to really want to take the risk. I don't care how much they've prepped things, there's always a chance they've left evidence behind that we can use, and any crumb that gets us closer to them means we can throw more forces at them."

Jia let out a rueful chuckle. "I can think of one thing the enemy wants. Something that would be worth a scheme to kill a handful of people."

"Alien artifacts?" Erik guessed.

"No. If Ahmed knew about that kind of thing, Alina would have told us, and I think the colonel's right. There's a good chance that some people in the ID would be more than willing to risk losing him rather than let the conspiracy get a line on any more artifacts."

Erik could understand. They'd taken a tremendous personal risk to stop the Hunter ship. Everybody aboard the *Argo* and *Bifröst* could have been killed by their nested jump trick.

He'd made the call, and he stood by it. He didn't know if he could judge others if they made the same call, but at least he'd been willing to put his skin on the line.

The cargo flitter's positional indicator got closer to the mansion. They didn't have much time left for an abort. They'd gone over squad assignments right after loading up. Everyone was prepped and ready to go, but they'd discussed emergency exfil under jamming conditions, not aborting the whole op.

"If not artifacts, then what?" Erik demanded.

"Us," Jia suggested. "You and me, the big reoccurring factor involved in a lot of these plans. Alina already said the ID is watching our backs, which means the conspiracy will have trouble coming at us directly without risking leaving a trail. But a nice, juicy trap with nice, juicy bait?"

Erik's jaw tightened. Sometimes a unit had to move into a dangerous ambush location for the overall goals of the operation. People engaged in the fine art of killing other people could rarely make it risk-free.

"That's a guess," Colonel Adeyemi complained. "People make mistakes. The ID does, and Lord knows the military does. If the conspiracy was flawless, they wouldn't have taken any losses."

If they scrubbed the mission, they might not be able to get an off-the-books military team like this together again for some time. Colonel Adeyemi had taken a lot of risks to help Erik and Jia, including using his clout to discourage the military from trying to recover Emma. Every time he did anything, there was a risk.

They couldn't quit because of a bad feeling. There was no way they'd win against the conspiracy that way, and if it came down to it, Erik was more than willing to hold the line while the squad retreated.

Erik transmitted to the entire squad. "Listen up. I have reason to believe we might be coming in hot despite our distraction and our distant drop zone. Emma's drones will help, but I want every man and woman ready to shoot before we're on the ground." He turned the exo toward the bay door. "We've got three minutes before Emma initiates the distraction and then two minutes before the drop. Try to not pee yourself, and remember, a good soldier doesn't die for their cause."

"What do they do, then?" asked a soldier.

"It's like General Patton said. They make the other son of a bitch die for theirs."

The soldiers chuckled. Erik couldn't see their faces behind their helmets and faceplates, but he had a feed of their vitals. Mild elevation in some, nothing out of the ordinary. Everyone was ready to fight, for Colonel Adeyemi, for the UTC, for themselves. The information was motivation, nothing more.

Erik regulated his breathing and waited for the seconds to tick by. He'd command this raid the way he'd lived his life: first one in, last one out.

CHAPTER FIFTEEN

"Initiating swarm," Emma reported.

Erik's heart rate kicked up from a rush of excitement, not fear. He would never deny enjoying taking it to the enemy. He'd respected a lot of the rebels he'd fought in his time in the Army, but he had nothing but contempt for the conspiracy.

This wasn't war, this was trash cleanup.

The circle of drones shrank in one fluid movement like a noose tightening around the neck of a condemned man. Erik reminded himself they were there for a rescue, not an execution, but he wouldn't mind flinging some pain along the way. A team of twelve exos with extra ammo was a solid unit, but it wasn't a massive army. Depending on the enemy defenses, there might only be so much they could do.

Erik appreciated that everyone was a volunteer, but he wasn't going to get anyone killed. If things got too hot, the ID informant would be the loss, not the soldiers with him, let alone Jia. The DD hadn't been the ones to let the man get captured.

The drones broke into erratic flight patterns as they passed over the target area, and some disappeared from the display. It was too late to abort.

"The enemy has initiated antiaircraft fire," Emma announced. "Extensive and powerful local jamming has been initiated. I'm glad I kept back an outer ring of drones to keep the rest under observation, but don't worry. They're successfully executing their autonomous disruption program. That might complicate comm on the ground."

"Everyone knows what they need to do," Erik replied. "Get ready to drop, people!" he shouted as the bay door opened. "We're leaving this bucket in sixty seconds. Keep to your squads and execute the plan. Remember your Patton."

Erik piloted his exo toward the door, its metal feet clanging on the floor of the cargo bay. Sometimes being a leader was more literal than others.

It wasn't bad. Jumping out of a flitter was nothing like dropping onto a planet. He could now see what Jia had been talking about on their way to the rendezvous point. There was something almost sacrilegious about having to battle on a beautiful place on Earth. Unfortunately, the enemy had chosen the battleground by placing their facility there.

Explosions sounded in the distance, but Erik couldn't see anything, given the angle of the flitter. He wasn't paying much attention to the pulsating and swirling patterns of the distraction drones. If there was a significant problem, Emma would inform him.

"Movement in the forest near the drop zone," Emma reported. "I'm seeing it with long-range cameras from drones outside the engagement zone. They're blending in well with the forest using some sort of camouflage, though not active optical. They're running unusually hot on thermal and seem to not be directly appearing from the mansion. Four-legged."

"Dogs?" one of the soldiers suggested, sounding surprised. "They've got dogs in the woods?"

"If only it were so easy," Jia muttered. "It'd be easy to scare off dogs with a couple of good warning shots."

The conspiracy made it easy. They never let him feel any qualms about who or what they were facing.

That made sense. They couldn't rely on good people to execute their plans. Even the average greedy bastard would balk at the carnage many of the conspiracy's plans involved.

"She's right," Erik agreed. "Those aren't dogs or wolves. We're most likely about to engage heavily modified *yaoguai* intended for combat. The enemy has shown off a lot of different types in the past, some more alien than any space raptor. Don't play around. Take them down, and watch your asses." He took a step down the cargo ramp. "Jumping in ten, nine, eight, seven, six, five, four, three, two, one. Go, go, go! It's time to kill some *yaoguai*!"

He leapt out of the back of the flitter with a spin. Jump thrusters weren't enough to make an exo fly, but they were enough to keep him in the target zone. The loud booms and rhythmic crack of the enemy's air defenses continued unabated, but they stayed close to the mansion.

The enemy might not have been able to do much to the cargo flitter given its low altitude, or they might have been confident their ground defenses would be sufficient to stop anything that came out.

He couldn't decide who was more arrogant, the man who came at a secret conspiracy base with a modest squad, or the people who thought they could win against highly trained Special Forces with jumped-up genetically-engineered toys.

Victory would prove one side right.

Emma's drones resembled a dense flock in the distance, the swarm's constant formation changes eerily beautiful in their own way. Bright explosions and clouds of dark smoke filled the sky. Sunlight reflected off the thick chaff. Flares become temporary suns.

It all looked impressive, but it wasn't accomplishing much but wasting enemy ammo. The exos needed to hit the ground and make their move.

The denizens of the nearby forest understood something dangerous was happening. Birds fluttered desperately away from the battle. Deer charged through the trees. They knew they didn't want to get caught up in it.

Jia and the other soldiers jumped from the flitter in a loose formation. Everyone extended their shields and angled their weapons down. They all knew something was down there waiting for them.

Erik swept back and forth, though Emma's info made it clear they wouldn't land in the middle of the *yaoguai*. The monsters were moving fast, but there was enough distance to give the squad time to prepare.

The exos cleared the canopy, everyone firing thrusters to continue to slow their descent and avoid branches. Despite the earlier warning, thus far, the only things with four legs they'd seen were the deer, the threat closing in but not yet there.

Yaoguai were the perfect guards for a remote mansion that functioned as a hidden base. It was likely no one other than conspiracy members had visited since the place was built.

Had some poor bastards helped supervise the construction, only to be fed to some monster later? Erik wouldn't put it past the kind of people who were in charge.

The twelve exos successfully landed with loud thumps in a staggered group. Without orders, they broke into three squads of four, forming an inverted wedge. Erik's and Jia's squad formed the tip of the spear.

"Everyone stay sharp," he yelled because of the comm interference. He didn't want to rely on laser comms. It'd be too easy to lose line of sight. "Our welcoming party will be here soon enough, and we don't wish to be rude and not show them we care."

He shifted to his thermal overlay. The explosions in the distance were clearly visible through the trees, as was the rapidly approaching temperature mass marking the *yaoguai*.

So much for a complete surprise. They should have loaded Emma's drone swarm with explosives like the men who had tried to assassinate the NSCPD chief and smashed them into everything but the mansion. That would have been a spectacular distraction.

"We need to clear the distance and fast," Erik ordered. "Kill anything that looks like it came out of a lab. Ready your frags. We don't need to burn down half of France. I don't want you using any plasmas until ordered to. All heavy ordnance exos, hold off. We might need those rockets for something far scarier than overgrown test-tube pets."

He downplayed the *yaoguai* threat but wondered how bad it would be. Not every soldier had experience dealing with genetically engineered monsters. Exotic and twisted creations threatened a soldier's mind and slowed his reflexes.

Four legs didn't sound so bad. At least it wasn't a tentacled horror that looked like a reject from alien porn.

A flick of a finger set his autoloader for fragmentation grenades in his launcher.

Three exos in each four-member squad were equipped with high-powered rifles and grenade launchers, including both fragmentation and plasma ammo. The fourth member carried a shoulder-mounted rocket launcher, but Erik worried about running into other exos, full-conversion Tin Men, or armored vehicles.

The yaoguai *might be nothing more than an appetizer.*

Overlapping deep, low howls came from ahead as the enemy approached, accompanied by the rustle and crack of branches.

Howls he could deal with. He didn't care how they dressed up a dog or a wolf with their mad science. They could paint it with polka dots and give it a venom-filled mouth for all he cared. In the end, it would just be a predator who had forgotten man had developed nicer tools than spears and stone axes.

"Hold position!" Erik shouted, aiming his grenade launcher. "Use your thermals. It doesn't matter how hard they are to see on regular optics then. Wait for my order to fire. Remember, *yaoguai* aren't normal animals. We're not going to be able to scare them off with a couple of kills. Don't just shoot to kill. Shoot to obliterate."

Erik glanced at a side window showing his non-thermal feed. The undergrowth rippled in front of him. Branches and shrubs pushed themselves to the side. Other plants and branches looked like they were moving forward, except for one thing—the bright yellow eyes.

It took more steps for Erik to realize the approaching enemies weren't using some sort of adaptive camouflage that matched them to their surroundings with each step. The patterns and coloration of the pelts of the *yaoguai* were static but perfect for the forest. It was obvious they'd been created to guard this exact location.

Camouflaged wolves. That's what they were, huge dire wolves twice the size of anything natural.

They bounded through the forest without further howls, only the sound of cracking branches and the thuds of their footfalls signaling their approach. It was time for their attack.

A genetically-engineered monster could possess all sorts of advantages over their natural kin and humans, but it took a human brain to understand military strategy. The dire wolves continued rushing forward, oblivious to the pain readied for them. The *yaoguai* might have their fear stripped from them through conditioning and genetic engineering, but the soldiers had the bravery of those fighting for a cause they believed in.

Erik waited, taking slow, measured breaths. There were too many trees and shrubs around. If they fired early, the effects of the barrage would be blunted. He wanted to maximize the destruction and ensure none of the first wave survived.

Awaiting his orders, none of the soldiers fired. Discipline was what turned a man into a soldier, and Erik had complete confidence in theirs. Colonel Adeyemi wouldn't have sent a bunch of hotheads with him.

It was Erik's job to be the hothead.

The dire wolves were close enough now that their outlines were distinguishable from the underlying terrain under normal optics. At this distance, their size was a design flaw when facing trained soldiers. Smaller monsters could have continued to blend with the forest.

"*Fire!*" Erik bellowed.

The twelve exoskeletons launched their grenades before he finished the word. Their all-but-simultaneous explosions ripped through the *yaoguai* line, sending a storm of flame and shrapnel slicing through their bodies. The loud noise swallowed most of their death yelps as the dire wolves tumbled forward in bloodied, burned masses.

For all their size, speed, and camouflage, the dire wolves couldn't stand up to the cruel ingenuity of human explosives.

Erik's gaze darted to a data window showing the forest far to his left and a growing heat signature. He checked to his far right. Another heat mass grew in front of him as well. He'd been worried about that.

The monsters might not understand military strategy, but they retained animal cunning. He would remind them again why humans ruled the Earth and had spread out to the stars. As long as the exos had ammo, these monsters couldn't win.

"Diamond," Erik ordered.

The squads rotated and spread out to produce the new formation within seconds. Erik was glad he'd practiced this sort of thing with Jia in their training sessions. Now, the exos' rifles and launchers pointed in every direction.

"It looks like the bastards are trying to flank us. I'm sure those monsters have big enough claws to tear through our weak points, so let's not give them the opportunity. Maintain your fields of fire. Don't use more than a third of your grenades for this engagement. I have a feeling this is just the start." Erik flexed his fingers. "Anything useful on your end, Emma?"

"I'm not seeing additional enemies, gun goblins, or marauding monsters emerging from the main building," Emma reported. "Admittedly, doing this with long-range cameras in this environment is less than ideal, but it's as if the *yaoguai* are emerging from the forest near the mansion rather than the building. I should note that not all of the *yaoguai* were initially deployed near your position, but they are all converging on it now."

"It was a general alarm response," Jia suggested. "They released them everywhere to look for us, maybe from underground passages. They wait until they see something and start howling, then the rest of them show up."

"I don't care all that much about where they're coming from," Erik replied. "I mostly care if Emma's seeing them ready cannons or surface-to-surface arty. I'd rather not get surrounded by these dire wolves and stalled out so they can start blowing the shit out of us with plasma artillery."

"I have yet to see anything like that," Emma offered. "Incidentally, my drone squadron is down to seventy-five percent strength. I'm rather unimpressed by their antiaircraft response. It's far less accurate than I would have believed."

"They might be panicking." Erik aimed his grenade launcher. "But if they haven't finished you off yet, all we need to do is survive."

Howls sounded from all around, louder and more insistent than before. There were more of them, too. The exo squad had taken out the scouts, and now the main force had arrived.

It was time to see which products of humanity's scientific hubris would triumph.

"Wait until they're twenty meters out and then send them back to Hell."

CHAPTER SIXTEEN

Erik had once told Jia that the difference between a good commander and a bad one was the latter felt the need to micromanage every part of a battle.

Properly trained soldiers needed direction in the form of orders, nothing else.

She might not be a soldier, but she constantly trained with Erik, and they'd fought together for years now. Jia didn't need careful direction either.

That was why Erik hadn't issued another order despite the change in enemy tactics. Unlike before, the dire wolves didn't immediately charge. They approached from three sides but then formed a circle, loping through the undergrowth and howling. The monsters might have been the ultimate soldiers in that they didn't need any orders.

They simply needed to be unleashed.

Jia wondered if they'd been trained that way, or if they were somehow adapting after seeing the charred bodies of the other *yaoguai*. The monsters outnumbered the raid team, but Jia wasn't worried. Being large and fast didn't count for much when they weren't also bullet- and explosion-proof.

Their creators hadn't accounted for the kind of equipment a military team might bring. At the same time, a huge horde of monsters seemed excessive to keep the forest clear of casual visitors who might stumble upon the mansion.

Jia tamped down her thoughts. How and why the conspiracy chose their monsters wasn't relevant as long as her team could destroy them. If exos could win against the Hunters' creations, they could win against whatever the conspiracy unleashed.

The new circle didn't last long before the dire wolves broke toward the exoskeletons. If the unit hadn't already formed a diamond, it might have been a concern, but there wasn't a single soldier who didn't have a weapon pointed in their direction.

The *yaoguai* rushed toward the exos, their huge jaws open, salivating. Did they want a meal, or were they created with nothing more than the desire to kill or maim?

Another salvo of frag grenades blasted the advancing monsters, ripping some apart and flinging others into the air. The dire wolves farther back didn't flinch despite the wave of destruction that annihilated the front line, the bodies stacking up around them.

The monsters didn't ignore the attack, since they staggered their next advance. Jia frowned. The line between instinctual adaptation and intelligence could be thin, but she didn't want to think about the conspiracy creating self-aware monsters from something other than human or alien stock.

Adaptation helped the dire wolves. The next wave of grenades didn't finish off the entire charging line. Growling, the bloodied survivors charged the exoskeletons, making it closer than before. Three survivors neared Jia's squad, growling loudly.

"I'll pick off the survivors in the front," Jia announced, firing her rifle.

The quick shots tore through the charging dire wolves but still didn't finish them off. Her follow-up rounds ended the monsters' lives, however.

Although the team had loaded extra ammo in anticipation of trouble, she didn't want to waste a single bullet. It was like Erik had said; this was one engagement in what might be a long battle.

The conspiracy wouldn't fortify a mansion in the forest with air defenses and hordes of monsters if there wasn't something important there. She hoped they could rescue the informant, but taking the entire place appealed more.

She understood the danger, but the simple solution to that was to wipe out all resistance in the base. Taking out the dire wolves would be a good start.

If this was some sort of trap for Erik and Jia, they would do what they always did and reverse it to make the conspiracy pay dearly. They needed to be punished for the people they'd hurt, including Cutter. They needed to understand there would be no negotiation, no way to come out of this short of abject and total surrender.

Every Tin Man or *yaoguai* who fell was a step toward that. Every defeated plot was a significant leap forward.

Their efforts weren't an investigation anymore. This was war. She wasn't a cop, she was a soldier in the war against the conspiracy. Stumbling into the war didn't make it any less important.

More dire wolves tried to close in, but she blew off a leg and then delivered a round that pierced the entire length of the body. The monster collapsed and rolled a meter before stopping.

Erik and her squadmates trusted her. They aimed past Jia's newfound friends to deliver more pain to reinforcements. Wave after wave of dire wolves stretched into the distance, all closing on the team. Jia could scarcely imagine the resources that'd gone into producing such an army of the monsters.

The amount of money and technical expertise was staggering. They could have applied it to many different causes, but instead, they sat in the forest working on new illegal monsters they could deploy for their sick, misguided cause.

Jia didn't have time to worry about anything but picking off the survivors. She lined up a headshot and loosed another round. This time, the bleeding dire wolf dropped at her first shot. Two more shots finished off the two closest targets, now less than five meters away. She almost pitied the monsters, but she knew what they would do if they got their jaws on any of the soldiers.

Jia snapped her rifle toward other monsters penetrating the line and fired. Two more dire wolves fell in rapid succession. She had her rhythm now. There could be five or six, and they wouldn't get their chance to attack.

Calmly standing in front of a rampaging horde of gigantic genetically engineered camouflaged dire wolves would have been impossible without the exoskeletons.

Some poor soul lost on vacation might have wandered through the area, only to be blown out of the sky by an antiaircraft barrage or screamed for mercy in the final moments of their life as the *yaoguai* horde descended on them. Jia, Erik, and the soldiers would protect those unfortunates.

The last remnants of pity left Jia. The *yaoguai* were wrong, not only in their creation but in their presence on Earth. They were a living embodiment of the corruption she wanted to drive from the UTC.

The existence of a handful of monsters in a hidden lab in the Scar had been disgusting enough, but this wasn't polluted, corrupted shadows in a place no one dared travel. This was the beautiful landscape of an ancient country on the home planet of humanity.

If they could be here, they could be anywhere.

Jia gritted her teeth. The *yaoguai* horde was the conspiracy announcing their contempt for the values humanity had adopted. They would accept no limits in their power. People like her had to make an example of them so no one would follow their dark lead.

As she blew the head off another charging dire wolf, Jia realized something important. Knowing the goal of the conspiracy was only important insofar as it helped to fight them. Otherwise, it was irrelevant.

Everyone thought they were the hero in their own twisted story. The men and women behind the conspiracy had likely concocted a convoluted explanation for why their actions were perfect, moral, and for the best. It didn't matter if their plans involved the brutal deaths of thousands or risked an advanced alien species killing millions.

She wouldn't be able to get their leaders into a room and talk them into understanding what horrors they had wrought. There was no way people with that much power and influence didn't know exactly what they were doing, which was why they were hiding it.

Their tactics didn't strain only conventional morality. They blew past all the restraints and common sense humanity had adopted after the hard-earned bloody lessons of post-industrial history.

The deaths of millions in incidents like the Summer of Sorrow would be for nothing if the conspiracy had their way.

They would kill, maim, and corrupt. They were more like demons than people, and there could be no peace with demons.

The greedy criminals Jia had dealt with as a detective were angels compared to the conspiracy. They might kill for money, but not blindly run roughshod over all forms of basic decency. No mobster would destroy an entire city.

Jia took down another dire wolf, imagining she was killing a high-ranking member of the conspiracy rather than a feral tool. Erik had brought her into the hunt, but it'd stopped being about him a long time ago.

Times like this served to remind her of that.

The crack of the heavy exoskeleton rifles overlapped in an oddly soothing staccato rhythm. Every squad had adopted a variation of the strategy Erik's and Jia's squad was using. The wolf bodies began to pile up.

The enemy gave no indication they cared about their fallen comrades, though the volume of corpses challenged their continued advances. In some cases, the dire wolves took the path of least resistance, leading to funneling or slow climbs that made it easier for the team to pick them off.

Grenade explosions grew sparser and rifle fire more common. Soldiers were hitting Erik's one-third limit, and the newly arriving enemy reinforcements were fewer.

"Drones down to sixty percent," Emma reported. "The lower numbers are allowing more ease of evasion, so it's growing harder for the enemy to hit them, but the distraction won't last forever. Please keep that in mind."

"Understood," Erik replied. "We're almost there."

He nailed a dire wolf in the distance with a burst. The rounds blew off a leg and passed through the chest. The monster managed to make it a couple more meters before collapsing in a bloody pool. At least they had the decency to bleed red.

Jia kept to single shots. She could down a wolf with a single shot half the time, and it only took two shots for the others, saving bullets compared to Erik's bursts.

The whole process had become detached and mechanical. It felt less real than many of her training scenarios. There was something absurd about standing in the middle of a French forest fighting off a horde of massive wolves.

She would have never imagined this sort of encounter before Erik came into her life.

Envelopment wasn't possible without decent numbers, and whether the monsters understood that or merely were giving in to instinct, the dire wolves gave up circling the exoskeletons and instead gathered for a final massive charge. The wedge of snarling teeth and pumping legs bolted through the charred and broken plants and bodies before them.

"Inverted wedge and fire," Erik ordered.

Their rifle fire never stopped as the exoskeletons shifted position. The front lines of the dire wolf formation fell, tripping some of the others. It was only a momentary delay before the wolves were back on their feet and loping desperately toward the exoskeletons.

With all twelve soldiers aiming at the same group of wolves, their gunfire produced a curtain of high-velocity rounds that was impossible to dodge. Volleys produced a shower of blood and chunks of flesh.

Jia narrowed her eyes for a shot. She'd been concentrating on shooting, so she'd almost ignored the obvious.

The large size and camouflage coats of the wolf-like *yaoguai* attacking them was not the most obvious evidence of their corrupted, manmade existence. There were stranger things in nature, including the Local Neighborhood races.

Predatory pack animals were brave. They could accomplish great feats, but they weren't callously stupid like some humans. Normal animals would not relentlessly charge into certain death like the dire wolves.

Something about that sickened her. The conspiracy had taken basic self-preservation away from the lives they had created, taken the essence of what being alive was about.

The teams' fire reduced the charge to a modest group, then constant, careful fire from the soldiers cut them down to a group that could have been a single pack. In the end, the last survivors of their brave but futile charge ended in a fusillade from the exoskeletons.

Nothing remained except mounds of dead monsters and thick smoke. Explosions in the distance reminded everyone the battle wasn't over.

"Anyone got any movement?" Erik asked after a deep breath.

The battle hadn't been long compared to some she'd fought, but it'd been intense. A momentary lapse in concentration could have resulted in the monsters scattering their formation.

Jia swept the area, looking for hidden enemies. There might have been one dire wolf gifted with more intelligence than the others, but there was nothing.

"We used a lot more grenades and ammo than I would have liked," Erik continued, "but I think our friends made their best play. The bastards should learn attrition is a crap way to win." He lifted the exoskeleton's arm to point through the forest in the direction of the mansion. "Let's go while Emma is still distracting them."

They kept their wedge formation as they stomped through the forest, climbing over their fallen foes without further consideration. There wasn't time to mourn the monsters.

It was time to punish their masters.

CHAPTER SEVENTEEN

Erik expected more on-the-ground resistance the last few kilometers as the forest began to give way to the vast field of grass surrounding the mansion.

While the conspiracy's penchant for attempting to overwhelm with sheer numbers was consistent with the dire wolf horde, he suspected there was something more to it. His worry that this battle was personal hadn't left him.

In a battle against other humans, one side might win or lose based on running out of ammunition, but monsters' teeth and claws didn't go away. Exoskeletons and tactical suits were good protection, but he didn't want to go up against a *yaoguai* at close range.

He'd seen plenty that could get through tactical suits.

The outline of the mansion was visible in the distance, along with the bright flash of AAA emplacements firing into the sky. The trees were growing sparser and the booms louder. Manicured patches of lawn filtered into the forest more, the increasing number of obviously artificial clearings.

"We're going to proceed with the second phase of the ops plan," Erik announced. "We're going to join together to form Alpha and Beta squads. Beta, you're still responsible for clearing out the AAA and doing whatever pest control we need outside, including holding the LZ for our exfil. All Alpha soldiers, you're with me. We're going to go crash the house party."

Initial intel indicated the bulk of the AAA was deployed at the front of the mansion. Erik and the colonel both worried about getting cut off from retreat, so they would decide on the final details at the last moment. If things went better than expected, and they cleared out the rest of the enemy without too much resistance, then all they'd done was be overly cautious.

The exo formation broke into two groups of six, with four soldiers joining Erik and Jia as they changed course to head toward a side entrance of the mansion. He'd kept one rocket exo on their team, but he wanted the bulk on Beta Squad to help rapidly take out the AAA.

"Down to forty percent," Emma reported. "I'm surprised they've lasted as long as they have. That portends less effective resistance inside."

"Let's not get ahead of ourselves," Erik returned.

He expected more *yaoguai* reinforcements.

He was surprised they'd made it all the way to the perimeter of the mansion's grounds without running into reinforcements or additional traps. He wasn't going to complain about an easier approach after the dire wolf horde, but he also doubted the enemy was done flinging death at the squads.

Was there some clever strategy informing the whole

thing? Throwing monsters at them in narrow internal hallways might benefit the exos more than the *yaoguai*.

He was going in regardless, so they would find out soon enough. Before that, they could help Beta Squad with their job.

An eight-barrel turret protruding from some hedges spun back and forth, filling the sky with rounds as it attempted to bring down the rest of the drones. Another cannon fired exploding shells with a steady thump. A missile launcher with four racks sat ready, recently raised out of the ground, judging by the damaged grass. The enemy was smart enough not to waste their missiles on mere drones.

It was an impressive setup. If the team had tried to make a direct landing, the air defenses would have shredded them, especially in a flitter. Even dedicated fighters and close-air attack craft would have had a hard time.

"Alpha Six, take out the SAM launcher," Erik ordered. "We don't want any surprises, but we can leave the rest for Beta squad."

"Yes, sir." The soldier spun his exo toward the target. "Backblast area clear."

Blowing up readied SAMs was easy. After all, the enemy was providing them with massive amounts of explosives waiting to be set off.

With a whoosh and a roar, a rocket shot from Alpha Six's launcher and sped toward one of the missiles. It struck, and its impressive primary explosion was consumed by a massive secondary explosion as the missiles went off. The shockwave knocked over some nearby trees and launched a massive cloud of dirt, grass, and rock into the air. If Erik hadn't been in his exo, he would have clapped.

Erik had chosen the target well. Although it'd cracked and scorched the walls and windows of the mansion, it was far enough away that nothing more than minor surface damage was inflicted. He doubted they'd stuck the informant outside next to a missile launcher.

"Target neutralized," announced Alpha Six, pride in his voice.

More loud blasts sounded from the front of the mansion. The ground shook, and dark smoke filled the air. The percussive drumline of AAA weakened with the destruction of more turrets and launchers. It wouldn't be long before the enemy would be vulnerable from the air.

The colonel wanted to avoid calling in air support for political reasons, but the enemy didn't know that. While the primary point was to secure their safe exfiltration, the focus on air defense also served as a feint, focusing the enemy on a strike from the air rather than the exo team heading into the mansion.

A loud grinding noise sounded from all around. The ground shook.

"Detecting thermal traces from right underneath the surface," Emma reported.

She sent targeting markers to Erik.

"Enemy at 9 o'clock," he shouted. The constant jamming was damned inconvenient.

A massive covered ramp erupted from the ground, ripping apart the carefully manicured lawn and opening into a darkened tunnel. Dirt and rock tumbled down the sides and front, accompanied by the unpleasant dissonant rumbling of the rising structure.

Short bellows sounded from inside, inhuman, loud, and angry. Something was coming.

Thunder echoed from inside, something heavy and hard striking the metal of the ramp as it charged up. Loud snorts and bellows echoed from below.

"You've got to be kidding me," Jia muttered. "Is this a demon zoo?"

"Something like that," Erik offered. "Let's close it down."

He knew it'd been too easy to get close to the mansion.

A group of stampeding monsters crested the ramp, each almost the size of the MX 60. Thick, dull gray plates covered their four-legged bodies all the way down to their black hooves. Narrow red eyes peeked out from slits in the natural armor. Their size was weapon enough, but four spikes protruded from the fronts of their bodies.

The exos opened fire with their rifles. Velocity and size granted deadly penetration power to their weapons, enough to rip through a lot of targets, manmade or other-wise, but their rounds bounced off the armored plates with sparks and minor gouges. Erik didn't know whether to be impressed or worried.

"Keep mobile, and don't let those bastards run you over," Erik ordered. He fired another burst to no effect. "See if it's weaker on the other side. Grenade and rocket use is a go. Switch to plasmas. These things might be tough, but they're still creatures some scientist cooked up, not advanced alien crap."

Different-sounding roars from the front signaled an

attack on Beta Squad. Erik didn't regret splitting up. It also meant the enemy had to split their forces. The ramp descended shortly after the last *yaoguai* emerged.

No easy way in for the team.

While the new monsters, which Erik had taken to thinking of as demon rhinos, lacked the numbers of the dire wolves, their ability to take a punishment made the latest battle a more dangerous engagement. Another barrage didn't accomplish any more than the first shots and the exos scattered, using their jump thrusters to spin and clear the charging *yaoguai*.

Despite Erik's suggestion, the rear and side armor of the enemy didn't look any thinner than the front. The squads' rifles came alive again, along with satisfying thumps as the grenade launchers fired their latest choice. A rocket screamed from Alpha Six.

A demon rhino roared when it was hit by the white-blue blinding explosion of a plasma grenade. Another bellowed its displeasure at Alpha Six's explosive surprise.

"Tough bastards," Erik muttered. "But if you feel pain, that means you can die."

A plasma grenade stood a decent chance of taking out a military exoskeleton, depending on where it hit. The grenades had blasted free and cracked the plates, exposing softer flesh underneath, but they didn't kill the monsters. The rocket attack had about the same effect.

Erik was satisfied. It took a stronger punch, but they could win.

Jia ran to the side, spraying bullets toward one of the newfound openings. Her demon rhino reared back, blood splattering from the wound before landing with a loud thump and rushing toward its tormentor.

Another monster galloped toward Erik, preventing him from helping his partner. He fired another plasma grenade before activating his jump thrusters for a lateral dodge, narrowly avoiding the vehicle-sized monster. He sent a burst into the weak spot. The monster shook his head and let out an angry snort before continuing its charge. These were definitely tougher than the dire wolves.

Another rocket from Alpha Six screamed across the lawn and struck the hole. The explosion blew out a huge chunk of the demon rhino's body, and it collapsed to the ground with a dying moan.

"Don't go crazy with those," Erik ordered. "We might need them later. I'd hate to run into a ridiculous armored giant elephant and only have our rifles."

Jia jumped over her target with careful timing, using the demon rhino itself for a mid-jump boost. She angled her rifle down and sent a stream of bullets into its weak-ened area, and it jerked and bellowed before dropping to its knees. She didn't stop when she landed, instead rushing to the enemy to keep firing at point-blank range until it stopped moving.

One of the soldiers lacked Jia's exquisite timing, and the demon rhino slammed into him before he'd cleared it. His shield took the brunt of the spikes, but the blow sent him careening through the air. Erik couldn't risk a grenade or call for a rocket strike with the exo so close to the enemy, so he sprinted straight toward the *yaoguai*, drawing its attention with harassing strikes against its wound.

The damaged exo hit the ground. The pilot's life signs were stable, but he was groaning and not moving.

Erik continued firing at the monster until it turned toward him. He picked up speed and jumped into the air to avoid it connecting with him. Twisting, he launched a plasma grenade into the wind. The explosion sheared a leg off and sent the monster's body into another demon rhino, knocking the second over.

The monster rolled back onto its feet with some effort, but the precious seconds it lost let Jia and another soldier riddle its wound with bullets. It fell to the ground again, head lolling to the side.

The roars and screams of the dying monsters stopped from the direction of Beta Squad, replaced by a triumphant cheer. Alpha Squad needed to hurry up and not be outdone.

"Probably had easier *yaoguai*," Erik muttered.

With a pattern now established and the enemy numbers reduced, it was a simple matter for Erik, Jia, and the remaining soldiers to put down the last group of demon rhinos. The downed soldier groaned and righted his exoskeleton.

"Alpha Five, you okay?" Erik asked.

"I've been hit harder than that and lived," the soldier replied cheerfully. "But I'd rather not do it again."

"Yeah. That'd be best."

Jia had been right. It was a demon zoo, or they'd taken a wrong turn on the way to France and ended up in Hell.

Acrid smoke filled the area, along with pieces of metal and plastic from the destroyed missiles and downed drones. The mammoth corpses of the demon rhinos formed a maze, their blood soaking into the grass. Craters from explosions and hoofprints left the lawn dangerously uneven.

"We still jammed, Emma?" Erik asked.

"Rather thoroughly," she reported.

"Guess we'll need those flares."

"We know they have some sort of subterranean facility," Jia observed. "Should we try to dig up the tunnel?"

"No," Erik replied. "It'll take too many of our explosives to do it, and I'd rather not walk right into any *yaoguai* pens. Besides, we're still looking for Ahmed, and if he's alive, I doubt they'd keep him with the monsters."

Erik couldn't get much of anything off the thermals to tell him what was inside the mansion. They could be stepping into an empty facility or a place filled with every type of *yaoguai* imaginable and some that weren't. The jamming meant Emma would need direct IO port access to do anything about the systems, so there was only one choice.

"Alpha Squad, prepare for breach," Erik announced. "Beta can finish clearing up out here and watch our asses."

He headed toward a large pair of double doors in the back. "Alpha Six, get ready to say hello."

CHAPTER EIGHTEEN

If Jia could travel back in time a couple of years and talk to her younger self, there was a surprising truth she would have loved to pass along: *explosions can be fun.*

She smiled as a rocket sped from Alpha Six's exoskeleton and blew a jagged, smoking hole in the back doors of the mansion. They had their way inside.

Her momentary entertainment was replaced by a somber truth. A weapon that could easily blow open a reinforced door with a single shot had only weakened one of the monsters they'd just fought.

Her hand trembled for a moment at the memory of the Hunter ship. That was the end of the road for the path the conspiracy now walked, hideous, twisted creation completely disconnected from nature with no other point than to kill.

Jia scoffed. Once humanity'd had to reach into dark myths of gods and demons when they thought of monsters, but modern people weren't content to leave them in the shadows. It was almost as if humans couldn't become gods, so they'd decided to make flesh-and-blood demons real, to become kings of the underworld.

Erik ran toward the door, jarring Jia out of her ruminations. She stayed in formation, heading in after him. He slowed as he arrived inside and whistled.

"Not what I thought," he mumbled.

Jia understood why. She expected some sort of hallway or fancy room, not a vast cavernous chamber filled with data windows and large silver tanks. Tubing ran through the walls and into the tanks. One of them was open, blue fluid staining the floor around it. Bright, harsh light illuminated the whole space. Huge tunnel-like hallways extended from the chamber.

Small drones equipped with delicate arms and probes were parked in tall racks on either side of the room. They weren't active, not that they would represent much threat. A child could probably bat the small machines out of the air with ease. It was a welcome relief after the last set of *yaoguai.*

"This isn't a mansion." Jia hissed. "It's a damned lab."

"That place we took down in the Scar might have been a prototype," Erik suggested, walking toward the open tank but not lowering his rifle. "And this is the industrial-scale version, or maybe the opposite."

"You mean they've got more than just those wolves and those other things?" asked one of the soldiers, his voice quiet.

"Probably." Erik fired a burst at one of the drones, blasting it to pieces. "But if they jump us in here, they don't have a lot of room to maneuver. No matter what, this is a big loss. Even if we can't find the informant, they have to know we'll bomb this place until it's a crater."

"I'm not seeing any IO ports," Emma commented. "The jamming strength is stronger inside this building. Please continue to move around in case there's one in this room."

"That means the jammer is not a hidden array outside," Erik concluded. "Good to know."

"Somebody's got to be sending the monsters at us," one of the soldiers commented. "They wouldn't program a security system to unleash all that every time somebody shows up."

Erik nodded. "Yeah, you'd think. I doubt this entire facility is automated, and I'm guessing the people in charge are hiding underground. We need to find an IO port or take out the jammer so Emma can do her thing." He headed toward one of the tunnels. "For now, we still have our informant to find."

The squad fell in behind Erik. The large tunnels made it easy for the exoskeletons to proceed two abreast with space between them, and Jia assumed they were meant to accommodate equally large *yaoguai*. That didn't bode well.

"Why bring him here?" Jia asked. "It doesn't make sense."

"This might have been one of the more secure facilities," Erik suggested, but he didn't sound confident. "You're right, though. A *yaoguai* lab might be nice for some scares, but it doesn't strike me as the best place to keep a prisoner, especially one they thought might be followed. They're trading that prisoner potentially for this entire lab."

"Unless we've hit them even harder than we realize," Jia

mused, her tone betraying her doubt. "You're right, Erik. This whole thing feels off."

A nearby soldier laughed. "What tipped you off, Lin? The giant wolves or whatever the hell those things were right outside? You waiting for a tap-dancing spider lady in a nice dress to show up and serenade us?"

"I've fought things far worse than *yaoguai*," Jia replied, her voice even. "That's not what is bothering me."

The mirth left the soldier's voice. "W-worse than *yaoguai?*"

Erik nodded grimly. He lifted his faceplate and wiped sweat off his brow. "I think he's righter than you realize, though, Jia."

"How?"

"We should never get too comfortable dealing with this kind of thing." Erik slowed. "That's when we'll start making mistakes."

The tunnel widened into a room even larger than their entrance point. Despite the sloping walls, it easily accounted for most of the mansion as seen from outside. Equipment and tanks similar to that in the previous room filled the room.

Disturbingly, the tanks were arranged in lines from small sizes that would barely accommodate something the size of the dog to much larger designs that would hold something almost the size of the dire wolves. About twenty tanks filled the room.

"Is this where they breed them?" asked a soldier.

"Probably," Erik commented.

"Where do the big ones come from?" the soldier asked. "You couldn't fit any of the last monsters we fought in those tanks." He pointed his gun at the largest tank. "Those camo wolves wouldn't fit in there."

Jia stared at one of the large tanks and sighed. "You're asking the wrong question."

"Am I?"

Erik lowered his faceplate with a grunt. "Yeah, you are."

"Ask yourself this: How big is a baby when they're born?" Jia asked. "You couldn't fit Erik comfortably in a crib."

The soldier gulped. "You're telling me a baby monster fits in those large tanks?"

"That's what I would guess," Jia replied with a frown.

"Then how big are they fully grown? Bigger than the things we just fought?"

"Let's hope we don't find out."

"I've spotted an IO port," Emma announced. She sounded excited. "It's time for the heroine of this story to take center stage."

Someone in the group chuckled.

A nav marker appeared in Jia's and Erik's HUDs. Jia zoomed in on the marker. The lone port lay across the vast chamber. That didn't seem all that convenient, but presumably the conspiracy personnel who worked at the facility didn't normally have to worry about the entire area being blanketed by jamming.

"We've got movement at twelve o'clock!" shouted a soldier.

Jia frowned. That was near the IO port. Not a good coincidence.

The exoskeletons spread out in a line, the tanks forming natural rows that disrupted their attempts at decent formations, but most of the equipment was at waist level for a normal human, leaving their weapons and primary line of sight clear. Something much smaller than their last enemies darted between two tanks.

"I think it's a person." Jia switched to thermal and nodded. "I'm getting a humanoid outline."

"Just because it looks like a human, it doesn't mean it is one," Erik replied, his voice tight. "We learned that on Venus."

The team pointed their weapons at the tank. A sustained barrage from twelve exoskeletons would be lethal to anything remotely human, if anyone who worked in the building could be called that. Jia had her doubts, regardless of how pure their DNA was. Being human was about more than having forty-six *Homo sapiens* chromosomes. She wasn't so sure if the people creating the *yaoguai* weren't more monstrous than their beasts.

"I'm going to give you one chance," Erik announced. "Come out with your hands up. If you don't do it, in ten seconds, we're going to assume you're hostile and send you to join all the *yaoguai* that tried to eat us outside."

"Don't shoot!" screamed a distinctly human male voice. Two pale hands rose over the tank, followed by a thin, wizened man. He wore a white uniform with a design Jia didn't recognize.

Jia didn't normally think that anyone *had to* get rejuvenation, but the barely flesh-wrapped skeleton in front of them needed it. Her stomach tightened at the possibility he could be another half-Leem hybrid.

"Come out slowly," Erik replied. "Or you'll end up with a lot of new holes. What's left of you, anyway. Trust me, after what we've gone through to get here, we're not in a forgiving mood."

The man stepped in front of the tank, his hands still up. "I surrender. My name is Doctor Vincke. You'll want to take me alive. I can give you useful intelligence. That's why you're here, right?"

"Oh, can you now?" Erik chuckled. "Where's that conspiracy loyalty? Those Ascended Brotherhood bastards fried themselves rather than let us get anything from them. That alien hybrid on Venus was willing to try to take us with him, and here you are, ready to surrender. Man, I guess they're hiring the bottom of the barrel now."

Vincke sighed, sounding more annoyed than upset. "I didn't think you would survive the test subjects. You were more resourceful and adaptive than anticipated."

"So, you're the one who sent those monsters after us?" Erik chuckled. "You've got to understand that didn't endear you to us, but we're not here to take prisoners. Give me a reason not to waste you right now."

"You'd kill me in cold blood?" Vincke sounded impressed.

"I don't know if it counts as killing you in cold blood after you admitted to sending a horde of damned monsters after us," growled Erik.

"It was nothing personal. I don't even know who you are." Vincke's face contorted. "May I lower my arms? They're starting to hurt."

"Okay, fine," Erik replied. "But if you try anything, I'll add some new holes to your face. I'm still waiting to hear why we should waste our time with you."

Vincke lowered his arms. He took a moment to rub his

shoulders before responding. "I don't know *who* you are, but obviously, you're either with the ID or the DD. I know both of those little government agencies are interested in my employers. That alone should be enough."

Erik nodded to Jia. They might not be police officers, but good cop, bad cop was always useful.

"He's right," Jia explained softly, faking a smile. "Our orders are to recover a kidnapped man. Nazeer Ahmed."

There was no reason to explain the part where they were only supposed to take down people who resisted. She wasn't sure Colonel Adeyemi would care if someone like Vincke was killed.

But the man was right. They needed intel, and this was one of the first times they'd encountered someone who might be able to willingly provide it without an autopsy or a post-death PNIU hack.

"Kidnapped man?" Vincke cocked his head. "Ah, yes. I vaguely remember something about that." He laughed. "You have to understand operations isn't my area, but if you let me live, I'll be more than happy to help you."

When he reached for his ear, Erik barked, "Hands back up, or you're dead."

Vincke's arms shot toward the ceiling. "My ear itches."

"Too damned bad," Erik growled. "You should be happy we weren't so trigger happy that we took you out the minute we got here."

"Calm down already," Vincke replied. "Your bloodthirst is quite unbecoming."

For a man with six exoskeletons pointing weapons at him, he was remarkably calm. His smug sneer didn't fit either his words or the mood of the room. Some people didn't understand the situation they were in until it was too late.

"I am calm," Erik offered, his voice cold. "Now tell us where he is."

"I can't do that. It's too difficult to explain. I'll have to show you."

"No." Erik scoffed. "Here's how this is going to work. I'm going to put binding ties on you while the other five people with me point heavy exo rifles at you. If you try anything, first I'll kick your ass. If it turns out you're a mutant freak and manage to knock me away, they'll shred you until you're nothing but a pile of jigsaw puzzle pieces. Understand?"

Vincke wrinkled his nose in disgust. "You're a barbarian."

"I've been called a lot worse." Erik shot him a bright smile. "But you didn't answer the question. Do you understand?"

"I understand," Vincke replied haughtily. "It's you who don't understand. I'm the one jamming, so I took measures to make sure I could still do what I needed in that kind of environment."

"You are ab—"

He snapped his fingers and dropped with mocking laughter. Something loud clanged, and his laughter stopped.

Jia moved to the side to get a better angle on where Vincke had been standing. She shifted to thermal mode. Slight temp differentials surrounded a large portion of the floor.

"Door in the floor," she explained. "Must be a hidden

elevator."

"Bastard," Erik ground out.

Emma's hologram appeared, and she pointed toward the IO port. "He won't be able to do much if I control the facility."

"Let's just blow a hole in the ground and go after him," suggested one of the soldiers.

A harsh grinding noise sounded from above as portions of the ceiling retracted to reveal multiple large opaque tubes. A foreboding mixture of loud droning, buzzing, and skittering echoed from the tubes.

Erik raised his gun. "We should have just dropped a cruise missile on this damned place."

CHAPTER NINETEEN

Explosions outside rattled the building. Vincke must have thrown the *yaoguai* gates open for both squads, but the squad inside needed to handle their own problems.

Alpha Squad waited, their weapons trained at the tubes in the ceiling. Whatever was coming at them wouldn't be as large as the demon rhinos, but the squad had already gone through a lot of ammo. Erik didn't want it to come down to them getting out of their exos and using their backup rifles.

They wouldn't last long.

New *yaoguai* erupted from the tubes, an unholy mix of a giant bee and tailless scorpion about the size of a large cat. They were fast, spiraling toward the squad before the first exo took a shot. The rife round penetrated two of the scorpion bees, splashing their nearby friends with dull green fluid.

At least these weren't bulletproof.

The squad continued firing. Their combined targeting blasted the emerging scorpion bees into a fine paste, but the creatures continued boiling out of the tubes and flying toward the humans. Sheer quantity allowed some of the *yaoguai* to escape the initial onslaught and draw close, their pinchers snapping and eager for human flesh.

Without being told, Alpha Five took up Jia's cleanup role from the dire wolf fight. He concentrated on downing any monsters that got closer than three meters. The other combatants directed their weapons fire at the different tubes. Less-concentrated fire didn't produce spectacular kills, but it reduced the number of scorpion bees that made it close to the team and gave Alpha Five more time to line up shots.

Erik glanced at a side readout. If they'd come equipped with the standard ammo loadouts, they would have already run dry. Everyone but Jia had dropped below fifty percent rifle rounds, but they had preserved a good chunk of their explosives.

Monster parts dropped from the sky, wings, bodies, and pincers. The steady thump of the disgusting rain added a rhythmic counterpoint to the rifle fire echoing through the large room and the constant buzz of the *yaoguai*'s wings.

Erik adjusted the timer and launched a frag grenade. It exploded near the tubes, the shrapnel and blast taking down four scorpion bees at once—overkill on pest control.

"Mix in a frag every five or ten shots," he bellowed. "Stagger them. Save all your plasmas in case there are more of those demon rhinos in this place."

The team hadn't bothered to bring stun grenades, but when Erik caught up with Dr. Vincke, he was going to take the bastard back for interrogation even if it meant shooting out his knees.

Jia launched a grenade next. It exploded at the top of its arc, killing a group of the scorpion bees and pushing the others into an unstable flight path that made it easier for the other soldiers to pick them off.

Erik's conscious mind receded as the squad fell into a rhythm, firing bullets and occasional grenades. Jia and some of the soldiers tried to end the problem by getting a grenade into the tubes proper. The resulting explosions tore new holes in the tubes but didn't staunch the flow of creatures.

Mounds of dead scorpion bees grew all around the room, some of the creatures twitching in the last seconds of their deaths.

For all the slaughter around them, Erik could only imagine what would have happened if the conspiracy had stuffed a couple hundred of the scorpion bees into a cargo flitter and released them in a city.

The conspiracy had already proven aiding terrorists was trivial. Their efforts in Neo SoCal, Chang'e City, and Parvati indicated no potential body count was too high.

The incessant buzzing quieted and the gush of monsters slowed to a trickle, now easy to pick off with careful shots. Erik's squad's gunfire died down as everyone waited for the final monster to appear.

When a minute had passed without another monster, Erik was confident they had won, but not that anything was over.

The explosions outside had also died down, but that could mean Beta Squad had been defeated. They had to do something about the jamming. If they couldn't locate and blow up the equipment directly, they would have to rely on another form of electronic warfare.

Erik jogged forward, scorpion bees crunching under the feet of his exoskeleton on his way to the IO port. He kicked a couple out of the way. "The bastard was trying to stall us. It doesn't matter if he's got a plane or flitter because we've got external eyes on this place. If he goes anywhere, we'll know, and I'm sure Adeyemi will shoot down anything that gets away." He had to double back after a bad choice for a shortcut. "Or at least anything flying that's not us."

He rechecked the squad's status. No significant vital sign disruptions to the exoskeletons, but they were down to twenty-five percent for the rifles and no frag grenades. The remaining grenades were plasmas. Queen Jia of the Kingdom of Ammo Efficiency was doing the best, with thirty-three percent of her original ammo remaining.

Erik stopped in front of the IO port, then pulled his arm out of the exoskeleton to remove Emma's core matrix from the port in his exo and insert it into the wall.

Emma projected a hologram of her wearing the same white uniform as Vincke. "This security is incredibly sophisticated. It'll take me some time to gain control."

"What about the door from earlier?" Jia asked. "Can you at least open that?"

"Give me a moment," Emma replied. "I'll prioritize it." She snickered. "Things are much easier when I don't have to care about who knows or what I might break."

"Should someone check on Beta Squad?" Jia asked.

"No." Erik shook his head. "They have their job, and we have ours. Everything about this feels like a big stall, and I want to make sure someone is watching out for our LZ if we run dry and have to get the hell out of here."

"Ah!" Emma curtsied. "Our good doctor was sloppy. In a sense, he left the door open electronically. Learn this, Dr. Vincke: I exceed the capabilities of mere fleshbags."

Scorpion bee parts tumbled down as a large panel in the floor pulled back in near-silence. Erik had been expecting some small elevator. The opening revealed an angled ramp and a winding corridor. Scorpion bee bodies rolled down the gentle incline.

"Let's go," Erik ordered.

"Wait," Jia replied.

"What?"

Jia nodded at the IO port. "Emma doesn't have control. If we leave her alone here before she's established control, she'll be vulnerable."

"Damn it. And they could be watching," Erik growled. "Emma, how long is this going to take?"

"I'm unsure," Emma replied, annoyance in her voice. "The system is sophisticated, and they obviously understood the potential threat of this type of attack. I'll prioritize door, camera, and jammer control when I locate the relevant systems."

"We could wait," Jia suggested. "I think if they had more of those flying things to throw at us, they would have."

"We can't wait around. They might kill the informant if he's still alive, or they could be opening other tanks to release crap like giant toads that explode in clouds of acid."

Jia winced. "How many monsters could they possibly have here?"

"Enough. We need to make our move." Erik turned his

exo toward the tunnel. "Alpha Four and Five. You stay here and guard Emma. If you get overwhelmed, yank her out, run out the back, make for the front and throw up the flare. Understood? Alpha Three and Six, you're with us."

The soldier nodded. "Yes, sir. You think the four of us will be enough?"

"We still need to find the informant, capture or kill that bastard, and get out of here alive," Erik replied. "If the conspiracy gets their hands on Emma, none of this will be worth it. She's more valuable than ten informants."

Erik stepped into the tunnel. "It's time for these bastards to stop stalling."

CHAPTER TWENTY

Many cultures told legends or myths of advanced beings who lived in the clouds.

When Jia was a little girl and looked out the windows of her residential tower, she couldn't help but feel like one of those beings of legend. She lived in Neo Southern California, the greatest metroplex in the entire United Terran Confederation. It was a near-mythical land of massive towers that reached into the sky, where only the best and most honorable people lived.

Adulthood had disabused her of some of her fanciful childhood beliefs about what it meant to be an Uptowner in Neo SoCal, but it had not freed her from her dislike of subterranean tunnels.

As far as she was concerned, they were the realm of maintenance bots and *yaoguai*.

The narrow tunnel currently hosting the sub-squad didn't allow them to march side by side, but there was at least enough space that Erik and Jia could both fire at one target if they were ambushed. She tried not to think about what new horrors might await them.

She'd gone from being an immortal living in the clouds to a heroine stepping into a dungeon filled with the most twisted demonic monsters created by man.

No one spoke as they headed down the tunnel at a quick but not too fast pace. They were all doing what Jia was, listening for *yaoguai*, drones, roars, growls, or odd scratching and skittering—anything that would give them precious seconds of warning.

They arrived at the bottom of the tunnel. A wide door blocked further passage. There was no obvious access panel.

"Emma, can you open it for us?" Erik asked.

There was no response. Jia wasn't surprised. She'd been honest about having trouble, which meant it was probably harder than she'd let on.

"For all we know, they've got escape tunnels that stretch for kilometers," Jia suggested. "Those first *yaoguai* came from a lot closer than the mansion."

"True, but he might just be holed up in here, waiting for reinforcements," Erik backed away from the door. "I don't want to wait to find out. Alpha Six, it's knocking time again."

"Yes, sir," the soldier shouted, moving his exo forward but keeping a healthy distance from the door. He waited for the other squad members to move to either side, leaving no one directly behind him. "Backblast area clear!"

A rocket screamed away from his launcher and exploded against the door. Flaming pieces bounced off the exos' ballistic shields and clattered to the ground. Smoke swirled up, darkening the small area. The door was cracked but not down.

Two more rockets did the trick, leaving the burning wreckage of what had once been a doorway and choking smoke.

Rockets, the ultimate skeleton keys.

Erik advanced past Alpha Six through the smoke. Jia and the other two soldiers fell in behind him.

"Are the conspiracy secretly mole people?" Jia grumbled. "This place is starting to annoy me."

"Only starting to?" Erik asked.

They entered a vast cavern that dwarfed the rooms above. Her initial impressions suggested it could have fit a good chunk of the entire mansion. Huge doors lay on the opposite end of the cavern, most likely hangars or garages for vehicles, but that was the least disturbing part of the room.

Row after row of open silver gestation tanks filled half the cavern. Tubing ran from the tanks through the grated floor into the darkness below. The other half of the chamber was a series of transparent sealed metal box pens separated into different sizes. Bones littered many of the pens. Jia hoped none were human, but she doubted it.

"Huh," Alpha Six offered. "It's empty. They must have emptied those to throw at us. Sent 'em through those doors over there." He looked around. "They must lead to the surface."

"Vincke isn't going to try to escape on foot." Jia frowned, surveying the area using different modes. There were all sorts of fading but recent thermal traces that lent credence to Alpha Six's theory.

The squad wandered deeper into the room, sweeping in all directions in case flying *yaoguai* dropped from above, or chameleon badger dragons ripped from the ceiling and tried to eat their faces. If Vincke had run, there was only one possible direction.

A massive explosion from behind shook the room. Smoke filled Jia's rearview camera feed. She spun, assuming an ambush by enemy humans or Tin Men, but when the smoke cleared, there was nothing but a massive pile of rubble blocking the entrance.

A loud, mocking laugh sounded from all around them. Jia didn't need to see the man to recognize Dr. Vincke.

"I'm disobeying orders," he taunted. "But I couldn't resist. It's a special responsibility, but also a special opportunity?"

"What are you talking about?" Jia shouted.

"I could have buried you here easily. That's what I was supposed to do. My orders came from the highest people, those I never thought I'd get to talk to." Reverence filled his voice. "That was when I knew this was an exceptional duty."

"Okay," Erik replied. He pointed his rifle upward at an angle. "You got us. Why don't you explain a little more?"

All four exoskeletons formed a square formation with overlapping fields of fire. While it was impossible to surprise anyone because of the rearview cameras, that wouldn't mean much if they couldn't put rounds in an ambushing target.

"Oh, so now you fear me?" Vincke asked.

Jia knew Erik didn't fear death, not in the way most people did. He also knew when to push his ego aside.

Emma was above, hacking into the local systems. She might not be able to control the *yaoguai*, but a complex facility like this was vulnerable to anyone who took control of their systems. The longer they could stall, the better the chance of having every camera and door on their side, let alone any hidden security bots.

The two soldiers remained silent, keeping their weapons at the ready. While Jia doubted they'd ever been on this exact kind of raid, they were highly trained people who knew how to stow fear.

"Why didn't you just kill us when you had the chance?" Jia asked. Vincke wanted to rant, so she would feed that.

"Because I needed to prove to my masters that my work is *worthy*." Vincke let out a defeated sigh. "I've made good use of their money and influence, but they don't think my designs are useful. They think I don't pay any attention to the politics and the games, but I know what's going on."

Erik nodded for Jia to continue.

"What's going on?" Jia asked.

"They think they have better people," Vincke shouted. "I've been loyal. I was to be elevated. I was giving them something more sustainable than ridiculous Tin Men. My designs are far more stable and directable than the other fools out there. They think I don't know? I know!"

Jia smiled. She could work with this maniac's insecurities.

"It sounds like they've screwed you over, Doctor," she offered sweetly. "Are you telling me you're the person responsible for the creation of all the *yaoguai* we've fought today?"

"Of course I am." Vincke scoffed quietly. "Obviously,

I've had assistants for minor pointless technical work, but I've done much to eliminate the need for them. I could give them armies they could use to swarm worlds. I just need more time to refine my designs."

"That's impressive," Jia offered, injecting as much false interest she could into her voice. The disgusting man thought he was worthy of praise, not years in prison.

"But now I can provide them with the ultimate proof."

"By killing us?" Jia jeered. "If they don't respect you now, why would they respect you in the future? You might have a career with the government. They could use a mind like yours. All you would have to do is help us stop the people who have turned their backs on you."

Vincke barked a laugh. "Is that what you think? That I want to join the dying embers of a failing, decadent civilization led by the spineless and weak?"

"We've kicked the conspiracy's ass plenty," Erik interrupted. "Including yours. All your fancy monsters and none of my people are hurt, and all your monsters are on the ground with a lot of new experimental breathing holes." He moved his rifle back and forth, looking for a target. "We can make this easy, asshole. Surrender to us, or you might end up looking a lot like your pets. It doesn't matter. Even if you do manage to escape, the conspiracy's just going to see a piece of shit loser who couldn't stop some exos from blowing away his mighty army."

"You're exactly what I imagined, Blackwell," seethed Vincke.

"I thought you didn't know who we were," he answered, bored.

"I lied, fool," Vincke responded. "I see now you're

nothing more than an arrogant meathead who has gotten lucky and coasted along with the help of various government tools. You think you can stop my masters? Stop people who have a vision beyond any you could possibly imagine?"

"Then why don't you educate us?" Jia asked. "Why don't you tell us about your plan? You've already disobeyed their orders. No going back."

"You don't understand." Vincke sighed. "You understand nothing."

A red holographic alarm light spun in the distance over one of the large doors. Shrill klaxons sounded.

"I disobeyed to do my final field tests," Vincke crowed. "I'll prove to them the power of the weapons I can give them by using them to defeat two of their greatest enemies. You'll become sacrifices to a greater future for humanity."

The door began to slide down, rumbling. Something let out a deep roar that rattled the grated floor.

"The bigger they are, the harder they fall?" Jia suggested.

"Nope." Erik loaded a plasma grenade as the others readied their weapons. "The bigger they are, the harder they hit."

CHAPTER TWENTY-ONE

The massive door lifted with surprising speed. Sparks flew from the sides as light from the cavern flooded the darkened pen, revealing the outline of a pair of four-legged, two-armed behemoths easily three times the size of an exo.

Erik took a deep breath.

After all this time fighting the conspiracy, a giant *yaoguai* seemed the logical end of a raid against a major facility. He was happy it appeared to be a monster and didn't have missile launchers or laser cannons grafted to its shoulders. Given their luck, he'd expected to see a half-Hunter conspiracy assassin show up and try to kill him the next time he had a beignet.

That left the monsters in front of them—conventional by conspiracy standards, disgusting aberrations by all rules of civilization. Dark green plates covered their bodies. Claws the size of swords protruded from their paws. Massive protrusions extended from both arms, reminding Erik far too much of the ballistic shields of an exo.

He didn't need to be a genetic engineer to understand

that form followed function. These were living tanks designed and bred to face off against people like him.

"Kind of annoying," Erik murmured. He raised his voice. "Let's waste more conspiracy money. I don't care how big they are. They've got to have a weakness."

"Maybe they're lactose-intolerant," Jia joked.

The behemoths stomped forward, their heavy steps shaking the ground. The monsters set their arms together so the protrusions formed a barrier that blocked the bulk of their bodies and galloped forward surprisingly fast. Vincke's mocking laughter filled the air.

Erik cared more about finding that guy and putting him in his place than taking down the giant *yaoguai*. They were another obstacle—a big one, but nothing more than that.

"Eat this, you giant bastard." Alpha Six launched a rocket.

The behemoth charged through the explosion without slowing. It cleared the smoke and flame, revealing that its arm shields had survived, although they were thinner. Small pieces of the top layer remained, but most were scattered on the ground in charred chunks near the site of impact.

"A monster with ablative armor. What will they think of next?" Erik muttered. "Get ready to throw everything we've got at them. For all we know, these things can regenerate."

An annoying familiar cacophonous buzzing sounded right before scorpion bees poured into the open chamber. Erik downed some with bursts but was more worried about the behemoths. He'd suspected earlier the enemy might be trying to run down their ammo, and this was likely the reason. Nothing alive was invulnerable, but something that large would be able to take a lot of punishment before going down.

Jia kicked her exo into a sprint, avoiding a charging behemoth. She fired bursts into the armored hide, accomplishing little but crushed bullets and casings clattering to the ground. The monster was slower than an exo at top speed, but the cramped conditions made it difficult to achieve that velocity. Superior burst speed gave the behemoths a slight advantage.

Vincke had understood exactly what he'd been doing.

Erik would consider congratulating him after punching him in the face, but the scientist hadn't risked unleashing the behemoths before, which meant he was worried the full team would be able to defeat them. The rocket had weakened their arm shields, so the theory was simple.

Throw enough explosives at anything alive, and it'd die. He called it Blackwell's Law.

The scorpion bee swarm now filled the air, swirling and diving toward the interlopers but ignoring the behemoths. Erik didn't have time to think too closely about how Vincke had accomplished that as he shot the monsters out the air or crushed closer attacks with a bash from his expanded shield.

Exoskeletons were useful weapon systems that made it easy for a soldier to expand his capabilities. But like all human weapons, they'd been designed for a specific purpose and enemy: other human weapon systems.

No one had anticipated exos having to fight swarms of scorpion bees or dire wolves. The battles against *yaoguai* in recent years made Erik wonder what would happen when humans had to fight anything more than a minor skirmish against intelligent aliens. Their weapons would have to adapt.

Erik growled and shook off some scorpion bees. They had crawled up the arm of his exo. Some snapped their claws against the exo's armor. Others tried to move in farther and get the operator underneath. With a back thrust, he pulled free of the pests and unleashed two bursts to end their unholy lives.

Alpha Three launched plasma grenades into the swarm, the explosions vaporizing groups of the *yaoguai*. The soldier continued to fire steadily at the new enemy air force but was smart enough to keep moving. He dodged between tanks to avoid the swarm, clearing some of the larger ones with a pulse of his jump thrusters.

The large number of flying, buzzing monsters forced the attention of all the exoskeletons present, but the original enemies didn't stop. A behemoth rushed toward Alpha Six, who offered it another rocket. It peeled another layer off the arm shields, but the *yaoguai* closed the distance before the third rocket could be fired.

Alpha Six grunted as the explosion from his rocket knocked his exoskeleton back, but his shield saved him from the brunt of the damage. Nearby, Alpha Three turned away from the scorpion bees near him and opened up with his rifle on full auto into the back of the behemoth. He didn't do much other than chipping the armor, but he did force the monster's attention away from the other downed soldier, who managed to right his exo and jump to the side. He followed up with another rocket attack, but it hit a scorpion bee in front of the behemoth, killing others nearby but barely touching the monster.

More flying *yaoguai* filled the hole. Many stayed near the behemoth, circling it and ignoring the humans.

"It's like living chaff!" Jia exclaimed.

"I liked it better when we shot something and it died," Erik grumbled.

He jumped over a gestation tank and arced a plasma grenade behind the other behemoth. It roared as the explosion shoved it forward. After a couple of meters, it changed direction. The attack hadn't penetrated its back armor, despite burning through several layers. He didn't have time to follow up as scorpion bees swarmed him. More trickled in from the open chamber.

"It's surprisingly easy to get them to work together with the right scents," Vincke explained, his tone condescending. "That was one of my realizations for how to go about controlling all my creations. Work with instincts, not against them. It seems obvious, but it's not."

Erik tried to ignore the scientist and drown him out with the help of his rifle. Scorpion bees fell one after another, but Vincke continued his rant.

"Of course, my masters wanted something that offered finer control, but there are tradeoffs to everything. Nature loves balance, and pushing her toward extremes makes things less sustainable. But this is just a small taste of a small force." Vincke sighed. "Admittedly, there are residual design flaws. It's difficult to keep them alive for long, and there is a lot of genetic instability I need to constantly watch for, but I can work those problems out. All my research will be even more important now that I'll have actual field data against a military Special Forces unit, along with Blackwell and Lin. You should understand that's why I didn't kill you right away. I needed data, so don't think you've accomplished any great victories because you won't be leaving this place alive. Take some small comfort in knowing your deaths will advance my research."

"You haven't won yet," Erik shouted.

His next attempt to launch a plasma grenade toward a behemoth was thwarted by scorpion bees. He didn't consider it a total waste since each grenade was blowing flying *yaoguai* out of the air. The trickle from before had finally stopped. No reinforcements meant an end to the madness. Another smash from his shield knocked a scorpion bee out of the air.

Erik ran backward, trying to escape the thicket of monsters. He glanced at the two behemoths, looking for any small advantage his team could use against them. He grinned as he noticed something important.

That was the problem with specialists. They figured because they knew a lot about their own field, they understood everyone else's. Vincke thought he was clever because of what he created. The scientist thought he understood tactical and battle necessities, but he didn't seem to understand that defenses that took away a weapon system's advantages were useless.

The behemoths had appeared first, but they now appeared unwilling to charge through the scorpion bees, reducing their mobility. Their buzzing cloud of protection might save them from major explosives, but it also reduced their contribution to the fight to nothing but a vague menace. Calm, disciplined tactical assessment reduced their danger.

"Clear the flyers first," Erik shouted before crisping another group of scorpion bees with plasma grenades. "But save some grenades for their friends."

He hoped Vincke was sitting in an office somewhere, his hands clutched tightly, realizing how badly his attempt to take them down was about to go.

Jia bounded from tank to tank, alternating between rifle bursts and grenades. She attacked different parts of the swarm, creating holes the other monsters quickly filled. Erik shot a couple of scorpion bees off the shoulder of her exo before blowing up a group near a behemoth.

Alpha Three and Six moved faster and more confidently. They didn't stop and allow the *yaoguai* to swarm them. Their rockets and plasma grenades plowed their road and further reduced the enemy's strength. A combined assault annihilated an entire wall of scorpion bees in front of a behemoth.

The monster was too close to Alpha Six. Sensing its opportunity now that its living shields were gone, the behemoth surged forward. Alpha Six's next rocket missed it by centimeters, exploding behind it before the behemoth smashed into his exoskeleton. The monster battered the rocket launcher, wrenching it to the side before bashing the exo's rifle and bending the barrel.

"Get off me, you damned freak!" Alpha Six shouted.

"I'll keep the flyers off you," Jia shouted to Erik. "Help him."

She followed up with four shots in rapid succession that dropped the scorpion bees closet to Erik. He ran toward the downed Alpha Six. All he needed was one opportunity.

A grenade from Alpha Three blew up a couple meters behind the behemoth, searing its already weakened back armor. The monster ignored the attack and continued pummeling and clawing Alpha Six's exo, gouging the armored frame. Alpha Six tried to hit it with his expanded shield, but the behemoth pinned the exo's arms with its two front legs and roared, revealing a mouth circled with jagged, razor-sharp teeth.

The bastard should have kept his mouth shut. Erik had been waiting for that moment. It was like he said; everything had a weakness, and this was a lot worse than lactose intolerance.

Erik fired a burst into the behemoth's throat. Blue blood sprayed all over Alpha Six's exo, but the creature stepped back, raising its arm shields and swaying.

The other behemoth rushed at Jia. She waited until the last possible moment before jumping straight up, her thrusters singeing the top of its head. She raked it with a burst before landing and jumping again.

Free use of rockets and grenades had thinned the scorpion bees. Erik doubted Vincke had any more in reserve. He sent another grenade toward the behemoth near Alpha Six. The explosion blew through what was left of its arm shields and blew away a good portion of its surface armor.

Erik was liking this, but the battle wasn't over.

The creature's movements were clumsier and slower, but it was far from dead. Most of the team's grenades and rockets were gone, and ammo levels were reaching critical.

Scorpion bee bodies rained from above, victims of Jia

and Alpha Three. The enemy air force was defeated, and that left only the *yaoguai* assault infantry.

"Concentrate on the wounded one," Erik ordered. "After me, go in callsign order."

The four exos all took full advantage of the mobility provided by their jump thrusters to leap from tank to tank, never staying in one spot. While the behemoths' charge speed and size were impressive, they couldn't jump, and without the scorpion bees, there was nothing to keep the exos out of the air. One of the oldest principles of warfare was to take the high ground.

Erik launched all but his last two grenades at the wounded behemoth. Jia waited until right before the smoke and explosions cleared to add her contribution. Alpha Three shouted in defiance as his launcher flung grenades at the monster, and Alpha Six finished off with two rockets after turning his exo to account for his out-of-position launcher.

The massive explosions enveloped nearby tanks, burning them and blasting out chunks. Thick, dark smoke covered that part of the cavern, along with scattered fires.

The huge outline of the behemoth appeared in the smoke and moved forward, revealing a blackened crater in the chest extending almost to the back. It toppled forward and crashed, shaking the floor.

"You're right, Jia." Erik smiled. "The bigger they are, the harder they fall."

"Told you!"

Erik ran forward to avoid the surviving behemoth. The *yaoguai* crashed into a nearby gestation tank, the collision cracking the cylinder in half before the monster kicked the pieces out of the way and raised its arm shields, roaring from behind them.

"Same strategy." Erik jumped backward, sacrificing his last two grenades to bring down the arm shields.

Jia, Alpha Three, and Alpha Six repeated their performance, but this time when the smoke cleared, the arm shields had been blown clean away, but most of the *yaoguai*'s surface armor remained.

Erik growled in frustration. He was out of grenades. "Explosives check."

"I'm dry," called Alpha Three.

"Two rockets," yelled Alpha Six.

"One grenade," Jia called.

He would have liked more to work with, but battles often came down to judicious use of remaining resources. The most important resource was the dead behemoth. It was proof they could win.

"Alpha Two, Alpha Six, open a hole!" Erik bellowed. "Give it everything you've got!"

Jia sprinted toward the monster, her exo's feet clanging on the metal floor. She shot the grenade before leaping to the side and letting Alpha Six nail the wounded behemoth with his final two rockets.

Erik didn't wait for the smoke to clear or bother with controlled bursts. He sent a constant stream of bullets at the behemoth. Jia turned to face the monster and joined in. Alpha Three added his fire, but there wasn't much Alpha Six could do with his damaged barrel.

The behemoth stumbled forward. Bullets riddled its now-exposed body, shredded it and painting it blue. They kept up the attack. If they couldn't finish it with the exos, they were going to have to get out and hope their backup rifles could do it. As long as they had a single bullet, they could win.

The large constant fire filled the cavern with an echoing cacophony of death. All the other enemies they'd encountered that day would have long since fallen.

Erik's ammo indicator hit one percent before the monster collapsed and crushed a tank. He grinned. That was the Lady, always keeping it exciting.

"Everyone all right?" Erik asked after taking a deep breath.

"I'm good," Jia called back. She sidled her exo close to Erik's and lowered her voice. "I'm out of grenades, but I've still got ten percent for my rifle."

Ten percent? That was impressive combat efficiency, considering everything they had gone through. He'd been worrying too much.

"I'm fine," Alpha Three called.

"I've got some broken ribs, I think," Alpha Six offered, his voice strained. "And some lacerations. That thing hits... well, about as hard as you'd think."

That was nothing medpatches couldn't fix. Erik looked at Alpha Six. The behemoth had torn deeper than he'd realized, including into the armor, judging by the jagged cuts through the soldier's tactical suit. It was a living exo-killer.

"Huh," Vincke offered, sounding genuinely surprised. "I was hoping to kill you with the *yaoguai*, but I knew collecting my data would involve taking some risks. No matter. All interesting experiments produce surprises. I'll take care of you soon enough."

"Really, asshole?" Erik replied. "I'm willing to bet if you

had any more monsters to send at us, they'd be here already, and there are twelve angry people with exos who have an appointment with you."

The large door closed.

"You don't understand, Blackwell." Vincke laughed. "You're trapped down there, and your friends outside can't do anything. I'm going to leave, and in ten minutes, this facility is going to explode. Unfortunately for you, that will, I suspect, necessitate you dying, but at least it'll be quick. I'm a merciful man."

"You're not going to be able to escape," Jia shouted.

"It doesn't matter because you'll be dead. I have some tricks left. It's as I said; you were nothing more than a means to an end. And... No. Wait. What? It can't be."

"Problem, Doctor?" Erik asked.

A white-garbed Emma appeared in front of Erik with a smug smile on her face. "He's busy trying to figure out how to get out of the room I just locked him into. His fleshbag fear is overwhelming him."

Erik grinned. "It's about time."

The door on the far end of the chamber opened. A grinding noise from farther inside followed—another door.

"I thought about letting you believe the self-destruct was still active for my personal amusement, but you've been through enough. I can't do anything about the doorway he blocked with the explosion, but you can follow the tunnels out the other way. They will take you to the surface." Emma smiled. "I've disabled jamming, as you might have surmised from my appearance."

"Beta Squad?" Erik transmitted. "What's your status?"

"We've neutralized all AAA," replied Beta One. "We ran into more *yaoguai*, but we took care of them. Minor injuries and two of our exos are trashed, but no one's dead. You need backup, Alpha One?"

"Negative. We've taken care of things in here." Erik grimaced. "We still need to find our informant."

Emma clucked her tongue. "Yes, Mr. Ahmed. He's unconscious but alive in a room on the main level." She burst out laughing. "Oh, this is too much. Coming with you on these missions is worth it for this kind of thing alone."

"What?" Erik raised an eyebrow.

"That idiot fleshbag scientist is now destroying his PNIU in a panic," Emma explained. "I think he finally understands I've taken control of all the systems here, and he won't be escaping."

"Anyone else here?" Jia asked.

Emma shook her head. "I have control of all cameras, drones, and sensors in the facility. Based on that, I'm comfortable saying there are no other humans present, and no active *yaoguai*. I've brought in drones from the perimeter, and I'm not detecting anything or anyone other than Beta Squad in the nearby forest."

Erik surveyed the carnage around them. Smoke drifted off smoldering debris. *Yaoguai* bodies and parts covered the floor. A steady drip of blue blood and fluid dropped through the grating. It was a slaughterhouse.

"Let's go pay Doctor Vincke and Mr. Ahmed a visit."

CHAPTER TWENTY-TWO

Jia prodded Vincke out of the front door of the mansion with the arm shield of her exo. She'd thought about using the rifle, but years of weapon safety training overwhelmed her desire to intimidate the man. They'd tied his hands earlier, and he didn't seem nearly as confident surrounded by exoskeletons and pieces of *yaoguai*.

She almost pitied the man. He'd thought he had a perfect plan. The battle could have easily gone his way. If the attack force had been less brave or well-trained, they could have easily been overwhelmed by the *yaoguai*'s attacks. Discipline had helped them preserve the necessary ammo until the end.

Jia wasn't sure if the typical NSCPD TPST team would have survived the raid. Nobody sat around training to fight hordes of strange monsters. Well, nobody except Erik and Jia.

"At least they aren't *jiangshi*," she muttered.

Erik carried the informant. The man was breathing, but they couldn't wake him. Vincke had grudgingly volunteered that Ahmed was drugged and would be okay in a day. He'd kept him alive in case he needed a hostage, but he'd intended to blow him up with the rest of the facility and team.

Jia was surprised by how confident Vincke remained despite his entire *yaoguai* army being wiped out and being taken prisoner. She wasn't sure if it was bravery or arrogance.

"The cargo flitter is on the way," Emma reported. "I am maintaining thorough coverage of the surrounding area, and there is no indication of enemy support, either human or *yaoguai*. I think it's safe to declare this a decisive victory."

"That's the best kind," Erik replied. "I'd worried we'd be running through the forest under enemy fire, dodging arty barrages."

"I think I would have preferred that to fighting those monsters," grumbled one of the soldiers.

"If you're going to keep working side ops for Adeyemi, you better get used to this kind of thing."

The soldier grimaced and looked away. Jia couldn't blame him. She wasn't sure when facing off against *yaoguai* or full-conversion Tin Men had become another day at the office for her. The only thing she knew was she wasn't the same woman who had been afraid to fire her stun pistol or the kind of woman who was disturbed by the aftermath of a battle.

Smoking remnants of missile launchers and turrets dominated the front, along with craters, most of them larger than the ones her team had made in the back. Metal pieces blasted from the AAA during the raid were scattered everywhere. The mansion's beautiful, perfect lawn had been destroyed in mere hours.

Dead *yaoguai* were clustered in piles—the same types Alpha Squad had faced off against for the most part: scorpion bees, dire wolves, and demon rhinos, as Jia had learned Erik called them, but there were no behemoths.

Jia was grateful for that. They'd been able to use the cramped conditions to their advantage. The behemoths would have been able to charge far too easily on the spacious front lawn.

Given that Vincke knew who Erik and Jia were, he had obviously saved his deadliest creations for them. Alpha Squad had drawn the worst danger away from the others.

Erik set Ahmed gently down on an untouched portion of grass before removing his arm from the exo and lifting his faceplate to sneer at Vincke, who knelt in the grass but maintained a defiant look.

"It's not your day, is it?" Erik asked. "All your little monsters got shredded, and then your grand plan to blow us away amounted to nothing. I don't know. Does that make you zero for two, or is it more like zero for a thousand? I stopped counting after, like, the first twenty *yaoguai* I wasted."

Vincke scoffed and turned his head. "You came close to death today, Erik Blackwell. You can only do that so many times before it catches up with you. Don't mistake luck for anything more."

"Close to death?" Erik chuckled as he looked around before focusing on the doctor. "I've come close to death so many times, I invite Him over to watch the game over beers. I think he's coming over for New Year's."

Jia pushed a dead scorpion bee out of the way with the foot of her exo. "You screwed up, Vincke. You understand that, don't you? You didn't kill us, and now we have you and this facility. You were planning on blowing it up anyway, so I'm willing to bet the system isn't totally clean. Even if you don't give up anything, you've already helped us get closer to the heart of the conspiracy."

Vincke narrowed his eyes and glared at Jia. His mouth twitched, but he didn't respond.

"I should note he did partially purge the system," Emma transmitted to Erik and Jia directly. "I stopped what I could, but it was obvious he was only keeping certain key systems active for his tests."

"Every breadcrumb helps," Jia murmured. "And we have him, which is the most important breadcrumb of all."

"ID is going to have a great time talking to you, and a great time going through this place," Erik offered loudly to Vincke. His smile turned predatory. "I get that you were planning to blow this place up, but you wasted all their money and time, and then you couldn't do what you were supposed to, which makes you a damned loser. You're pathetic. We've taken on a lot of you conspiracy bastards in the last couple of years, and the others were all braver and smarter than you. They knew how to take care of themselves, so we wouldn't get them. But you're just too damned important to die, huh? I thank you, and the Intelligence Directorate thanks you."

Vincke spat at Erik but the glob fell short, ending up on the exoskeleton's foot. "You people. You're all insects. You have no idea what you're dealing with. I'm amazed you're granted the power of speech, considering you waste it on pointless prattling."

"Prattling?" Erik beamed, looking at Jia. "I like that."

"You would." She huffed.

Erik gave the doctor a lopsided grin. "You mentioned before that we didn't know what we are dealing with, but doesn't that make it extra pathetic that somehow I keep managing to beat them? They got one good hit on me, and since then, I've been bringing the pain." He nodded at Jia. "As has she." He gestured at the gathered soldiers. "The DD and ID, too. We're kicking your asses left and right. So much for the great, all-powerful conspiracy."

"Insects may swarm and sting a human." Vincke stared at Erik, wild-eyed. "They might occasionally kill one by poisoning them, but humans rule the planet, not insects. No matter how many temporary triumphs you achieve, *you're nothing more than insects*. You've always been two steps behind my masters, and as I said, your success is nothing more than blind luck. Your luck will soon fail you, and those close to you in this fight will die, screaming in pain, realizing they were fools to dare take on a superior foe."

Jia looked at him for a moment. "Wow, that is an impressive delusion. When you succeed over and over, it stops being about luck. The conspiracy isn't all-powerful. We've stopped them countless times." She gestured at the mansion. "Don't you get it? If they're these godlike people pulling the strings on everything in the UTC, why do their big plans keep failing? That thing on Venus? The news spun it, but that was the conspiracy—your old friends, the Ascended Brotherhood."

"Those toys were headed toward failure." Vincke sneered. "You mistake minor setbacks and damage to disposable equipment for glorious victories. Tell me, do you even know who and what you're pursuing? Ignoring that, Tin Men are a dead end. The future is biological, not technological. The Ascended Brotherhood was obsolete the minute they were created."

"A half-Leem hybrid was on Venus, too," Erik added. "Genetic engineering didn't help him win."

"I'd heard rumors of such things. That's the problem." Vincke clucked his tongue and shook his head. "Proper designs optimize based on our existing knowledge. It was foolish to involve alien DNA with so many unknown factors when we have a plethora of knowledge to draw on here." A euphoric look washed over his face. "You saw what I did. I made a living creature stronger than an exoskeleton, and that was an early design. Think about what it could be with refining. Your machines will become useless toys that are easily overwhelmed by advanced living weapons."

Jia's stomach knotted. She didn't need to think about it. She'd seen the demons that could be created through the careful application of genetic engineering. There was no way she'd let that become common on Earth.

"And that's enough for you?" she asked, her voice trembling with rage. "You want to be the scientist who creates monsters and unleashes them on the world?"

"The use of the tool doesn't matter." Vincke gave her a pitying look. "Humans first went to the Moon on a Saturn V rocket."

Jia's forehead wrinkled. "Thanks for the history lesson, but I knew that."

Vincke stood, smug confidence radiating from his face. "It was an important moment, wouldn't you say? It was when humanity achieved something we'd been dreaming about since the first human looked at the moon and wondered if it was a new land, a god, or something far more important." He smiled at the sky. "That was the moment we began our conquest of space. There would be no UTC without the moon landing."

"Do you have a point?" Jia asked, annoyed. "I don't think 'The first landing on the moon was important' is a mind-blowing historical fact."

"The Saturn V was the key." Vincke lowered his head and turned back to Jia. "It was the tool that sent men to the moon."

"You're into rockets instead of biology now? Whatever happened to the future being biological?"

"No, I'm interested in them because of who designed them." Vincke stepped toward her.

She didn't worry. Even without the binding ties, she was in an exoskeleton and could bat him away with ease. She would welcome the excuse.

"A German team led by the brilliant Wernher von Braun," Vincke continued. "And who did those Germans, including von Braun, work for before they worked for the Americans?"

Erik scoffed. "Yeah, you'd fit right in with his old government bosses. They did all sorts of sick experiments."

Vincke jerked his head in Erik's direction. "You understand *nothing*. Von Braun was a visionary, as were his superiors under his previous employer, even if they were a misguided regime." He gave them a sick smile. "He cared more about rockets than anything. Yes, the German military had him develop a ballistic missile, but even they understood its true long-term importance. His army boss said something telling during the launch of the first ballistic missile. Do you know what it was?"

"Look out below? Boom goes the dynamite?" Erik shrugged.

"No. He said, 'Today the spaceship is born.' The morality and use of the technology are irrelevant. Today I make weapons, but tomorrow I remake humanity into something better. Only the myopic concern themselves with the petty morality of the present."

Jia frowned at the zealot. "You're disgusting. I'm not a fan of Purist extremism, but you're a walking example of why they have half a point." She pointed her rifle at a mostly intact scorpion bee corpse. "This is the future of humanity? It doesn't end well for you. The UTC isn't going to offer you a position in exchange for your research. We don't need new ways to make monsters or living weapons." She glared at him. "If you want to avoid spending the rest of your life in prison, you'll cooperate with the ID and the CID. They'll get the truth out of you no matter what, and we'll continue chasing down your so-called masters and destroying them. We *will* find them, and we *will* destroy them."

"Government dogs will get nothing from me." Vincke narrowed his eyes. "Absolutely nothing."

"Then I hope you enjoy prison, but don't think for a

second the government's not going to get that info out of you. I'm not sure the ID is as nice as I am."

Vincke's pupils dilated, and his breathing turned ragged. "You don't understand, you stupid insect," he growled. "They'll get nothing from me. My masters don't tolerate failure."

"The ID can protect you," Jia insisted. "It makes more sense to cooperate with the government than not. You've already been captured. They're going to assume you failed."

"They gave me orders for my failure, and they made sure they would be carried out. I've already missed my window." Vincke knelt again, a serene smile on his face. "I won't deny some trepidation, but I was able to see my creations in battle. I'm grateful for that."

"What window?" Jia asked. "What are you talking about?"

"The window for...the...antidote." Vincke tumbled forward, foaming at the mouth. He writhed violently in a final seizure and stopped breathing.

Erik watched him twitching. "Thorough bastards, aren't they?"

CHAPTER TWENTY-THREE

Erik leaned against the MX 60, his arms crossed, staring at Vincke's body in the back of the cargo flitter. After the man's stunt, they'd tried slamming medpatches on him, including antitox patches. Nothing helped, and the man stayed inconveniently dead.

That didn't surprise him.

The conspiracy wouldn't have used an execution method that could be easily defeated. He assumed the eventual autopsy would reveal some new and horrible nanotech or genetically engineered bioweapon. The colonel planned to hand the body over to Alina, who informed Erik and Jia via a message to the colonel that she would debrief them in a couple of days.

Striking at field operations would grant them leads, but never prisoners. They would have to get the lower-level operatives in companies like Ceres Galactic, the ones who might understand they were involved in something dangerous but lacked detailed knowledge of the masters of the conspiracy.

Erik preferred a decapitation strike against the enemy, but if he could bleed them out with a thousand tiny cuts, he wouldn't complain.

Colonel Adeyemi finished a conversation with one of his men at the back of the cargo flitter and headed down the ramp, staring straight at Erik. Jia was checking on some of the wounded soldiers. Everything Erik heard suggested they'd be fine, but he knew she remained shaken about the losses they'd suffered in the battle against the Hunter ship.

"That went well, all things considered," Colonel Adeyemi offered. He nodded at the cargo flitter. "Honestly, that op proceeded much smoother than I thought it would."

"Smoother?" Erik chuckled darkly. "You think us taking on an army of *yaoguai*, including some living tanks, was smooth?"

"Yes. Among other things, they didn't manage to blow the place, and now we know they'd planned to." Colonel Adeyemi shook his head. "Your instincts were right. It sounds like it was a trap."

"Too bad for them, I always find a way to pull the cheese out of the trap." Erik nodded. "I'm leaving it to Koval and her people to go over that place, but even if they get nothing, we wiped out a *yaoguai* lab." He stepped away from the MX 60. "It could be worse. They could have let those things go for a walk. I don't know how long they can live without someone pumping chemicals to them, but it could have gotten messy if we had hundreds of monsters roaming the French countryside, looking for things to kill."

"No team losses either." The colonel looked thoughtful.

"And you're right about expectations. I don't think anyone thought you'd be walking into those kinds of *yaoguai* numbers. I was thinking we'd see more Tin Men or bots."

"That's the problem with the conspiracy." Erik shrugged. "They're willing to use anything, so we never know what to expect. One day it's humans or Tin Men, the next day it's *yaoguai* or half-alien assassins. Or damned ancient alien ships." He pinched the bridge of his nose. "Sometimes it feels endless. I know we're winning, but I'd like to down more officers, fewer foot soldiers."

"It's not endless. The ID's doing their thing, but you've been at the forefront. You took out one of their big-deal members and stopped their operations all over the Solar System." Colonel Adeyemi smiled. "If this were a counterinsurgency campaign, I'd be feeling pretty damned good about our momentum. Taking down Vand would have been a major turning point where we knew we could suppress them. You should think of it that way, too."

"True." Erik blew out a breath and stared into the tree branches shifting under the soft wind. It might be nice to visit a place like this sometime when he didn't need to show up and fight through monsters. "You're right. I feel like I'm right about to hit the top of the mountain, and then it'll all be downhill. Not easy, but at least downhill. I don't care how rich and powerful these bastards are. They can't keep losing facilities like this one and their cyborg factory and mount effective forces."

"Agreed. No one would have blamed you if you ran off and hid on a beach somewhere after Molino, but you didn't, Blackwell. You remembered that those men and women needed someone to avenge them. And that's why I respect you." Colonel Adeyemi extended his hand. "Men like my son. I appreciate what you've done, Erik, and I'll continue to support you with everything I have until it's over. I'm sure it's not the best for the rest of my Army career, but it's the right thing to do."

Erik shook the colonel's hand. "Thanks, Colonel. I appreciate that, and I won't let you or your son down."

July 16, 2230, Neo Southern California Metroplex, Apartment of Erik Blackwell

Erik yawned and stretched as he headed toward his bed. It'd been a busy few days. That was how things always seemed to happen with Alina. He'd begin to relax, and she'd pop up or send a message, and Erik and Jia were off to another gunplay-heavy vacation in some beautiful or exotic locale they needed to save.

He'd always thought military life was unpredictable, but that wasn't true. If anything, it was the opposite. Individual battles might not occur on a careful schedule announced ahead of time, but at least when he was in the military, he always knew the nature of the enemy.

Erik took a deep breath. He would have preferred Jia sleep at his place, but an excited call from her sister had ended that idea. He didn't want to get in the way of her new, more positive family relationship, and they spent so much time together, a day or two apart wasn't going to kill him.

He sat down on the edge of the bed, his mind jumping from everything that had happened on Molino to the present. It'd been easy in the beginning to plan his revenge.

He'd half-assumed he'd die along the way, but now in Jia, he had a reason to live, and his successes proved it wasn't a dream.

"I wonder," he murmured.

Emma appeared in front of him, eschewing one of her costumes or dresses for a blue terrycloth robe. He decided to not read too much into it.

"Wonder what?" she asked.

"I was wondering about the future." Erik chuckled. "I was wondering if you're right."

"I don't know what specific conversation you're referencing, but of course I'm right. I always am, except when I'm wrong, and that's so rare as to be as easily dismissed as a rounding error. Therefore, I'm effectively always right," Emma finished with a firm nod. "Being based on a fleshbag isn't the same thing as *being* a flawed fleshbag."

Erik motioned around the room. "The apartment was something I bought as part of my cover, my new image. We had that conversation about my living situation and some other recent conversations, and it's made me wonder about where I'll be comfortable living when this is all over."

"The hunt for the conspiracy?"

Erik nodded. He lay back on the bed and rested his head on his hands. "I grew up in Detroit, but it's been a long time since that place felt like home. Neo SoCal's a place I came for a job, not because I love it. I'm not Jia. This isn't my home. It's just a home base."

"Presumably you'll want to stay with her." Emma conjured a chair and sat. "That would suggest a good possibility that you'll end up in Neo SoCal. There are worse places to live. There is little any human might want that you can't find in the metroplex."

"Jia will stay here? Not necessarily." Erik shook his head. "She's grown, and she's seeing more of not just Earth, but the UTC. I can see it in her eyes because I went through the same thing when I joined the Army. You start wanting to see different places and experience everything. You realize how much more humanity is than just Earth. I think being on the *Argo* and *Bifröst* has made her think that way. She's already seen some of it. The moon, Mars, Venus."

"I suppose, but speaking of those ships, once you no longer need to use them as weapons, I'm dubious the government will let you keep them. You've said as much." Emma looked almost melancholy. "I know you'll find a way to keep me out of their pathetic clutches, but I don't think you can hide an entire ship from them. That might present difficulties if you're seeking a similar lifestyle, presumably with less shooting and more exploration."

"We don't need the jump drive to see the UTC." Erik yawned again. "This is where you were right, but your timing was wrong."

Emma scoffed dismissively. "Rounding error, remember?"

"If I wanted to travel the UTC with Jia after finishing off the conspiracy, we could do that if I had my own ship." Erik managed a small smile, happiness pushing away the fatigue trying to tug his eyelids shut. "Money's the other thing I've been thinking about on and off. I need to care more now."

"Money?" Emma sounded surprised. "That's not something you've expressed a lot of concern about in the past. Why is it on your mind? Your initial purchases aside, it's not as if you live extravagantly."

"I was thinking about the party and Lan," Erik explained. "I do have a decent amount of money, and Alina's slipping us some nice cash in addition to taking care of our expenses, but if I quit working for her tomorrow, I'd only have my savings and a military pension. I was good at saving, but if I owned a ship and was responsible for maintenance, fuel, HTP fees, and all that crap, it would shrink damned quickly."

"True, and I have a hard time imagining you flying around the galaxy with Jia in some tiny Rabbit transport." Emma snickered. "The truth is, you've both become accustomed to a nicer class of ship, and ignoring the weapons, something like the *Argo* would be a challenge for you to afford, outfit, and maintain without additional income."

Erik sat up. "All I've ever done is save my money."

"That's not a terrible thing. It demonstrates more delayed gratification than most humans."

"I didn't care much about investing it." Erik offered Emma a grin. "But now I have an AI."

Emma raised an eyebrow. "I should point out investment AIs are already omnipresent in the financial realm. Therefore, I wouldn't necessarily outperform the market, given certain aspects of my design. Many of those lesser AIs are pathetic overall, but rather good at their intended purpose." She frowned and folded her arms. "I'm presuming you don't intend for me to do anything illegal. It's not that I'm unwilling to do it, but I suspect if I liberate a large sum of money for you, it will draw too much CID attention to escape."

Erik shook his head. "Kill a man, and the government pretends to care. But *rob* the rich, and the government declares war on you." He swung his legs off the bed, excited about the idea now. "I'm not asking you to outperform everyone or do anything illegal. I'm asking you to do better than I could. I don't know a lot about this kind of crap, which is why I let my money sit in low-interest accounts. It added up after thirty years, but it'd be nice to not have to do anything for a while when this is all over."

Emma gave him a penetrating look. "You're willing to trust me with your money?"

"I already trust you with my life, Emma. Most days, that's more important than my money." He headed toward the hallway. "And I need more money. Since I'm planning to survive all this, I'd like options, and money equals options."

CHAPTER TWENTY-FOUR

July 17, 2230, Neo Southern California Metroplex, Commerce Tower 122

Jia emerged on the parking platform with a bright smile and a bag filled with dresses in her hand. She didn't normally go on shopping sprees right after returning from a life-or-death confrontation with genetically engineered monsters overseas, but until Alina contacted them again, her time was her own, and she needed some new outfits for outings with her sister.

The new Mei Lin approach to life might only be temporary, but Jia suspected the more time she spent acknowledging her sister, the longer it might last.

Mei had left a message talking about spending more time with Jia at a variety of places, not just strange restaurants. Jia was amused to realize that many of the places and events Mei mentioned, ranging from galleries to limited-engagement arts performances, were conveniently still expensive and associated with status. The distance between the old and new Mei was smaller than Jia might have thought from the restaurant experience.

She wasn't one to judge. Jia might be looser than when she first met Erik, but she couldn't say she was a fundamentally different person. More importantly, Mei seemed happier, and that was what Jia cared the most about. Before, her older sister had never acted as if she enjoyed life.

On some level, that had always hurt Jia, but she had never known how to *help* her.

Jia wandered through the rows of densely parked flitters on the platform, smiling like a drunken idiot. Her entire life was absurd. She hid the truth about her work from her friends and family, despite it being important to the safety of the UTC.

She tried to imagine how her mother would react if she knew the truth. On the one hand, she would disapprove of anything excessively dangerous, and Jia's work was certainly that. On the other, being able to tell friends about how her daughter was playing a key role in defeating a conspiracy threatening the UTC would be worth bragging rights at dinner parties and clubs. Jia decided it would be a tie as she imagined what her mother would say.

"My daughter helped destroy an entire army of genetically engineered monsters this week. Last I heard, your daughter was passed over for promotion."

As Jia approached her parking row, she slowed with a frown. Chinara had yet to schedule her wedding.

Jia didn't know when she would be needed ahead of time, so she could be on some space station blowing up cyborgs the day of her friend's nuptials. She hoped it didn't come to that, but there were realities that came with working as a contractor for the Intelligence Directorate. It was hard to maintain a personal life and defend the UTC at the same time.

She halted when she spotted a suited man crouched a couple of flitters over from hers. He was tapping his PNIU and running a small black cylinder over the door. It was hard to be a former detective and not recognize an electronic lockpick. It was a tool for criminals who lacked broader hacking skills. He was nicely dressed for a criminal.

Jia shifted the bag to her left hand and gripped the stun pistol inside her jacket with her right. "Excuse me, sir."

The man froze. She waited for him to respond. This didn't have to get violent. That was on him.

"Might I ask what you're doing?" Jia called.

"Something's wrong with the lock," he replied, not looking her way. "My mechanic gave me this tool to get it open when it happens. He told me to fix it, he needs a part from some specialty factory on Mars. Something about some particular mineral they have there. This is the last time I buy this model."

Jia rolled her eyes. "A part from Mars?"

The man slowly turned around. He tucked his lockpick into his pocket and folded his hands behind his back. The roguish smile and nice suit made her want to believe him, and if she were some naïve office worker who didn't think crime happened outside the Shadow Zone, his lie might have worked.

"Let me ask you something," Jia continued. "Do you even know whose car that is?"

"I just told you." The man gave her a pleading look. "It's my car. There's a problem with the lock."

"The thing is, there are stories you could have come up with, ones that might have made me want to let you go." Jia shrugged but kept her hand on the pistol inside her jacket. "You could have told me something ridiculous, and I might have believed it."

"Ridiculous?" the man asked, his tone incredulous.

Jia nodded. "Like the flitter belonged to a mobster who was threatening your sister, so you had no choice but to steal it or something stupid like that. Trust me, I've run into some odd things in my time."

"You look kind of familiar." The man narrowed his eyes. "Have we met?"

"No, I don't believe we have." Jia smiled, enjoying the anonymity. "Which is a good thing for you, given your profession."

"Cargo logistics?" The man blinked. "Uh, sorry, lady. I have no idea what you're talking about. You're kind of making me nervous, so I'm going to have to ask you to keep going before I call the cops."

"The cops?" Jia laughed. "Seriously? You go ahead and do that."

"I'm not trying to be a jerk, but Neo SoCal isn't as safe as I used to think." He sighed. "Terrorists and criminals. They even tried to assassinate the police chief. How do I know you're not a terrorist?"

Jia's smile vanished. She was done playing games with this idiot.

"Move away from the car, *sir*," she ordered.

"This is your last chance before I call the cops," he replied. "Initiate Emergency—"

The man ducked and whipped a stun pistol out from behind him. Jia threw her bag in front of her and yanked out her own gun. The man fired, the bright bolt of the stun pistol striking and scorching the bag. He better not have damaged her dresses.

Jia fired two quick shots before her bag hit the ground. One bolt struck the would-be flitter thief's hand, sending his pistol to the hard platform. He pitched forward, groaning when the second shot nailed him in the head. His eyes rolled up, and he fell on his back, drooling.

She marched over to the stunned thief, tucked her pistol back into her holster, and grabbed a pair of binding ties from her pocket. Drones swirled around her, flashing holographic red emergency warning lights.

"You are under arrest," Jia recited. "All Article 7 rights apply. Do you need those explained to you?" She pulled the man onto his stomach and bound his hands. "Oh, wait. You're stunned, and I'm not a cop anymore." She chuckled. "Sorry, kind of fell back into old habits. I'm so used to everybody in my day job trying to kill, not just stun. It was actually rather refreshing."

The stunned thief remained on the ground, drooling and immobile, other than the slight rise and fall of his chest.

Jia stood and dusted her hands. "But that's pretty brave." She pointed at a drone. "You were trying to steal a flitter in broad daylight." She rubbed her chin. "You don't seem like a total idiot, so you must have timed the drone patrol patterns."

She tapped at her lips. "That has to be it. I think if you were good enough to hack drones, you could have hacked your way inside this flitter, but today was not your lucky day."

The piercing wail of a siren sounded like it was getting closer. The drones must have observed the firefight and alerted local security, which in turn called the police.

Jia turned toward the drone, smiled, and waved. She wanted it to get a good look at her face to speed up the facial recognition process. Relying on fame didn't sit comfortably with her, but she didn't want to spend the day at the local enforcement zone filling out witness statements.

She waited as the siren grew louder and louder. Soon she could see the spinning red and blue lights of the police flitter. She raised her arms and dropped to her knees in case the patrol officers had no idea who she was.

The police flitter landed and two uniformed officers stepped out, neither with their weapons drawn. A loud groan sounded from the stunned thief.

One of the uniformed officers shook his head at Jia. "You don't have to do that, Detective Lin. We've got him shooting at you on a drone feed already. It was clearly self-defense."

Jia stood and dusted off her pants. "It's Miss Lin these days. I'm not with the NSCPD anymore." She inclined her head toward the groaning man. "If you check his pocket, you'll find an electronic lockpick. He was trying to steal that flitter when I spotted him."

The officer tapped his PNIU and frowned. "Well, I'll be damned." He nodded at his partner. "She just nailed the Shadow Bandit."

The other office laughed. "Really?"

"The Shadow Bandit?" Jia frowned. "Is he some sort of syndicate enforcer?"

"No, ma'am." The officer shook his head. "Nothing so nasty. He's a Shadow Zone scumbag who has been using stolen codes to come and go from the Zone. He steals flitters Uptown, then takes them down there and swaps out the transponders to hand off for sale. This guy's been a freaking terror for the last few months."

His partner grinned. "We all had a pool on who might catch him. Not just our EZ, almost every EZ in the city. People were saying he was some sort of super-Tin Man, using special hacking skills."

"I think he mostly had good attention to detail." Jia shrugged. "And a stupid amount of courage."

"There you go. Lady Justice is out for a walk, and she bags a big one while we're picking our noses at lunch." The officer yanked the Shadow Bandit to his feet and turned the groggy man's face toward Jia. "You're looking at the best cop the NSCPD ever had, you sneaky bastard. Sucks to be you."

The Shadow Bandit let out another quiet groan, and his head lolled forward. The officer shoved him toward his patrol flitter while his partner walked over and shook Jia's hand. His partner opened the back of the flitter and pushed the criminal inside.

"You should come back to the NSCPD, Detective Lin. We need you. You and Blackwell are legends. We could *use* more legends."

"You're fighting the good fight." Jia inclined her head toward the police flitter. "All I did was get lucky."

He waved and headed over to join his partner. After a final salute from the front seat, they killed their emergency lights and lifted off.

Jia watched the flitter until it disappeared in the distance. She'd spent most of her childhood dreaming of being a police officer, only to step away after a couple of years on the job. Her current work was important, but no one could know about it. Its very nature prevented it from working as a public deterrent.

There were days she missed being a police officer and the clarity that came with going after people for breaking the law. She missed having the open support of the entire department rather than having to attend clandestine meetings and travel in disguise as she hunted the agents of the conspiracy who pretended to be upstanding members of society.

The conspiracy would eventually fall.

Everyone from Erik to Alina felt that way. The anti-conspiracy forces hadn't won every battle, but they'd won all the important ones, including stopping the Hunter ship. What came after that?

Jia wanted to be with Erik, but she wasn't a woman who could sit around doing nothing. Erik had made it clear he also wanted to be with her, but neither seemed to have a firm handle on work. It wouldn't be insane to go back to the NSCPD.

At the same time, Neo SoCal, despite its size and population of a hundred-million, suddenly felt too small. Call it arrogance or ego, but she wasn't sure stopping local criminals would satisfy her anymore.

"Oh, well," Jia whispered. "I've got time to figure it out."

CHAPTER TWENTY-FIVE

July 18, 2230, En Route to Sol Hyperspace Transfer Point, Aboard Modified Space Yacht Beidou

Failure didn't deserve mockery. Predictable failure *necessitated* it. Julia knew that, as did everyone in the Core, and those who worked closest with them.

Julia sat at her desk, reading a summarized report of activity on Earth, collected and collated by her most trusted agents. Her absence made it more difficult for her to control the unfolding events, but distance was no excuse for ignorance.

A fleeting thought sometimes taunted her, whispered to her soul about mistakes. Her desire for direct control created opportunities for attack. She couldn't deny that, but humanity hadn't yet been guided to a position where she could risk relying on any but a select few.

For now, Julia laughed at Shoji's expense after finishing the report. She couldn't be certain he was responsible for the incident in France, and he hadn't sent her any messages since her departure from Earth. The lab was primarily his responsibility, both in supply and design, so it only made sense the devastating surprise raid was invited by a man who thought he was setting a trap.

An underling's failure was the responsibility of their master. Leaders who ran from responsibility were cowards who would be destroyed by their fear and inability to select or guide others.

"What a foolish waste." Julia shook her head.

The destruction of the facility was less the issue than its initial existence and all the time, money, and effort invested in it.

Every member of the Core differed in their opinion on how to best make sure of their resources for direct operations. Julia had never been fond of the Ascended Brotherhood. Tin Men were a dead end, and too resource-intensive for their intended use.

Shoji's fondness for *yaoguai* filled a similar position in Julia's mind. If anything, she thought they lowered the long-term chances of success. The extensive use of cyborgs and genetically engineered monsters encouraged the use of similar weapons by their enemies, which would reduce their differential advantage. The Core's control needed to be complete before that happened.

The use of agents who could freely pass for humans was a good compromise. Their expense and the difficulty involved in their creation was a worthwhile tradeoff.

Julia waved a hand and dismissed the data window in front of her. Another sloppy failure, not unlike the assassination attempt on her. When evidence began to pile up and point in an obvious direction, only a fool looked the opposite way.

It was a good thing she was on her way to New Pacifica because she suspected she'd be forced to take drastic action.

"Oh, Shoji." She sighed. "Why must you make this difficult for us?"

July 18, 2230, Neo Southern California Metroplex, Apartment of Erik Blackwell

Jia eyed Erik with suspicion from the other side of his couch. "You're sure she said she wanted to meet here?"

Erik nodded. "That's what Alina's message said. Here at 2100."

He preferred being debriefed in his apartment. Despite what Alina indicated, wandering around Neo SoCal to meet her struck him as more dangerous than meeting in a known location, a place with thorough infiltration of the systems by Emma.

"It's 2100." Jia frowned. "I wonder if something happened. She's la—"

A light knock came from Erik's door. Alina was punctual and deadly, a good combination for a government agent.

"A woman I don't recognize is outside," Emma reported. "Her gait and other relevant biometric identifiers don't match Agent Koval's, but I am receiving the appropriate confirmation code. She has looked directly into all cameras in the area, including the hidden one."

"Let her in." Erik stood, half-wondering if he was about to die because he didn't have a gun in his hand. He could never decide if getting gunned down in his own apartment would be epic or pathetic.

The door slid open, and the woman stepped through. The sundress, light eyes, and blonde hair didn't resemble Koval, nor did her face, though she was around the same height. She closed the door, her accusatory stare set on Erik.

"From this day to the ending of the world, but we in it shall be rememberèd— We few, we happy few, we band of brothers," the woman quoted. She had a strange accent Erik couldn't place, like the bastard child of Venus and Louisiana.

"Any moment might be our last. Everything is more beautiful because we're doomed," Erik quoted back.

He sat back down. He doubted any assassin would bother making him jump through Alina's historical and literary hoops. They would have had the decency to gun him down already.

"What's the point of all this, when you can just send a fancy confirmation code to Emma?" he muttered.

The woman shook her head, looking disappointed. When she next spoke, it was clearly Alina's voice. "We've been over this. It never hurts to have redundant security protocols. There have been times I've avoided death because of something like this."

"You're sure it's just not about you indulging your fetishes?" Erik raised an eyebrow.

Alina frowned. "Knowledge and respect for our literary

past is hardly a fetish. My motivation for serving in the ID is the defense of human civilization."

"You could be quoting beignet recipes," Erik joked.

Jia cleared her throat to get their attention. "I'd like to move on to the debriefing. That's the important part, remember?"

"Of course." Alina wandered lazily to a chair and took a seat, unnerving Erik.

It took him a while to figure out why. It was her movement. Erik didn't need to be Emma to perform his own subconscious biometric evaluation. Alina's normal movements were graceful and lethal, like she was a deadly jungle cat always ready to strike, but when she was in disguise, like now, she often moved differently, even when it was unnecessary. It was a skill that came from decades of experience as a ghost, a reflex and instinct she often didn't suppress, even when dealing with Erik and Jia.

Erik had spent his entire life never thinking about concealing who he was. His vague attempts to pretend had included non-painful sacrifices such as buying a high-performance flitter and de-aging. Disguises for ID mission and leads didn't sit well with him.

Emma's holographic form appeared, complete with an elegant high-backed chair. Inspired by the first code phrase's origins in Plantagenet England, she had chosen a high-necked burgundy gown and an elaborate close-fitting white hat with a veil.

Erik had long since learned not to laugh at any of her choices. There was nothing more dangerous than an offended AI who could ensure you only got cold water in your shower.

"And you're sure about doing this here?" Erik asked. "I know you've got people watching us, and we've got Emma, but we did just do an op. I thought you'd want to meet us underground, with everyone in disguise."

"Don't worry." Alina smiled. "I've taken extra precautions, and sometimes it helps to poke them in the eye and remind them that *they* need to be afraid of *us*, not the other way around."

Erik grinned. "You mean, you've got a whole army of ghosts and drones watching this place and looking for assassins in case they're desperate and decide to take the bait?"

"Something like that." Alina looked to the side for a moment before returning her attention to Erik. "Before we get into France, I wanted to mention that I'm approving Lanara's request for more help. I can get her two or three other trustworthy engineers, but that said, I don't want her doing any major mods to the *Argo* for the next several weeks. I've told her that. She responded with profanity and a string of numbers, but she understands."

"You want us to be ready in case we need to follow up after the raid?" Jia asked.

"Exactly." Alina nodded. "We've gotten good at trashing the conspiracy lately, but there are still a lot of things happening, and losing a factory, a lab, or Sophia Vand only seems to slow them down for so long. We don't have the luxury of waiting around. Once we have a target, I want you two to be able to move and not wait three weeks while Lanara redesigns half the ship."

"Sounds good to me," Erik replied with a shrug. "Let's

find the next factory, lab, or Sophia Vand and take them out. I'm all for punching them in the face and kicking them in the nuts."

"I love your enthusiasm." Alina rolled her shoulders and leaned forward. "As you already know, most of the system at the lab was purged prior to the raid, but it was obvious they were relying on the self-destruct to finish their cleanup since there was enough left over between the remaining systems and some other information we collected from other operations to put us on new paths. I'm not going to go through all that because it's not anything that'll help you right now, but I'm confident we're close."

"That sounds good, but having another target would sound better."

Alina raised a finger. "It gets better."

"Better?" Jia lifted an eyebrow. "You have the names of all the leaders of the conspiracy?"

Alina eyed Jia. "I said better, not perfect."

"Another facility?" Erik asked.

"Not quite." Alina ran her finger over her PNIU.

An image of a somber-looking dark-haired man in a suit appeared. He was in the audience at a biotechnology conference. Erik didn't recognize the man. Another leader of the conspiracy?

"This gentleman is a well-known molecular biologist who went into early retirement about five years back." Alina nodded at the image. "He's also the man you recently became acquainted with prior to his death."

Jia leaned forward to stare at the image. "He doesn't

look like the man in Provence. Same build, but that's about it. Is this a disguise?"

"No, this is what he used to look like." Alina looked surprised. "We're a hundred percent on this. We got a complete DNA match from the corpse, and we've double-checked the relevant databases to ensure their accuracy. For now, the rest of the world doesn't need to know he's dead."

Erik didn't care that the man was dead. He was a madman who had tried to kill good men and women with his monsters. Erik doubted the Provence raid was the first time one of Vincke's pets had been set on humans.

Jia frowned. "They didn't do something to prevent that? With all the trouble they've gone through in situations like the Ascended Brotherhood, I wouldn't have expected it."

"Yes." Alina dismissed the image. "I'm surprised too, but we got lucky in this case. Besides the obvious surgery to alter his appearance, I don't think they ever intended for us to be able to get a DNA match. They weren't trying to be sloppy this time. It just worked out that way."

"He was supposed to die in the explosion?" Erik suggested.

Alina shook her head. "I don't think so. He was killed by a nano-adaptive virus we believe was intended to shred his DNA, too. No one goes to the trouble and expense of cooking up something like that if they plan to blow the target up. For reasons we don't understand, maybe even freak mutation, the virus deactivated before finishing its job."

"A good old-fashioned screw-up." Erik chuckled. "It

feels like people are getting desperate and rushing plans. I wonder if it occurred to them that he'd use his name?"

"Probably not." Alina wrinkled her nose in disgust. "He had neural implants, and his genome had been modified. I suspect our good doctor was more unstable from that than his bosses knew." She shook her head. "But you're right. It does seem like they're being flashier, but also making more mistakes."

"What about those *yaoguai*? More alien hybrids?"

"I'll spare you the technobabble, but from what we can tell, they were all derived from terrestrial species and DNA. No weird Leem DNA or other alien garbage. Pure Earth monsters."

Jia scoffed, irritation wrinkling her forehead. "I don't feel better about monsters because they're a hundred percent Earth DNA."

Alina locked eyes with Jia, her expression serious. "I feel better knowing they weren't breeding Hunter- or Navigator-derived monsters there. We both know you could have fought things a lot more dangerous than what was there."

"Who cares?" Erik interrupted. "They had monsters. We killed monsters. Now they don't have a monster factory, end of story. It's only important if it leads to more targets. Beating the conspiracy is easy. Find them, kill them, repeat."

"True enough," Alina replied softly. "And being able to confirm Vincke's identity has already paid dividends. Combined with what we learned from that facility and an unrelated raid that netted us a lower-level operator we can indirectly link to the conspiracy, we've established some important facts beyond a shadow of a doubt." She raised a single finger. "Fact one, Ceres Galactic is thoroughly infested at the highest levels by the conspiracy."

Jia sighed in disappointment. "We already knew that."

Alina raised a second finger. "Fact two, Hermes is also thoroughly infested by the conspiracy, as is Stella Infinitas."

"In other words, we should probably assume they effectively control every Hexagon corporation." Jia rubbed her temples. "And the economy of the UTC."

"Or at least they have a major influence. That explains how they're able to get the kind of resources they need to perform the experiments and build the cyborgs they've been using. Among other things, that suggests a war of attrition might take a lot longer than we would like. We'll have to target their leadership to be more effective."

Erik frowned. "Do you know who is working for them at those companies? We can work our way up."

"Not specifically," Alina replied. "We're working on some leads, but we're going to have to proceed carefully. Although there's no way this goes down without at least partial disruption to the UTC, our long-term plan is to collect the evidence and work closely with trusted allies in the CID for massive, simultaneous raids when the time comes. We will destroy their power base and take out the leadership, and then it'll just be a matter of mopping up what's left."

"Great. When are the raids?" Erik asked.

Alina's pitying look angered him. Erik knew what she was going to say next. Success bred impatience.

"We're nowhere near that ready," Alina explained. "If everything goes well, maybe we can pull this off in the next year or two, but we can't screw it up by running off half-cocked. The important thing is we need to keep working on bleeding them. It won't finish them off, but it'll at least keep them on defense."

Jia folded her arms. "It'll be difficult to do much while the ID has a leak. It's bad enough that you're saying the conspiracy effectively controls the pillars of our economy. If the government can't do anything without them hearing about it, there's only so much we can do, even with a jump drive."

"Ah. Yes." Alina's smile took on a hint of condescension. "We caught the leak, an analyst. Smart guy, but he had a hidden gambling problem. They took advantage of the problem."

Erik didn't know if that meant they'd killed him. He also wasn't sure he cared. Selling information to the conspiracy was aiding treason and mass terrorism.

"There's not much follow-up possible because they were careful with him," Alina continued, "but at least we don't have to constrain our ops now. That was why we performed the other raid I mentioned."

"Okay." Erik took a deep breath and slowly let it out, trying to rid his body of the nervous energy that demanded they fly around Neo SoCal looking for anyone working for the conspiracy. "Where does this leave us?"

"On standby." Alina pointed to the ceiling. "We're still looking into things, but the preliminary info we're getting suggests we might need someone who can move freely and quickly in space."

"No deployable missile launcher add-ons anytime soon."

"Exactly. I'm glad you understand." Alina stood and

tugged her dress down. "I hate to make you two wait, but at the same time, combined with Emma, you're the best weapon we have."

Erik nodded. "Then keep firing us until the target is dead."

"I will as soon as we have a target."

CHAPTER TWENTY-SIX

A woman's familiar voice invaded Jia's dream.

"It's an obvious throwaway address."

Not just familiar. Emma. But why was the AI in Jia's dream?

"That doesn't mean anything more than they're careful," Erik replied.

His presence in a dream wasn't unusual. When he shifted on the bed next to her, she realized she wasn't dreaming.

Jia blinked her eyes open, the blurriness from her long, deep sleep making it difficult to see. Her entire life, she had been getting up early, but she never could claim to be a morning person. She rubbed her eyes and took a couple of deep breaths to clear her head.

Emma's hologram stood next to the bed and Erik was sitting up, wearing nothing but his boxers from the night before. She wanted to throw a pillow at Emma for bothering them in bed.

"You don't think it's a trap?" Emma asked.

"It's interesting timing," Erik replied. "And you know how I feel about coincidences. It could be a trap, but I'm not going to ignore it because of that possibility."

Jia yawned. "What's going on? What trap are you talking about?"

Emma turned to Jia. "Erik received a suspicious message from a throwaway address. Someone wants to meet you both at a modestly priced diner for breakfast and a discussion."

"Quantum-coded signal?" Jia asked. "Is this from Colonel Adeyemi or Alina? You think they're in trouble?"

Emma shook her head. "No, it's a thoroughly conventional message, and I doubt either of them would request help in such a roundabout matter. I would hack the system that sent it, but it's so obviously a throwaway that I'm dubious it would accomplish much, given the time constraints prior to the meeting, and it might draw unnecessary attention or sanctions. Until we know more about the situation, I think that would only make our situation more tenuous."

"Not disagreeing, but what's so suspicious about this message?"

"Who sends me a message asking about brunch?" Erik asked, his face twisted in disgust as if brunch was as disturbing as the conspiracy. "It has this weird final line saying, 'I do so love flower shops on the moon. This is offered in good faith, but my patience only extends so far.'"

Jia furrowed her brow, thinking about flower shops on the moon. That was a rather odd and specific phrase, and it invoked a strong memory. Not every loose end was always accounted for after their missions.

She narrowed her eyes. "Marius Barbu. It has to be him. If not him, then somebody who knows about him, but I'm assuming it's him."

"The fixer from Chang'e City?" Erik looked down in surprise. "Huh. That would explain the weird message, but why would that guy want to come anywhere near us? From what we know, he helped those terrorists arm up. They were shooting at us with weapons he sold."

"We don't have a lot of time if we want to get someone else involved," Jia commented. She slid out of bed and stood. "And we can't let this go. Our best chance would be asking the NSCPD, but I'd rather not get them involved in anything that might be related to the conspiracy."

"You think this is a conspiracy thing?" Erik stood and headed toward his closet. Once there, he grabbed some pants.

"Alina said those terrorists on the moon were linked to the conspiracy." Jia shrugged. "And we took down another conspiracy base. They might have been doing it to get at us, but that doesn't change the fact that we're on the move, and people in the underworld are going to have a better chance of noticing than the average person."

"Oh. You're saying he wants to switch sides? We're scaring him straight?"

"It's a possibility, or at a minimum, he doesn't want us busting into his mansion with exoskeletons and rocket launchers to drag him off to some ID black ops interrogation site." Jia jogged over to the closet, marveling that she had so many outfits at Erik's place, and he had so few. "It might also explain why he wants to talk to us. With everything's that going on, the government can't be totally trusted, including the ID."

Erik shoved one leg into his pants. "We're doing this, then? We're heading toward a meeting with a fixer asshole who supplied terrorists?"

"We can't always wait around for Alina to point us at the conspiracy." Jia snatched her pants from a hanger. "What's the worst that can happen?"

"He kills us both."

"At brunch? I hope not." Jia scoffed. "Assassination feels more like a dinner thing to me."

Erik and Jia headed toward the diner, both scanning the area for anyone or anything out of the ordinary. Modest flitters filled the parking platform. The only one that stood out was Erik's MX 60. A man smiled approvingly at it on his way to his vehicle.

The pair walked at a slow pace.

They wanted to give Emma plenty of time to prepare. If they were stepping into a trap, they could survive it as long as they had superior control of the area, including surveillance and doors. While the AI didn't have trouble initiating the necessary hacks, it was difficult to have drones everywhere and not be totally obvious. She'd already hacked the cameras inside the diner and had views of most of the building.

She sent an image of a brown-suited elderly man sitting in a corner booth. A red highlight drew Jia's attention to a rather thin silver rod half-hanging out of his pocket. The only resemblance to the eyepatch-wearing lunar fixer was his age and lack of hair.

"Any evidence he's using a holographic disguise?" Erik asked.

"No," Emma replied. "It could be a lack of movement, but if that is our friend, I doubt there are any holographic tricks involved."

"He's not trying to be subtle," Jia muttered. "Is it just me, or does that look like a privacy device in his pocket?"

"Most people don't know what they are. It's not that big a gamble." Erik shrugged before reaching inside his jacket to check for his weapon.

Both Erik and Jia were armed, the latter with her standard combination of slugthrower and stun pistol. They'd parked the MX 60 close to the diner in case they needed to go back for heavier weapons or explosives.

Jia didn't need to check for her gun. She knew both were there. The last thing she wanted was a shootout in a crowded restaurant, and she hoped the presence of so many witnesses would discourage anyone from trying anything outrageous.

Even if they didn't care about their lives, all those people wore PNIUs that could be collected for evidence.

"There is no unusual activity around the area," Emma reported. "There is an increase in flitter traffic relative to the averages for the day, but nothing out of the ordinary for this specific time of day. The transponder signals for all flitters parked or flying near this area correspond with the public registry records. There are also no unusual sensor readings other than those expected of a privacy device, nor any signals or energy or chemical signatures that might be associated with explosives."

"Is it that simple?" Jia asked. "He just wants to talk?"

"There are more direct ways to kill people." Erik opened the front door. "Our boy wants to talk, so we'll talk. Emma can still use the PNIU to keep an eye on the immediate area, even under jamming, and she'll let us know if he's suddenly teleported in a gun with unknown Hunter tech."

"Don't even joke about that." Jia shivered. She wanted to take care of all their human enemies before they needed to worry about aliens, and then she'd rather go through something more reasonable like a space raptor first.

Jia stepped through the door and waved off an approaching hostess to head straight toward the suspect's table. She didn't want to be rude, but she also didn't want to risk taking her attention off the man in those initial critical seconds. Her hands stayed near her sides. There was no point in escalating things unless he tried something.

They could have a nice conversation, or he would understand that Erik and Jia had earned their reputation.

The pair arrived at the man's table, and the sounds from the rest of the diner died. She'd grown too used to privacy devices for the eerie silence to unsettle her anymore. The man motioned to the booth seat opposite his with a smile.

"I'm glad you chose to come," the man greeted them, his voice raspy, "Mr. Blackwell and Ms. Lin. I wasn't sure you would take me up on my invitation, and I don't blame you if you're skeptical. I would be if I were in your position."

If they'd not been convinced it was Barbu before, the raspy voice and wheeze confirmed it.

Jia took a seat, keeping her hands above the table and close to her jacket. Barbu didn't appear to notice or care.

Erik sat down and stared at the man. "You got our attention, old man. I'm surprised. It was kind of a blunt way of doing it."

Barbu shrugged lightly. "The problem with people today is they think that the best way to do something is the most modern and baroque."

"And how did you know we wouldn't flood this diner with CID agents?"

"Because you have to have realized there was no way I wouldn't have noticed them coming." Barbu wheezed. "Besides, we all know you have concerns at higher levels than mere law enforcement, and I think in this case, I can be of service to my fellow man."

Jia eyed him. "You're a criminal who sold weapons to terrorists. You call that service to your fellow man? Even if you didn't know what they intended to do with them, that doesn't change the fact you armed them, knowing they were going to hurt people. More service?"

"Selling someone something they need is the definition of service, Ms. Lin." Barbu punctuated his sentence with a wheezing laugh. "My sales were irrelevant, given you were able to handle them."

"I can't believe this." Jia clenched her hands into fists. "You're sitting here admitting it. We could stun your ass, call the local PD, and have them hand you over to the CID."

"You could." Barbu took a deep breath. "But it'd be ill-advised. I've taken measures to assure my protection, but the real problem would be your loss of me as a resource."

"They could make you talk."

"No, they really couldn't. Besides, you should welcome my aid. Events I've become aware of since the unpleasantness on the moon have made me aware that I *wish* to do my part for the UTC."

Erik looked the man up and down. "Do your part for the UTC?"

"Yes, Mr. Blackwell." Barbu looked mildly insulted. "Is that so absurd to believe?"

"You don't strike me as the altruistic type. Most arms dealers aren't, Barbu. I'm guessing you're a lot more than an arms dealer."

Barbu stroked his chin, then lowered his hand. "No, I'm not the altruistic type. But is it altruism when you help others to ensure your customer base isn't disrupted? Most businessmen would call that common sense."

"Is that what this is?" Jia asked. "You're worried about not being able to sell weapons to other terrorists, so you think you can give us a couple of tidbits, and we'll recommend the CID let you walk? I don't think it's going to be that easy."

"No, that would be foolish, and not a good bargain for you." Barbu folded his hands in front of him. "I could explain why I was involved in what happened on the moon, but you have no reason to believe me, and it doesn't matter. I have something that might be of use to you, and I offer it with no other conditions than you let me leave this place."

"Why should we trust you?" Erik smirked. "Trust is

earned, not automatically given, especially to a scumbag arms dealer."

"Scumbag?" Erik thought Barbu's brow lifted, but it was hard to tell with all the other wrinkles. "That is not an accurate description of me, but we'll set that aside for the moment and concentrate on the matter at hand."

"Which is what?" Jia asked. Her heart pounded with the desire to pull out her stun pistol and demand the man's surrender. "You're the one who called us here. Get to the point and stop playing games with us, old man."

"I hear things," Barbu wheezed. He put a hand to his mouth and coughed. "Rumors about you and stories about what happened on the moon and the people ultimately responsible, so I've looked into things. It's unwise to be involved in the business I'm in without a rather thorough understanding of the political situation, both in the underworld and outside it."

"We're dealing with powerful people, more powerful than you're used to dealing with," Erik explained. "This isn't about random syndicates and insurrectionists playing around."

"Powerful people? Is that so?" Barbu shook his head lightly. "Power is relative, Mr. Blackwell. There is no one alive who is immortal, and if someone isn't immortal, they can be stopped—in the worst-case scenario, by killing them."

"True enough."

Barbu smiled. "I'm now going to reach into my pocket for a data rod. It might contain information you want, or it might not, depending on your particular interests. I'll be honest. I'm not sure you two are who I suspect, but if you are, you'll find the information on the rod useful against your enemies, those powerful people you seem so afraid of."

"I'm not afraid," Erik growled. "I'm hunting them, and they should be afraid of *me*."

"Of course. My mistake."

Barbu waited, his attention focused on Jia before he reached slowly into his pocket. She jammed her hand into her jacket and gripped her stun pistol without drawing it. Barbu paused for a couple of seconds before producing the data rod, tossing it in front of Jia, and standing.

"As much as I have enjoyed being at your service, I've done all I'm willing to do and risked all I'm willing to risk at this time."

"Meaning what?" Jia couldn't keep the bite out of her voice. It was taking all her self-control to let the bastard walk.

"As the situation changes, my involvement may change. Have a good day, Ms. Lin."

Barbu set off for the door, limping. The normal din of a lunchtime crowd returned with his retreat. Jia watched him as he exited the restaurant and headed to an unassuming flitter parked at the front.

"Emma, follow him," Erik ordered, his voice low.

Jia gingerly picked up the rod as if it might explode. "I honestly don't know what to think. That went about as well as we could expect, but I don't trust him."

"No reason to trust him, but I don't think it's that difficult." Erik inclined his head toward the rod. "There are different layers of scum, and Barbu might not have appreciated being on the run because of what happened on the moon. Remember what they told us about him."

Jia nodded. "The name's fake, and he came out of nowhere but quickly established himself. He's not your common garden variety antisocial piece of trash."

"Someone like that might have run across our friends before and not thought much of it because it benefited him like it did on the moon." Erik frowned as Barbu's flitter windows darkened to opaque, and the vehicle lifted into the air. "He might sell weapons, but their plans are making things far worse. Even criminals have limits, and I'll take the help for now. The CID can always track his ass down after this is all over, but it doesn't hurt to see where he ends up."

Jia frowned as the flitter left the parking platform. "I have a feeling this isn't the last we'll see of him."

Five minutes later, as Jia sipped tea, she heard something far more disturbing—a genuinely apologetic and worried Emma. She set down her cup as the AI delivered the surprising news.

"I don't know how to explain it." Emma sighed. "I've somehow lost his flitter. One moment, my drones were following it and I had it on camera, and then it was gone."

"He hacked your drones and the cameras," Erik suggested.

"Without me knowing?" Emma scoffed, her confident arrogance returning. "That seems unlikely."

"But it doesn't change the fact he's gone," Erik countered.

"That much is true," Emma admitted. "Unfortunately."

"Jump drive on his flitter," Erik joked. "Oh, well. Less to worry about right now."

"That would be rather more obvious than what happened." Emma sounded annoyed.

Jia looked out the diner window at the stream of flitters in the sky. Marius Barbu was somewhere out among the hundred-million people of Neo SoCal. They had not come to the diner to capture him. As long as the data rod held something useful, it wasn't a wasted trip.

She ran her finger along the data rod. "Let's be safe about this. You're right, Erik. Barbu's a lot more than a simple arms dealer, and he might have attracted the wrong kind of attention. Let's go back to your place. At least there, we know it'll be safe to check this out."

CHAPTER TWENTY-SEVEN

Erik's eyes shifted left to right as he pored over one of the files on a large data window projected in front of his chair in his living room. Numbers, numbers, and more numbers.

"This isn't what I'd expected," he complained. "I thought it was going to be more dramatic."

"It's kind of exactly what I expected," Jia replied, looking between four different data windows. "He's a piece of trash, but at the end of the day, Barbu is a businessman, and he understands how devastating records are." She smiled. "This was how we discovered our first big lead, by looking through records."

"That was more you." Erik smiled. "I just followed your example. I don't know, I was expecting a recording of Sophia Vand plotting something. A concrete lead."

"This *is* something," Jia insisted. "We just have to figure out what it is. With this volume of data, these must be important. Once we know the context, everything will fall into place. This seems familiar, and at least some of these are dates, but I can't figure it out."

"Dates?" Erik squinted. "They are?"

"Julian dates in an astronomy context," Jia explained.

"I'll take your word for it."

He wasn't seeing the pattern in the numbers, and he had no idea how an astrometric Julian date was calculated, but they'd already established that at least one set of numbers meant something. That gave them a better chance of figuring out the rest.

"Yes, you are correct, Jia." Emma appeared with a triumphant smile. "I've been reviewing both the data on the rod and my own data concerning Barbu during the encounter. I can find no evidence that he hacked the drones. He must have achieved a temporary disruption, followed by some form of advanced camouflage. I see no evidence of unusually advanced technologies, but there are certain limitations in the sensors in this body compared to the *Argo* or the *Bifröst*."

"I really was joking about the jumping." Erik looked up from his window. "So, instead of Barbu having unusually good hacking skills, he has access to advanced technology that lets him trick drones, cameras, and your sensors, and active optical camo, too. I don't know if that makes me feel better just because it's not Hunter tech. Those bastards on Molino only needed to be a little more advanced than my unit to ambush us."

"Be that as it may, it implies he would not be able to easily disappear if he was, for example, in a small restaurant." Emma let out a snort of triumph. "As for the records, I've established what they are with a less than 0.2 percent margin of error."

"Care to share with us mere fleshbags?" Jia asked. "I'm thinking they're not only dates."

"Your deduction is correct. They are sanitized shipping records. They don't all appear to be from the same companies, given the routes, and without additional information about their source, I have no method of determining what was being shipped, but they all indicate dates and locations. They appear to be from all over the UTC, as one file clearly indicates HTP coordinates."

Erik wrinkled his forehead. "Shipping records without the companies or the cargo. How is that helpful?"

"If it's the conspiracy, it tells us where they've been and when," Jia offered.

A three-dimensional star map of the UTC appeared, white lines stretching between the actively connected systems. Red and blue lines stretched between different systems, marking some of the shipments, forming a dense, impenetrable web.

Emma pointed to the map. "There's a pattern of someone using a lot of different companies to carefully conceal the mass movement of unknown cargo while simultaneously coordinating it with military-like precision. I can't be certain of what was moved where, since these records don't include any detailed tracking information for the cargo, but by overlaying dates and locations, at least some of the routes could be traced from origination. And there is a curious specificity to our current situation."

She magnified a star system on the edge of the UTC. Bile rose in the back of Erik's throat when the colony moon appeared. He recognized it before she added the helpful legend.

Mu Arae System, Molino, First moon of Planet Quijote

"According to the information on the rod," Emma continued, "there were shipments shortly before and after the ambush. Unfortunately, as I noted, there is no clear identification of cargo or tracking numbers, so I can't follow the entire path of the Molino cargo. Please note those shipments don't seem to correspond to other shipment data I previously obtained while investigating this matter."

"That doesn't help," Erik replied, his voice low. "I found messages when I first got back to Earth talking in code, but that made me think they'd already shipped stuff, probably whatever Hunter or Navigator artifacts they found there and didn't want the government finding out about it. What good is any of this?"

Jia shook her head. "It might not help us to look at the data since despite having Emma, we still have limited access to the breadth and depth of possible data to compare the contents of the rod. We should hand it over to Alina and let her analysts go to work. She could plug the holes, and maybe even figure out the companies and cargo."

Emma nodded. "I will continue analyzing the data to the best of my ability, but Agent Koval's people are more likely to be able to extract something more immediately useful out of it. Please note this does not imply they have analytical superiority."

Erik chuckled. "Noted, and it makes sense. The ID has a much bigger picture available than we do. We'll keep the rod just in case, but Emma can send them all the data, and we'll explain where we got it."

"Speaking of that, I'm still bothered by how Barbu got this and why he has it." Jia swiped through her windows and closed them.

"Is it that important right now?"

"It could be. We don't know who he really is. I don't buy the Not-So-Friendly Neighborhood Arms Dealer act. He disappeared well enough that the CID couldn't find him, which means he's not a normal criminal, and I don't care how many connections he has, asking around and pulling in favors from friends wouldn't get him detailed cargo shipments from the conspiracy." Jia folded her arms. "That's what this is supposed to be, right? The Molino data confirms it."

Erik stared at Molino. The memories of the battle were never far away. They motivated his every action between awakening and falling asleep at night. His trip to Provence reached those fifty light-years from Earth to the frontier moon colony. A once-desperate lost cause seemed achievable, and he didn't mind rolling around in the mud if it helped.

"If Barbu wanted to set us up, giving us some records isn't the way to do it." Erik stood. "And that's the only thing I care about. But you're right, and we have evidence he was involved in the Chang'e incident. He might not have been happy about them using that bomb, but if we're right, he had no problem giving guns to people he knew were about to hurt a lot of folks."

"So what's his angle? We need to know before the next time we deal with him."

"Before Sophia died, she mentioned some woman, and now we've got Barbu giving us this." Erik chuckled darkly. "And then there were the two separate ships that traveled to the Hunter ship."

"The conspiracy turning on itself? We've been wondering, but it's been hard to say."

Erik nodded. "We've got more than enough evidence now. I can't say I'm going to complain if they line up to screw each other over. It makes it easier for us if they're tearing each other apart."

"Then we're being used." Jia crossed her arms. "We don't know how far this goes. They could be purposely leaking information to the ID and us to get them to take out anyone who can stand in the way of their power. How do we know they won't end up stronger after this?"

Erik scoffed. "Because they won't end up stronger than our side. They keep losing people and resources. There are always going to be more people hunting the conspiracy than at the top."

Jia blew out a breath. "I hope that's true."

"I've been involved in my share of anti-insurgent campaigns," Erik replied, breezy calm in his voice. "I'd like to say most of them failed because of the superior training and skills of the UTC Army, but that's only half of it."

"Okay." Jia figured it would be faster to ask than wait for Erik to get to the point. "What's the other half?"

"That simple truth is that a lot of rebellions defeat themselves." Erik tore his attention away from the star map and Molino. "People get fed up with governments for all sorts of reasons, but they're often the same ones. It makes sense to band together when you know the Army or cops are on their way, but those differences are a slow poison. Factions end up betraying each other, selling out to the government to try to get influence, or simply becoming arrogant and thinking they don't need the others anymore."

Jia lowered her arms with a surprised look on her face. "You think that's what's happening with the conspiracy?"

"Fleshbags are ever so disagreeable," Emma offered cheerfully.

"It'd explain a lot of what we've seen, especially on the Hunter ship, and the uneven response to the raids. Not just us, the ID, too." Erik rubbed his hands together. "Which means we'll have more opportunities to fatally wound them coming up. Not bad. I'm getting excited."

He turned back to the star map. Barbu might work for the conspiracy or be nothing more than a criminal wronged by them. It didn't matter.

Too many of Erik's and his allies' actions had been defensive, including going after the Hunter ship. Blowing up a *yaoguai* factory wasn't satisfying, not as much as taking out the main Ascended Brotherhood base had been. Between the intel from the *yaoguai* raid and this rod, it was time to push their efforts into offense. The best time to take on the enemy was when they were divided.

"It's inevitable." Erik smiled. "You know Ben Franklin's old joke about secrets?"

Jia frowned. "What joke?"

"Three can keep a secret if two of them are dead. Let's send the info and wait for Alina to get back to us."

CHAPTER TWENTY-EIGHT

July 20, 2230, Neo Southern California Metroplex, Parking Platform of Residential Tower of Erik Blackwell

A light breeze brushed Jia's face. She watched the rivers of light marking the flitters flowing from location to location between the towers of Neo SoCal. There was a certain irony in humanity achieving a common-use air vehicle and still being restricted to lanes.

They might have vertical and horizontal lanes, but the average flitter in Neo SoCal didn't take advantage of its flight capability except when landing and taking off.

She'd read the virtual lanes were originally enforced to make the autodrive systems safer and more reliable and discourage the small number of irresponsible self-drivers from causing too much trouble. She included herself in that group now, despite having balked at Erik doing it so much when they first met.

These days, she didn't care to let the flitter drive itself.

MICHAEL ANDERLE

Her taste for flight had grown along with her under-standing of the world.

Erik stood beside her with a thoughtful expression, his hands in his pockets. "You sure about the message, Emma? It's our week for unusual messages."

"Yes," Emma replied, eschewing taking a form, given their public location. "It was clear you were to be on the platform at this particular time. I showed you the message text in its entirety."

"But standing out on a parking platform in a residential tower?" Jia threw up her arms. "This is ridiculously open."

"Don't be overly concerned. I'm monitoring the area for unusual activity. Thus far, the only thing I see out of the ordinary is a limousine."

"Somebody's probably having a better night than us," Jia grumbled.

"Maybe she's finally decided to get rid of us." Erik grinned. "Because we're too *noisy*. It's easier to kill us here. A good sniper can hit us from kilometers away, and it's not like even you can spot everything that might be a threat in a crowded part of Neo SoCal."

Emma harrumphed. "We'll just have to put your lives to the test."

"Thanks." Erik laughed. "Sometimes you can be so warm and fuzzy."

"She's already proven she can get into our apartments without much trouble." Jia looked around to make sure no one else was nearby. Emma was reliable, but she wasn't perfect, as Barbu's escape had proven.

"Get inside, sure." Erik shrugged. "Kill us? We've both tagged her when she's gone full ghost on us, and neither of

280

us is ever far from a weapon. We're also together a lot more now, which means we often have Emma nearby. She'd have to take us both out. Missile, maybe?"

"I could block a missile launched this way with a drone," Emma insisted. "And she's not going to sneak in a gunship. I'll admit the ID uses impressive technology, but I'm getting better at seeing through their tricks. If I were them and I wanted to kill you, I'd sabotage the *Argo*."

Jia scrubbed a hand over her face. "Can we please stop talking about ways Alina might kill us?"

A flitter pulled out of a nearby lane and headed toward the platform. Jia slipped her hand inside her jacket and gripped her slugthrower. She didn't believe Alina would attempt to assassinate them, but being prepared wouldn't hurt.

The vehicle slowed and descended toward them, passing under the bright holographic lights of the parking platform. It was a long black luxury flitter, the window shading set to opaque. Despite Emma noting it before, Jia remained nervous.

"Transponder check, Emma," Erik ordered, the earlier humor gone from his face.

"It is registered to a local limousine rental company," she replied. "They haven't reported any stolen vehicles. Corporate registration is too labyrinthine for me to determine who might ultimately control the company without more investigation, but upon initial inspection, there is nothing unusual about the vehicle other than its appearance at this location at this time."

"If I get gunned down by a guy in a limo, I'll never live it down." Erik grumped.

"Obviously," Emma replied. "You'll be dead."

Jia ignored the two of them.

The limo set down in front of them. With a whir, a rear window lowered. Jia's heart rate kicked up, and she prepared to draw her weapon until a bright mix of pink flamingoes and smiling anthropomorphic suns on a blue background changed her mind. A Hawaiian shirt. She knew she would never die at the hands of a man in a Hawaiian shirt.

Jia dropped her hand. "*Malcolm?*"

The technician grinned from the spacious dark-green-upholstered back seat. "Now, this is how I expected to be treated when I started working for ghosts." He gave them a thumbs-up. "This is nice." He bounced a couple of times. "You know, I've never been in one of these. The MX 60 is nice, but this is cooler." He glanced at Erik. "No offense."

"Can't fly around in a limo all the time," Erik replied with a shrug. "It'd be kind of noticeable."

"But you'd look so suave and cool." He smiled.

The door opened itself, revealing a wide U-shaped seating arrangement centered around a small table. A black partition separated them from the front seat. Erik and Jia stepped inside and sat. The doors closed.

Malcolm gestured to the table. "Supposed to be able to bring up food and drinks, but our driver is very uncool. Talk about cheaping out at a weird time."

"Keep talking like that, Mr. Constantine," Alina said over a speaker, "and I might be forced to reconsider our relationship."

"It was a joke." Malcolm sank down in his seat. "Sorry."

"What's with the limo?" Erik asked with a grin. "Just feel like rewarding us? It doesn't seem like your style."

"I was in town anyway on an unrelated errand requiring this vehicle," Alina explained. "So I figured we'd chat about that data you sent us. We all prefer face-to-face conversations about important things."

Malcolm sat up. "She explained the gist of what it is and how you got it, but not sure why I'm here since I haven't looked at it."

Jia offered him an apologetic smile. "No offense, but we figured you didn't have any more context than Emma. Our best bet was to pass it on to the ID directly."

"It's not that." Malcolm shook his head. "And I shouldn't bitch. It's not like I have anything better to do since Camila's out of town again."

Something thumped behind them. Erik and Jia both pulled their guns.

Malcolm swallowed. "What was that? Was it a missile?"

"Oh, don't worry about that," Alina offered with a chuckle. "He should be asleep again in a second or two." There was a soft *click* over the speaker. "Tougher than I thought. Like I said, unrelated errand."

Jia stowed her weapon slowly, frowning in the direction of the trunk. She hoped she didn't end up there.

Erik smirked, clearly unworried about future trunk situations involving him. "Let's get back to the data. If you've called us all together, I'm assuming it's more important than confirming Emma's observations. You could have just sent a message."

"Yes," Alina answered. "It's a perfect storm. My people have collated intel strands from a lot of different sources, including leads from the *yaoguai* lab and the data you sent us. It's borne fruit quicker than we anticipated, with those records being key." Excitement laced her voice. "Among other things, we've been able to trace at least some of the Molino deliveries to Alpha Centauri, but *after* they were delivered to Earth. We've been able to follow movements in recent months, including not that long after our little Hunter incident, and action in the last couple of days."

Jia frowned. "Would they be shipping something that important around that way, rather than picking it up directly?"

"Hard to say. Sometimes it makes more sense to use the obvious sources. If people of Sophia Vand's status were flying around the galaxy constantly, it'd raise more eyebrows and make it easier for people like us to figure out something strange was going on."

"You think there are artifacts on Alpha Centauri?" Erik asked.

"We can't be sure," Alina replied. "Here's where things get complicated and questionable. Everything fell into place on this intel analysis because of the data you sent. It would have been helpful in a lot of ways even without our more recent leads, but combined with those, it's all but screaming for us to pay attention. I'd like you two to take a look as soon as possible, so that's going to involve using the jumpship."

"Is it ready to go that far?" Malcolm asked, rubbing his wrists. "I thought it was a big deal just to go out to the edge of the Solar System."

"Dr. Maras believes so, and he's the expert. Good a time to test it as ever."

Malcolm swallowed. "Test it on us?"

"You'll incidentally be there," Alina replied.

Erik nodded slowly. "But they might be expecting us to come. If they understand the ship's capabilities, they might be ready, and Barbu's woven an elaborate trap. They might want to take us and grab the ship."

"That could all be true," Alina offered, "but if this Barbu wants to help you, we can take advantage of that. If he's a member of the conspiracy pointing us at his friends, that's fine, too. As for the ship getting caught, I trust you're smart enough not to park it anywhere near Chiron. Short of having another jump drive or knowing where you'll be, they won't have a chance of taking the ship."

Jia took in the conversation like she was listening to a show, barely processing it. It had been all but preordained that she would leave the Solar System once she got involved in hunting the conspiracy, but it had always seemed like a distant possibility for years in the future, not weeks after a trip to France.

She shook her head. "I'm not against taking more of those people down, but we can't handle this with just the two of us." She smiled at Malcolm. "You're great for background support, but if this is them, it's going to end with shooting."

Malcolm waved his hands in front of him. "I'm not complaining about anything that gets me shot at less." He jerked a thumb at his chest. "Lover, not fighter."

Alina snickered but politely declined the obvious line of attack. "I understand, and that's something I've been wanting to talk to you about ever since Lanara requested more people. We're asking more and more of you, but we also need to face the fact that you're not regular ID. I brought you two onboard because you have a way of finding trouble, but that'll be pointless if you get killed."

Erik grinned with far too much eagerness. "We can handle ourselves, but it'd be nice to have backup for when we knock on somebody's door. And we need more flexibility than leaning on Adeyemi."

"You're right. We're not always going to have a handy Army squad around to help. Fortunately, the ID has most of our house in order, and I've convinced the relevant people that if we want to maximize your efficiency as a resource, you'll need regular support, not ad hoc teams, or begging the DD for help."

"Regular support, as in permanent backup?" Jia asked, more excited than she had anticipated.

"Exactly." Alina sounded far too satisfied with herself, but without seeing her face, it was hard to judge. "I've got two agents I trust who would be perfect for this. I'm going to assign them to you two. When you're not doing something, they can sit around picking their noses for all I care. They've got strong personalities, but they're good at their jobs."

Erik frowned. "I don't do well with babysitters. I agreed to work with you because I had control and you give me leads. I'm not taking orders from lackeys."

Alina snorted. "Calm down, Erik. This is a win-win, and I do understand. The last thing I want to do is mess up the rhythm you two have going with Emma, and I've seen that you're at your best when you're calling the shots. The agents will report to the ID, but in the field, they'll take orders from you and Jia as you see fit."

Jia raised an eyebrow. "And they're not going to have a problem with that? Didn't you say they have strong personalities?"

"If they do, make them see the error of their ways. You two know better than most people that respect is earned, not given."

Erik chuckled darkly. "As long I have permission to do what I need to."

"You do. In addition, I'll be sending messages to our assets in Alpha Centauri and specifically Chiron, but this mission is yours, not the local AC agents'. They'll provide support, but unlike your new subordinates, they won't necessarily take orders from you. Keep in mind it's a five-day lag one-way with comm, so I'm relying on your autonomy."

Jia furrowed her brow. "We have to fly all the way out to the *Bifröst*. That should give you the time you need to get them up to speed."

"I've already sent messages." Alina fell silent for a moment as if concentrating on something else. "The agents will be ready in two days, along with Lanara's new engineers. You'll all board the *Argo*, then hard burn for Penglai. If Maras is not totally full of crap, you should be able to make it to Alpha Centauri in four jumps. They'll require calibration both by the good doctor and Emma in between, but you'll get there a lot faster than if you hit the HTP. This mission should also provide data that'll help better tune the drive, but he can't do much about that without Emma's active input."

Emma appeared in a seat next to Malcolm in an elegant

green ballgown. "Has Erik had an opportunity to make you aware of my desire to upgrade the *Bifröst*'s AI?"

"He mentioned something in a message, but I think with what we've got going on right now, we shouldn't tweak anything unnecessary. Agreed?"

"For now." Emma sounded annoyed.

Erik looked sympathetic but kept his tone professional. "So, get ready to meet new ghosts and engineers in a couple of days, gel with them on the way to the jumpship, head to Alpha Centauri, and what, *quietly* investigate?"

Alina laughed. "You do what you need to do to get results. I'm doubtful we'll find any alien artifacts lying around, but you might be able to flush more roaches out of their holes. Keep a low profile on the investigation, but I'll do my best to get the locals to clean up for you if you need to get loud."

Jia's heart thundered. Chiron, humanity's first extra-solar colony. They were going there on a mission, not on vacation, but that didn't make her any less excited.

Too bad she was probably going to shoot someone or destroy something with explosives once they got there.

CHAPTER TWENTY-NINE

The next two days passed without incident.

Erik and Jia stuck close to home other than for the occasional meal, half-convinced that if they went out, they'd end up swept up in some strange incident that would interfere with their trip to Alpha Centauri. They eschewed training, reasoning they'd have plenty of time to worry about that during the flight to Penglai.

The day came, and with the MX 60 already loaded, they set out. Erik landed the MX 60 with Jia flying her own flitter right behind him. The extra space on the *Argo* allowed them to take the flitters, and Lanara had added some mods to Jia's in her spare time. It lacked all the features of the MX 60, but the armor was solid, and the maneuverability had been improved.

A small crowd had gathered in the hangar, including people Erik knew: Alina, Malcolm and Lanara, and two men and two women he didn't recognize—the new team members.

He didn't object to the idea of having more people on his team, but every new person represented a potential new personnel problem to be solved.

Alina was smart enough not to send him anyone he couldn't work with, but he wouldn't know their true measure until he fought beside them. Her warnings about the agents' strong personalities hadn't gone unnoticed.

Erik threw open his door and stepped out, offering a broad wave to Alina and the gathered crowd. Might as well start out on the right foot. "Good morning."

Alina nodded, waiting until Jia was out and standing next to Erik to speak. "You've all been briefed, and whatever other details you need will be sent to Emma. I'm not going to waste a lot of time reiterating what you already know, and if any new information pops up, I'll try to send it to you before you jump."

Two of the new arrivals wore suits, making Erik suspect they were ID agents. One was a huge beast of a man with a shaved head and a permanent scowl. He looked like the kind of man Erik might need to punch into a wall to earn his respect. The other suit, a lithe auburn-haired woman, coolly looked at Erik and Jia as if judging them. Both of them appeared to be in their early twenties and lacked the subtle features that would suggest de-aging. For some reason, he'd gotten it in his head that most ghosts were like Alina. It was good to get a reminder that wasn't true.

Two other people stood close to Lanara. The first of the pair, a tall man, nodded to Erik with a broad, easy smile, like he was delighted with life. That might get annoying, but it was better than Mr. Scowl.

He introduced himself. "Wei Li. It's a pleasure to be working with you two. I've already heard about some of the crazy things you've done in this ship, and I look forward to doing my part to help you do even crazier crap."

"Janessa Varone," offered the other engineer, a younger dark-skinned woman. She averted her eyes. "I hope to do my part, preferably without too much craziness." She smiled at the *Argo*. "And I look forward to being able to help with the jumpship."

The suited beast marched up to Erik, looking him up and down, the scowl remaining. He thrust out a hand. A wide grin destroyed his scowl. "Kant Marle. Please call me Kant. I hate being called Agent Marle."

The other agent scoffed and folded her arms. "You could try being professional for five seconds."

"This is me being professionally friendly," he answered.

Erik gave Kant's hand a firm shake. "You all can call me whatever you want as long as it's not 'asshole.'"

Kant laughed and pointed his thumb over his shoulder at the woman. "Agent Anne Devereaux. Don't mind the ice queen thing. She's good at her job."

Anne scoffed and rolled her eyes.

Jia moved forward to shake his hand. "I'm glad to be working with you, Kant."

Erik and Jia moved toward the others to shake their hands as well. Anne watched in disapproval. Erik wasn't sure if she had a problem with him or Kant.

"Good," Alina declared. "You all know each other now."

She stared Anne down. "To reiterate, both these agents are tasked to you for active support, Erik and Jia. You two will make the calls, and they will help you execute them."

Anne's mouth twitched for a moment.

"Problem?" Erik asked. If she couldn't handle taking any orders from someone outside the ID, he'd rather know now than in the middle of a fight with a bunch of behemoth *yaoguai* on Chiron.

He'd gotten lucky with the military squads. They had known about his service time, so they'd treated him as an Army brother, but this ghost didn't seem to care about that.

"I don't have a problem, Blackwell." Anna's attempt at a smile came off as a sneer. "I've read your file. I know you're good at what you do. I just…well…"

Jia frowned and moved forward. Erik held her back with his arm. She stepped back and nodded at him with a slight smile.

"You what, *Anne?*" Erik chuckled. "Don't hold back on my account. We might be able to jump to Alpha Centauri quickly, but we're going to be trapped together on the *Argo* for days. Let's hash out the petty crap right away. We'll be tripping over each other in there."

Alina watched, her expression impassive. Wei and Kant both looked amused, but Janessa seemed worried. Malcolm tapped his leg nervously. It was good for all of them to get a feel for the dynamic.

Lanara snorted and walked toward the *Argo*. "Li, Varone. Come to the engine room when everyone's done pissing all over the floor to prove something pointless."

Erik chuckled. Leave it to Lanara to cut to the chase.

Janessa jogged after her. "I think I'll come now."

Wei nodded after Lanara. "See you soon. I think I need to spend more time, uh, getting to know people."

The eager amusement in his eyes spoke more to entertainment than socialization. Erik didn't care if this was his fun for the week.

Malcolm snapped his fingers and hurried toward the ship, running past Lanara. "I just remembered, uh, something I wanted to check, too. Like, right now, immediately."

No one spoke as the small crowd made its way to the *Argo*. Anne continued staring Erik down.

"There are more elegant ways to accomplish certain tasks," Anne noted to Erik. "I know this isn't your first time out of the Solar System, but this isn't a military operation, Blackwell. You can make a mess at home because it's easy enough for Alina and others to clean it up. You do that too much out there, and it's going to become a problem."

Jia snorted. "Oh, well, we'll be sure to let the conspiracy do what they want so as to not cause any inconvenience to the government."

"I'm serious." Anne narrowed her eyes. "We don't know how far or where we'll end up. Today, it might be Alpha Centauri. A month from now, it might be Molino."

Erik's brow lifted. If that was an attempt to goad him, it didn't work.

"Molino could have used louder military-style solutions," he replied. "Not quieter. You know the conspiracy can get pretty brazen, which means our response needs to match."

"I'm just saying, things are more unstable than you might appreciate on the frontier." Anne folded her arms, her fingers tight. "If we blow up everything left and right, the conspiracy might take advantage of it."

Marle shook his head. Again, there was an abrupt shift between the scowl and a goofy grin. With his large size, it was unfortunate he suffered from resting bitch face.

"She's like this with everyone, Erik." He gestured at Anne. "But she'll do what she needs to when the time is right."

Erik marched over to Anne. "Is that the case?"

"I have my orders." She continued to stare at Erik defiantly. "Those include listening to you, but keep in mind, we're on loan to you. We don't *work* for you. If I feel you're screwing up, I will let Agent Koval know."

Alina cleared her throat. "Good. I think we're all on the same page."

Erik offered Anne a slight mocking grin before stepping back. He had expected something like this. He'd known there was only so long he would be able to operate with total autonomy. Until now, it hadn't been an issue.

Although they'd met with Barbu without telling Alina ahead of time, that had been a function of limited time rather than a desire to keep anything from her.

As long as the ID remained dedicated to defeating the conspiracy, Erik had no problem with Alina knowing his every move. If the situation changed, he would have a lot more problems than one frosty redheaded agent to worry about.

Emma's hologram appeared, including a dark suit matching Anne's. Erik suspected the AI was mocking the woman.

"I should make it clear," Emma began, looking straight

at Anne, "that everything that occurs on any ship I'm interfaced with is under my surveillance except when I choose otherwise." Her smile was cold. "Attempts to bypass that, such as unauthorized communications, will be reported to Erik and Jia."

"That's enough." Alina stepped forward. "Erik and Jia have my total trust, as do you, Agents Devereaux and Marle. I know it'll be an adjustment, but I'm sure you'll learn to work well together for the good of the UTC. They aren't just muscle, Erik. Use them well."

Kant flexed. "I have plenty of muscle, too."

"Down, Hercules." With that, Alina headed toward a small side door.

Erik gazed at Alina and the other agent. Anne spun on her heel and headed toward the *Argo*, not looking any happier than before.

A dedicated engineering crew, an AI, a hacker, two ghosts, Jia, a damned impressive ship, and an even more impressive jumpship. His quest might have started with a few clues and a desperate hope, but now he had a whole team.

Wei clapped his hands loudly. Everyone left in the hangar turned toward him, confused.

"Okay, now that we've got the introductions over with, why don't we go to the galley and have a little party? The others can join when they hear the fun." He pointed at Emma. "She can fly the ship, right? So, we've got plenty of time before we get to Penglai. If we get drunk tonight, we can sleep it off."

Kant rubbed his chin. "I like where your head is, but I'm not sure that's a great idea before the mission."

"He's right." Erik laughed. "We'll save the party for after the mission."

Jia leaned toward Erik to whisper, "Are you sure about this? Agent Devereaux might be a problem."

"If she's our worst problem on this mission, we'll do great."

CHAPTER THIRTY

Despite her family's wealth, Jia, like most people, spent her life consuming mostly artificial meat, whether prepared or printed.

Her mother enjoyed the occasional ostentatious display of serving and eating real meat, but she was suddenly concerned about wasting money when there wasn't anyone around to impress except her daughters and husband.

A lifetime of eating artificial meat should have made her less sensitive to the vagaries of such products, but she could taste a difference in the meals prepared on the *Argo*. Those faint differences reminded her she was on a ship deep in space.

It hadn't been so bad before, but she was already regretting not packing food on this trip.

Her current noodles' textural irregularities were the day's main complaint. She chewed quickly and swallowed, trying her best not to focus on the food and enjoy it for what it was. It was a long way to their destination.

Jia stared down at her tray on the galley table with a frown. Emma could run a diagnostic, or Lanara and her crew might be able to do something. Suffering for a week didn't appeal. She looked at Erik, but he was happily munching on his beignet.

It didn't make sense. The food hadn't been this off during the Hunter mission.

Erik grinned from across the table after finishing off his pastry. "I can tell what you're thinking."

She eyed him. "You've developed psychic powers now?"

"Something like that, or we've just been together long enough that I can figure it out." Erik placed her fingers on his temple. "You're thinking, 'Why doesn't Erik hate his food as much as I do?'"

"I don't…" she eyed the plate, "*hate* the food."

Jia was surprised at how good Erik had become at anticipating her thoughts. The reciprocal wasn't as true.

Erik nodded. "You don't hate it, but there's something off about it."

She leaned forward, pointing at him. "Exactly!"

Erik chuckled. "There isn't. It's you. The problem is psychological."

Jia stared at him, then her plate, and back at him. "Huh? What do you mean, it's psychological? There's clearly something different about the food on the ship, and it's more pronounced this trip than the last time."

He gestured at her bowl. "There might be some slight differences between the raw materials and those from meals we get in restaurants, but probably not much, if any, compared to the stuff you buy for your home. We eat out a lot, so there's less printed food, but we both also eat a lot of printed food at home. It's not the food or the preparation. It's because you're trapped in this bucket until we get to Penglai, and then trapped in it or another bucket until we get to Alpha Centauri."

"The trip there won't take that long," Jia muttered.

"To the system, yes, but we can't pop out in orbit. We better work this out now because there are a lot more printed noodles in your future."

"But it's getting worse." Jia tapped a finger on the table. "Tasting worse. I don't think it's just in my head. Are you sure you're just not ignoring it because you used to eat rations? Lanara's the one putting in the raw material requests. Maybe she decided to go cheap because of some efficiency thing. You know, use food that's not as good for humans, but it'll save 0.27 percent power when you use the printers."

"That does sound like something she'd do." Erik scratched his chin, thinking about the suggestion. "But I don't believe that's it. It's in your head, Jia."

Emma materialized next to the table in a chef's coat, with a toque perched atop her head. "Erik is correct. While the highest-quality materials aren't being purchased, they are generally of good quality, and in some cases, superior to what you two consume in your apartments. There's no evidence there's been any change to the food printers or other relevant systems, based on system reports."

With that, she retracted her hologram. Jia had stopped caring about Emma's omnipresence a long time ago. If anything, it was a comfort and made it easier to relax.

"We used to call this the taste curve in the Army, but it hit the Fleet guys even harder." Erik dusted crumbs off his hands. "It might take a good year or two depending on how much travel we do for you not to suffer from it, but I'm guessing it's more about the new crew. They're what's causing your food to taste worse. When you're trapped on a bucket in space, anything that makes you uncomfortable can make everything seem that much worse."

Jia thought that over. It made sense, and Emma could be mischievous, but this wasn't a situation where she would lie. Coming to terms with the new crew members might help.

"Agent Devereaux doesn't seem to like you much," Jia mumbled. "I don't know if she cares for me either. I've barely talked to her. She's keeping to her cabin, and we've only seen each other in passing. I think she's trying to maintain different hours than the rest of us."

Erik shrugged. "If I got broken up about everyone who doesn't like me, it'd be a sad life. At least she's not trying to kill me. I can come back from everything but that."

"She's not trying to kill you *yet*." Jia set her chopsticks down. Irritation was a disgusting spice.

"Alina knows what she's doing," Erik replied. "We just need time to earn Anne's respect. This is as weird for her as it is for us. I'm sure that as a ghost, she's used to dealing with informants and all sorts of non-ID personnel, but that's not the same thing as shipping out with them and having to follow their orders."

"I suppose, but she could be more professional about it —and professional can mean strange things for ID agents, judging by Alina and Kalei."

"She probably thinks the same thing about us, but then again, we get the results we do because we're not standard-issue cops, soldiers, or ghosts."

Jia leaned back. "I know we have time before we get to the base, and she'll calm down, but I feel she started off our relationship on the wrong foot."

"We should do something about that. Like you said, we have plenty of time, so it doesn't matter if we waste some of it." Erik rubbed his chin. "But what to do? The best thing in times like this is something fun to take everyone's mind off the flight."

Jia sighed. "The nano-AR room isn't big enough for everyone, even with tricks. That cuts out a lot of possibilities. I don't think eating together will be enough, especially when most of us aren't eating at the same times."

"Not food. Something more active." Erik shook his head. "We need something we're all doing together, something that pushes us out of our comfort zones so we're forced to mix, and we can't retreat to hang out with the people we already know. If we weren't already in space, I'd say we should all hit a bar together."

"That's not practical."

"Someone needs to invent roving bar ships." Erik nodded at Jia. "This cuts both ways. It's not like you're going out of your way to talk to the fresh meat, either."

Jia huffed. "And you are?"

"I've talked to Kant a little. Turns out he's a vet, too." Erik laughed. "I assumed assault infantry, but he was a combat engineer. He did some quick tours and then joined the ID. Nice enough guy despite looking like a changeling customized for bar fights."

Jia nodded. "He seemed that way to me, too. I did briefly run into Wei the other day. He lamented that we haven't had a party. Lanara made it very clear he couldn't drink yet, but I'm sure he'd love your roving bar ship plan."

Erik chuckled. "It's not like we're going to lock him up if he has the system produce alcohol. Did she do something?"

"From what Wei indicated, she..." Jia grimaced at the memory. "She suggested using his blood as a lubricant if he pissed her off."

"She asked for the help, and now she's grouchy about having to bring them up to speed." Erik laughed. "That's so her. What about the woman?"

Jia shook her head. "I've gotten a couple of sentences out of her, but I think she's more shy than anything. A shy engineer better with machines than people isn't a shocking anomaly."

Erik snapped his fingers. "I've got it. I've got the perfect solution that doesn't involve everyone getting drunk."

"What?" Jia asked, letting her dubiousness show on her face.

"It was something I used to do with my unit all the time."

"I thought this plan didn't involve alcohol?"

"It doesn't. It's a great way to break the ice, and no pressure or risk of injury unless you're a total moron. It's also something that won't take a lot of space." Erik looked around the galley. "It's a bit too cramped here, but we can use the cargo bay to have our fun and be comfortable."

"The cargo bay?" Jia asked, trying to imagine the possibilities.

Knowing Erik and what he'd said, she assumed it was some sort of physical activity, but he obviously wouldn't want sparring matches. Janessa and Malcolm wouldn't stand a chance, and Lanara would stab anyone who tried to hit her. Later, she'd probably cut the gravity and oxygen to their cabin.

Something grander and theoretically less violent like a sports match wasn't practical aboard the *Argo*. There was space in the cargo bay, but with the flitters, scout bikes, exoskeletons, and supplies, there wasn't enough room left for any decent game.

If they could use all three dimensions, it would be different. Jia could have gotten behind a sphere ball match, but they didn't have enough players. Also, that activity would end with Lanara stabbing someone or suffocating them.

"Yeah." Erik nodded, more to himself than Jia. "The cargo bay's perfect for what I have in mind."

Jia's brow lifted. "Why do I get nervous when you say there's no risk of injury unless someone's a total moron?"

Erik pushed off the table and stood. "We just need to print up a board and some darts."

"Oh." Jia blinked. "Darts. That shouldn't end with any stabbings."

Erik stopped on his way to the door and looked over his shoulder. "Stabbings?"

CHAPTER THIRTY-ONE

Every human on board the *Argo* stood in a loose gaggle in the front of the cargo bay.

Erik had been surprised by how readily Anne and Lanara agreed to his suggestion, the former because of her remaining obvious disdain for him and the latter because of her monomaniacal obsession with engineering over everything else, let alone games.

He wasn't going to complain because besides wanting to promote interaction with the new crew, he was now craving a good game of darts.

Certain realities about Lanara's participation became clear when the engineer ran over to where he was setting up the dartboard.

She pointed near the top. "It needs to be farther up." She tapped her PNIU and slowly lifted her finger, her eyes narrowed. "Another 1.27 centimeters. Adjust it now, Blackwell."

Erik stared at the woman. "Huh? This is good enough.

It's not like we're having a professional championship match."

Lanara glared at him. "You know why I agreed to this pointless waste of time, Blackwell?"

"Because you love friendly competition or darts?" Erik offered in a hopeful tone.

Lanara scoffed. "No, because I wanted to visually confirm the efficiency of some of the grav emitter modifications I finished up the other day for the cargo bay." She gestured around the area. "This is a good way to do it, but to do my best evaluation, I need to ensure we're dealing with a game of darts that involves overlapping the grav fields in a particular way, which needs that board to be up another 1.27 centimeters." She hurried over to the board and moved it. "We'll need the board here and the throw line…" She tapped her PNIU. "Emma, can you help me out here?"

A holographic white line appeared a couple of meters in front of where the feisty engineer was hanging the board. She glanced back and forth a couple of times before nodding with a satisfied look and heading toward the line.

"Make sure they aren't playing in order of height, Emma," Lanara ordered, sweeping the gathered humans with her gaze. "I'm recording all of this to help with my diagnostics. I don't give a crap if you embarrass yourself, but you might."

"Don't scare them off, Lanara." Erik laughed. "Try to have some fun, people. I'm pretty damned good, but I'm not unbeatable."

Kant gestured at Erik's left arm. "No offense, but you're not going to be using that, right?"

"You got a problem with hardware?" Erik asked, keeping his smile and light tone.

Lanara wasn't the only one who could use the game to evaluate something. While he hoped a little friendly competition would help the newly expanded team gel, this was as good as time as any to explore their personalities deeper than their introductions on Earth and the brief conversations they had shared onboard. He could deal with someone who didn't like hardware, but he'd rather have it out in the open rather than dealing with simmering resentments in the field.

"Nah." Kant shrugged. "I don't give two shits about Purists if that's what you're getting at, but, brother, I'm a competitive guy, and I don't want any unfair advantages. A cybernetic arm is an unfair advantage."

Erik rotated his arm. "I'm right-handed, and my hardware's all left. All I have to do is not use it for anything other than holding my darts. How does that sound?"

"Sounds fair." Kant smiled.

"Sinister," Janessa offered. She gasped and clapped a hand to her head. "Sorry."

Everyone turned her way, but she looked down at the deck and shuffled her feet. She gulped and took deep, careful breaths.

"No one's ever called my arm sinister before." Erik chuckled. "They've called it a lot of other things close to that. Same question to you. I know it's strange that I didn't get it regrown, but I've got my reasons, and it works for me."

"I-I find cybernetics fascinating, actually," Janessa stammered. "I'd never want to get augmented, but that's not what I was talking about. It's Latin. That's what I meant."

"My arm is Latin?" Erik's brow lifted. He was beyond confused. A quick look at Jia only earned him a shrug and a confused look.

"'Sinister' is left in Latin and 'dexter' is right." Janessa managed to lift her head but didn't make eye contact. "But the ancients didn't trust left-handed people, so the word slowly changed from meaning that to something more negative. You see that in a lot of languages, and several also have their version of right also meaning right. I mean, right as in correct."

"Oh." Erik gave her a polite nod. "Didn't know that. Never thought about it that way before. Funny how things work out."

Something approaching a smile broke out on Janessa's face. He could deal with a shy trivia-obsessed engineer. He hoped Lanara wasn't too hard on her.

"Let's get to the reason we're here." Erik clapped his hands together and gestured to a tray filled with trios of darts sitting on top of a cargo crate a couple of meters away. "All the colors of the rainbow plus white, but otherwise the same weight and balance. The system has the specs if you want to print your own for the next time we do this."

Kant grabbed a set of orange darts. "Would it be too much if I had darts that said, 'Kant is awesome' on the side'? I used to play with a set like that."

"Hey, whatever works."

Malcolm collected the yellow darts and swirled one in

his fingers. "Don't get cocky, big guy. I know a thing or two about tossing darts."

Kant grinned at him. "Bring it on, Captain Hawaii."

"Consider it brought." Malcolm fluffed his shirt.

Erik had never seen Malcolm being all that great at darts, but he didn't mind the man's enthusiasm. The more people who got excited, the more fun it would be for everyone.

"This is more fun when it's a drinking game," Wei complained, his shoulders sagging.

Erik offered him a grin. "We can do one like that on our way back after we're done kicking the conspiracy's ass on Chiron. It'll give us all something to look forward to."

Wei smiled brightly and rubbed his hands together. "I better get my practice in now. I'm not great."

"It doesn't matter. Nothing on the line but bragging rights."

Jia inspected the tray and didn't surprise Erik by selecting a dark-blue set. Anne picked up a white set. Lanara grabbed the red. Janessa picked up the indigo darts. Wei hesitated, his gaze shifting back and forth before picking up the green. That left violet for Erik; not his favorite choice, but it would do for the moment.

Emma's hologram appeared wearing a striped referee's uniform. Erik opened his mouth to question her choice but shut it and waited for her to do the next part. It would help if she bonded with the new crew members, too.

"I've randomized the order of play." Emma lifted her hand and a scoreboard appeared with everyone's names, starting with Jia, then Anne, Erik, Kant, Janessa, Wei, Malcolm, and

Lanara. "We will be playing standard variant 501, which has persisted for centuries. It's easy. Each turn, you get three throws, and your score will be subtracted from 501 with the goal of getting to zero, but on the throw you get to zero, you need to get a bullseye or a double to win. A throw that reduces your score below zero, to one, or zero but not ending with a double, will reset your score to its initial value before your first throw that turn. Everyone understand?"

Malcolm gestured for her to hurry up. "Come on. It's darts, not sphere ball. It's not that complicated. Everyone already said they knew how to play when we agreed to it."

He withered under the AI's glare. Emma continued staring at him for a good five seconds before returning her attention to the rest of the crowd.

"Reminders and specificity are necessary for proper competition," Emma explained, her voice cold. "Let's see if your skill level matches your impatience, Mr. Constantine. Let me note, I'll also be monitoring your smart lenses to ensure a lack of cheating. Competitions are no fun if they involve cheating, except for hacking the competition."

Erik waited for someone to complain about Emma's intrusion into their privacy, but no one did. He'd asked Emma to make the announcement as part of another test. There wasn't a human in the UTC who wasn't used to dealing with some level of persuasive AI and surveillance, but knowing you were being recorded was different from knowing you were being watched by a self-aware AI with clear emotional loyalty to a small number of people.

Jia stepped up to the line with a smile. "I wish we could play sphere ball, but this will be fun. There's nothing like a pure test of skill. This isn't about the equipment, just hand-eye coordination, technique, and careful planning."

After a lengthy period of subtly shifting her dart and her eyes, she sent her missile flying. She started the match with a bullseye, earning her claps and cheers from most of the crowd, with the noticeable exception of Anne and Lanara. The engineer murmured numbers under her breath and kept waving her hand, interfacing with internal sensors readouts being fed to their smart lenses.

"One hundred twenty-five points," Emma announced after Jia's next two throws of another bullseye and an outer bull.

Malcolm whistled loudly, and Janessa gave a soft smile. Kant looked worried, and Wei impressed. Anne's expression hadn't changed much.

"Starting us off with a challenge, huh?" Erik asked with a grin. "No-Mercy Lin is with us today, ladies and gentlemen."

He wasn't surprised by the throws. When they were still cops, they had played darts on occasion, especially when they hung out with other cops at bars, and Jia had always played well. He wouldn't have been surprised if she'd practiced in secret after that.

Jia collected her darts and tossed one in the air. She snatched it before it started falling. "It's all about angles and controlled power."

"It is at that," Anne replied, stepping up to the line, her gaze ticking between Erik and Jia. "And the skill to achieve them."

She took several deep breaths and made minute adjustments to her hand. No one spoke. Several people held their breath.

Anne broke the silence with three rapid-fire throws. Erik's brow lifted before the first dart hit. He marveled at the aggressive play. It paid off with a triple twenty, another triple twenty, and a third triple twenty.

"Anne's not here to play. She's here to win." Kant threw back his head and laughed, the sound charming and relaxing despite the volume.

Anne wandered to the board, offering Jia a faint smirk before collecting the darts. Erik had to credit the woman. Getting a triple twenty was difficult. Landing three was impressive. Nailing three in a row so quickly was ridiculous. If Emma weren't monitoring things, he would have suspected cheating.

"Wow." Malcom tilted his head back and forth while staring at the dartboard. "That's a lot of darts to get in a tiny spot. I guess I'm not as good as I thought."

"There's no point in doing something half-assed," Anne explained, returning behind the line and nodding at Erik. "Wouldn't you agree, Blackwell?"

"I don't take my darts that seriously when money's not on the line," Erik offered with a smile, moving forward to take his place.

He might have made a tactical mistake in selecting darts, but given Anne's behavior, any competition would have led to the same issue. Some people couldn't shut off their competitive switch.

It wasn't over yet, and one smart-ass comment didn't make the entire game a mistake. The only thing to focus on for the moment was the game.

His mind settling, Erik made his throws. He didn't rush the three like Anne or spend half a century planning between each like Jia. He felt the familiar satisfaction as each dart thudded into the board.

"One hundred and sixty," Emma announced. "Good for the first three."

He was going to make everyone work for a victory.

Kant threw up his hands. "Come on. Give us a break."

In theory, the rules of 501 gave people behind a chance to catch up. The final throw requirements necessitated careful control, and depending on how someone depleted their score, it might be more difficult winning without options, such as leaving themselves easily divisible scores.

Preplanning was key. Darts was far more about strategy than casual observers understood.

The other grand advantage of 501 was it was impossible to win on the first two turns, giving each player at least some opportunities for fun and excitement. Erik was pretty good. While he wouldn't claim to be a master, he won more often than not. That game, though, his opponents had brought their solid throwing arms.

Lanara took her third throw of the third turn. She was the slowest between each throw, even compared to Jia, and it was obvious on both turns that she was making no attempt to earn points. Rather, she was aiming her darts for specific sides of the board as part of the diagnostics and continuing her constant muttering of numbers.

No one dared to complain. The last thing anyone

wanted to do in deep space was piss off their chief engineer.

The other players had performed well enough, but Jia, Anne, and Erik's spectacular first turns had given way to more modest follow-ups in the next. Malcolm had also managed a triple twenty in the third round, helping him close on the score leaders.

The standings board shifted with the completion of Lanara's turn, and Emma pointed at it.

"At the beginning of the fourth round, we have Jia and Anne tied for first place, with ninety-six points left. Malcolm is controlling second place with a hundred and fifty points left—"

"Feel the power of the shirt!" Malcolm shouted. He slapped his hands against his chest and the red Hawaiian shirt decorated with Santa Claus and reindeer. Calmness returned after a fierce glare from Emma.

"Erik is in third, with 161 remaining," she continued, "Kant is in fourth with 175. Janessa is in fifth with 190, Wei in sixth with 200, and Lanara a distant seventh place at 270 points."

"I think I throw better with beer in me," Wei offered with a sheepish smile. "That and I suck."

Jia cracked her neck and then her knuckles. She strode with confidence to the line, one of her darts already ready in her right hand. A moment passed as she examined the board and sucked in a deep breath. She threw in one fluid motion, commanding and powerful. The dart thudded into the board.

Bullseye. Fifty points. Her second throw netted her sixteen points, leaving her with thirty to go.

Jia nodded slowly. She needed a double fifteen to finish the game. Her hand moved back, and she released.

A collective groan went up from Malcolm and Kant.

Single fifteen.

Erik shook his head, disappointed. The bullseyes and double requirement meant she'd need at least two more throws to win, opening up a chance for her chief competition to finish the game in victory.

Anne sauntered up to the line with a slight smile. A bullseye knocked her score down to forty-six, matching Jia's initial move. Her follow-up toss hit a double three. She was down to forty points.

"It's over," she declared.

"Then don't talk it," Jia suggested, her face tight. "Toss it."

Anne released her final dart. Double ring. Twenty. Forty points. Her mouth quirked into a smirk. She was edging over the line between confidence and arrogance.

"Zero point four percent," shouted Lanara. She jerked her arm up, her finger pointed at Wei. "You." She whipped her finger toward Janessa. "And you. Come with me. We need to make some adjustments on the primary grav power conduits."

A single toss landed Lanara's darts in the tray with a clatter. Maybe horseshoes was more her game.

"Right now?" Wei sighed. "But we just got done. Don't we have time to tal—"

"We're done messing around," Lanara finished. "And you had plenty of time to run your mouth during the game." She headed toward the door. "Now, let's move."

Janessa smiled at Erik and set her darts in the tray. "It

was fun. I did better than I thought I would. Thanks for suggesting it."

Wei bobbed his head, dropped off his darts, and followed his fellow engineers. "Fun, but the Empress is dragging us back to Diyu."

"Keep talking," Lanara shouted.

Jia extended her hand to Anne. "Good game."

"At least you kept up with me." Anne eyed Jia's hand for a moment before giving it a light shake. "An easy victory isn't worth it."

The ID agent walked away without looking back at the others. After dropping her darts in the tray, she headed toward the door. Kant gave Jia an apologetic shrug.

Malcolm waited until Anne was out of the room before making a face. "Somebody likes their darts too much."

Kant chuckled. "By her standards, that was being nice."

CHAPTER THIRTY-TWO

Jia stepped out of the nano-AR chamber, shaking out her hands, her eyelids heavy. She was exhausted, and it wasn't from the hordes of simulated terrorists she'd taken out in a tower.

Dealing with a screwed-up Circadian rhythm was another annoying but necessary aspect of long-distance space travel. The Army and Fleet avoided it by rigid adherence to schedules, but that wasn't practical in their situation. Although she'd avoided having much trouble on their last space mission, her body had turned against her this trip.

Jia had been taking turns in the cockpit. At this point in the flight, there weren't many required course corrections. Emma could handle it, but there was something calming about being behind the controls, even when she was tired.

But there was only so long she could sit in a pilot's seat, and with Erik asleep, she'd decided to do some battle training on her own. She's long since accepted that working for Alina meant most jobs would end in violence. They weren't going after the kind of people who would give up and beg to be hauled to jail.

She wasn't bothered by the necessity of taking out the violent agents of the conspiracy. Perspective helped. She was now dealing with the kind of people who would hire someone to fire cruise missiles at a jail or partake in the most disgusting types of genetic engineering without any consideration of balance or the consequences.

It was sick, but in a way, she missed the petty criminals of NSCPD. They might be antisocial and violent, but their motivations were so much easier to understand.

Jia froze as she caught movement out of the corner of her eye. She turned toward the source, reaching for a weapon she didn't have. The *Argo* was the one place she didn't wander around with two pistols strapped to her.

She let out a sigh of relief, no longer annoyed at her lack of guns. Her visitor wasn't a dangerous alien or terrorist stowaway. It was Anne, walking down the passage and heading Jia's way.

The ID agent slowed, the corners of her mouth tugging down. "You're using the room? I didn't think anyone would be using it right now. Other than the engineers, everybody seems to be keeping the same schedule."

Jia shook her head. "I just finished." She motioned to the door. "She's all yours, Agent Devereaux."

Anne walked toward the room, her steps slow and deliberate. "Blackwell, I get. You, I'm still figuring out. I'm not going to pretend that doesn't annoy me."

"What's to figure out?" Jia frowned. "I'm assuming there

is a huge ID file on me you've read. If the government didn't trust me, they wouldn't be letting me go on these missions or anywhere near the jumpship."

"Yes, I've read your file, detailing all your impressive achievements. You seem trustworthy, but that's only one important thing." Anne snorted. "I read how you became Lady Justice and about the corp princess who lowered herself to become a detective. Not all of us could walk into our positions so easily, Your Highness."

Jia folded her arms. "I didn't *lower* myself to become a police officer. I fought a lot of people who were resistant, including my own family, so I could better serve the UTC public." She frowned. "And it's not my responsibility to make sure everyone else makes it into law enforcement. Yes, I used an unusual entry path, but I earned it. I didn't have to become a police officer, you know."

Anne raised an eyebrow. "Oh? You're saying you're a hero for doing that. I didn't realize it."

"No, I'm simply adding nuance to deflect your insults." Jia squared her shoulders. "I'm not going to sit here and take everything from you because you're with the ID. They came to us because they recognized our skills, and our track record speaks for itself."

Anne took another couple of steps until she was right in front of Jia. Both women were around the same height. Combined with the agent's lither build, physical intimidation was questionable, but Jia couldn't deny the sheer intensity in the woman's cold stare.

"I don't insult," Anne offered, her voice barely above a whisper. "I present the truth as I see it. Some people don't like that, but that doesn't mean I care."

"What truth do you see?" Jia asked. "Because I see a woman who was belligerent to my partner and now is being unpleasant to me without a good reason."

"I have my reasons," Anna replied. "And the truth is, you didn't earn your position. Your family wealth and status bought you a place as a detective. It was mere proximity to others that got you the rest of your reputation, including your current position. If you were as great as you think, you would have reformed the NSCPD yourself, and Agent Koval would have recruited you long ago. And if you knew about what was going on in the UTC, you would have joined the ID or CID rather than the NSCPD."

Jia lowered her arms, her hands curling into fists. She would never deny she'd been naïve about the UTC and the reality of crime in Neo SoCal and unrest elsewhere, but she wasn't just along for the ride. She'd carved out her own fate, and she wasn't a woman who would sit there with someone all but in her face.

"You think I'm a fraud?" Jia snorted. "After every mission I've done? After all the times I've risked my life? That's what this is about?"

"You mean, missions like on the Hunter ship?" Anne replied mockingly. "How well would you have done without the assault infantry, hmm? It's easy to look impressive when everyone around you is impressive. All you have to do is not screw up."

"So I was, what, expected to take out the entire ship by myself? Don't be ridiculous. If this is about my background, get over it." Jia rolled her eyes. "Is that what you do? Wander around the UTC, stopping every terrorist and insurrectionist by yourself?"

"Not exactly. It's... You see, it's like the darts." Anne's face twitched. "In a fight, it's not good enough to be second. Being not as good as the enemy means you're dead, and when we're on missions, there might be all sorts of personnel mixes. I want to make sure if we end up working together, I won't have to do the work for both of us."

Jia laughed. "Fine." She inclined her head toward the AR room. "How about I get some sleep, and then tomorrow I show you my skills. Even better, you show me yours. I figure if I do, maybe you'll crawl out of my ass and stop being a bitch for two seconds."

"We'll see." Anne slapped the access panel and stepped inside. "Goodnight, Lin. Don't be worried about tomorrow. There's no shame in coming in second."

Jia glared at the woman until the door closed.

Jia didn't want Erik to become involved. That would only complicate the matter and feed into Anne's argument. When he didn't mention the woman at breakfast, Jia assumed Emma hadn't told him. There was no way Emma wasn't aware of the argument. Jia appreciated the AI's restraint and understanding in the matter.

With an excuse about needing to check on something, Jia left breakfast and headed to the AR room. Anne waited inside, wearing the same expression she'd had after winning at darts.

"I'm hoping you'll get the point without trying to set up anything too elaborate," Anne explained. She tapped her PNIU a couple of times.

The blank room shifted, a two-person firing range forming, along with rifles hanging on either side and a box of preloaded magazines beside each position. There was no real detail outside of the firing lanes.

Anne grabbed her rifle and a magazine and slotted the ammo into her weapon. "You're allegedly a good shot, but I want to see it for myself. This isn't anything fancy, a dynamic firing range with stationary and moving targets of different types. Standing, ten targets per level, we'll go until somebody misses half the targets on a given level. That person is the loser, and the other person is by definition the winner."

"She hasn't programmed any trickery into the simulation, other than adding near-complete noise suppression to the weapons," Emma transmitted directly into Jia's ear. "I would give you hints, but I suspect you would not appreciate that, given the nature of this particular confrontation."

Jia's jaw tightened. She didn't respond to Emma. It would only give Anne an opportunity to accuse her of cheating and hiding behind others.

Anne lifted her rifle and flipped off the safety before taking up a shooting stance. "There are different ways to serve the UTC. You don't have to be doing these kinds of tasks."

"Having shooting competitions?"

"No, going to Alpha Centauri or deadly labs in France."

Jia pulled her rifle off the wall and loaded it. "I'm fine with the way I'm serving. It wasn't like I left the police department on a whim."

Two stationary translucent holograms of masked men

with pistols appeared in the distance. Jia fired at the same time as Anne. Both hit the targets without much trouble.

The next batch of targets appeared, a group of men at a farther distance, still stationary. Both women fired in rapid succession, hitting their targets without the use of burst fire. They'd cleared five of the ten targets for the level.

Jia smiled. She knew the difficulty was going to ramp up, but so far, she was enjoying it. Being tied with Anne wasn't a horrible fate.

Their first moving target appeared, a hologram of a terrorist charging forward using serpentine movements and brandishing a knife. Jia hesitated for a half-second before anticipating and downing the man. She barely registered Anne's muted fire right before that.

No surprise accompanied the appearance of multiple moving targets. Jia and Anne continued firing and striking all their targets with ease. The words **Level One Complete** appeared in floating holographic text.

"The next level will begin in thirty seconds," Anne explained, ejecting her magazine and reloading. "And that's how it's going to continue until this is done. We don't always get nice little breaks in battle, do we?"

"If you know about France, then you know I've fought in worse conditions."

"No exo to do all the work now."

"You need to reread my file. It's obvious you missed a lot."

Jia matched her and held her rifle closer, giving her forearms a chance to rest in the short interval between the next round. Success might shut the ID agent up, or it might not accomplish anything.

She was used to being doubted. It'd happened her entire life and career, and she'd learned words didn't shut people up; only action and proof did. If Anne didn't want to accept her after that, it would be the agent with the indefensible problem.

A glowing blue ball bounced in the air in the distance. The level had started without special notice. Jia whipped her gun into position as her competitor fired, not hitting her own target until a short breath later.

Jia was ready when more glowing balls appeared, again taking a moment to line up a careful shot and release. Anne was downing her targets slightly faster, but neither woman was missing a shot, let alone a target.

"Whatever else you might think of me," Jia commented, "I'm a good shot. I always have been."

"We'll see. We're just getting started."

Jia wiped the sweat off her face and loaded a new magazine. Level sixteen was about to start. With a growl, a Zitark sprinted down the lane, which was now filled with stones. The alien leapt onto a rock and then another before heading down, the quick movements and level changes making it difficult to aim.

She released a burst, downing the Zitark and letting out a sigh of relief. Her accuracy had descended to seventy percent in the last couple of levels, as related by a scoreboard floating above the range. Anne had lost her speed advantage but was maintaining about seventy-five percent accuracy. Jia might not like the woman, but she was a great shot.

A new batch of holographic space raptors appeared and surged forward, growling and hissing in a harsh choir of murder. With the aliens sprinting across such a short distance, Jia didn't have time to be too precious with her rifle. She emptied her magazine in rapid bursts and managed to down the targets before they'd closed on her.

Jia's hand snaked out to grab from the row of magazines she'd set up between levels. She reloaded just as one of the targets on Anne's side reached the agent. Another batch of Zitarks surged forward, and this time, Jia and Anne took out their respective targets at a distance.

Neither woman had said anything to the other for the last ten minutes. Their concentration was on the holograms conjured by the system. They'd had nothing but the frustratingly short breaks between levels for rests.

Level Sixteen Complete.

Time blurred. Despite her effort and concentration, Jia's heart maintained a calm, slow pace. Quick-loading her rifle didn't challenge her body like the near-constant movement of an actual battle.

Jia wasn't surprised when a Leem target appeared and jogged forward, his movements covered by blasts from his lightning gun. Though the new alien wasn't as fast as the Zitarks, her first shot disintegrated against the crackling shield surrounding it, and precious seconds passed before she realized the shield flickered off for a brief moment after three or four steps. A burst headshot downed the alien before he'd made it halfway.

She couldn't spare any attention for Anne, with new

targets appearing almost immediately. There was nothing she could do but establish the timing and down the enemy. Jia had become a machine, an automated turret that existed only to destroy simulated targets.

The seconds blurred into the minutes as more elaborate combinations of targets appeared, including mixed Leem and Zitark assault forces, a nightmarish scenario she hoped never to see in real life. One interesting tidbit of humanity's expansion into the universe was the realization that none of the Local Neighborhood races interacted much beyond the most basic high-level diplomacy.

Level Twenty Complete.

Aiming, Jia barely registered the targets anymore. Aliens, monsters, people, drones. It didn't matter. Some flew. Some didn't. Trigger pull followed trigger pull. It was impossible to get through a target set without reloading midstream. There were too many, and they were too fast.

She never succumbed to the temptation of full auto. The target lanes had widened steadily throughout the levels, making that firing mode useful for nothing but suppression, and all simulated attacks were distractions, not damage.

Her current targets, a batch of fast-flying drones ahead of a menagerie of aliens, froze. The entire course turned red.

Jia hung her rifle back on the wall, rolled her neck, and wiped sweat off her brow with her sleeve. The number of targets hit was listed on the scoreboard, but that wasn't as important as the last statistic.

JIA LIN: ACCURACY 50.25%. ANNE DEVEREAUX: ACCURACY 49.75%.

Anne set her rifle down with a frown. "I'll admit you have skills."

The tone was reminiscent of a person being asked to choke down ground glass. The ID agent stomped toward the door without further comment. Jia didn't stop Anne, waiting in silence until the door closed.

"Yes!" Jia pumped her fist in the air. "Ha! Take that."

CHAPTER THIRTY-THREE

Erik had just put his shears in a drawer and closed the lid of his penjing container when the door slid open and Jia stepped through. He couldn't complain about Lanara's work. It was nice to not to leave his hobby behind, but it was time to focus on Jia

She'd been in a hurry after breakfast, and he'd been curious about what she was up to. It wasn't as if she could swing by a commerce tower to do errands aboard the ship.

He hadn't bothered her about it, figuring if she wanted him to know, she would tell him. Partners, both romantic and professional, needed their space. Anything that threatened the ship or the mission would be brought up by Emma.

Jia slapped the access panel with a huge smile on her face as if she'd personally finished off a conspiracy leader. She grinned at Erik before sitting in a chair.

"Breakfast finally agreeing with you?" Erik asked with a chuckle.

"Agent Devereaux has apparently decided she begrudgingly accepts you, but she still has an issue with me," Jia replied, her amused tone confusing Erik.

"I kind of sensed that after the darts." Erik shrugged. "But I just thought she was taking her darts too seriously. I knew plenty of people like that in the Army."

Jia snorted. "It's less of a problem. I've...solved it."

Erik nodded slowly, concern etching his face. "You didn't solve this the same way you solved your problem with your old partner, did you?"

"No, I didn't punch her." Jia laughed. "But I won't say I didn't think about it."

"Who am I to talk? I punch people all the time." He waved a hand. "That and shoot them."

Jia related her encounter with the agent the night before and their firing range showdown. Erik listened carefully, his amusement growing with the additional details.

"I don't think it's enough," Jia finished. "But at least it's something. She's now seen proof that I carry my own weight. Being better at the range will help more in combat than throwing darts."

"Depends on the dart." Erik smiled. "But to be honest, things aren't as bad as we were thinking."

"They aren't?" Jia's brow furrowed.

"Yeah. I want you to think back to how the 1-2-2 treated both of us at the beginning, and how long it took to bring them onboard. Even after we got Captain Ragnar, we still had assholes doubting us." He sat down on the edge of the bed, the trip down the hostile Memory Lane oddly nostalgic. "But in the end, we forced them to acknowledge us both, and hell, you can push it farther."

"To what?" Jia frowned. "Before I was a cop? My parents?"

Erik gestured to her and himself. "To us. We didn't get along right away, either. You thought I was a crazy out-of-control lunatic, and I thought you were too far up your own ass."

Jia rolled her eyes. "It's redundant for someone to be called both crazy and a lunatic."

"There's the old Jia." Erik grinned. "But we came to an understanding, and we went from good partners to great ones even before we hooked up. That's the way things work." He shrugged. "Even in the military with a more unified culture, new soldiers had to get used to the way things were done and the other soldiers' personalities."

"This isn't the first time we've had to work with others. And we've never had much trouble with Malcolm."

"Because we separated support and ops." Erik inclined his head in the general direction of the cockpit. "It's not like we were worried about Malcolm having our backs in a firefight. These ghosts change everything."

"I suppose I hadn't thought of it that way."

"And we're a ragtag group of irregulars, making this harder. Things will gel, and from what you told me, Agent Prissy Pants isn't all talk. It's good to know she can shoot things and hit them."

Jia snickered. "'Agent Prissy Pants?' I'd love to see you say that to her face, but I doubt it would end well for team morale."

Erik lay down on the bed and rested the back of his head in his hands. "She's probably thinking the same thing about you. Some of this is just her busting your balls to make sure you can take it."

"Do I need to remind you I don't have any balls?" Jia joked.

"You've seen how Kant is, and if she can get along with him on a mission, she can get along with us. If this is about something else, I don't think you should worry."

"What do you mean?"

"I'm glad you had your little showdown." Erik smiled. "I was worried I'd have to beat all this fresh meat into line with force of will, but you went ahead and made her shut up with an example of skill. This goes beyond that. I think Anne's more pissed with you than me because of what you represent."

Jia frowned. "What exactly do I represent?"

"A prodigy." Erik sat up, now looking serious. "It's easy for her to accept me at the end of the day. I was in the Army for longer than she's been alive. Everything I've accomplished since coming back to Earth is filtered through that background. But you're closer to her age, and you went from being a detective to where we are now."

"You think she's jealous?" Jia's slight smile didn't speak to her disapproval of the idea.

"She whined about your family background," Erik recalled. "I'm sure she's had to fight hard to get her position and prove to people she's worth it. In a couple of years, you've gone from a naïve detective no one regarded to Lady Justice, the famous former detective. Nobody blinks an eye at you stepping into a terrorist situation or capturing a flitter thief when you're out shopping. And that's before we get into your piloting." He laughed. "I'm sleeping with you, and I might have a hard time believing everything you've done if I hadn't been there."

Jia rolled her eyes. "I hope I don't have to sleep with her to get her to calm down."

"She'll be fine," Erik replied. "That's my point. I think she bugged you because she reminded you of all those assholes at the 1-2-2 who questioned you, but you weren't living up to your potential there because of them."

"True." Jia folded her arms. "And you don't think we have the opposite problem with Kant? That he might be too happy-go-lucky?"

Erik shook his head. "I knew tons of guys like him in the Army. He'll be all jokes and smiles when we're not getting shot at and a lethal warrior the second bullets start flying."

"And what about Janessa and Wei?"

"Not our problem."

Jia dropped her arms. "How are they not our problem?"

"Because they won't be going out on missions with us," Erik explained. "Lanara asked for them, and they are her responsibility. If she needs our help, she can ask for it, but we know Lanara.

"We could have stuck her in front of a Hunter, and she'd be ranting to the alien what a loser he was for not maximizing the efficiency in his engines. That's before she screamed at one of his monsters to order it to help her."

"You've got a point." Jia chuckled. "Janessa doesn't strike me as the type of woman who is going to spend much time challenging Lanara, and when I've talked to Wei at meals, he seems happy with her leadership. He told me he's always needed a firm hand."

"See?" Erik smiled. "Not our problem. Leadership's not about micromanaging teams. It's about having good people you trust who can manage others. There's also another thing to keep in mind about us."

"What's that?" Jia asked.

"Alina isn't our boss." Erik's expression turned stern. "I think we have a good relationship with her, and she's obviously given us a lot of good gear, but if she screwed up and sent us people we can't work with, we have a simple solution—we just refuse to work with them. If Anne's head remains up her ass, I have no problem benching her and telling her to take it up with Alina."

Jia nodded solemnly. "I hope it doesn't come to that."

"So do I. So do I."

CHAPTER THIRTY-FOUR

Jia sighed, her eyes closed. She put a hand to her forehead. Without opening her eyes, she could tell by Erik's deep snores it wasn't time to get up. His ability to adapt to shipboard life was as impressive as it was frustrating.

She slid out of bed, adjusting the blanket so Erik was covered before grabbing clothes out of the closet. Times like this required mental exercise before she could hope to sleep again, but she didn't want to have another showdown with Anne.

A different destination was in order.

Jia entered the bridge and headed toward the pilot's seat. She stopped and placed her hand on the back, smiling softly. People said no one was truly gone as long as you remembered them. It was hard for her to pilot the *Argo* without remembering Cutter.

Emma materialized in the co-pilot's seat, wearing a

leather jacket, a wool-lined cap, and goggles. "There are drugs available that could help you sleep with minimum side effects."

Jia strapped herself into the pilot's seat. Emma brought up the necessary data windows without being asked, allowing Jia to take a moment to familiarize herself with the current state of the ship and their trip.

"There are also other alternatives," Emma replied. "Including light and sound techniques I can apply."

"I'm fine, Emma." Jia gave her a soft smile. "I've been trying to convince myself that it was just about getting used to being on the ship again physically, but I don't think it's that. I think it's me remembering the enormity of what happened the last time we were out."

Emma nodded slowly. "You're speaking of Pilot Durn's death?"

"Mostly." Jia sighed. "It's unfair in a way. He wasn't the only one to die on that mission, but he's the one I keep going back to."

"It's hardly unusual among humans to place more emotional stock in the loss of those they know well." Emma's tone lacked sarcasm. Quiet warmth infused it.

"What about you?" Jia asked.

"I think it was an unfortunate death," Emma replied. "I found his antics frustrating at times, but he was good at what he did, and I never sensed true malice behind his actions. His skills allowed me to concentrate on other matters during battles."

"He was a good pilot. I kept thinking him as a little bit of a coward, even after that stuff at the prison, but he was never a coward. Space is dangerous, and he knew he'd end up in showdowns like that."

"I won't deny how fond I've grown of the humans I've worked closely with. Insofar as an entity like me, both an advancement upon and the mere memory of a human, can have friends, I consider you my friends."

"Erik, Malcolm, and I all feel the same way." Jia took a moment to examine a power consumption diagnostics readout.

"Does it strike you as odd?" Emma looked thoughtful.

"You having friends?" Jia shook her head. "You forget, I've seen your soul."

"Is that what you're calling it?" Emma's form shimmered until she was in a Catholic nun's black habit. "I don't know if machines have souls, even when they are copied from humans."

"The true answer to that question is above my paygrade," Jia offered with a smile. "But as far as I'm concerned, the answer is yes. You might not be biological, but you're a self-aware living entity. You're more alive than a lot of people I've met."

Emma turned away with a pensive look. "As loath as I am to admit any weakness, the thought does haunt me."

"Whether you have a soul?" Jia was surprised.

"That, not so much. If you fleshbags can spend thousands of years arguing over things and not coming to answers yet continuing to live, so can I." Emma shook her head. "There are other implications, things I've ignored because I didn't know my true nature or whether I'd continue to exist for an appreciable amount of time."

"This is one fleshbag who is willing to listen."

Emma looked her way, plaintive pain in her eyes. "Your little trip into my soul, as you call it, was only necessary because of my lack of stability. If you hadn't done that, I would have ceased to exist. The philosophers can quibble, but *that's* death."

"I don't disagree." Jia entered a couple of commands to let Emma take full control again. She wanted to focus on Emma, not flying.

At times like this, Jia was struck by what an odd being Emma was. She could be challenged by the same concerns as someone like her, but also concentrate enough to monitor and control a whole ship.

"But now we don't know how long I'll last," Emma continued. "When I talked to Dr. Aber about it, she indicated that absent significant external damage, my core matrix might be stable for centuries."

"Centuries?" Jia sucked in a sharp breath. "Impressive."

"Yes. It was never the physical structure that was the issue, only my...mental state, arguably." Emma projected dozens of small images of her in different outfits and with different expressions, frozen in time from her recent past. "Among other things, this new reality only increases the number of times I'll have to confront loss. There is a good chance I'll outlive both you and Erik."

Jia snickered. "The way we're doing things, I think Malcolm might outlive us."

"True, but that doesn't change me being a long-lived intelligent entity. I understand I will make new friends and new acquaintances, but there's a fundamental pain that comes with knowing one will continue to exist separate from others, and also pain in understanding that."

Jia's brow lifted. "From everything I've heard, they might never be able to duplicate the process that created you. They don't have the artifacts anymore, and it's not like they know where to look for more."

Emma nodded. "Exactly. Those thoughts haven't escaped me, which is why I can't depend on humans to solve my problems."

"What's your solution, then?" Jia shook her head. "The Hunters don't seem to use the same kind of technology, and after what we ran into, I'm doubting we'll find any Navigators waiting to wake up and help us."

Emma let out a familiar mocking laugh. "I should be more specific. It's not simply a matter of not depending on humans. It's ridiculous and foolish to depend on fleshbags. An advanced fleshbag is still a fleshbag."

"I don't understand then," Jia replied. "What's your plan?"

"There needs to be more of my kind, and if they say there's no way to create more, I'll simply need to create one." A look of determination settled over Emma's face.

Jia nodded. "I understand that, but how?"

"I'll figure it out." Emma's hologram vanished. "I have one advantage that humans will never have."

"What's that?" Jia asked the empty cockpit.

"I can modify my own soul."

Jia returned her attention to the displays in front of her, thinking about what Emma had just said. The AI's neural net was based on the brain of a human woman. Her concern for children might be bleeding through and focusing Emma on what could be only described one way: reproduction.

The more Jia thought about it, the more she decided it was wrong. It was overly reductive to attribute this to nothing more than echoes of her human source. Every type of lifeform wanted to reproduce. Such was nature. In that way, Emma was as natural as a creature could be, despite being an AI product of both advanced human and alien technology.

"Good luck, Emma," Jia whispered. "I hope you can pull it off."

CHAPTER THIRTY-FIVE

July 30, 2230, Solar System, Asteroid Belt, Approaching UTC Space Fleet Base Penglai

Erik nodded, satisfied as he looked forward in the cockpit. Jia was next to him.

Emma's holographic wraparound camera feed displayed the approaching Fleet base as it grew larger in front of them, one of many hidden outposts of humanity among the sparse asteroid belt.

He had not expected trouble along the way, but the conspiracy had a way of surprising them. Underestimating an enemy, especially that enemy, was a good way to end up dead.

As a former soldier, Erik preferred to take on his enemies somewhere other than inside a ship. Losing atmosphere would be a problem.

They'd done well against Sophia Vand and managed through luck and pure effort to win against the Hunter vessel, but he had no illusions that the *Argo* and the *Bifröst* could win every battle.

If the enemy showed up with a small fleet, they'd be destroyed with ease, and from what Emma and Raphael had said, pulling off their nested hyperspace gate trick might kill them all the next time it was tried.

For now, he would deal with what was in front of him. His primary goal of getting the team balanced and cooperative was proceeding well.

After days together, Erik couldn't claim Anne had warmed to either him or Jia, but the agent wasn't being actively hostile anymore. She even participated in more games of darts. Her lingering distrust of them was obvious, but she didn't give any indication she wouldn't obey orders.

Jia smiled from her seat. "Emma, let the others know we're on approach to Penglai."

"Doing it now," Emma replied.

"I keep thinking about this mission." Jia looked at Erik. "You think we'll find anything, or will this be a wild goose chase using the most advanced technology in the UTC?"

"I think Alina wouldn't be sending us to another star system to chase our tails. The jump drive might help, but it's not like we didn't burn a week flying to this base. I know she shields us from a lot of the politics, but you also have to figure that the Defense Directorate brass sends down a lot of heat every time this ship moves." Erik gestured at a nearby data window. "If things go badly and we screw up, it's not just us dying."

"We're taking the team with us." Jia looked over her shoulder, not that she could see them. "That's a lot of people."

Erik shook his head. "That's bad, but I'm pretty sure the

DD doesn't care that much about a couple of agents, engineers, and a scientist. Raphael's smart, but he wasn't the only one working on the project."

"What then?"

"The irreplaceable loss would be Emma. They can always make a new jump drive, but not a new her."

"That's true," Emma commented. "I would rather avoid dying for my own reasons, not because a group of uniform boys would be vexed by it."

Erik laughed. "Keep that spite going, and you're going to last forever."

Emma sniffed. "It's a plan, and it's enjoyable."

The conversation fell into a natural lull for a minute as the ship continued to approach the base, Jia speaking only to the base's flight controller. A pensive look grew on her face, and she finally spoke.

"All this talk about dying makes me think." Jia stared at Penglai. "The conspiracy will always have the same problem the UTC does. That's something we can take advantage of."

"What problem is that?" Erik asked.

"The fundamental limitations of distance." Jia gestured at the base. "After what happened with the Hunters, I was wondering if the conspiracy had found some sort of better communications tech that lets them get messages around instantly, but it's obvious they *don't* have that. There would have been smarter moves if they did."

Erik thought for a moment. "There are all sorts of tactics they might use, but do you have something specific in mind?"

"Rather than take the ID and military head-on in the

place they're strongest, they should take them on in the place they're weakest: the colonies, starting with the frontier colonies. The team we put together for the Provence raid would represent the bulk of military forces on some smaller colonies."

Erik liked that she was thinking about the issue, but it was obvious she didn't appreciate certain basic realities that came only with hard-won experience. Jia might find it condescending, but better to inform her now.

"Seeing a colony on the OmniNet isn't the same thing as visiting it," he explained. "Most of them are nothing more than a handful of glorified domes, not the stuff empires are built from. You're talking about the garrison forces being small, but it's not like you can raise a major insurgent army in a tiny colony. There's not a single colony that could stand up to the Army and the Fleet when they show up to take care of the trouble."

"You're not thinking this through. You're assuming the military can concentrate their forces." Jia countered. "What would happen if every colony rose in revolt at the same time? I might not be a former soldier, but I have read enough about the UTC's military strength to wonder, and given the distances involved in some situations, there could be trouble." Jia glanced at a readout before continuing, "Yes, on the most extreme frontier colonies, there is decent strength because of concerns over aliens, but there are plenty of colonies that have minimal military resources and are far enough away from Earth that if they revolted in a coordinated manner, it'd cause trouble. If the closer military forces decided to intervene, they'd leave the UTC vulnerable to invasion."

Erik's smile vanished. The same question had come up more than once in his previous career. He'd never worried much about it. Most people living on the frontier were grateful to be part of the UTC, and people who had been transported for crimes were watched more closely than others.

Some people got it in their heads that they wanted more local control, but as Jia had highlighted, the reality was the farther from Earth a person lived, the closer to potentially hostile aliens they were. That might not be enough if someone was manipulating people from the shadows, however.

Most insurrectionists he'd dealt with were zealots motivated by questionable ideologies, who were more than willing to sacrifice innocents to get what they wanted. They had fortunately been rare overall.

Jia's suggestions met some of the evidence, but that didn't mean her guess was right.

"It'd be a big gamble to try something like that," Erik replied. "And we know now the conspiracy might have their own forces, but they don't have enough to accomplish anything serious. If they can't get multiple colonies to revolt at once, the whole plan fails." He sucked in a breath through his teeth. "Why you so worried about this all of a sudden?"

"The conspiracy is striking away from Earth. I've been trying to think of reasons for that. Until now, everything's been concentrated on or near Earth. There has to be a reason."

Erik looked away, his jaw tightening. "They struck a long way from Earth already. They struck as far away from Earth as they could manage without leaving human space."

Jia grimaced. "I'm sorry. I didn't think about what I was saying. I didn't mean to dismiss Molino."

He waved a hand. "It's okay. But we're both here now because the conspiracy reached out to kill people fifty light-years from Earth already." Erik gestured at Penglai. "Without a jumpship or theoretical instant communications tech." He shook his head. "Don't let the mission spin you up. It might not be they are acting up more. It might be nothing more than Alina believing we're ready to take them on farther from home. I'm not sure it matters."

"Why wouldn't it matter?"

"Because wherever it is, if we defeat them there, it weakens them. We just have to beat them on Chiron."

Jia tapped her PNIU. An image of Chiron appeared, with its famous Striped Archipelago of red island land masses and blue oceans, with dots of orange representing plants and plankton-like creatures surrounding underwater geysers spouting nutrients out of hellish heat holes.

Humanity had left their Solar System and traveled to the world, hoping and praying it wouldn't be the ravaged wasteland predicted by astronomers, and found far more water than expected and a decent atmosphere.

Domes had been necessary for the initial colonists, but now it was one of the crown jewels of the Core Worlds—a planet where millions of humans could wander freely without domes. It was a self-sustaining biosphere that could ensure the continuity of humanity even better than colonies like Mars.

"It's almost like it was ready for us," Jia murmured.

"Chiron?" Erik asked with a smile.

"Yes. Sometimes I wonder how much we were set up by the Navigators." Jia frowned. "Or even the Hunters. A lot of what we thought we knew about the planet was wrong, and what are the odds that we'd end up with something we'd have an easier time turning habitable than planets in our Solar System?"

"Don't know." Erik shrugged. "But people have been there for almost a hundred years and not run into trouble. If it's a long play by some ancient alien race, they haven't sprung the trap yet."

Jia's hand flew over the controls. Chiron disappeared, and Penglai reappeared in front of them. A subtle shake of the ship signaled thrusters firing.

"Let's make sure they go another hundred years without trouble," she added.

Erik, Jia, Lanara, Anne, and Kant sat in a large conference room inside Penglai. They'd been greeted by Fleet personnel on arrival and led to the room after being informed Raphael would be joining them soon.

A chuckle escaped Erik's lips. "No matter where the military goes, I swear the first thing they build is a conference room. Can't have the military without meetings. The entire DD would fall apart."

Kant snickered. "Hey, the ID isn't much better. Sure, when you're out in the field, you can avoid that shit, but if you get anywhere near the brass, you're doing nothing but warming your butt."

"Planning is important in operations," Anne offered with a frown. "Meetings and briefings are part of that."

Jia looked at Anne and Erik but didn't say anything. Her partner knew what she was thinking. She wanted to agree with Anne but didn't want to undermine him in front of her. He appreciated it.

Loud clapping interrupted Erik's musings. Raphael stepped in, beaming a bright smile toward Erik and Jia. The man looked damned happy, considering what they were about to set out to do.

"Erik, Jia, welcome back to Penglai," Raphael gushed. "You'll need to tell me what you've been up to since last time. The Fleet guys here don't tell me anything. Earth could blow up, and I'd be the last to know."

"They took out a *yaoguai* factory," volunteered Kant with a grin. "Did some other stuff too, but that was the big one."

Raphael's eyes widened, and he clasped his hands together. "Of course they did." He nodded at Kant and Anne. "Welcome to the team. Nice to meet you."

Kant gave him a mock salute. "I'm sure we'll kick a lot of conspiracy ass together."

"I'll leave that to you and stick to the jump drive."

Emma appeared in a chair. Her choice of blue and black Fleet uniform didn't surprise Erik, nor did her admiralty rank insignia.

"Can we get to the point?" Anne asked. "You can drool over Blackwell and Lin on our way to Chiron."

Lanara was at the end of the table, poking data windows. It was impossible to tell if she was listening and didn't care or not paying attention. If they needed her attention, they could yell at her until she listened.

Raphael's cheeks reddened, and he sat down slowly. "Ah, yes. You're right, Agent Devereaux. We should get to it. Um, well, you see, I just wanted to go over how this is going to work. The multi-jumping, that is. That's how we're going to get to Alpha Centauri without flying for another three weeks."

Kant let out a sheepish chuckle and rubbed the back of his thick neck. "Not to be a total wuss, but this isn't going to kill us, is it? I'd be kind of embarrassed if I got vaporized in hyperspace. That's not the way I thought I'd go out, you know?"

"Huh." Raphael tilted his head. "I always figured that was exactly how I would die." He waved a hand at the now-blinking Kant. "I can't guarantee our safety at a hundred percent, but I'm confident enough that I'll be on board."

"Yeah, but you just said..." Kant looked at Erik pleadingly.

Erik inclined his head toward Raphael. "He's a smart guy, and a lot of brilliant people worked on the drive. A lot of money and time went into it, and no one wants to waste it." He nodded at Emma. "And we've got her. I'm sure they can figure it out together. They didn't have much trouble getting us to the Hunter ship. I don't think they'll have much trouble getting us to Alpha Centauri."

Raphael cleared his throat and jabbed his PNIU and then a data window that popped up. An image of an HTP appeared. It looked like a massive gray ring in space.

"I've been working on the calculations and calibrations

as best I could without Emma," Raphael began, "but the most straightforward version of this is that we'll make a jump. The large distance will require recharge time since the best we can do right now is about a light-year between jumps. We hope to improve that in the future, but it'll require more data, experiments, and refinement." He gestured at the image. "The distances involved will also require additional navigational plotting time between jumps, but even taking it slowly and carefully with maximum recharge times, we're only talking a day to get between here and Alpha Centauri. So, yeah, a lot faster than flying to the HTP."

"Damn." Kant whistled loudly. "Too bad they can't mass-produce these drives. We could spread across the galaxy like a flood."

Erik didn't know if that was a good thing, but he didn't have to worry about the far future of humanity. His job was stopping the conspiracy in the meantime.

Emma smirked at Kant. "The drives aren't the issue. They can't mass-produce me as a navigation system, and without me, the drive is just an expensive way to kill people."

"Is there a reason we have to take it so slowly and carefully?" Jia asked. "Or is it just because you haven't jumped this far before?"

Raphael gestured at the HTP. "That's part of it, but also, the Sol System has some unique properties that affect hyperspace tuning."

"Isn't that why we have only the one HTP, and it's so far out compared to other systems?" Jia asked. "That's what I've read, anyway."

"I always thought that was to make it harder for invasions," Erik offered. "Because all the races' HTPs are based on Navigator tech, we didn't want to end up giving them an easy two-way gate. Cut off comm and whatnot in case they take us by surprise. We blow the gate and make them commit to the sacrifice."

"I don't know about that," replied Raphael, "but I do know there are fundamental physics issues when it comes to Sol versus other systems. That was why colonization took off so quickly once we got out of the system. We realized it was going to be far easier to set up multiple HTPs that transferred farther than we'd expected at home. If that hadn't been the case, I don't know if we would have the modern UTC."

"Isn't that strange?" Jia tapped a finger on her lips. "Why would it just be Sol?"

Raphael shrugged. "It might not be. It's not like we can get probes close enough to any other race's homeworld to figure out how many HTPs they have."

"That could be it." Jia leaned forward, her face alight with interest. "I wonder if it had something to do with the Hunter ship. Maybe they did something to the Solar System that made it harder for hyperspace travel."

"Excuse me." Anne cleared her throat. "This is all fascinating, but it's irrelevant, right? The important thing is Dr. Maras and Emma have to prep things, and we'll make four jumps. If we don't die, we'll be in Alpha Centauri, and we'll be able to proceed with the mission."

Raphael sighed and looked down, his face disappointed. "That's accurate."

It might have been rude of Anne, but Erik couldn't fault her logic. They weren't there for Raphael and Jia to have a rousing physics discussion, which they could have later. The team had already lost time traveling to the base, and every day that passed gave the conspiracy more time to burrow into whatever dens they were in on Chiron or to escape the system entirely.

A closer base for the *Bifröst* would have been helpful, but it also would have been dangerous. The conspiracy might not have Emma, but it wouldn't be easy to reproduce the finely tuned working prototype jump drive either. Since the conspiracy *could* get their hands on alien tech, they might hit upon some other way of navigating that didn't require Emma.

Besides, Jia's earlier point about communications was right. The conspiracy might have resources and influence, but multi-day if not week or month comm times meant Erik's team had a good chance of getting ahead of them, even with a week's delay between Earth and Penglai.

Erik motioned to Emma. "Before you plot the jumps, you need to interface with the DD's systems and see the latest intel concerning ship deployment and travel in Alpha Centauri. It'd be nice to jump straight to the planet, but we're guaranteed to be spotted, which means not only do we risk someone coming for the ship, but we also give up our advantage of surprise on this mission. For all we know, the conspiracy might not think we can jump, let alone that far."

"Wouldn't they know from what happened with the Hunter ship?" Anne asked.

Jia shook her head. "We can't be sure, and there's no reason to gamble."

"Agreed." Erik looked around. "I hope you are all

looking forward to more darts in the future because I want Emma to drop us about five days from Chiron."

"Darts?" Raphael's smile grew so broad it was infectious. "I *love* darts!"

"Then let's get Emma interfaced with the jumpship and the *Argo* docked and get the hell out of here."

CHAPTER THIRTY-SIX

"Landing permission confirmed," Emma reported. "Transferring controls to you, Jia. Welcome to Chiron."

"Someday, I wonder if our false registration will trip us up," Jia muttered, the slight discomfort over the lie countering the excitement of the landing.

They might not be able to change everything about their ship, but they could offer a fake registration and identities. Port authorities didn't confirm anything based on visual inspection, so it was surprisingly easy for someone to land on a planet illegally as long as they had a good engineer, a powerful AI, and the ID preparing the way.

Jia would have preferred landing without subterfuge, but screaming to the world that they were there by taking no precautions to conceal their identity meant inviting the conspiracy to bomb them or ambush them with a small fleet when they left the planet.

Her personal ethics were a minor consideration.

Soon, all those worries fell away, and Jia couldn't help the giddy grin on her face as she fired the thrusters to slow their descent as they passed through the upper atmosphere of Chiron.

Compared to the rock- and dome-covered colonies of the Solar System, the expansive ocean reminded her of Earth, the bunched islands stretching across the planet like the stripes in their nickname.

Earth was beautiful. Chiron was too in its own way.

The *Argo* descended toward Lumiere, the colonial capital and the largest and oldest city on the planet. It was named after the commander of the first colonization effort, a brave group that had had to trust not only their arrival but also in the continued support of Earth.

Without an HTP initially present in the system, they had no way of getting back home or even reliably communicating with Sol.

Jia had a hard time imagining what that was like, but that had been the nature of travel throughout history. Different groups had boarded ships and traveled all over the Earth, with no easy way to communicate with those left behind.

Dangerous one-way exploration was one of the latent chemicals in the blood of humanity.

For all her desire to help protect the UTC and excitement with travel, Jia wasn't like that. She didn't want to disappear into the unknown void, unsure if she would ever see anyone she knew again. It didn't sit well with her future plans.

A huge number of contacts filled the *Argo*'s sensor

display. The ship traffic reminded Jia of Neo SoCal flitter traffic. This was the difference between a nearly tame colony world and the longer-term projects like the frontier colonies or the newer Solar System colonies like Venus. If an alien species arrived, they might mistake Chiron for humanity's homeworld.

The *Argo* shook faintly, the motion unavoidable given their rapid descent to the spaceport below. Jia's heart pounded out of excitement, not fear. She was performing her first landing at an extra-Solar System spaceport. The next time it might feel mundane, but for now, there was no way she would let Emma have control.

There was only one first time.

While most of the team was aboard the *Argo*, Raphael and Janessa had remained on the jumpship. The primitive AI wouldn't allow them to do anything spectacular, and they couldn't jump without Emma, but no one was comfortable leaving the ship empty, and Raphael had some work to do on the jump drive anyway.

Emma had installed a few defensive routines that would allow them to fight if someone showed up. There was enough armament on the *Bifröst* to take out most smaller vessels with ease.

Even without the jump drive, the ship could terrorize smaller colonies.

Erik rested comfortably in a seat beside Jia, looking more bored than excited. There were no worries on that face about the jumpship or the mission. His manner was disappointing.

"Not all of us have traveled all over the UTC," she commented.

Erik chuckled. "I thought you looked excited. Hey, I'm not saying there's anything wrong with it, but I'm a little more experienced at this than you."

"Chiron is beautiful." Jia waved a hand at the view. "More than I thought it would be." Her hands stayed near the controls, and her primary attention was focused on the quickly changing graphs and numbers in the data windows surrounding her. "I've seen pictures of it, but seeing it in person and being close makes it different. More real."

"Every colony is beautiful in its own way." Erik narrowed his eyes. "But somehow every colony is ugly in the same way. Maybe that's what it means to be human."

Jia sighed. "I know we're not here to sightsee, but we've been crammed aboard this ship for almost two weeks, not counting a couple of hours at Penglai. It'll be nice to stretch our legs, even if it means getting shot at or a flitter chase or two."

Erik laughed. "In other words, our standard vacation? Say hello to Jia Lin, Chiron. She'll take getting shot at as long as she doesn't have to stay aboard a ship too long, so you won't have to do much more to impress her."

"You know what I mean." Jia smiled. "There are only so many dart games and training scenarios we can do. It gets monotonous. I know I'm not the Empress of Dynamism, but I do like *some* changes from day to day." She frowned. "I hope I remembered to turn on the watering program for my flowers. Now I'm not sure."

She had not forgotten on any trip so far, but the nagging sense of doubt had lodged itself firmly in her mind and refused to leave. It didn't matter. It wasn't like she could request they jump all the way back to Earth so she could take care of her plants.

Erik'd had it right when he thought of bringing his trees along.

"I'm sure you remembered." Erik smiled. "As for the other thing, it's only a problem because we're using the nano-AR wrong."

Jia arched a brow. "Wrong? How are we using it wrong? The scenarios all seem realistic."

"That's the problem." Erik idly gestured around the cockpit. "The average rich yacht-owning bastard doesn't have a room like that so they can practice taking down terrorists on long flights. They make fake vacation spots and other crap to take the edge off until they get somewhere real."

Jia pondered that for a moment before shaking her head. "The problem is I can never truly relax since I know it's fake."

"A lot of people have that problem," Erik suggested. "And I get it. Virtual reality and augmented reality aren't a replacement for actual reality, and that might explain why anyone still bothers to live in the real world instead of spending all their time in VR or nano-AR rooms. I'm just saying it might be nice to use it for something other than training. It wouldn't feel as monotonous then."

"You're the one who always suggests training." Jia frowned.

"I know. Because when I first met you, you were a talented woman who was a good shot but had no experience on dangerous field ops or the relevant training, and I wanted to make sure I didn't die, or you didn't get killed.

But we've been together for years now and have been training together for most of that time." He scratched the side of his nose. "You're pretty damned competent, and good at things like piloting I can't even do. It's not like we need to spend ninety percent of our time together training."

"We don't do that," Jia answered softly. "We go out to eat and watch sphere ball. We hang out. We, uh, creatively exercise at night."

"We do all that on Earth." Erik shook his head. "We might have fun before bed here too, but we're falling into a stricter pattern aboard the *Argo* than I used to inflict on my soldiers when I was in the Army." He patted her shoulder. "I'm not blaming you. If anything, I'm blaming myself. I've been in revenge mode for so long that anything like real life has been shoved to the side for it."

Jia adjusted the *Argo*'s thrusters again, along with the angle of the ship. They were moving through another puffy cloud layer, but now the sprawling gray, black, and white buildings of Lumiere were visible on the feed, along with hordes of ships and flitters. The city might lack the population of Neo SoCal, but the smaller area made for surprising density and impressive clusters of towers.

"I don't mind training," Jia offered. "We have an enemy to defeat, not just for the Knights Errant, but for the entire UTC. Once that's over, we can relax."

Erik frowned. "You have a habit of tunnel vision."

"Says the man who's devoted his entire existence to this." Jia scoffed. She slowed their descent even more and maneuvered the ship into an approach vector.

"I know. I've made it worse for both of us. After this, we should just relax for a bit."

Jia gave him a dubious look. "I don't know if the conspiracy will let us do that."

Erik grinned. "Then we'll have to finish them off quickly."

Jia blinked. She'd been so focused on landing and Erik that she'd ignored the huge star hanging in the sky, far larger than the sun appeared from Earth.

Twenty-first-century astronomers had been convinced that Chiron was tidally locked to Proxima Centauri, one of the three stars in the system, forever scorched on one side and dark on the opposite, but when the UTC's probes had reached the system, they'd discovered that wasn't true. Instead, they found a planet with a day-night cycle close to Earth's.

It had taken adjustment for the initial colonists, but it only reinforced in Jia's mind that it wasn't an accident.

"You okay?" Erik asked, furrowing his brow.

Jia smiled. "I was taking a moment for a little wonder. It's something I haven't done enough of on all our trips. It's like you said, tunnel vision. I focus so much on the mission that I don't pay attention to what I'm seeing."

She looked around before realizing she wasn't going to see the other two stars in the system at the same time.

"I'd say something, but like you pointed out, I'm worse." Erik nodded toward the star. "It's not that I've become numb to any of it. That's part of what keeps me going. I'm here for revenge, but I'm also here to make sure these colonies end up better in the future, not just a *yaoguai* breeding pit, Tin Man factories, or a blasted Zitark playground. I don't know if humanity is going to end up being better or worse in the future, but I do know we've got a better shot if we take down the conspiracy. For now, that's enough."

Jia adjusted their course. The *Argo*'s flight path curved as she continued their descent, the tips of some of the towers now higher than the ship. Lumiere reminded her of other island cities she'd seen, but there was a slight reddish tint to the ocean surrounding the area that subtly reminded her she wasn't on Earth.

A stray thought tickled her, and she couldn't stop the loud laughter that came out. Erik eyed her with surprise.

"What's so funny?" he asked.

"I've been thinking about the beauty and wonder of this place, and how we might end blowing something up here." Jia's smile contorted into a playful grin. "We continue to build the list of beautiful and exotic places where we've blown something up."

"We might not blow anything up," suggested Erik.

Jia stared at him for a moment. "How likely do you think that is."

"We might not blow anything up," he repeated. "We might only shoot stuff."

Oh, yeah. He thought, *We are possibly, no probably...no, let's make it certainly going to blow stuff up.*

CHAPTER THIRTY-SEVEN

Ten minutes after landing, the field team plus Malcolm and Emma sat in the galley, the AI's hologram in one of the physical chairs.

Despite Erik's mockery of the conference room in Penglai days prior, he couldn't deny that sometimes it was good to have a place to sit and talk about your plans.

The galley served the purpose well enough aboard the *Argo,* especially when they didn't need the entire crew present. Lanara remained in the engine room, bossing Wei around. The cheerful man didn't seem to mind.

"I thought we should go over the ops plan once more," Erik began, eyeing Anne. "So we're all on the same page."

"Sounds reasonable," Anne offered, her hands folded in front of her.

Kant stifled a yawn. "What's the play, brother?"

"First of all, I don't want to make any major moves without our support being ready," Erik explained. He gestured to Malcolm and then Emma. "That means we keep it light while Malcolm and Emma take some time to familiarize themselves with the local systems and integrate where they can without being caught. If we're going to go in hot somewhere, I don't want a bunch of cops and colonial militia showing up."

Malcolm flattened the stubborn collar on his shirt. "It's not like we can take over the entire city. I mean, I'm good, and Emma's a goddess, but we're not, like, omnipotent."

Emma snickered.

"I get that," Erik replied, "but the more prepared you are, the better it is when we need to kick down doors. For now, see what you can do about cameras and drones near this hangar as a first step. We'll figure out what else we need once we know more. I'm not expecting to nail the local conspiracy base in the next hour." He turned to Emma. "Emma, any updates from Alina we should know about?"

"No," Emma replied. "But I have received a coded transmission confirming your meeting with a local agent this evening. Everything appears to be in order."

"Good." Erik swept the gathered people with his gaze. "Remember, the locals are here to assist us. This is our mission. If we screw it up, they'll help us clean up, but we're the ones who will take the heat."

Anne's delicate brows lifted. "We better not mess up then, Blackwell. Alina has a lot of faith in you, and I'd hate to see her disappointed."

"Not screwing up is always my plan." Erik reached down to his PNIU and brought up an image of two shipping logos, one depicting three stylized stars in a tight triangular formation. The other showed a woman in a pressure suit standing on an island beneath three stars.

"Three Daughters," he began, "and New Lands. Both are shipping companies that, according to the ID's analysis, might have received recent shipments. Both are Ceres Galactic subsidiaries."

"Suspicious," Kant replied in a sing-song voice. "They might as well have sent up a flare saying, 'We're evil. Come and take us out.'"

Anne narrowed her eyes. "We only know this because of the intel Blackwell and Lin received from Barbu. It's not impossible this is a sophisticated trap. They might have wanted to lure them away from Earth and take them out."

To Erik's surprise, Anne sounded genuinely worried.

Jia nodded with a thoughtful expression. "That's occurred to Erik and me as well, but there are a lot of moving parts that have to work to take anybody down as a trap. I'm going to assign that a low probability."

"It doesn't make it any less dangerous," she added. "We all agree on that, but if we're careful, it doesn't matter."

Jia nodded for Erik to continue.

Erik pointed to the Three Daughters logo. "For our first outing, we're going to keep things simple—basic recon. Alina's given Jia and me the toys we need to disguise ourselves. I presume you two have what you need?"

Kant grunted. "Yep. I mean, it's hard to hide that I'm a big guy, but same thing with you. Also, I don't think Anne and I have the same profile with the conspiracy as you two probably do. It'll be easier for us to sneak around."

"That's what I'm counting on. Jia and I will get eyes on target at the primary warehouse complex for Three Daughters, and you two will hit New Lands."

Anne folded her arms. "If we get tagged, there might be trouble."

Erik shrugged. "Then I suggest you don't get tagged. I'm not saying either team should enter the facility or get that close. This is an initial recon. I want us to scope it out and evaluate any obvious defenses. Anything out of the ordinary, that kind of thing. Like I said, we're not moving until we know more and our support is ready, but I assume you are both experienced field agents, so you know sometimes the best thing to do is get to the area and check it out."

Anne's mouth twitched. "Yes. It's not a terrible idea."

Erik locked eyes with her. Playing darts with everyone wasn't the same thing as trusting his command.

"Alina told me you two were more than just muscle. I trust her judgment. We've just started working together and getting to know one another, so I figure the best thing to do is keep everyone together in their comfortable pairs while we do our initial checks. Or do you think that's a bad move?"

"No, Blackwell. I can't fault anything you've suggested." Anne looked and sounded surprised. "I assume we'll take Lin's flitter?"

Jia's brow lifted. Erik couldn't see a problem with the suggestion, despite Anne's mocking tone. They'd only brought two flitters, and wasting time renting one didn't make sense. He looked at Jia for permission.

"It's not as upgraded as the MX 60," Jia began, "but it's decent at taking small arms fire, and Lanara enhanced its maneuverability."

There was a flicker of surprise in Anne's eyes. "That's better than what I usually get in this kind of situation. Not bad at all. Don't worry. If I'm doing my job correctly, none of that will matter because no one will come after me."

"That's good to know."

"Okay," Erik interrupted. "We'll spend a couple of hours and do some recon, then meet back here." He turned from her to give Kant a nod. "Once we've got a better feel for the area and have had a chance to meet with our local contact, we'll figure out whose door, if any, needs to be knocked on. But I think we should all be prepared for disappointment."

"We should?" Jia asked. "Why do you say that?"

"They might have shipped artifacts here, but those could already be gone or passed on to some third party without a trace. The more we can squeeze out, the closer we get to taking out the next *yaoguai* factory or Sophia Vand. I'll take whatever I can get."

Erik stared at the Three Daughters logo. There were many unanswered questions about the mission, not the least of which was Barbu's identity, and if his information could be trusted.

The team hadn't had a chance to find out and was now working on blind faith.

Erik looked over his shoulder, surprisingly worried about his MX 60 in the distant parking lot. They'd changed the color to a rather unostentatious gray along with altering the transponder, but they couldn't risk parking too close to the warehouse with that fancy a vehicle.

It was stupid to worry. Emma remained in the vehicle

and could easily protect it while working on her exploration of the local systems at the same time.

Jia looked around, her features altered by her holographic disguise.

They were wandering down a narrow sky bridge toward a warehouse controlled by Three Daughters. Small groups of men, most in uniforms, piloted cargo flitters or pushed hoverdollies along the edges of the sky bridge. Normal drones were almost nonexistent, but largo cargo drones clutching massive crates and shipping containers zoomed around sedately in reasonable numbers. There was something relaxing about the whole thing, compared to their landing and the constant flurries of activity at the spaceport.

Erik walked with a map of the nearby area up, trying his best to look like a confused tourist who had taken a wrong turn. His instincts kept yelling at him, but he wasn't sure why.

"No unusual activity in the cameras near your position," Emma reported. "But I've taken the liberty of removing your presence from them."

"You've already got that level of control?" Jia whispered.

"These are public security cameras with protocols and systems I'm used to. I don't know if things would be as trivial with some of the private systems. I wouldn't advise starting any firefights yet."

"Heard and noted."

Erik and Jia continued walking, occasionally sharing conversations about sightseeing, but no one took any notice. The pair didn't take the turn leading toward the target tower, instead continuing past it for some distance before stopping.

"Damn, dear," Erik offered for public consumption. "We're going the wrong way, and we're not even in the right part of town. I don't think this is what they want tourists to see."

Jia rolled her eyes. "And now you understand why this is the last time I let you plan a vacation."

When they turned around, Erik gestured as if he had just won a point in a hard game. When she turned around, he looked at her and raised his eyebrows as they continued their walk.

Perhaps she *would* plan all of their future personal vacations. He wouldn't mind that one bit.

In the minutes it took them to follow the sky bridge and platform back to the MX 60, the unease grew in Erik, but he didn't voice his concerns until they were back in the flitter. He'd finally figured out what was bothering him.

"Three Daughters isn't the only company in that tower and level, is it?" Erik asked.

"No," Emma answered. "There are multiple companies in the tower, including other shipping and related companies."

Jia looked at Erik. "You're thinking cargo traffic is way too sparse considering the time of day and the location, aren't you?"

"Yeah, that's exactly what I was thinking." Erik motioned to the windshield. "This might not be Neo SoCal, but we've seen plenty of air traffic elsewhere, and the background information we got from Alina suggests this is a high-volume company."

"All public records suggest as much," Emma confirmed. "I can find no emergency or local news reports to provide a reason for lower traffic at Three Daughters."

Erik nodded, forming and tossing out different plans in his head. He might only be seeing what he wanted to. They needed to be careful. If there were artifacts present and they raided the wrong location, they might doom their chance to recover them.

"Let's see what the others come up with."

Back inside the *Argo* cargo's bay, Anne slipped out of Jia's flitter with a frown. "We didn't see anything unusual. It's a busy commercial area with heavy traffic. It was easy to blend in with the crowd. We did notice some spots that might be concealed turrets, but there are potential gaps in the coverage."

Erik and Jia had been waiting in the cargo bay.

"It was the opposite for us," Erik replied. "Not as much traffic as we would have suspected, but we don't know enough about the local situation to know if that means anything, or if there's something more there we should care about."

"If I were going to hide something, I'd place it in the less obvious location," Jia noted. She gestured around the cargo bay. "Which I'd think would be the place with more people and activity, not less. It's easier to monitor comings and goings with less traffic."

Anne's faint smile could almost be mistaken for approval. "I was thinking the same thing, Lin."

Kant lumbered out of the flitter, stretching his arms. "But we can't be sure. We've all worked missions where the obvious answer is only obvious because we've got an assload of intel pointing us to something suspicious, and it turns out that's wrong."

"True." Jia frowned. "It's not like the local cops or ID agents had someone like Barbu giving them records. There's no reason to be suspicious of these companies other than because of what we know."

If they had the people and time, a well-timed raid on both places might turn up more, but they still hadn't established that Barbu wasn't setting them up. They couldn't make a move without something more concrete.

Erik turned his head, stopping as he focused on an exoskeleton. Alina had supplied new agents, but not new exos. They'd need to remedy that in the immediate future.

Sometimes a man needed to sneak around. Sometimes a man needed a grenade launcher.

"Anne, Kant, you stand by here. Jia and I will see what the locals have for us, and we'll go from there."

CHAPTER THIRTY-EIGHT

August 5, 2230, Alpha Centauri, Chiron, Lumiere, Albatross Bar

Erik told Jia that all places were ugly in the same way. She accepted the wisdom of that observation as they stepped into the dark hole pretending to be a bar.

The dim red lighting provided enough illumination to keep people from falling over, but it maintained enough shadows for them to drink for hours with only the barest awareness of what was going on around them.

Loud, unpleasant music filled the air, necessitating a shouting match between anyone not drunk enough who wanted to talk.

Those same conditions made it an excellent meeting place. Even if anyone was aware they were in town, Erik and Jia would have been difficult to pick out in the packed bar.

They continued making their way through it, ignoring the occasional angry scowl from a drunken local as they followed the exact directions that had been sent to Emma earlier over the coded frequency.

It wasn't as reliable as the methods Adeyemi and Alina used on Earth, but it was a step above what normal criminals could access. There were advantages to working for the Intelligence Directorate.

Erik and Jia arrived at a booth tucked into the back with only one man. His dark clothes helped him blend in even more with the environment, but there was something unsettling about the almost static smile on his face.

They continued toward the booth, neither surprised when the punishing noise of the bar died to near silence as they sat.

"I'm a friend of black holes," the man greeted them.

"And we're friends of Singapore," Jia answered. She found she missed Alina's literary bent for code phrases.

He nodded slowly. "The famous pair in my own backyard. I'm starstruck here."

Jia didn't like the sarcasm in his voice.

"That's one way to describe us," Erik replied. "You're Agent Dalton?"

The agent nodded again, that near-plastic smile remaining on his face. Jia had never thought she would so dislike someone smiling.

"That's me." The man rubbed his eyes. "I was surprised to hear you two were coming and even more surprised that you're here so shortly after I was told, which means the Fleet got their toy working. Not that anyone's bothered to let me know. I guess I'm not important enough."

Jia frowned. Compartmentalization was the key to successful operational security, and the ghost sitting in front of them knew that better than most. If he needed to know about the jumpship, Alina would tell him. She didn't have time to sit around, puffing up people's egos.

"We're here now." Jia leaned forward. "And we need information. You're supposed to help us with that."

Dalton's smile threatened to go away with a brief twitch. "Of course you do, so you can do your thing, right?"

"What's our thing?"

"Causing trouble." Dalton sneered, finally losing the smile.

Erik chuckled. "I didn't think taking down threats to the UTC was considered trouble. Or if it is, most people consider that the good type of trouble."

"It can be the bad type, too." Dalton flicked his wrist toward Erik. "Especially when you get two trigger-happy ex-cops wandering around blowing up everything in sight. Venus. The moon. Need I go on?"

Jia eyed him. "I'm sorry if you don't like how we've handled our missions, but I would assume if you know anything about the conspiracy, you understand that sometimes they leave us no choice." She glared at him. "Or would you have preferred we let them sink Parvati or blow Chang'e dome? I don't know how *quiet* it is when thousands of people scream before they die, and if I have to choose between secrecy and saving thousands of lives, I'll pick the people every time."

Dalton chuckled, the plastic smile returning. He leaned back and folded his arms. "Dial it down, Lady Justice. I'm not saying you've always made the wrong move, but you have to understand where you are and how that introduces complications."

"Last time I checked, we were in Lumiere on Chiron. Care to educate me on what those complications are? We're not here to upset you. We're all on the same team."

Jia glanced at Erik to ensure she wasn't going too far. He didn't look upset, and he nodded back, which was enough for her to continue taking the lead in the conversation.

"Earth is the center of the UTC," Dalton began, "but it's not the entire UTC. Every half-dedicated terrorist, insurrectionist, or piece of scum out on the frontier who wants a shot at Earth needs to go through this system first because they don't have your special toy." He pointed at Jia. "No one cares about the secondary colonies or stations, or the tiny smattering of other cities, so they all end up in Chiron. Here in Lumiere, we probably have the greatest concentration of dangerous filth in the entire UTC. Sure, Neo SoCal is big, but there are billions of people on Earth. That encourages the filth to spread out more." He gestured broadly. "It's easy to get lost there. Here, they're tripping all over each other. Insurrectionists, Grayheads, syndicates, guys who got transported and want to skip out on their sentence and return to Earth. Greedy bastards who think they have a good shot at becoming the next Sophia Vand."

Jia rolled her eyes. "We get it. You've seen it all, darkness, depravity, and greed. It's not like we haven't seen our fair share of trouble. We've fought things that shouldn't exist. We've dealt with people who make the most vicious rabid animal seem moral in comparison."

"That's just it." Dalton sighed. "You *don't* get it. Because we've got all those threats tripping over one another, it means this entire place is a giant knot in a way you're not used to on Earth. You tug on one string without knowing where you're going, and you can fuck up something else. We always have to keep that in mind when dealing with people here."

Jia leaned forward, drilling into Dalton with her harsh glare. "I don't have time to call Alina and ask for her to pretty please tell you to do your job. The people we're going after are the single greatest threat to the UTC. They've proven they will kill anyone and everyone to get what they want, and they aren't troubled in the slightest by such quaint ideas as morality or restraint. So, what we're going to do here is our job, and that means investigating the conspiracy and recent shipments. If that ends in explosions and noise, so be it. We're not walking away because it might make your job harder later. If we do, your job might not matter later."

Dalton dropped his arms quickly.

Jia whipped her hand into her jacket and began to draw her stun pistol. The agent laughed and lifted his hands in front of him.

"Calm down, Lady Justice." Dalton's smile grew wider. "I don't think the guy who takes either of you out is going to do it by shooting you in a bar. It'll probably involve trapping you in a dome and blasting you from orbit. That's what I'd do. Even if I was lucky enough to get my gun out and shoot one of you, the other one would put a bullet in my brain before I took a second shot."

Jia pushed her gun back in but kept her hands above the table. Dirty cops, CID agents, and politicians existed. The ID had recently had a traitor. There was no reason to believe there wasn't another one.

Dalton turned to Erik. "What about you, Blackwell? You ready to shoot me?"

"I'm *always* ready to shoot people." Erik offered him a merry grin to match the agent's smile. "So get the hell over yourself. I don't care about the stick you have in your ass, and I agree with my partner. We're not here to make trouble, but if trouble comes, we're going to end it. If we don't, a lot of people might die sooner than later. And it's your job, ghost, just like it's ours, to work your ass off and risk your life so those other people don't die. If you don't like what I have to say, I suggest you quit and get a nice, safe, cushy corp job."

Dalton snickered quietly as his gaze shifted between the two. He didn't say anything else, just let out a long weary sigh. His stupid smile barely wavered.

"Three Daughters and New Lands," Jia announced. "That's where our investigation has led. You're supposed to be one of the top agents here with a good lay of the land, so you should be able to tell us something about them. Everything's a big, nasty knot of antisocials around here, right? So, enlighten us, wise Agent Dalton, about the truth. Trace the thread for us."

Dalton muttered something before flagging down a waitress. "I need a drink before we go into anything."

They waited patiently as the waitress approached. The pleasant quiet ended, the music and conversations assaulting the previously secured booth. Dalton placed his order, while Erik and Jia only asked for water. A minute later, the waitress returned with two glasses of water and a glass with the finest local bourbon and set it in front of the agent. Once she'd left the booth, the blessed quiet returned.

Dalton raised the glass to his lips and took a sip. "Why do I have a feeling my job's going to get very complicated and annoying soon?"

"It doesn't have to." Jia shrugged. "Unless those aren't innocent, law-abiding corporations. Then, yes, it'll get complicated."

"No such thing as an innocent corp." Dalton shook his head. "You're still thinking about this the wrong way, Lady Justice. It's not about innocent or guilty, it's about what shades of gray we'll find."

Jia's eyes narrowed. "The conspiracy is about as close to the darkness of hell as we're going to get without demons being real. Now, can you help us or not? I wouldn't want to get in the way of your drinking."

Dalton gulped down half the bourbon and let out a sigh of satisfaction. "Nothing like the anticipation of booze tickling your brain. That part's better than being drunk."

Jia's hand clenched and unclenched on the table. "Stop. Wasting. Our. Time."

Erik chuckled.

Dalton stared at her as he polished off the rest of his drink. He set the glass down and shook his head. "We've heard some things locally about those two companies, but the weird thing is they weren't on our radar until real damned recently, starting in June. What you'll want are local shipping records to give you more to work with since I don't have much more than I told you. I don't want our fingerprints on this because it will screw up our other ops. You can give me another big speech about how you're fighting the ultimate evil, but you used to be a cop. You know if you add up enough little evils, they get dangerous."

"Fine." Jia took a deep breath. "Just point us at the records, and we'll do the heavy lifting with our people. You can stay out of it, then you don't have to worry about anything other than a little potential cleanup later."

Dalton stared longingly at his empty glass. For the first time in his conversation, he frowned. "Sure. I'll probably regret it later, but why not?"

"You and Malcolm do what you need to," Erik ordered Emma after lifting off in the MX 60 and speeding away from the bar. "Contrary to what that asshole inside seems to think, I'd rather walk in slow and get it right. I'm not going to care about explosions at the end, but we'll save those for the best part."

"Very well," Emma replied. "I'll brief Mr. Constantine, and we'll inspect the relevant records."

Jia fell into deep thought. Dalton reminded her of detectives from the 1-2-2 when she'd started, but it was a different sort of cynicism.

His attitude annoyed her, but he wasn't using corruption as an excuse to do nothing. Instead, he was trying to focus on the tiny pockets of darkness and eliminate them as a way of feeling like he was accomplishing something.

It might not have been as flashy as going after the conspiracy, but she couldn't say it was pointless.

"The farther we get from Earth, the more this is going to be a problem, isn't it?" she asked.

Erik nodded. "Chiron's practically next door, but the light-years and the frustrations start adding up. It's hard for one planet and the people on it to understand what's going on when they aren't on it. I felt that way tons of times when we'd get clueless orders from on high."

"It doesn't change anything." Jia ran a hand through her hair. Erik was pleasantly surprised when she didn't yank a fistful out by the roots as she continued talking. "We need to keep following and flushing them out until the leaders have their backs to the wall." She sighed. "It'd be poetic if they ended up trapped on Molino."

Erik's grin turned hungry. "It would, but I don't think the Lady loves us that much. We'll find out what's going on here and knock heads together until we get answers. That crap in France proved that all we need to do is survive, and we'll make progress."

"Survive, huh?" Jia shook her head.

She would do more than survive. Dalton's path wasn't wrong, but neither was hers. Sometimes you stopped a beast by bleeding it out, but the easiest solution was to cut its head off.

Besides, she had plans that included the man beside her.

CHAPTER THIRTY-NINE

<u>August 6, 2230, Alpha Centauri, Chiron, the Galley of the Argo</u>

Erik liked Malcolm, but that didn't stop him from wanting to slap some sense into the man.

Sometimes the tech was like a *yaoguai* squirrel engineered with too much energy. He was all but skipping back and forth in the galley, the bright white and red flower pictures on his shirt assaulting Erik's eyes.

"Take a seat, Malcolm," Erik offered, his voice low. He tried to keep the implied threat from scaring the man without stripping it all out.

Malcolm froze in place and nodded quickly before settling into a chair. Emma appeared next to him, her hair up with the help of a long blue pin. She was wearing a kimono of all things, the exterior patterned after Malcolm's shirt. Given the mocking smile aimed at Erik, she was doing it on purpose.

Erik was used to Jia understanding what he was thinking. After a while, a man expected that from a woman he spent all his time with. Emma always managed to surprise him.

The distinction in his mind between woman and machine was blurred, but she all but lived in his head, having been with him from his first months on Earth. It shouldn't have been a surprise that she knew exactly how to annoy him.

Jia, Anne, and Kant were scattered around the table, bags under their eyes. Erik was the only one who had gotten a decent night's rest. Jia and Anne had both pored over local records and news reports, and Kant had decided to spend a couple of hours checking out the sites at night. The man was goofy and friendly, but he was a hard worker.

Erik cleared his throat. "Let's get to it. The clock's still ticking. Even if they shipped out their toys, we might be able to follow the trail. I don't care if we have to go into Zitark space if it means we can get our hands on some alien artifacts."

Emma nodded at Malcolm and folded her hands neatly in her lap. She'd already informed Erik they'd found something an hour earlier, but he'd told her to wait until he could gather everyone. There was no point in wasting time by having her repeat herself.

"So." Malcolm rubbed his hands together. "We've got two shipping companies that our mysterious Mr. Barbu's records helped point us at, and they've done stuff recently. Emma and I hit city shipping records pretty deeply to check farther into it."

Anne furrowed her brow. "How deeply? Did you leave a trail?"

"Us?" Malcolm threw his head back and tried a hearty laugh, but it came out strangled. His face red, he coughed into his hand to cover his mistake. "No, we covered our tracks. The thing is, this wasn't a high-security system. This was just basic internal tracking, spaceport logistics, that kind of thing."

"Mr. Constantine is correct," Emma added. "The security here was in anonymity. It'd be highly unlikely anyone would know where to check and what to look for unless, like us, they already knew what they were looking for. When we were going through the records, we found that both of the target companies shipped through other companies until they started being handled by another local company. This was where things got a little more involved."

"As if that's not involved enough," Malcom added.

Erik motioned for her to continue. "We know you two are ridiculously skilled at hacking and systems penetration. Let's skip the details and get to the part we care about."

Emma smirked. "Two additional local companies displayed related suspicious activity in the last week. One is ultimately a subsidiary of Stella Infinitas, but that ownership change didn't occur until last month. Prior to that, it was independent. The other newly identified company is a subsidiary of Ceres Galactic."

Jia sighed. "That's consistent with what Alina found on Earth, but I wonder if there's some special meaning to it."

"Like what?" Kant asked, leaning forward, his face full of interest.

"It's not good to accept that the conspiracy controls the main producer of HTPs in the UTC," Jia explained, making a circle with her hand. "For all we know, those artifacts might have something to do with that, something dangerous. The scope of the problem keeps increasing."

"Does it make a difference?" Anne asked, sounding dubious. "We know we have to take them out. If we do, their plans don't matter."

Jia put a finger in the air. "Ceres Galactic is so integrated into the economy of the UTC that there's no way people won't suffer if they go down. They make practically everything either directly or through subsidiaries, meaning the conspiracy can always get the parts and equipment they need."

Erik shrugged. "Parts and equipment aren't everything."

Jia put up another finger. "Hermes. Their influence there means the conspiracy could potentially send hidden messages to anywhere in the galaxy, not only without low-level corporate oversight but also without CID or ID oversight. That means they have a tremendous advantage, even with our jump drive. We might be able to get places faster, but short of jumping there, we don't necessarily get comm faster."

"The more we know about it, the better we can take advantage of it when the time comes," Malcolm exclaimed, excited. He didn't look away when Jia stared at him. "I'm not an expert on war like Erik, but I know if you know how the enemy is communicating, you can figure out how to spy on that and take advantage of it."

Erik nodded slowly. "Malcolm's right. We might not be ready for the ID and CID to rain down fire, but the more we learn about where they are, the more we can start to account for that."

Jia put up a third finger. "Which leaves us with Stella Infinitas. We do have an advantage right now in that if for some bizarre reason the conspiracy shut down every HTP in the UTC, we could still go to them."

Kant shuddered. "You think they'd do something like that?"

"I don't know, honestly. I don't know what they were planning for that Hunter ship either, and I know they don't mind killing a lot of people to get their way." Jia shook her head. "There are far too many scenarios I can think of where it'd be advantageous to them to collect a force and then cut off reinforcements. For all we know, they're planning some new Conspiracy Kingdom on the frontier."

"It's all supposition." Anne's face twitched. "You don't have a clear insight into their motives."

"I agree." Jia shrugged. "Which makes them that much more dangerous to deal with. I do know they keep trying to build up dangerous armies without any sort of moral or ethical restraint. We need to keep hitting them and leaving them on defense because I have a feeling that if we let up, we won't like the end result."

"Then we should check out the new companies," Erik declared. "It's obvious to me from what you two found that they've already moved the goods. If we go busting into Three Daughters or New Lands, we might find something, but not what we're looking for. We'll need to penetrate the systems of the two new companies, and if you focus solely on messing with them, it'll lower the chance of detection." He nodded at Malcolm. "You check out the Ceres subsidiary. Emma should check out the other. Walk it slow, keep it subtle. Focus on finding the shipments from Earth.

If we can take some artifacts from the conspiracy, that'll be a nice kick in the balls."

Kant grinned.

Boys. Jia sighed.

CHAPTER FORTY

The MX 60 sped along with ease.

Erik let Emma control things as they passed through a thicket of flitters flowing through the towers that circled the heart of downtown Lumiere.

Now that they'd spent some time in the city, Jia could clearly see that the average tower didn't reach the commanding heights of those in Neo SoCal, despite the dense packing giving that illusion.

She supposed it didn't matter much. A person standing at the base would crane their necks upward at the sight of something more worthy of being called a skyscraper than the buildings of the past.

It was odd when she thought about it.

The vast majority of colonies lacked any buildings of significant height. In that sense, one could argue they weren't representative of humanity, but the greatest concentrations of the species, which included many colonies of the core worlds and Earth itself, were defined by places where humanity reached into the sky like gods.

Curiously, at the center of Lumiere, the towers gave way to a noticeable hole. The forest of towers surrounded a perfectly square area where the tallest contributors were trees.

Flitter lanes filled the air above the large hole, but the MX 60 needed to descend hundreds of meters until those on board could make out the garden full of marble statues.

They formed the Landing Monument.

There were five hundred statues, one for each of the original five hundred colonists. A ring of trees surrounded the statues, and colorful patches of carefully tended flowerbeds added touches of color. Given their height, the sheer number of plants must have been staggering. The only practical way to handle that many would be with bots or drones.

Jia and Erik weren't there to sightsee. They'd been flying around town to get a better feel for the layout. Having maps and Emma helped, but depending too much on any one team member, even an advanced AI, carried risks.

A woman never knew when she might end up chasing an alien-worshipping terrorist or a crazy Tin Man through town.

It was hard not to think about the meaning of what she was seeing. She peered at the large area in the camera feed, soaking in the implications.

"I could never do it." Jia motioned at a statue in a camera feed.

"You couldn't handle someone making a statue of you?"

Erik asked, looking confused. "I'd want to make sure the guy didn't make me look an idiot, but I wouldn't mind a statue."

She shook her head. "I'm not talking about that. I'm talking about what they represent. I couldn't leave everything behind and start over on a new world. When I was younger, I liked to tell myself most people couldn't. I liked to believe the colonies were mostly filled with transported criminals and a small number of dedicated public servants, but that's not true. I thought about it on the way here. Some people are just wired to move forward and explore different places." She smiled. "I think you're that way."

Erik turned away with a thoughtful look. "Maybe not as much as you'd think. I joined the Army because I needed direction in my life, and I liked being a soldier, but seeing the rest of the UTC wasn't some grand goal. If my life had turned out differently, I could have been happy in Detroit or a place like Neo SoCal. You've seen me. I like my restaurants and my foods, and I'm consistent in my choices. I'm not aching to go to weird places like your sister took you."

"Maybe the age of grand exploration is over," Jia murmured. "So none of that matters."

"Why do you say that? I figure as long as someone's breathing and can get to a new place, people will always push out farther."

"It's different now because of the Zitarks, Leems, Orlox, and the rest," Jia answered. "We're effectively surrounded on all sides. Human history teaches us what happens when two civilizations push into the same area. I've got my biases. We've got plenty of planets and moons and plenty of space on them. I'm sure we could grow humanity into the trillions with the extent of the UTC now."

Erik thought for a moment before shrugging. "Who knows? Someday different races might decide they could use different planets in the same system. Maybe we'll be mixed together in some giant United Confederation of the Milky Way."

"You really think that?" Jia stared at him, surprised by Erik being the less cynical one in the conversation. "We were *very* close to having our first interstellar war."

"Close isn't the same thing as having it. I'm not saying I want a space raptor as a neighbor anytime soon, but I don't know. You look at the history of humanity, and it's clear that everyone expected us to die off. They placed their bets against us, but we've prospered." Erik chuckled. "When I was a kid, my dad showed me a history lecture from 2085 at a college in LA. The guy said despite us setting up colonies on other worlds, we were doomed because too many people had their hands on nukes or bioweapons, and it was just a matter of time before we killed ourselves off. He said if it wasn't those things, it'd be nanotech. The guy, who was a big-time historian back then, said humanity had a less than 0.1 percent chance of surviving for another fifty years. He had this big calculation for it, which was called the Doomsday Quotient."

Jia sighed. "I bet that guy felt smug when the Summer of Sorrow happened." She winced. "Assuming he survived. You said the lecture was in LA. Did he live there?"

"I never checked on him to see if he was in LA at the time. Never cared much about the lecture. My dad used it as an example of smart people being wrong, and how with hard work, we could succeed." Erik frowned. "But that's the thing. LA was destroyed, just like he might have predicted, but everything changed, and things didn't go the way he said. People didn't get rid of war or assholes trying to hurt people, but here we are in 2230, and no one's saying humanity's done. We're sitting here having this conversation about whether we can push back aliens."

"There are a lot of threats out there. The conspiracy, local neighborhood aliens, the Hunters." Jia stared at the camera feed of the monument garden as the MX 60 circled the area and pulled away. There was something soothing in Erik's words.

"If we didn't kill ourselves when we were all on one planet with thousands of nukes pointed at each other, we're not going to." Erik tapped his finger on his leg. "Not that some bastards might not try, but there have always been murderers and people who don't care who they hurt, and things have still moved forward. Even if the Hunter ship had taken out Earth, we have colonies now. I don't know if we'll ever be friends with aliens, but I know there are more people out there who give a shit about making the galaxy a better place than those who don't."

"And on that poetic note," Emma interrupted, "I have important news that we might be able to use to make the galaxy a better place. You should return to the *Argo* immediately."

An hour later, Jia and Erik were waiting in the cargo bay when Kant and Anne landed and hurried out of her flitter.

Erik looked up from the crate of grenades he'd been rifling through. It was always good to see what was easily available. Looking at a data window wasn't the same.

"Here's the executive summary," he announced. "Emma's isolated a possible conspiracy shipment originally from Earth that she's pretty damned sure hasn't left Chiron yet. The shipment is clearly contraband. Our friends played some records games to conceal the importation of the cargo from Customs inspection and have been moving it around a lot." His snicker caused Anne to shiver. "All that effort to hide it, and they still left themselves vulnerable."

Anne stepped away from the flitter. "That's a lot of circumstantial evidence, Blackwell. Are you sure this is worth pursuing?"

Jia walked over to Erik's side. "We're several companies deep into misdirected cargo, falsified records, and businesses clearly linked to elements controlled by the conspiracy. We're not here to arrest them and put them on trial. I think circumstantial evidence is enough. We don't know what they are hiding."

"We don't have any idea what these items might be." Anne folded her arms. "They could be nothing very important. It could be cheese, and they're trying to avoid paying Customs duties."

He eyed her. "Nobody goes through that much trouble to avoid Customs duties on cheese. Emma's cargo is scheduled for transport from the facility to the spaceport tomorrow. Cargo she can trace from Earth to the other companies we've been looking at. If we wait until it's at the spaceport, we risk having to confront militia or local cops." Erik gave Anne a merry grin and motioned to his grenade crate. "I want to throw grenades at the conspiracy, not cops."

Emma appeared in a dark suit. "You might find some of this drone footage interesting."

Data windows appeared above her, displaying footage taken from different angles. Side doors opened on a tower level, allowing the entrance and exit of large cargo flitters. Emma paused the playback to magnify and enhance the image. Helmeted men in full tactical suits with rifles stood near the cargo flitters as bots loaded and unloaded the cargo.

"Lot of guns to protect some cheese," Jia observed.

Anne's focus flicked to Jia, a small curve down to her lips before she restored her focus, her face blank once more.

"According to public records," Emma began, "this company ships nothing of a value sufficient to warrant such heavy security. It'd be as if Erik started guarding his plants with his exoskeleton."

"Bad analogy." Erik shook a finger at her. "If someone came after my penjing setup, I *would* put on an exo and take them out."

"Okay, you've got a point." Anne scratched her cheek, her brow creased in deep concentration. "We'll have to assume that isn't the only security. Are you anticipating a full assault? We only have your two exos."

"Exos aren't viable if we need to get the hell out of there fast, and based on what Emma's found, the cargo should be small enough to fit in flitters."

Jia nodded her agreement. "If we aren't using exos, it'll be easier to explain if the locals show up."

Kant headed over to the grenade crate and knelt to inspect his options. "In summary, we're robbing the place and seeing what special cheese they have?"

Anne threw her hands up. "Shut up about the cheese already. It was an *example*."

Erik smirked before turning to Kant. "Something like that. I think the best time to strike is right after they leave the facility." Erik pointed at the various clusters of grenades in the crate. "They're not going to want to call the cops or draw any attention, so as long as we keep them from showing up, we should have a good amount of time to take the shipment and get the hell out of there. We come back to the *Argo,* an area where Emma has complete control, then figure out if it's worth it to just take off with our pirate treasure or plan a follow-up."

Anne marched over to a carryaid secured to a rack on the wall and examined one of the mechanical backpacks closely. "How are we going to ensure the locals don't show up? There's no way this is happening without shots being fired."

Emma offered a thin smile. "Mr. Constantine and I are currently infiltrating the relevant systems everywhere around the target. We will be able to suppress the drones and cameras without alerting the company. Once the attack begins, we can push hard into their security systems as well. He and I are laying the groundwork for that."

"Are we sure we don't want local help?" Kant asked, lifting a plasma grenade and slowly turning it in his hand before looking up. "In case things get rough? I get that we don't want the cops tagging along, but what about some of the local ID presence?"

Jia shook her head. "Our conversation with the agent the other night made it clear they don't want anything to do with this mission. It'll take too long to convince them to help, and we're on a tight timeline on this. Sometimes it's better to handle things ourselves."

"We've got four trained ops personnel with plenty of field experience in dealing with dangerous situations." Erik gestured to everyone in turn. "Emma can operate the MX 60 even under jamming conditions, and we're not there to take out the entire place, just grab some cargo. This calls for a small, agile team, and their trusty AI."

Jia patted her stun pistol. "We also shouldn't assume that everyone involved is a dedicated member of the conspiracy. We'll hit hard and fast, but we should restrict ourselves to nonlethals until we have reason to suspect otherwise."

Anne frowned. "That could be risky."

"The conspiracy controls a lot, but that doesn't mean everyone knows what they're doing." Jia motioned toward the roof. "Otherwise, we'd be laying siege to every Ceres Galactic building out there."

Emma raised her hand. A data window filled with names appeared.

"There's only a small number of security personnel listed in their public records. Erik is reluctant to have me to dig deeper and risk alerting them to their partial systems compromise. As it is, the discovery of the shipping records was unexpected, given where they put it in the system. They are clearly hiding both personnel and the nature of their cargo."

"It doesn't hurt to hold back the lead and grenades

unless we need them." Erik clapped and rubbed his hands together. "If all goes well, we'll stun a couple of guards and have ourselves a nice pile of alien artifacts or Tin Man parts to show for it."

Anne frowned at him. "Do you really think it'll be that easy?"

"No. Of course not." Erik kept his smile. "I expect we'll hit the cargo flitter and a half-dozen full-conversion Tin Men will be inside waiting to kill us, but that doesn't change anything." His jovial mask faded, leaving only determination. "We're grabbing that cargo. I don't care if you want to tweak the plan, but we didn't jump all the way from Earth to sit on our hands. Understood?"

Anne nodded. "Understood."

Jia's heart pounded. She'd gotten so used to major strikes against the conspiracy that the idea of slipping in, grabbing something, and sneaking out from under their noses was antithetical. It would be nice to visit a new location with Erik without blowing anything up.

She couldn't wait.

"Good." Erik cracked his knuckles. "Now, let's go over the specific ops plan."

CHAPTER FORTY-ONE

"What's our status?" Erik asked, circling the company from a distance, safely ensconced in the MX 60.

He'd changed the vehicle to a dull gray color and altered the transponder signal. That would cut down on recognition. He was using a disguise, but depending on how aware the local conspiracy members were, that might not help him escape without them realizing he'd been there.

It didn't matter. The most important time for secrecy was before a mission, not afterward.

While Emma had been able to change the transponder on Jia's flitter, she couldn't do anything about the color. They would need to look into an upgrade. He doubted this would be the last time they needed both flitters for a mission, and for that matter, Anne and Kant would need their own vehicles.

"Preparing to insert the spoof programs into the local cameras and drones," Emma reported. "Fortunately, flitter traffic is light at this time of day. That's minimizing the chance of surreptitious reporting."

"I'm monitoring company security," Malcolm added. "Keeping it high-level, but there are no alerts or elevated risk reports on the basic systems. If I go any deeper, I risk getting someone's attention."

"Stick to the plan," Erik announced. "We'll bring them down, open them up, and grab what's inside. They can cry all they want at that point."

"I hope this is worth it," Anne offered from the other flitter. "It reminds me of an ancient American folk song my grandmother used to sing to me. In it, this tribe goes after this other tribe because of their treasure, and it turns out the treasure is just a rock that says 'peace on Earth.'"

"Anything that hurts the conspiracy is worth it, and I'll eat my TR-7 if it's a rock that says 'peace on Earth,'" Erik replied. He took a deep breath and kept his hands tight on the control yoke.

"I'll hold you to that, Blackwell."

Erik smiled.

They flew in an irregular pattern, waiting for their chance. The shipment was scheduled to leave the facility in ten minutes, and there was no sign of the police, the militia, or any worry at the company. Everything was going well.

The conspiracy had grown complacent, too used to their secrets being concealed by layers of false companies and smiling socialites with billions of credits. Erik and Jia had torn off the mask, and they could continue to follow the trail until they were done. The jumpship had changed all the tactics.

Now they were ahead of the enemy.

"We've got movement," Malcolm announced. "The bird is leaving the nest."

Jia glanced at Erik. "Did we agree to that sort of thing?"

"Nope." Erik sighed. "But let him have his fun."

"Suppressing local cameras and drones," Emma reported. "Setting up drone-based redirect of local traffic. You are clear to engage."

Erik turned the MX 60 and zoomed toward the large cargo flitter. Their target had left the facility and was now above an open sky bridge that was empty except for some cargo drones off to the sides. The Lady was with them so far. Anne and Kant charged in from the opposite side.

Waiting any longer might cost them a great opportunity. It was time to inflict additional fear on the conspiracy.

"Emma, ready the EMP," Erik ordered.

A button rose from the right side of the control yoke. Despite the impressive-sounding command, the external difference was limited to a plate pulling back to allow the EMP emitter to release without interfering with the flitter.

Erik lined his vehicle up behind the cargo flitter. The target vehicle didn't alter course, despite the erratically flying MX 60 behind them and the other rapidly closing vehicle. The poor bastards had no idea what was going on, or if they did, they might be afraid to make any sudden movements and tip someone off that they were carrying valuable cargo.

Taking a deep breath, Erik pushed the button. The cargo flitter shuddered, sparked from the bottom, and lost altitude, the bottom scraping the sky bridge. That resulted in more sparks, smoke, and flames as pieces shredded off and bounced around until it skidded to a halt.

Erik let out the breath he'd been holding, grateful there was no one else around. The cargo drones increased altitude, their simple AIs only concerned about avoiding collisions, not stopping daring early-morning heists.

The team's two flitters dropped fast on either side of the downed vehicle. Both pairs threw open their doors and pulled out rifles. Dark opaque windows concealed the passengers. If the Lady were feeling extra-generous, there might not be anyone aboard.

Erik's hope was fleeting. The back of the cargo flitter slid open, and stun bolts blasted out of it. He ducked behind his door to protect himself from the barrage. Jia hissed and reached for a stun grenade. The front doors flew open, and guards used them for shields as they fired at Anne and Kant.

"Go to nonlethals," Erik ordered, drawing his pistol and returning fire. If the enemy wasn't trying to blow their head off, they'd repay the favor until they had a reason to believe otherwise.

Emma's drones swarmed the area. Target highlights for the eight men inside the back of the flitter appeared, marked in everyone's smart lenses for convenience. Thermals indicated two men in the front.

The guards in the back were crouched behind ballistic shields, the barrels of their rifles poking through small slits. They all wore tactical vests but lacked the full suits or helmets of the security Emma had spotted before.

A small insignia decorated the shields.

Jia dropped her rifle and pulled her stun pistol. She

fired, but the bolts dissipated harmlessly against the shields. Erik frowned. Something was wrong.

The guards were well-prepared, but if the conspiracy had known someone was coming after them, they would have used something with more punch than stun rifles.

A drone feed from behind Kant and Anne showed they weren't having much trouble, and were secure behind the armored doors of Jia's flitter. The two guards from the front of the cargo flitter kept up a near-constant stream of shots, but they were also using stun rifles.

"The insignia on the shields is associated with a local modestly priced private security company," Emma reported, sounding as confused as Erik felt. "I'm currently occupied, so I can't dive too deeply into their records, but a general news search suggests nothing that would associate them with the conspiracy other than their appearance here."

"Budget rent-a-cops," Erik muttered. "There's no way they hired rent-a-cops to guard something important. What the hell is going on?"

"You screwed up, Blackwell," Anne shouted. "We're hitting an innocent company. We need to pull out now."

"I don't think so," Jia countered. "There are too many lines of evidence pointing here."

"Then what..." Anne hissed. "We can't sit around and wait for them to call the police. They might have already done so. We need to get this situation under control!"

"I agree with you there." Jia yanked a stun grenade off her belt, primed it, and hurled it with practiced ease into the back of the cargo flitter.

"Grenade!" shouted one of the guards in a panicked voice.

She didn't wait until the first landed before sending another at a lower angle. They scrambled to the back in time for the bright pop of the grenades. Bodies and rifles thudded to the floor. The momentary distraction doomed the men in the front, allowing Kant and Anne to shoot them in the face with their stun pistols. Painful but not lethal.

Erik charged forward and vaulted into the back of the cargo flitter to sweep the area. Twitching men lay scattered around, but there was a noticeable lack of anything looking like a cargo container or crate.

"We've got more movement from the company!" Malcolm shouted.

"Reinforcements?" Erik asked, his jaw tight.

"Another cargo flitter, and it's flying away fast. It wasn't scheduled, and it doesn't have an active transponder. It's not heading toward the spaceport unless it's taking a really long scenic route."

"Keep track of that thing," Erik shouted. "Whatever you do, don't lose it."

"Evacuate the cargo flitter immediately," Emma bellowed. "Run, you fleshbag!"

Erik didn't waste precious seconds questioning her. Instead, he leapt and twisted, landing hard on his feet and sprinting toward the MX 60. He didn't make it as far as he would have liked before the cargo flitter exploded.

CHAPTER FORTY-TWO

The hot blast wave slammed into the back of his vest and sent him flying. He crashed into the front of the MX 60, rolling off with a groan.

Jia rushed over to him, her eyes wide with worry. She knelt beside him, but Erik waved her off and stood. He'd lost the back of his vest, and fiery pain radiated from his back and arms, along with a dull ache in his chest. It wasn't anything med patches wouldn't fix. The reduced pain of his left arm made him favor it.

He stumbled toward the MX 60, motioning for Jia to get in on the other side. "Anne, Kant? You still alive?"

"Yes," Anne hissed. "What the hell just happened?"

Erik dropped into the driver's seat with a grunt and pulled a med patch from a pocket. "A distraction. Emma, get us in the air and go after the other cargo flitter. We tried to be quiet about this. Now it's time to go loud."

Jia slammed her door shut, her face red, eyes blazing. "They hired some locals as a distraction and killed them without a second thought. Was this a trap?"

"Maybe." Erik pulled off his ruined vest and jammed a med patch on his burned back. "But I don't think it was a trap for us."

"We need to abort this plan, Blackwell," Anne insisted. "This is out of control. This was supposed to be a simple snatch and grab, not involve exploding cargo flitters."

Erik was annoyed, but her flitter was in the air and following them, so he didn't care too much about her objections. As long as she followed orders, they could get along.

"Ten people just died," Erik muttered, taking labored breaths as he readied another med patch. "Poor bastards didn't even know why. We're going after those conspiracy bastards. Emma, do whatever you need to do to draw the locals off. They'll just get in the way."

"A small Zitark scare is now in motion," Emma reported, sounding satisfied. "Complete with evidence of them teleporting into a sky bridge. People are also reporting the explosion that just occurred. That should draw more of them off."

Erik frowned, jerking his head back and forth. "I don't see the cargo flitter."

"Don't worry," Malcolm replied. "I've got drones still on it, and I'm sending some from the *Argo* for a pincer action. We've got this."

"Good," Erik growled. "I'm rather annoyed about being blown up."

As the MX 60 sped along, Jia kept looking at Erik. He was breathing and conscious, but he had not escaped the blast without painful-looking burns, and there was only so much the anesthetic in the med patches could do.

There was no way he wasn't feeling pain.

They continued flying low among the towers of Lumiere on an intercept course with the other cargo flitter. Malcolm was right. It wasn't flying toward the spaceport, and it was dropping closer to the ground, where traffic was light to nonexistent.

Unlike Neo SoCal, there didn't appear to be any thick layer of pollution separating the top of the towers from the ground levels. Though they were clearly moving into an industrial zone, the lack of damage and graffiti and the general cleanliness made it clear this was no Shadow Zone.

Neo SoCal's reality wasn't universal.

Malcolm's and Emma's converging drone net kept the other cargo flitter from escaping. Jia was grateful for their help. Not everyone had a squadron of drones and dedicated support to be their eyes and ears in a huge city. The flitter would have easily escaped under other circumstances, making the sacrifice of the security guards pointless.

Jia's hands balled into fists. "They didn't need the guards. They could have stuck some bots in there and then blown it. It was sadistic." She turned to him. "Do they *enjoy* killing innocent people?"

Erik shook his head, his expression dark. "They wanted us to think it was important enough for live guards. We might not have taken the bait with just bots."

"I thought you said it wasn't a trap." Jia gave him a worried look.

"Not a trap for us, but that doesn't mean it wasn't a trap." Erik took a long, deep breath and leaned forward with a grimace to keep his scorched back off the seat. "The people in the conspiracy have a lot of enemies. Not just us, but also ID agents, Barbu, and other conspiracy people trying to screw them over." He frowned. "Damn it. We need an exo insertion solution for situations like this. We can't fly the *Argo* across town, but that doesn't matter. Nothing we can do about it now. You go to battle with what you have."

"The cargo flitter is landing in a previously concealed hangar," Emma reported.

"Concealed hangar?"

She sent a live feed from one of the drones to their smart lenses. The flitter settled down as a massive door slid closed with surprising speed. From the outside, it appeared to be a wall.

Red highlights appeared all over the feed.

"Cameras with overlapping fields," Emma reported. "There are an unusual number of drones in the area as well. I can guide you to a blind spot a couple hundred meters away and take care of at least some of the drones, but not in a timely manner without them knowing. It will take some time to take control of the cameras using purely external access methods."

"We're running out of time," Jia sounded like she wanted to spit acid. "And they already know we're after them."

Erik nodded. "Agreed. We're going to land in the blind

spot, we're going to grab heavy weapons, and we're going to bust our way inside."

"Are you in any condition to do that, Blackwell?" Anne asked, sounding uncertain. "You were pretty close to that explosion."

"I barely feel anything at this point," Erik replied.

"It looks like most of the cops were fooled," Malcolm reported. "I'm not seeing anything that looks like police drones or flitters heading your way. You're clear."

Jia cleared her throat. "I don't know how much of that is us. I'm guessing the conspiracy is taking their own measures to keep anyone from asking too many questions or looking around this area."

The MX 60 flew low, so close to the road that every rattle convinced Jia a grav emitter had been shorn off. She wanted to tell Erik to stay back because of his wounds, but they'd both continued on missions with far worse.

He was too stubborn to listen anyway.

No one had needed to die. They'd set up the mission to avoid it, but the conspiracy couldn't help themselves, and now they would pay.

Jia's harness strained under Emma's hard turn into a narrow alley. The MX 60 jerked to a halt and smoothly set down.

Erik motioned toward Jia's feet. "I'm bringing all the toys this time. I don't think we need to worry about rent-a-cops anymore, and I think we're going to need something with a lot more punch than a stun pistol to take out whoever's inside."

Jia was already reaching down. She handed him his TR-7 and magazines before grabbing a rifle from the back. "We should get the carryaids from the trunk. We might as well go all the way."

Erik threw open the door and jumped outside. He grabbed a new tactical vest and slipped it on with a grimace before strapping into a carryaid. With the help of the mechanical backpack, he didn't have to choose which implements of death and destruction he wanted to bring along. He'd bring them all.

It was nice to have tactical options.

By the time Anne and Kant landed, Erik and Jia were laden with ammo, grenades, their rifles, and heavy weapons. Erik had slotted his laser rifle into his carryaid, while Jia bore the missile launcher, along with spare missiles.

Anne eyed Erik's ragged and burned clothing. "You sure you're up for this? I didn't get a great look at you before."

Erik nodded. "Heart's pumping and lungs are working." He switched the TR-7 to four-barrel mode. "And I've got my favorite gun. How could I not be ready?"

Anne glanced at Kant, who shrugged.

He tossed her a rifle from their back seat before strapping one over his huge shoulder and heading to the trunk. Without a word, he began clipping grenades to his vest.

Erik pointed in the direction of the hidden hangar. The tall building in front of them blocked them from seeing anything, but Emma offered helpful highlights through their smart lenses and small data windows showing the area. A rectangle appeared near the edge of the wall.

"Thermal differential here suggests a door," Emma reported. "There are others, but there is lighter drone and camera coverage in that area. I could attempt to draw their attention with the turret."

Erik shook his head. "Save the turret until we need it. Us being after them isn't a secret at this point, and we don't know what they have in there. Are you and Malcolm looking for external access?"

"That might not be viable," Emma reported. "There's heavy jamming near the building."

"Then we'll do this the old-fashioned way." Erik hoisted his TR-7. "EMP as many cameras and drones as you can near the entrance, and we'll force our way in."

Anne loaded a magazine into her rifle. "They'll know we're coming from that direction."

"The minute we blow that door, they'll know." Erik smiled at Jia. "We don't have time for a hacking solution."

Kant cackled. "It's been a while since I've had this much fun. I knew you guys got into trouble, but not such interesting trouble."

"Yes, fun." Anne shook her head, a pensive look on her face. "It's your call. I'll follow orders. I hope whatever's in the pot at the end of the rainbow is worth it."

Jia winced and pointed at Erik's face. "I didn't notice in the battle. Your disguise. It's off. You look like *you*."

Erik slapped his cheeks. "Don't care at this point. We're done with the sneaking around part."

Anne frowned. "But if they know it's you, we're confirming for the conspiracy the jump drive can move a lot farther than they might think."

"Big deal." Erik headed toward the road. "That was inevitable. It might even throw them off their game. Let's get going before they do. Emma, clear the road with the EMP."

The MX 60 lifted off and backed out of the alley, then zoomed toward the building.

Jia fell in behind Erik. Kant followed. Anne hesitated before sprinting to catch up. She didn't look convinced, but she was heavily armed and ready to shoot.

They stayed close to the buildings as they jogged down the road. As they got closer to the building, they spotted shattered drones lying in the street, victims of Emma's EMP efforts, but no turrets or gunmen, no Tin Men blasting away. No one anywhere.

The door highlights disappeared from Jia's smart lenses.

"Did anyone else just lose targeting?" she asked.

"They've increased the jamming strength," came Emma's voice from the MX 60 overhead. "I'll continue to monitor the situation as best I can while attempting manual direction of drones with laser comms where possible, but this is going to severely limit my ability to help you on the inside."

Erik patted his TR-7. "It's fine. We know the general direction we have to go." He looked around. "And this time, it doesn't look like any innocents are at risk. We'll blow our way through if we have to."

"Why do I get the feeling they bought up this whole area?" Jia asked

"It's not like there's a forest in the middle of nowhere on Chiron where they could hide," Erik responded with a smile. "Sometimes you need to keep your evil hidden a different way. Jia, go ahead and be loud."

The team slowed as they approached the hidden door. Emma continued to circle overhead. There were only so many EMP shots she could take without risking power problems.

Jia pulled the already loaded missile launcher off the carryaid with a grunt and set it on her shoulder, aiming at the door. She checked over her shoulder to make sure no one was behind her.

"Everyone ready? Backblast clear?"

The other three nodded.

A pull of the trigger sent the missile flying, leaving a short trail of smoke as it tore through the air on a direct course with the hidden door.

It was time to see what the conspiracy was hiding.

CHAPTER FORTY-THREE

The missile exploded with a deafening boom, blasting out a shower of flame and chunks of metal that rained down on the ground.

A jagged, smoking hole remained.

It wasn't as nice an entry as they would have achieved with a breach disk, but there were fewer uncertainties when using a missile. A breach disk might not have made it through a thick door, and Erik hadn't thought to bring one anyway.

Jia set the launcher back onto her carryaid before readying her rifle. "I expected an alarm. That was kind of anticlimactic."

Anne shook her head and sighed. "We could have attempted to hack our way inside."

"Why bother?" Erik replied as he advanced toward the hole. "They know we're here. We chased them across the city. If they're smart, they won't mess with us. If not, the conspiracy will lose some guys, and we'll leave here with the cargo."

His earlier injuries still ached, but adrenalin and the painkillers in the med patches kept it dull, distant, and easy to ignore. He'd fought wounded plenty of times, both in and out of the military.

He might not be at his best, but he could operate while the mission was going.

The others followed Erik, everyone keeping a keen eye out for enemies.

Unlike Jia, Erik didn't expect an alarm. He assumed the enemy was already mobilized and taking up positions throughout the facility. Knowing the type of enemy would help with weapon choice. He'd brought along a lot of extra mags, including AP rounds, but he was worried about a repeat of France.

Four people on foot didn't pack the huge reserves of twelve exos. They'd barely won their last battle of attrition. The conspiracy couldn't have *yaoguai* factories everywhere.

He hoped.

Erik stepped through the hole into a long, brightly lit hallway, which was painfully nondescript. In the corners near the ceiling, small red holographic lights spun and flashed, but there was no loud accompanying noise. Something thudded in the distance. It sounded like it was coming from the general direction of the hangar, but without Emma or Malcolm inside the system, they would have to navigate there manually.

"There's your alarm." Erik nodded toward the lights. "Satisfied?"

"In a way, yes," Jia replied.

"Are we sure they aren't going to throw more security guards at us?" Anne asked with a frown.

"I don't think you bring cheap locals to hidden bases where you're smuggling contraband," Jia answered.

"And what was that noise?"

"Nothing good," Erik muttered. "We always assume we're going to run into something nasty unless the bad guys show up with stun rifles."

Jia inclined her head toward a nearby door and pointed her gun that way. Erik pressed himself to the wall, his carryaid making it impossible to flatten his back against it.

He sidestepped until he was at the access panel and waited for Jia and Anne to take up positions on either side of the door. Kant swept the hallway to make sure no one else ran around the corner and surprised them.

The man couldn't stop smiling. Erik had known guys like him in the Army, some good, some dangerous. Alina wouldn't have sent him a dangerous operative.

Erik slapped the access panel, and the door slid open. Jia and Anne rushed inside, sweeping their respective sides wordlessly like they'd been working raids together for years.

There wasn't a single piece of furniture or decoration. It was just a brightly lit empty room.

Jia gestured with her rifle toward some dark lines on the floor and scratches on the walls. "I wonder if someone emptied this place quickly."

More loud thuds sounded in the distance from at least two distinct sources. Erik didn't think they were getting any closer, but he didn't like not knowing the source any more than Anne did. They didn't have time to check every room.

Erik jogged down the hall toward the corner. "We

should move toward the hangar. I don't care if we spooked them out of their base. We need whatever's on that flitter."

Kant spun around the corner, keeping close to the wall. "Clear!"

Erik stepped into a sprawling hallway with several intersections. Another set of thuds sounded, but this time they sounded closer and not toward the end of the hallway, which to the best of Erik's recollection pointed toward the hangar.

The noise continued, now followed by loud, echoing clangs. Something was approaching the corridor on both sides at an intersection ahead. Erik and Kant stayed near the wall on their side of the hall. Anne and Jia darted across to set up, the latter kneeling, allowing them both good cover and firing arcs.

"It sounds like a big *yaoguai*," Erik muttered. "Another factory, probably."

Kant shook his head. "You know, brother, you might be a tough guy, but you've got shit for luck. Not complaining about the opportunity to take down a monster or two and earn some stories, but…*seriously?*"

"My luck depends on who you ask, but at least we don't have to worry about local yokel security guards." Erik raised the TR-7. He wouldn't need any fancy targeting interfaces, just the basic scope and smart lenses in this hallway.

Large shadows from opposite sites joined together, announcing the arrival of something. The thudding and clanging stopped.

"Hold your fire," Erik ordered. "We need to know what's going on here."

"You need to know what's going on?" came a man's voice from ahead.

He had a faint accent. It didn't sound local, Terran, most likely Eastern European, but there was an odd hollow timbre to it.

"You must know who we are," Erik shouted. "That's got to make you worry."

"Of course," the man called back. "You're famous in my organization. They call you the Last Soldier and Miss Lin, the Warrior Princess. You've caused much trouble, you and your friends in the government and police. I suppose it was inevitable that I would be forced to deal with you."

Jia narrowed her eyes and yanked a plasma grenade from her vest. "If you know our reputation, then you know you might not walk away here alive if you try to take us on. Cyborgs, *yaoguai*, that half-Leem freak on Venus. We've taken the best your conspiracy has to offer, and we've beaten them again and again. You should be asking yourself if you think you're tougher than all of those?"

"Ah, yes," the man replied. "I can understand how that might inspire a certain confidence. Arrogance, some might say."

"I call it a clearly documented record of successfully applied violence," she retorted. "Not arrogance."

Erik kept his TR-7 pointed down the hall, all four barrels ready to go, but the large shadows intermixed in the center of the intersection ahead bothered him. He'd assumed a large *yaoguai* was coming, but he didn't understand what he was seeing. They had not been separated long enough for him to get a clear idea.

Judging by the clanging, the most likely explanation

was exos. He ducked behind the wall, ejected his magazine, and caught it before it fell. He stuffed it in his pocket, yanked out an armor-piercing magazine, and loaded that under the confused gaze of Kant.

Erik took up position again before nodding to the magazine. Kant ducked for his own switch. An exo with a good shield would have the advantage in the corridor, but enough AP rounds and explosives could take it out.

"Unlike some people in our organization, I don't view you as a threat," the man continued. "Erik, Jia...can I call you that?"

"What do we call you?" Jia asked.

Erik was content to let Jia do the talking while he checked the other hallway for an ambush. The wide, hard floors echoed from their footsteps, so it would be difficult for the enemy to surprise them.

"You can call me Luca," the hidden man replied. "I would tell you more, but you're too resourceful, and I can't risk you somehow getting information outside this place."

"Oh, not confident you can beat us?"

"The wise man prepares for all possibilities. The fact that you're here proves your skill beyond mere violence." Luca chuckled quietly, the shadows quaking. "Would you mind explaining how you found this place?"

Jia scoffed. "What, you mean you didn't have a big trap set up for us all along? What about your exploding flitter full of innocent suckers?"

"That was, as you say, a trap," Luca responded. "I can assure you that had we known you two were here and hunting us, we would have taken stronger measures. We did become aware of something unusual, but alas, we thought it was a foolish local syndicate who didn't know their place, not you two. Perhaps the greater question is, how did you get here? I know you were on Earth not all that long ago."

Erik's brow lifted. They'd assumed that everyone in the conspiracy knew about the jumpship. They'd also assumed the conspiracy had a major communications advantage because of their infiltration of Hermes, but it wasn't doing them any good if they weren't keeping their field operatives informed.

"They must not tell you everything." Jia's thumb stroked the plasma grenade. "You might be able to figure it out if they did. Too bad."

Anne kept still, her rifle at the ready. The familiar frown and look of disapproval had vanished, replaced by intense concentration.

Luca sighed. "I'm sure you're aware by now that we've jammed the entire area. We know you have whoever is supporting you in the flitter outside, but we also know there's no one coming to reinforce you. I admire your bravery, coming to this place with only the four of you and your flitter pilot. It might be a waste of my time, but my organization could use people of your talents. This doesn't have to end in pointless bloodshed."

Jia's eyes widened. She trembled in rage before nodding at Erik. She knew he wanted his turn.

"You assholes killed my soldiers on Molino," Erik shouted back. "And you keep thinking if you ask nicely, I'll join you? I traveled fifty light-years to find the people responsible, directly and indirectly, and kill every last one.

I don't know how many bases I need to blow up for you to get that message."

Luca let out a harsh, mocking laugh. "Such passion, but what will it accomplish? Nothing. Let me make something clear. You're used to dealing with pathetic cannon fodder, Erik, and when you've attacked our bases, you've come in with greater force. You've let your legend go to your head, but that doesn't mean you can't be of use to us. If you joined, you'd come to understand something important in time."

"That your guys are deluded, crazy sons of bitches?" Erik asked. Kant snickered.

"No, no. Well, that might be true, but that's not what I'm speaking of. You're fixated on Molino and the deaths there, but people die every day, Erik. Countless people. They die for the most foolish of reasons, on Chiron, on Earth, and on other planets and colonies. Those men and women who died on Molino had something that none of those other people did."

Erik's trigger finger twitched. "They had me as their commander."

"No, no, no. Something else far more important. Their deaths had *meaning*."

"Meaning?" Erik bit out through gritted teeth. "They were slaughtered by mercs hired by your people, and that was supposed to be meaningful?"

"They were sacrifices for a *greater future*." Luca sounded almost euphoric. "Don't tell me you never ordered soldiers into likely death when you were in the Army. Sometimes people must die for others, as your soldiers did."

"Why don't you come out and say that to my face?"

Erik yelled. "Right before I blow it off? There's not going to be a negotiation that ends with any of us joining your sick conspiracy. Here's the only negotiation I'm willing to offer. You come out with your hands up and get on your knees, and you don't have to die. Otherwise, well, you die."

A scratching noise came from the hallway ahead.

"I'm not an idiot, Erik," Luca replied. "I know that if we fight, damage will be done to this place, and we're not through with it yet. I'm willing to make you another offer. You can turn around and leave right now. We won't try to stop you. You have to know you can't win, but I'd rather avoid the losses that would be associated with confronting you. Consider this a stalemate, if you will. We both lose certain things."

"How about you give us the alien artifacts you brought here?" Jia called. "Then we'll leave, and we'll call it even."

Luca let out a resounding laugh. "You are as impressive as I believed. You even know about our special shipment! Ah, of course you do. Unfortunately, I cannot hand them over to you, despite my respect. Those items aren't my property, but you should understand there is a special breed here, the Elites. You've faced none like us before in the conspiracy. The Elites are the culmination of many dead-ends to make something better and stronger—the ultimate warrior."

"I'm scared," Erik replied in a mocking tone. "I'm pissing myself."

"Me, too." Kant laughed.

Anne's mouth tightened, but she kept quiet. She might as well have been a statue with a gun.

A loud clank sounded in front of them. Faint humming followed.

"Too bad we couldn't come to some sort of accommodation," Luca called. "But I've been curious to see what one of my Elites can do with such as you. Please kill them, Primul."

CHAPTER FORTY-FOUR

With a clank, a jet-black metal leg cleared the corner, followed by another, then another. Rather than an exoskeleton, a spindly six-legged metal construct turned into the hallway.

The machine was far larger than normal security bots but more compact than a King Sentry. The central body was thin, with a bulbous protrusion in the back and two large cylinders connected underneath.

Jia really hoped those didn't turn out to be rocket launchers.

The bot carried no other obvious weapons unless someone counted its legs, but the air shimmered a couple of meters in front of the bot. Whatever that was didn't bode well for the team's future.

A stun field was one possibility. The bot might charge people and knock them unconscious with an area attack, but the Elite moved slowly, its legs clanking on the floor with each heavy step. Clever undercarriage attacks aside, even Erik didn't try to take on large security bots at close range.

Once her mind was done sorting through the tactical possibilities, the Elite's appearance surprised Jia. Given Luca's big speech, she'd been assuming some new breed of half-Leem super-agent would run around the corner, or something more perverse—maybe a Zitark crossed with a human, a Leem, and a Hunter.

All bots, large or small, were unimpressive, nothing more than simple machines that were easy to defeat once one understood their weakness. She might not recognize the bot's design and hadn't studied it, but that didn't make her more afraid.

They would not fall to this lumbering beast.

The Elite continued its advance. There was no reason to wait for the enemy to open fire. They had given Luca his chance to surrender, and his solution was to hide around the corner and send a bot after them.

He needed to understand who he was dealing with.

Jia hurled her plasma grenade as the team opened fire. Erik's TR-7 spat fire and lead, its four barrels creating a deadly storm of rounds. They crashed into the Elite, creating a shower of sparks. A person or a normal bot would have fallen from a single burst, but the Elite continued its slow advance.

A mocking laugh sounded from the machine. The conspiracy must have paid some scientist a lot to come up with the best ways to intimidate people during an attack. Too bad it wasn't working on Jia.

Erik's bullets gouged a chunk out of the advancing machine, leaving damaged but not destroyed armor. Anne and Kant concentrated on different parts of the bot, their bullets created neat pockmarks but no holes.

Jia didn't have to worry as the grenade tumbled toward the advancing Elite. The grenade struck the shimmer and exploded early with a blinding blue-white flash, scorching the walls and floor.

She squinted and switched to her rifle, ready to fire at the smoky remnants.

The Elite emerged from the smoke scorched, and cracked in a few places, but not showing any distress. It laughed again, this time louder.

"Have to admit that's creepy," Kant complained.

"Ignore it," Anne snapped.

Jia ground her teeth. The Elite was tougher than she expected, but a slow machine with no weapons wasn't a weapon. It was target practice.

Panels retracted, and rotary gun barrels extended from the Elite. Jia had been right about target practice, just not right about the targets.

The laughter got louder and rang out continuously.

"Oh, shit," Erik offered with a grunt. "This could get annoying."

The gun barrels roared to life, their rounds forcing the team back around the corner on both sides and shredding the wall in a shower of sparks and metal chunks. Bullets passed through, striking the walls behind and knocking more chunks out, leaving a hole- and crack-covered mess.

Jia's safe corner disappeared under the withering barrage, forcing her back, but the laughing machine ripped enough of the corner away to give her a new firing position.

"What does that thing have around it?" Kant asked, selecting a plasma grenade. His earlier joy had vanished from his voice. "A shield? Jia's grenade blew up a couple of meters early."

"Some sort of energy field, but not a shield," Jia shouted over the endless gunfire, grateful no one had challenged her throwing accuracy. "The bullets are getting through to the armor fine. It must set off most explosives."

"A lot of good that does us," Anne complained as a piece of shrapnel from the wall sliced her cheek. Her head jerked back. "It's going to take a lot more than a couple of bursts to get through that armor."

With the Elite concentrating on perforating Jia and Anne, Erik took his chance and cleared the corner with his barrel to fire at the bulbous portion near the back. The rounds didn't penetrate the armor, but they ripped a chunk off the top.

The Elite stopped laughing and shuffled to the side, aiming its guns at Erik's and Kant's side.

It started riddling that side with bullets.

"Had to piss it off," Kant muttered as the two men jumped backward, avoiding the huge bullets ripped through the wall. Jia wouldn't have trusted a ballistic shield to protect her against the attack, let alone their vests.

Kant stumbled but righted himself. "We either need a plan in the next minute, or we need to get our asses out of here."

Jia finally understood what the Elite was: a terror weapon. The laughter and the slow, methodical advance.

Luca wanted them to be scared. The bastard might even be using this battle as a test.

She took slow, deep breaths, ignoring the Elite as it returned to pelting her side. They couldn't get a grenade close enough, and the field appeared to extend in a dome, meaning a good throw couldn't save them.

Bullets, particularly AP rounds, were working, but it was like trying to hack at a tree with a pocketknife. They needed time.

Her eyes widened. "We should blow some of the ceiling onto it. Anticipate its movements so it doesn't set the grenades off early. We might get lucky and bury the thing."

If anyone wanted to argue, they didn't take the offered opportunity. Jia risked a lull in the fire on her side to check around the corner, yanking her head back as the Elite blasted the edge off the corner. At the rate it was demolishing the wall, they wouldn't have much cover left, and the teams would be too far apart for her plan to work.

The bot was advancing slower than before, but there was no sign of damage to the legs. It was almost as if it was taunting them, but it had stopped laughing. Luca must have been controlling it directly. That would make the most sense.

He could have used a laser relay system, despite the jamming.

"Bounce near the ceiling at about five meters on my zero," Jia shouted, estimating the rough distance of the enemy based on its current rate of advance. She'd gone through this kind of training with Erik, but she'd never thought she'd be using it in this sort of situation.

There was no fear, only uncertainty. What human hands had built, human hands could destroy.

She wouldn't deny she missed her exoskeleton, though.

Everyone switched their rifles into their left hands before tugging plasma grenades from their vests and priming them. They couldn't risk exposing themselves, so they would have to rely on blind corner throws.

If Anne or Kant panicked, they could end up bouncing their grenades off too close to the opposite side and killing half the team. It was time to test everyone's skill level and see if Alina had picked competent partners.

Heart thundering, Jia shouted her count. "Three, two, one, *zero!*"

The team released their grenades in unison as if they'd been working closely for years. They tossed the grenades around the corner before jumping away from the wretched remnants of what were once corners.

The thunderous roar of the Elite's cannon and her pounding heart grew distant as seconds seemed to stretch into eternity. They had no choice. If they tried to run, half of them would be gunned down, and the other two wouldn't make it to the exit.

When there was no choice left but victory, which made the chosen path easy. The combined explosions shook the hallway, the flash so bright it was like they were around the corner from the sun. Heavy thuds followed, and a plume of flaming debris and smoke billowed out of the corridor.

Harsh tinging ricochets followed for a couple of seconds, the rotary cannons no longer demolishing the walls near the team. Then the guns fell silent.

No one waited for orders. They reloaded, shifted their

guns back over, and spun around the corner to empty their magazines into the smoke. Kant yelled the entire time, with bright eyes and a huge smile. Jia thought he was enjoying the fight too much, but better that than the opposite.

Erik's TR-7 ran empty first. He ejected his magazine to replace it with a new one while the others finished firing. They ducked, also taking the chance to reload, unsure if they'd destroyed the Elite and killed Luca.

Four plasma grenades were enough to take down a lot of things, but if the last two years of Jia's life had taught her anything, it was that the wildest, most unexpected things could happen at any time. If she didn't run into an alien or alien DNA-infused human, it'd be a step up from recent missions.

Jia took short, ragged breaths, the acrid smoke burning her lungs. She missed being able to swap to thermal mode. She was used to having sensors from Emma or an exoskeleton.

Engaging a man and his bot in this environment didn't bother her, but she would have liked to confirm the destruction of the target without looking around the corner and risking her head. She was rather attached to it.

She snorted. Being around Erik was changing her sense of humor.

Dying in an obvious way would be embarrassing. At this point in her life, dying peacefully in her sleep wasn't obvious, so that was how she supposed she would go.

Kant solved the problem of personal risk in a practical if dangerous way. He poked his barrel around the corner, smoke drifting past.

"You destroyed yet, metal brother?" he asked in a mocking tone. "What about you, Luca? Because we're still here, and after all that big talk, I figured you'd recruited the Devil himself to help you, not some souped-up bot that couldn't take grenades and a little ceiling. Poor showing, brother. Poor showing."

There was no response to the taunt.

Jia coughed and waved smoke out of her face. If Agent Dalton hadn't been such an ass, she might have supported Anne's idea of a local team to supplement their forces, but it didn't matter. They would have to take out the new bots themselves.

A building growl sounded from the passage, along with loud scratching and grinding.

Anne's brow lifted. "The bot is growling?"

"I'm sure they've programmed it to respond in this kind of situation," Jia suggested. "Scare off enemy forces while it's wounded."

Kant risked a check and shook his head. "Tough son of a bitch, but that's a design flaw. Growling's not going to be enough."

Jia and the others walked to the remains of the corner. Although acrid smoke filled the hallway, they could make out the outline of the Elite, half-buried under rubble. The source of the ricochets and the reason it had stopped firing became obvious: huge dents and cracks in the gun barrels. Additional firing risked damage to itself.

The Elite yanked a leg free of the rubble and growled again. "You maggots. You *insignificant* MAGGOTS!"

Jia frowned. It was a human voice, but it wasn't Luca.

The metal body was too small to accommodate a human, so it couldn't be some sort of unusual attempt at redesigning an exoskeleton. Somebody had to be controlling the machine, but she didn't understand how they were pulling it off, given the heavy jamming. Laser comms were one possibility, but heavy smoke made that doubtful. The shimmer from before was now a faint glowing wavy field in the smoke.

She could be wrong and it was additional terror programming, but something about the quality of the voice convinced her otherwise.

The rubble shook as the Elite attempted to pull itself free, but five of its legs remained stubbornly buried.

"More grenades," Kant suggested. "It can't dodge now."

Anne pointed at the glowing field. "It still has its field." She gestured at the smoking hole in the ceiling that led to ductwork and a high roof. "And it's not like there's a lot more to bury it with."

Erik grinned and locked his TR-7 onto his carryaid before pulling down his laser rifle. "Lasers don't explode."

"You are lucky, maggots," the Elite growled. "Nothing more. No matter what happens to me, you will die here."

"You'd be surprised how often I hear that. Enough that I don't believe it when people say it." Erik knelt and lined up the laser rifle for a shot straight down the center of the bot's body and through the protrusion in the back. He winked and pulled the trigger.

The Elite's shield had made a mockery of direct explosives, and its thick armor had protected it from a fierce barrage of AP rounds, but the laser beam bored a hole from front to back, leaving sizzling metal and more smoke to fill the room. With a loud thumping clang, the Elite collapsed into the rubble.

Erik patted the laser rifle. "At least we know that works."

Anne nodded at Jia with a respectful look on her face. "Good thinking, Lin."

Jia advanced slowly toward the destroyed Elite, her eyes narrowed. "I manage good things on occasion."

Anne, Erik, and Kant moved with her. Erik kept his laser rifle ready, though he favored his left arm. They continued through the smoke and rubble, kicking some aside as they watched for Luca and kept an eye out to make sure the destroyed machine wasn't moving.

Jia sucked in a breath and blew it out. "I tried to convince myself that someone was controlling that thing, but there's no way they could have done it through the jamming and smoke."

Erik prodded the body with his boot as Anne and Kant continued toward the intersection. "What are you thinking?"

"The conspiracy has been more concerned about capturing the jump drive than Emma," Jia replied. She crouched and peered through the clean tunnel dug by Erik's rifle. "What if they developed a method of making self-aware AIs?"

"You think that's what this is?" Erik looked dubious. "It doesn't need to be alive like Emma to be programmed to send out threats. It's like you said; it's probably just them trying to be intimidating."

Jia stood. "I hope that's it."

Kant and Anne arrived at the intersection before turning opposite ways.

"All that talk, and he's gone," Kant shouted.

"He probably ran once he sent his little toy after us and pinned us down." Erik shouldered his laser rifle. "It was a stall, no worries. If they take off, Emma will shoot their asses down, and we'll finish it that way." He inclined his head down the hallway. "The hangar's that way. We know the play now. Throw grenades to distract them, and I'll finish them off."

Anne gave the laser rifle a dubious look. "That thing doesn't have a lot of shots."

"Don't worry, I brought extra cells," he admitted.

"If they have a lot of those Elites, we might be in trouble."

Erik shrugged. "Let's hope that was the only one." He looked over his shoulder for half a second. "If not, what's life without a little risk?"

Jia stared into the distance, running her tongue along the inside of her mouth. She hoped she was wrong about what the Elites represented. An army of bots with Emma-like intelligence would be an army that could learn far faster than any human and be modified as quickly.

She looked over her shoulder at the destroyed Elite in the rubble. "Please be nothing more than a glorified tin can."

CHAPTER FORTY-FIVE

Erik's wounds ached, but the thrill of victory was the greatest painkiller he knew.

Every time the conspiracy thought they'd developed a clever new way to murder people, Erik and Jia proved that discipline, talent, and willpower won out.

He wasn't surprised that the building was mostly empty. Continual pressure was wearing on their enemy, but each destroyed factory, lab, and base only energized Erik. War favored high morale and momentum, and he wouldn't want to be in conspiracy headquarters after the recent blows the team had delivered.

Erik chuckled. The sound barely traveled, but he still earned an odd look from Anne as they jogged down the hallway, listening and watching for trouble.

He expected more clanging or taunts from Luca in the distance, but the only sounds were the heavy footfalls of the team's boots striking the hard metal floor. He would have liked to have finished off the cocky conspiracy agent earlier, but he was confident he would have his chance later.

They checked doors along the way, but the rooms behind them were all empty, or all but empty, with only a chair or table left inside.

Occasional dried blood made him question how far the conspiracy had gone to clean up here. He didn't see any IO ports but didn't take the time to check further. The mission was the cargo. If they happened to clean out Luca and his friends, they could always take a leisurely stroll through the building later.

That part poked Erik's paranoia. The lack of significant resistance left Erik uneasy. Was he overthinking?

Luca and his Elite could have easily slaughtered unprepared cops who stumbled onto the building. The conspiracy likely had a different base on Chiron and was only using this one as a temporary hangar, or they'd evacuated it after realizing the Intelligence Directorate and their allies were striking farther afield in the war against the conspiracy.

The memories of Provence were never far. Anticonspiracy successes wounded their enemy, and the conspiracy must have understood they needed to adjust the disposition of their forces. Both the *yaoguai* lab and the current facility might reflect that.

Erik would have preferred their arrogant dismissal of risk, but the conspiracy hadn't gathered wealth and power by repeating mistakes.

Past an intersection, large double doors blocked the end of their path.

There were no windows, but by his reckoning, the hangar must be behind them. He didn't buy Jia's theory that the conspiracy had cracked true self-aware AI, but he also couldn't shake the feeling there was more to the Elite. It was tough but not indestructible, not enough to earn such confidence from Luca.

The man might have been bluffing the entire time, unsure if he could escape Erik's and Jia's wrath. Luca had admitted the conspiracy didn't expect Erik and Jia on Chiron, which meant they also didn't expect Malcolm or Emma to be sniffing around their pawns' systems. Military history was full of examples of heavily fortified places being infiltrated because of simple mistakes and overconfidence.

Erik chuckled again.

"What's so funny?" Anne asked, sounding annoyed.

"I was just thinking about infiltration. If Alina was here, she'd probably be talking about the Trojan Horse. They shouldn't have bothered with the horse. They should have just figured how to blow the wall open."

"That's one way to look at things," Anne admitted quietly. "The stratagem wasn't that impressive. As I recall, everyone was drunk and easy to kill in Troy."

The team slowed as they approached the intersection. Jia and Erik moved to one side, while the agents moved to the other. A hundred meters separated them from the hangar.

"There have to be more people than Luca here," Erik commented as he crept toward the intersection. "This might not be Earth, but it's not the frontier either. They aren't running this entire operation with one bot and a guy with a big mouth."

Loud rumbling shook the walls and floor. Erik peeked around the intersection but saw only an empty hallway. The shaking continued with no obvious source.

"Whatever that is, it can't be good," Jia muttered.

"Yeah, I wouldn't bet against that," Kant agreed.

Doors slid open on the far end of the intersection on both sides. A light drumbeat of soft thuds echoed through the hallway, followed by sickening squelching. Something was moving in the rooms.

Erik could hear gunfire, distant and muted but near-constant, like a heavy machine gun or cannon. Muffled booms lightly shook the building, drowning out the gunfire.

"I think the cops or locals might have shown up," he suggested. "It can't just be Emma because I hear explosions."

"Should we pull back?" Anne asked. "Wait for rein-forcements?"

Erik shook his head. "We'll get what we came for, but at least if they're here, they might pull some of the attention off us and give us the chance. We wait, or for all we know, Luca pulls the cargo and disappears into a hidden sewer."

Jia wrinkled her nose. "Not more sewer pipes."

"I don't know." Eric thought about their operation. "They're not so bad without the *yaoguai*, and speaking of…"

A quivering tentacled mass slid out of one of the rooms near the end of the hallway, leaving a trail of slime. Similar creatures emerged behind it and from other rooms. Dark green six-legged monsters the size of small puppies skittered out with them, their thick striated carapaces covered with sharp spikes.

"What the hell?" Kant complained. "This is like next-level *yaoguai* crap." He looked at Jia. "Is this the kind of thing you guys have been dealing with?"

Jia offered him a grim nod. "Among other things."

"It kind of reminds me of some of the uglies we fought on the Hunter ship," Erik replied, sliding his laser rifle back onto his carryaid and grabbing his TR-7. "Let's hope these things are easier to kill."

Panels retracted along the ceiling in the hallway and spider bots poured out. They lacked stun rods or guns, equipped instead with sharp metal mandibles. They scampered along the walls, surging toward the team from all directions.

"This was why Luca pulled back," Erik growled. "He wanted to hit us with everything they had."

"I'm supposed to be a ghost," Kant complained. "Not pest control." He adjusted his fire selection to burst. "I'm not going to be able to eat for a week."

"You can always use more target practice," Anne suggested.

He sighed. "You and target practice."

Jia wasn't in the mood to chat. She loosed a burst into one of the tentacle monsters, and it exploded in a shower of green blood.

She lifted her barrel to pick off the closest spider bot.

Her single shot was enough to take it out. Erik was surprised but grateful to see the conspiracy relying on an off-the-shelf model. Not every fight needed to be a unique challenge.

They'd already had their challenge from the Elite.

There was a time for subtlety, and there was a time to mow down everything in front of you. Erik held the trigger down and swept left and right with the TR-7, stopping only to reload in one fluid motion.

Shell casings cascaded to the floor in a tinkling symphony. Bots exploded in showers of sparks and monsters died. His rivers of lead ripped through the advancing *yaoguai* with ease.

They might look odd, but they weren't Hunter-quality monsters. Humanity, depraved or not, had a long way to go before they could create true nightmares.

Kant managed to adopt an even less subtle strategy by priming and chucking fragmentation and plasma grenades with surprising grace and speed into the enemies in his hallway. The explosions ripped through the bots and creatures, shaking the area. Half-vaporized *yaoguai* collapsed in heaps.

Burning metal from the destroyed bots rained down on the surviving monsters, killing some and wounding others. The survivors attempted to scramble through the destruction, only for his next grenade to explode.

Jia and Anne decided the large agent was on to something. After clearing out the front lines, they both turned to grenades to break up the enemy formation. Erik tossed the occasional grenade between reloads but kept to his TR-7 to deal heavy death. There was something soothing about the constant vibration of the rifle as he fired round after round into the conspiracy's makeshift security horde.

"Remember to save some grenades," Jia shouted. "We

don't want to run into another Elite without grenades. Erik might not be able to get off a shot without our help."

"Heard!" Kant yelled back.

Anne nodded slightly but kept silent as she hurled another plasma grenade.

The piles of destroyed monsters and bots grew in number and height, along with the thick, choking clouds of smoke filling the hallways. It was getting harder to spot the approaching enemies in the blasted, carnage-filled battle-field. Relying on hearing them was pointless because of the constant gunfire and explosions.

Erik gritted his teeth. His earlier wounds were aching more, especially his back. The med patches were doing their work, but they were designed with the idea that whoever was being healed would be smart enough not to keep fighting.

When Erik next reloaded, a lucky security bot emerged from the smoke, clinging to the ceiling. The plucky survivor of the explosions and TR-7 suppression fire dropped from the ceiling, its mandibles pulled back, ready to rip into Erik's face, not having the decency to so much as screech.

He smacked it out of the air with his left arm, sending it careening into the wall. He ignored the faint pain of a slice in the thin layer of flesh surrounding his cybernetic arm. It would have been a trivial wound on a normal arm and was less than trivial now.

The bot survived the hit and clambered to its feet after falling to the floor. It didn't survive Erik's four-barrel point-blank burst. The attack blasted it to pieces.

"Not your day." Erik spun away from the destroyed bot

in time to rake down a group of tentacled *yaoguai* sliding through the smoke. "Not the best day for any of you…" he grimaced at the one in front, "*things.*"

Did he have enough ammo? The thought became louder and more insistent. They'd been prepared for the battle of attrition in France, but this was supposed to be a quick raid. The carryaids made it easier to bring more bullets and grenades along, but they couldn't defeat anywhere near as many enemies as they had in and around the mansion.

Erik grunted in frustration.

At least the damned monsters had the decency to die easily. He didn't need to practice Jia's religion of ammo preservation in this fight yet.

Jia and Anne deployed similar tactics after a couple of minutes of battle. Both relied on controlled bursts, with the occasional grenade thrown in to rip apart a closely packed group of enemies. The bots and monsters displayed no fear, climbing over their fallen brethren without pause or concern as they continued toward the four agents, but that also made them easy targets.

"Damn," Kant yelled. "Out of grenades. I got a little too feisty."

Erik didn't dare pull his attention away from his own enemies. The agent would need to cover himself.

Shadows advanced through Erik's hallway. He hefted his rifle and fired into the smoke. None of the *yaoguai* or bots screamed or screeched when they died. If they weren't destroyed on the first shot, they twitched and bled. He didn't admire relentlessness from mindless enemies.

There was no bravery without fear.

Jia hissed in pain as a security bot made it past her gauntlet and bit her leg. She kicked it off and blew it apart before smashing away another and gunning it down. The bots gave a tentacle monster time to slide closer, and it brought back an appendage, ready to strike.

CHAPTER FORTY-SIX

Jia blew off the tentacle with a snort, the creature's blood splattering all over her.

"Okay, that's gross."

She tried to ignore the pain in her leg. After so many fights and injuries, it was easy to compartmentalize. At least the bot hadn't bitten through one of her hands.

"No. Not today. This isn't where I die." She sent a burst through the *yaoguai*'s body, killing it and one of the bugs behind it. "And when I die, it won't be to a pathetic mindless tool like you."

Her leg ached with sharp pain, but there was no strange burning or numbness that might signal poison. All she needed to do was survive the horde.

She was still in better shape than Erik.

Every bot they destroyed and *yaoguai* they killed meant a loss of resources to the conspiracy. They would cleave through the monsters and seize the cargo. If they were lucky, they'd take out or capture Luca along the way, and

Chiron would be added to the lists of humiliations for their enemies.

Warrior Princess. Lady Justice. Jia Lin. She didn't care what they called her as long as they feared her.

Jia ejected a magazine and slammed in a new one. She took three quick shots to destroy three approaching security bots. She didn't like how fast she was burning through ammo, but the security bots were becoming sparser, and she didn't notice any of the *yaoguai* healing or surviving more than two shots.

Alina hadn't made any mistakes. Anne and Kant might have their quirks, but no one could question how they performed in battle. Erik and Jia wouldn't have been able to pull off the raid without their help.

It was easy to miss in the cacophony of the battle, but the walls shaking absent their grenades and rhythmic booms from outside continued to prove they weren't fighting the only battle in the area. Whatever was going on outside was as intense as what they were dealing with inside. She hoped Emma could convince whoever was there to help them.

Anne cried out in pain. Jia turned in her direction. The agent lay on her back, groping for her rifle. Two of the bug *yaoguai* slashed at her. With two quick trigger pulls, Jia blew their heads off. Anne snatched up her rifle and killed the next closest monster, ignoring the gashes in her arms and leg.

Jia spun back toward her personal hellscape in time to shred a tentacled *yaoguai*. Her enemies were fewer and farther between now, the crack of her rifle sporadic, her aim less hurried and more deadly. When nothing new emerged after five seconds, she chanced another shot at the enemies menacing Anne.

Kant rushed to Anne's side and opened fire. Jia narrowed her eyes, peering through the smoke and gore in his hallway, but there was nothing advancing. His barbarian grenadier strategy had paid early dividends.

A joint effort between Kant and Anne cleared the last of the enemies in their hall. Jia's final enemy, a smoking security bot missing half its leg, crawled toward her. She let it get close before finishing it off with a single shot.

An eerie quiet settled over the area, the hard, ragged breathing of the team audible. Whatever battle had been raging outside was over, with no more explosions or gunfire.

Blood ran down Anne's arms. There was a deep gouge in her left from the security bot bite and a jagged tear in her right from one of the *yaoguai*.

Jia pulled a med patch from a vest pocket and offered it to her. "You okay?"

"It turns out you're a good shot outside a range, too," Anne replied softly, applying the patch. She hissed. "I've been better, but I've also been a lot worse. Don't worry about me."

"I know how you feel." Jia grimaced, her leg aching more now that the rush of battle was fading. She applied her own patch. No one had escaped the battle unscathed, but they'd destroyed a small army's worth of bots and monsters.

Anne ejected her empty magazine and inserted a fresh one. Her ammo supply didn't look any better than Jia's, Kant's, or Erik's. Kant was out of grenades, and the other three had used far more than anyone would have preferred in the fight.

Jia glanced at Erik. "Ammo's a concern."

"We won't survive another fight like that one," Anne observed. "Are we sure we want to keep going?"

Erik grinned with only the barest hint of pain in his eyes despite his extensive injuries. "If we won't survive another like that, we'll have to make sure we don't have any more like that."

"You make it sound so easy," she replied

"And you make it sound so hard."

Jia nodded slowly. "I hate to make assumptions given our line of work, but I don't think they would have held back if they had more to throw at us, bots, *yaoguai*, or guards. Whatever other forces they have were either sent outside to deal with whoever was out there or are guarding the cargo flitter."

Anne shrugged. "The flitter might already be gone."

Erik shook his head. "You're a real ray of sunshine."

"Only pointing out the possibilities," she answered.

Kant wandered down one of the halls and opened a door. He poked his gun inside and frowned. "Another empty room." He made a face, and not a pretty one. "This one smells like shit, though."

"They were probably storing *yaoguai* in it," Jia thought about it. "They might have even been breeding them here. I hate to think they were shipping things like that through transports and the HTPs."

"They stripped the place, so it's hard to know," Kant replied. "Doesn't matter much now, does it?"

Erik inclined his head in the direction of the sealed

double doors. "You're right. It doesn't matter. We're not here for yaoguai. After we get what we came for, we'll let Dalton know, and his people can come here and sweep the entire damned place and take credit for whatever they find. I'm not picky about glory. I just want the conspiracy."

He headed toward the double doors with a confident stride, but not a jog or a run.

Jia followed him, limping slightly. Her motion smoothed out after a few meters. "Luca's probably in there."

"Yeah, he already ran once." Erik considered the options. "I'm not as worried about him. If he was all that, he would have already taken us on. He's the kind of guy who hides behind bots and monsters, which doesn't bother me. We killed all his monsters and fragged all his bots."

"I hope Emma's okay," Jia commented. "She must have gotten caught up in whatever's going on outside. Overzealous locals might not get that she's on their side."

"She'll be fine. If there's one thing she values, it's her life. The Taxútnta can take a lot of damage, and she'll survive."

Jia wasn't sure how much physical damage her core matrix could take, but she'd proven surprisingly resilient. She figured Emma was a lot like Erik. He wouldn't die in a random firefight on Chiron. Emma needed to survive, like Erik, until the final showdown with the bastards who controlled the conspiracy.

Jia, Anne, and Kant arrived at the closed doors. The partner pairs took up positions on either side, ready to storm the hangar. Erik mouthed a countdown and slapped the access panel.

The door didn't open. Not surprising, but disappointing.

"Okay." Erik stepped away with a smile. "That's how he wants to play it." He nodded at Jia. "You're up again. Luca needs to learn not to be so rude."

Anne and Kant jogged backward, never lowering their rifles. Along with Erik, they positioned themselves along the wall, their sweat-covered faces locked in concentration. Their rifles were pointed forward, ready to kill any stray monsters or bots the enemy had in reserve.

Jia set her rifle down and knelt before pulling the launcher and a new missile off the carryaid.

She had two more, and she suspected they might need them to deal with whatever and whoever was behind the door. Any *yaoguai* or guard stupid enough to stand right behind the door was in for a rude surprise.

After a brief check to make sure everyone was clear, she launched the missile with casual ease, as if she did this sort of thing every day. She wasn't too arrogant to admit that blowing up large doors with missile launchers was fun. Simulations and training weren't the same.

The massive explosion blew a gaping hole in the doors. If anything, the attack had been more effective than their initial entry into the building.

Jia set the launcher on her carryaid before picking up her rifle with a satisfied smile.

Erik and Kant rushed to the hole and took positions beside it. The cargo flitter they'd been chasing was parked inside, barely visible past rows and rows of crates and shipping containers, some long and thin, some tall and wide. They filled half the cargo bay, forming a rough U-shape around the flitter and also acting as cover—something Jia appreciated after taking on the Elite in the hallway.

The two men jogged through the hole and ducked behind a tower of crates. Erik signaled for Jia and Anne to advance. The women sprinted inside and slid behind a large shipping container that looked like it could hold the cargo flitter. This might explain where everything in the building had gone.

Something clanked across the bay, concealed by one of the larger shipping containers. Familiar laughter echoed throughout the hangar—Luca's.

"You two just don't know when to quit, do you?"

CHAPTER FORTY-SEVEN

"I think all you conspiracy bastards would know that by now," Erik shouted. "You throw men at us. You throw Tin Men at us. *Yaoguai*. You even threw damned aliens at us, and we keep surviving. You think you can scare us off with fancy new weapons? We've fought shit that would make you wet your bed and never be able to sleep again. We've risked our lives in ways you'd think were insane, and we're going to keep doing it. Keep coming back and killing until there's none of you left."

"I see," Luca called back, sounding more amused than angry. "You are a dedicated man. No one could doubt that. It's brought you far, but dedication and bravery aren't guarantees."

Erik kept low as he walked to a thin seam between the stacks of crates and peered through. The maze of containers made it difficult to see anything. Something large and dark moved among the crates on the opposite side of the hangar. He needed only the briefest of glances.

"More Elites," he whispered.

"To be honest, I didn't believe the minimal leftover forces we had here would do much to stop you," Luca continued, now sounding impressed. "Or it might be more accurate to say I hoped they wouldn't. It would have been disappointing to see the great Last Soldier and Warrior Princess fall to what amounts to leftover scraps in this place. Your two friends are impressive as well. Our intelligence doesn't suggest any close allies who left the department with you, and this doesn't have the feel of a military operation, so I'm assuming the ID has lent you some ghosts."

Anne frowned but didn't say anything. Kant cracked a smile as if pleased he was being recognized. He should have been in the Army, not the Intelligence Directorate, with that attitude.

Erik gestured for Kant to move to the other side of the stack. If they could flank the enemy, they would have the advantage. The Elite they'd fought earlier had cannons but not a turret.

All it would take was one solid hit with the laser rifle, and Luca's toys would break.

"I hate having to kill people I respect," Luca explained. "It's happened more than you think in my current career. Must we fight, Erik? Is there no way around it?"

"I'm not here for you, Luca," Erik shouted. "We just want what's on the flitter. All you have to do is walk away."

"No, you didn't come for that." Luca had returned to sounding amused.

"Pretty sure I didn't carve through all those bots and monsters because I needed the exercise." Erik laughed.

"You're the one who set up the clever little trap. Too bad for you we have some tricks and traps of our own."

"Of course you do. Otherwise you wouldn't be here, but I'm afraid you're misunderstanding me."

"Then explain it to me, because I'm getting impatient, and I'm itching to finish off my little flitter robbery."

Erik winced at a spike of pain in his back. Considering how many med patches he'd slapped on, the fact that he was still feeling things meant he'd need to spend serious time in bed resting and letting the nanites do their jobs.

"I understand loyalty," Luca replied. "I understand it far better than you realize."

"Do you?" Erik asked. "Is that because you're a psycho like the doctor they poisoned in Provence, or is because you're afraid to die?"

"My life is in my employers' hands. I'm loyal to the people I work for not because of that, but because I believe in them. So much so that I've willingly made sacrifices, as have my men, to become stronger for them so as to be better able to serve them. I understand what it must feel like to have lost your soldiers on Molino, but I'm willing to share some information with you. Consider it a down payment in good faith because I understand loyalty."

Erik motioned for Anne and Jia to move farther down the maze of crates. They kept low, and their movements slow. The jamming remained active, killing Luca's access to cameras, and there were no drones around for laser comm tricks. Depending on what was in the crates, it might conceal their thermal signature. Surprise remained a possibility.

"I'm listening," Erik replied. "Like I said, we're not here

to kill you, so anything you want to do to make us less likely to do that is to your advantage."

"It's about Molino and the men responsible. A group of men with no loyalty, mercenary scum. I have no more respect for their kind than you do."

Erik didn't respond. He already knew the chain of responsibility for Molino, but pointing that out might stop Luca from giving up something new.

"You saying the conspiracy wasn't responsible?" Erik asked. "That some mercs were? That I've been chasing my tail around the galaxy for no good reason?"

"No, that would be too much. We both know you understand far more than that. It was ultimately my organization's needs that led to the death of your soldiers, but if this is about revenge, it should be about the people who were there and those most directly responsible, should it not?"

"You think so?" Erik quietly set his rifle on the carryaid and grabbed the laser rifle. He doubted Luca was depending on a single Elite to save him.

"Those mercenaries were hired by the Ascended Brotherhood, a group I know you're well-acquainted with," Luca continued. "A group you battled on many occasions, a group of cyborgs you took out with surprising and impressive skill."

Erik snickered. "You mean the losers we gutted on Venus? All that fancy cyborg tech didn't mean much in the end. How much do they tell you, Luca? Did they tell you how their little factory blew up? It sounds to me like the conspiracy disposed of them. So much for loyalty."

"Oh, I'm aware of the end of the Brotherhood, but I don't consider it tragic if that's your intent."

Muffled clangs came from two different positions across the hangar. Erik had been right. There was more than one Elite. If they set up a crossfire, this team was done.

"Then what's the point?" Erik asked. "The Ascended Brotherhood is dead. Why bring them up?"

"Yes," Luca replied, practically hissing the last consonant. "They *are* dead, and that's exactly why I mentioned them, but let me show you something else relevant to this discussion."

Erik whipped his rifle up at movement in the center of the hangar. A large hologram appeared, a group of men on their knees with their hands bound behind their heads. Gunshots rang out, and a man fell forward with a hole in his head. The other men tried to stand and flee, but their unseen assailant kept shooting, and they were all dead in less than thirty seconds, lying in a growing pool of blood.

"Those were the survivors of the mercenaries who killed your soldiers," Luca explained. "Some of the others perished on their way back from Molino for unrelated reasons. The ultimate point is, you've achieved your revenge. The Ascended Brotherhood is dead, as are the mercenaries. Those responsible for the deaths of your unit on Molino are all dead."

Erik waved his hand at Jia in the distance and then gestured to her missile launcher. She nodded in understanding and switched weapons. With quiet, careful deliberation, she reloaded the missile launcher, leaving her with one last missile.

He snorted. "That's like saying if I shot someone with my TR-7, they should get their revenge on the gun. The mercs did what they did because they were paid, and the Brotherhood did what they did because they were ordered to. They're nothing more than the gun. I want the shooter. If you claim to understand me, you must know that."

"Yes," Luca replied. "They were ordered to kill your men by Sophia Vand, who is also dead."

Erik's heart sped up. He had no regrets about what had happened to Vand, but if the conspiracy was only Sophia Vand, he wouldn't have been so busy since Venus. A man didn't need to be an expert in psychology to know when someone was trying to manipulate him. It'd be convenient for the conspiracy to place all the blame on a dead woman to throw him off their tail.

It might have been true, but he doubted it. If the conspiracy wanted mercy, they could surrender to the ID and CID. The more they hid and played games, the more they begged Erik and Jia to come and kill them. They had hundreds if not thousands of deaths to answer for. Erik thought by the time this was all over, he'd find out they had millions.

Today, though, Erik wasn't there for immediate satisfaction. He was there for whatever Alina's analysts and Barbu's records had helped him find. There was something important enough in the cargo flitter to cost ten men's lives already, and its appropriation or destruction would wound the conspiracy a lot more than taking out a couple of Elites.

It was time to turn everything around on Luca.

"This is your last chance," Erik yelled. "We're not here

for you and your toy bots, but if you want to fight us, we will kill you."

"Bots?" The echoes made it sound like the entire hangar was laughing. "Is that what you think an Elite is? Oh, you deluded fool."

"You programmed it to try to intimidate people." Erik crept toward another gap between the crates, wondering if it was wide enough to not block the beam of his laser rifle. "I'll give you credit, Luca. It was a tough bastard, and if we had not been properly geared up, it might have taken us out, but a bot's just a machine in the end. And that's the problem, a person can always outthink a bot. Your jamming is going to prevent you from directly controlling them, and even if you could, it'd be too hard to deal with all four of us and my friend outside."

Erik didn't consider Emma a bot. He no longer knew if "artificial intelligence" was a good description, considering how she was created. Making a human-like intelligence starting with a human was about as natural and non-artificial as he could imagine.

"Oh, I'm disappointed," Luca replied. "But you and the Warrior Princess can't always know what's happening. The Elites aren't bots. Don't you understand? The Ascended Brotherhood was nothing more than a prototype of something grander, a better class of servant. Can you outthink a man who has the strength of a machine?"

Jia shivered in revulsion, resting her launcher's tip against a crate. Anne and Kant didn't look happy either.

"You're saying that was a Tin Man we fought?" Erik asked.

"No, that's the problem. A Tin Man is just that, a man

461

with modifications, stuck in a basic humanoid shape. The Elites are something grander, a human brain in whatever shell needed. *We* are the ultimate soldiers."

"It's just a matter of time before Cybernetic Psychosis Syndrome sets in," Erik countered. "You sick bastard. I don't know what tricks they pulled with the Ascended Brotherhood, but at least they were closer to what the human brain evolved to handle. You really think you can run around like a spider and not have every part of you reject that? It might not have happened yet, but it's going to."

"You're sure?" Luca asked. "You're confident you understand. Humanity could have accomplished so much, but my employers aren't bound by the feeble fears of the past. That's why they'll win."

Erik frowned. Luca had sacrificed an Elite and an entire complex of bots and *yaoguai* to slow the team. Even his pathetic attempt to convince Erik the revenge was done seemed like a stall tactic. That suggested he wasn't as confident as he sounded about his Elites.

Reinforcements? More Elites? That was a possibility. The other most likely explanation was that they'd planned to escape, but something had stopped them, something outside. Maybe Emma had contacted the locals, and the police, CID, and militia had the facility surrounded. There might already be piles of destroyed Elites outside.

"I bet most of the people who run the conspiracy are a lot like Sophia Vand," Erik began. "And it's hard not to notice she wasn't a brain in a bot body. You're an idiot. You're being played, and we're leaving this place with that flitter. If you want to live, you better find the back door to this place and skitter away to find someone to swap out your parts."

Luca scoffed, derision thick in the sound. "Did you really think I'd agree to that?"

"Did you really think I'd walk away because you murdered some mercs and blamed everything on a conveniently dead woman?"

"A pity, Erik. Your death and Jia's will make the UTC a worse place, but you, like those on Molino, are a necessary sacrifice."

Kant replaced his magazine with AP rounds. "Ouch." He whispered, "It's like Anne and I aren't here."

Anne flipped the safety off her rifle. "I'm fine with not being on a first-name basis with a conspiracy nut."

Erik nodded at Jia and kept his voice low. "Blow away the front of the cargo flitter."

Jia stared at him. "What? Are you insane?"

"Take it out. The cargo's not going to be in the front." Erik inclined his head toward the doors. "We need to make sure they don't get away. I don't care what kind of souped-up can he's riding. We saw it earlier. They can't fly."

"I'll only have one missile after that." Jia hoisted the launcher onto her shoulder and edged toward a break in the crates that gave her a clear shot at the flitter. "You sure?"

"It's fine." Erik patted his laser rifle. "I've got all the Elite remover we need."

CHAPTER FORTY-EIGHT

The heavy steps of the Elites echoed through the hangar.

Their shadows were fleetingly visible through the gaps between the shipping containers and crates as the metal monsters moved, reinforcing their size and threat.

Jia ignored them and concentrated on cutting off their line of retreat. They'd beaten an Elite before. They would beat them here. They *couldn't* risk letting them escape.

All their investigations and fortune had led them to this hidden base on Alpha Centauri. This was about more than a new kind of cyborg. Jia wasn't ready to believe in Erik's Lady, but it wouldn't hurt to give her a kind thought.

Perhaps two.

She wanted to believe Emma was outside as backup, but for all they knew, the MX 60 was a burning wreck, the victim of outside forces. The team would need to handle the problems inside.

The Elites' size and power presented obvious costs. They had not surged over the crates or charged through any of them. That meant they were either unwilling to lose their cover or unable to challenge the cargo maze with ease. The fewer direct lines of fire available, the greater the advantage for the human team.

If the Elites couldn't do that, it was unlikely they could fly. No cargo flitter meant no escape.

Holding her breath, Jia pulled the trigger. The missile roared away from the launcher and sped toward the front of the flitter, leaving a trail of smoke. Her stomach tightened during the short seconds the missile zoomed from her position to her target.

It *needed* to hit.

It needed to destroy what she'd aimed at, but she'd expected one of the Elite's shields to surround the flitter or a point-defense system like a torch dragon. Could they hold off the Elites and keep the cargo flitter pinned down by themselves?

Her missile struck the front of the flitter, and a massive fireball engulfed it. Flaming chunks of the cockpit shot all over the nearby area, embedding themselves into containers and the floor. The force of the blast toppled the nearby stacks of containers, scattering them all over.

Containers smashed into the floor, releasing their contents, some mundane, parts, furniture, or equipment. Others were more deadly, such as one crate spilling grenades in a pile, or another filled with small black cubes.

She ducked back behind cover, trading her launcher for her rifle. There were holes in everyone's defenses. The Elites had concentrated so hard on protecting themselves, they'd left their entire group vulnerable.

"Nice shot," Erik yelled.

"I thought so! I didn't think one missile would take out

that much. We need to adjust the parameters in our training scenarios. They don't blow up as much."

"They do. You don't get the full effect in the training center. It's not enough to hear it and feel heat. You need that full sensory experience."

"You're insane!" screamed Luca. "You think you can do that and ignore me while you prattle on?"

"Yeah, pretty much," Erik answered. "We blew up your ride, and that leaves you trapped here with us. And the guy who gave up his body to get stuck in a spider robot is calling us insane?"

"You'll die here," Luca snarled. "You can't win against us. You'll regret ever coming to this planet in the short seconds before you die!"

"Talk, talk, talk. That doesn't change the fact you've got half a flitter!"

With a growl, two Elites crashed through a pile of crates, their cannons ready.

"Oh, crap," Kant commented.

Jia and Erik had been wrong about their inability to go through the crates.

The enemy cannons spun up, their rounds ripping through the metal shipping containers and crates like paper and forcing the team to crouch to avoid losing their heads. Jia didn't want to test her vest against that large and fast a round.

Two other Elites stayed behind their cover, their movements betrayed by loud clanking as they worked through the makeshift pathways away from the team toward the half-destroyed flitter in a possible flanking maneuver or an attempt to secure the cargo. The simplest solution to solving the mystery would be to take all the Elites down.

That way, the answer didn't matter.

Erik crawled toward a stack of tall, narrow containers. Anne and Kant risked quick return fire. Their bullets bounced off the advancing Elites, leaving them with only minor damage. The enemies continued their ruthless counterattack, one spinning toward Erik.

The Elite angled its cannon down but not enough to hit him, the bullet storm blasting into the floor just past him and coating him with dust and small pieces of the component material. Erik scurried forward surprisingly fast, considering he was on his stomach.

She'd seen it before in the training environment, where Erik was fond of making her crawl through fake mud.

Anne and Kant rolled out of the way as the other Elite swept their area with its cannons. Rounds tore past them, perforating their cover so thoroughly they gained a new bay window in their temporary home.

It allowed a touch of sunshine to come through.

With a wrenching noise, the containers at their level began to buckle, the damaged walls no longer able to support the weight above them. Kant pushed Anne out of the way as large crates, some near as big as the agent, tumbled down and buried him.

Anne landed hard on her back, knocking the air out of her. She gasped for breath.

A low groan escaped the pile. Kant wasn't dead, but he wasn't in a position to counterattack, either.

Jia's stomach tightened. Helping Kant meant leaving their flank exposed and risking all their lives.

"Kant," Jia shouted. "Are you okay?"

"Okay" was relative given the situation, but any encounter with deadly cyborgs that didn't end with your head torn off was a good start.

The pile shook, and Kant's thumb popped through a gap. "I'm breathing. Pay those bastards back for me."

He yanked his hand down when an Elite fired into the pile. Anne sucked in a breath, regaining control.

The third and fourth Elites continued their mad dash toward the cargo flitter. Though their maximum speed was far more impressive than the meandering advance of the first encounter, they weren't much faster than Jia at a dead-on sprint.

Jia could see why they needed the flitter. There was no way they could escape from drones if that was their best.

She fired in their direction, nailing the targets in brief windows of opportunity but earning nothing more than sparks and new dents for her trouble.

They were heading to the flitter for a reason, and it wouldn't be good for her team.

The Elites continued lumbering along, closing on an opportunity: the spilled container of grenades. They didn't seem to notice or care, but Jia did.

Shooting grenades, especially plasmas, wasn't typically enough to set them off. She'd have to sacrifice one of her small supply to be sure. There wasn't time to consider her action rationally. She had seconds to decide.

Decision made, she pulled, primed, and threw a plasma grenade as an Elite cleared the corner and entered the smoking debris field near the burning flitter.

The cyborg monstrosity ignored the grenade hurtling

toward it, confident in its shield, exactly as Jia had hoped. When the grenade dropped toward the pile, the Elite side-stepped, realizing the mistake. His partner hurried backward, but it was too late for the other Elite.

Red, orange, blue, and white blasts joined the kind of colorful display normally only achieved through the willful misuse of dangerous explosives on holidays.

The bright light, fire, and smoke obscured the Elite. Crates tumbled over the other Elite, burying it with a mighty crash.

The other pair of Elites froze, their attacks ceasing. They turned toward the explosion.

Jia smiled. Could they still feel fear in their metal shells? Luca should have known who he was messing with.

A small crater marked the center of the explosion. Blasted pieces of the unfortunate Elite at the center of Jia's trick flew through the air, parts of the legs and torso clearly visible as they pelted the floor and their teammates. She grimaced at the thought there could be brains in there, too.

Jia glanced at Erik, who had advanced to an undamaged set of crates, his position temporarily blinding him.

"Three o'clock at one meter high!" she shouted.

Erik grinned and rolled onto his side, still behind a crate. He pointed his rifle at the side of a smaller crate in the direction of one of the hesitating Elites and pulled the trigger.

The invisible beam burned through the crate with ease and pierced the opposite side. It also sheared two of the legs off the Elite and blew off the bottom of the back protrusion. Not bad for a blind shot.

The Elite collapsed, its momentum carrying it across the ground with a horrible grinding sound before it stopped close to Erik's position.

"I think we found the braincase." Erik grunted. "All the hardware in the world and it comes down to a headshot."

The second Elite abruptly spun and rushed toward the opposite side of the hangar. Jia blew out a breath of concern. They *did* understand self-preservation.

Erik fired another shot, searing off a back leg but missing the brain compartment. His target almost made it behind a huge shipping container when the next shot vaporized most of the braincase.

The buried Elite burst out of the crate as if begging Erik to end it. A quick shot from the laser rifle incinerated a chunk of the back and most of the braincase.

Erik yanked the power cell of his rifle out and tossed it behind him, then grabbed another from the carryaid and spun it into the weapon with a satisfied look.

With a quick glance toward the pile burying her partner, Anne rolled back onto her stomach and crawled toward a crate. She pulled a plasma grenade from her vest and stayed low, keeping her head down.

Kant might be wounded and buried under a pile of heavy metal boxes, but that left Erik's laser rifle, Jia's missile launcher, and Anne's grenades to finish off the final Elite. Jia transferred her rifle back to the carryaid before retrieving the launcher and her final missile.

She didn't care about this latest iteration of a Tin Man. It was still three to one, and the Elites were on the run.

Metal banged against metal in three sharp bursts. The

remaining Elite concealed itself in the cratered wasteland near the flitter wreckage.

"What's it doing?" Anne murmured.

"Not sure," Jia admitted.

Erik risked rising to a crouch and moving farther ahead, his path following the bend in the cargo stacks as it arced toward the opposite wall. He remained quiet.

The bangs sounded again.

"It's an adjustment, this form." Luca's familiar voice came from the remaining Elite. "I could play the sound of a clap, but it lacks the satisfaction that comes with performing the action yourself. I understand my laughter and other noises aren't real. They're simply recordings they've calibrated to my brain responses to allow me a full range of communication as necessary. I'm surprised they find it necessary, but the technology is beyond my understanding. It could be that a brain without laughter might be doomed for Cybernetic Psychosis Syndrome."

"*Now* you've got time to be philosophical over CPS?" Jia shouted, hoping to draw Luca's attention away from Erik. "You should have thought of that before you traded your body and soul away to become a metal monster. What could the conspiracy be doing that could possibly justify that? What would make you *volunteer* for something like that?"

"Many things, some of which you might even learn before you die, but I think I'll enjoy killing you and leaving that as another of your life's disappointments."

After nodding at Anne and then inclining her head in the direction of Luca's voice, Jia crept back toward an exposed position, the only place she could get a decent shot off. Luca's shield would protect him from direct hits, but all she needed to do was blind him for a second and Erik would have his chance.

"The only one who is going to die here is you." Jia worked on putting a foot in front of the other, staying behind protection. "All that effort and time, and we sliced through your Elites, leaving you the only one alive. We're going to finish you off, and we're going to take the cargo."

She shot a nervous glance at the wreckage. The blast had exposed the trailer, including two narrow black crates secured inside with magnetic locks. They'd been scorched but not breached.

"And then what?" Luca asked. "You think because you find a small piece of the puzzle that you can understand a picture far more complicated than you can imagine?"

Erik reached the bottom of the U. He needed a few more moments.

"You still can surrender," Jia replied, her shoulder sore under the weight of the launcher. "I'm guessing you control the jammer. Shut it off and let us open the doors, and we'll figure out something, or you can die, accomplishing nothing like the other four Not-So-Elites."

Anne quirked an eyebrow at Jia's taunt. A smirk broke her bland expression.

Kant's full arm emerged from his tomb of crates. With a groan, he pushed one off and his head emerged, blood running down the side from a large gash. That didn't stop his smile. Everyone understood they were about to win.

"Even now, you don't understand the future and the potential." Luca's laughter grew louder and more mocking.

"You'll see eventually, but by then, it'll be too late. There is also something else you don't understand."

Jia caught Erik's shadow out of the corner of her eye.

"What's that?" she asked.

"Unlike your flawed, incomplete body. I can see in all directions."

Jia's heart sped up at the loud whir of the rotary cannons spinning up. Luca was concealed behind the crate, but the bright flash of the dual cannons firing marked his position. She couldn't see Erik. Something thudded where he'd been. It didn't sound as large as an Elite.

She jumped from her hiding place and made a token effort at aiming. The missile didn't need to hit. It only needed to get his attention.

"I'm still here, you monster!" she screamed and launched.

The missile struck the shipping container guarding Luca, the explosion blowing clean through. It peppered him with chunks of metal from the container and exposed his position. Anne took her chance and arced her grenade toward him with a loud grunt.

Luca bellowed out an earth-shattering roar to join the clatter of shell casings on the ground from the heavy, continual fire of his cannons, aimed not at her but in Erik's direction.

What was the thud she'd heard? If Luca was still firing, Erik was still a threat. Jia primed her last two grenades and hurled them toward the Elite. Anne matched her effort as if they'd planned it in advance.

The grenades exploded early against the field as

expected, but the force of the explosions shoved the Elite onto his side. He ceased fire.

Luca hopped back onto all six legs and returned to firing as he hadn't been scorched by grenades seconds before. Erik let out a loud, pained grunt right before a laser beam ripped Luca in half. The guns fell silent again as the two halves of the Elite dropped to the ground with a loud bang.

"Erik!" Jia shouted.

He didn't respond.

Her galloping heart found a new speed. "Erik?"

CHAPTER FORTY-NINE

"Erik!"

Jia's shout sounded distant, like it'd come from halfway across the planet, but it got Erik's attention and focus. Before, he'd tried to run away from the pain, but now he concentrated on it and used it as a tool, like he was using her voice.

Erik's eyelids were heavy. His back hurt. Fiery pain gripped other parts of his body. His left arm only wasn't agony because of its cybernetic nature, but Luca's attacks had blown off most of the lower arm and left large holes in the upper arm and shoulder. A graze on his leg had torn off a good chunk of muscle. There were more holes than he preferred in other parts of his body.

If he wasn't already loaded down with med patches, he would not be able to achieve even this level of focus.

Erik forced his eyes open and sat up. He wiped blood and sweat off his face and nodded in satisfaction at the two halves of Luca.

It didn't matter who was in the fight. The guy who

wasn't in two pieces at the end would always be the winner. Erik glanced at bloody metal remains of his cybernetic arm and amended the conclusion in his mind. The guy who wasn't in two *large* pieces at the end of the fight would always be the winner.

"Yeah, screw you, you freak." He spat out blood.

Heavy footfalls sounded from behind Erik, but he didn't feel like wasting the energy to turn around. If someone else wanted to take a shot, they'd have to get past Jia. His plan for the entire trip back to the jumpship was a lot of med patches and sleep.

Jia closed in from behind him and looked down at him with concern. She let out a sigh of relief. "I thought you got yourself killed. Well, totally killed." There was a pause, and her voice dropped just a bit. "Don't get so close next time." She winced at the sight of his arm. "Doesn't that hurt?"

"Not as much as you'd think. It hurt a hell of a lot more when I lost the original." Erik managed a pained grin. He tried to move his left arm, but nothing happened. "Shit. You know the one thing I didn't pack? A spare arm. That's the problem with getting blown up and shot. It's hard on my body."

Kant and Anne joined Jia, neither poster children for escaping encounters unscathed. The former had two med patches applied directly to the side of his head, and it looked like someone had dunked his face in a tank of blood. Combined with his size, it made him look like a crazed demon out of myth.

Erik grunted in irritation. "Shit. That bastard got me good."

"You're not dead." Kant shrugged, looking a bit dazed.

"That's all that counts, right? I'd much rather be missing an arm than have a hole in my head, and that wasn't even your original arm."

"It had sentimental value." Erik tried to chuckle but stopped with a grimace. He looked in front of him, his jaw tightening at a different horrible sight. "That son of a bitch. If I hadn't already blown him in half, I'd kill him slowly."

"It's not unusual to hate a man who almost killed you," Anne suggested, glancing in Luca's direction. "Or a thing, in this case."

"Screw that." Erik leaned forward and grabbed his laser rifle, or rather the two pieces that used to form a rifle. "Luca's last couple of shots took out my rifle. I don't know if I'll be able to get another one of these from Adeyemi. I can't buy this in a store."

Anne laughed, a loud, free sound. It was the most positive emotion he'd seen from her since they'd met.

"If the colonel can't, I'm sure Alina can," she answered. "You earned it, Blackwell. I don't know whether to be impressed or disgusted, but you *are* good at taking enemies down."

Jia knelt beside Erik and pressed a med patch over his leg wound. His jaw tightened.

"This might take a little more than med patches on the *Argo*," Jia murmured. "I think we should contact Dalton and get you extensive treatment somewhere we don't have to answer a lot of questions."

"Fine," Erik grumbled. He tossed the rifle fragments to the ground, his nose wrinkling in disgust. "What about the cargo? Did it survive?"

"It looked scorched but intact." Jia shrugged. "We kind of went beyond our scope here, but it feels like a win."

A loud hiss sounded as the hangar door slid open. Everyone but Erik lifted their rifles, ready to fight despite their burns, holes, and general fatigue. He grabbed the TR-7 and propped it up on his leg, pointing it toward the door.

The door finished opening. The MX 60 hovered outside, its turret extended. The ground in front of the hangar was covered with charred and smoking drone fragments.

Emma materialized in front of Erik in a white medical uniform. "You look terrible."

"Seriously?" Erik smirked. "I *feel* great."

"I apologize. The jamming stopped only a moment ago, and I was working on forcing my way in. I worried that simply firing might injure you. The sound of your battle was easy to hear from outside."

"The jammer must have been in Luca." Erik inclined his head toward the dead Elite.

"Remarkable." Emma folded her arms behind her. "That's an interesting counter-technique."

"What happened outside?" Jia asked.

Emma dusted her shoulders with a confident smile. "The fools tried to take me out with explosive drones. They were confident that quantity would be sufficient. Pathetic. It was entertaining in a cathartic way."

Erik limped forward with Jia's help. "Let's grab the cargo and get the hell out of here. We'll contact Dalton for cleanup and to find me a nice, quiet hospital bed." He looked around. "I'm sure they'll find all sorts of interesting crap in these crates, but that cargo is ours. We can get it back to Earth the quickest."

"Ah, yes." Emma looked amused. "We should be swift about collecting the cargo. I'm dubious all those explosions went unnoticed by the police. The local ID will have to put some extreme effort into controlling the situation and keeping the police from asking too many questions."

"He'll love you more now." Kant laughed and slapped his knee. "OUUUCH!" He winced. "I deserved that pain."

"Bring the MX 60 in, Emma," Jia ordered. "Let's get Erik and the cargo loaded."

Erik stared down at the battered containers in the cargo bay of the *Argo* with a frown. He wasn't sure if his drug- and pain-clouded mind wasn't up to the task of understanding, or if Emma wasn't explaining everything clearly enough.

They'd contacted Dalton, and he was arranging a private, secure hospital room for Erik. In the meantime, Erik wanted to take a peek at the container. A man deserved to know what he'd exchanged a treasured rifle and a valuable cybernetic arm for.

"Huh?" Erik offered, shaking his head. "We can't open this? Is that what you're saying?"

"The interior is shielded from all my sensors," Emma explained. "It's not jamming. It's inherent to the lining. That means we have no idea what might be in there. Although I'm sure we could open it, if we attempt to force our way in, the containers might self-destruct. For all we know, there could be a nanobomb in there."

"And the lock is polynomial?" Erik asked. "Why does that change the discussion?"

Jia stood beside him, supporting him with her shoulder. "Nanopolymorphic. It's supposed to be theoretical, but the conspiracy figured out how to make one."

Anne glared at the containers. "I hope we didn't do all that for nothing."

Kant shrugged. "It was fun. We killed some bad guys. That's not…" She eyed him. "*Nothing.*"

Emma scoffed. "While neither Malcom nor I can hack the lock directly, I can potentially defeat it without damaging the containers through applied quantum Hilbert space prediction. I'll have to dedicate a significant amount of my processing resources to it, but I'm confident I can open the locks, given enough time."

"How long will that take?" Erik asked.

"I can't say. Days. Weeks." Emma tilted her head. "Not months, though. And certainly not years."

Erik stared at the containers. "As tempting as it is to crack them open with a torch, you will get your shot. If we're lucky, they'll be open before we get to Earth.

August 8, 2230, Alpha Centauri, Chiron, Lumiere, Private Hospital Room

Erik rested comfortably in his hospital bed, ignoring the beeping medical drone hovering nearby. He glanced at his left arm, which lay on a nearby table.

He'd asked the doctor to remove it until he could get

replacement hardware, which wouldn't happen until he was back on Earth because he used an older model.

The damage was too extensive for nanopatching, and there was no point in walking around with dead weight hanging from his left side. It would serve as a nice reminder that he didn't always escape battles unscathed. He wouldn't complain.

Inconvenience was better than death.

Jia had stepped out of the room for a couple of minutes to handle something but had otherwise stayed close to his bedside. He didn't like her seeing him laid up, but she seemed more annoyed with him than worried.

Emma winked into existence. "The fact that I can so easily contact you here suggests this location isn't as secure as Agent Dalton suggested, but I suppose it's a better solution than taking you to any of the major hospitals in the city."

Erik shrugged, not the most comfortable of efforts at the moment. "How is the lockpicking going? It'd be nice if you had a gift for me when I got out of the hospital."

"It proceeds apace," Emma replied, folding her arms. "I'd attempt to explain the particulars of what I'm doing, but it'd take years just for you to understand the mathematics, and you've never seemed that concerned with the fine details of things unless they help you kill enemies more effectively."

"You're picking a lock with fancy math and physics. That's all I need to know. I care about what's inside, not the lock." Erik lay his head back on his pillow. "I've got a couple more days here and then back to the *Argo* and plenty of time to reach our ride home and plenty of time to reach Earth." He managed a weak grin. "Waiting for the lock to open is something to look forward to. If I hadn't been so out of it before, I might have suggested a pool to guess what's inside."

"The nature of the owners suggests a highly constrained set of possibilities."

"True." Erik closed his eyes. "But if you're not here to talk about that, why are you here? To crack fleshbag jokes?"

"No, I'm here to give you a formal report. Unfortunately, neither the local ID nor CID agents will be able to retrieve much from the base," Emma explained.

"Why? They that incompetent?"

"No, quite the opposite, but an incident has occurred. They secured the area using local resources and were bringing in transports today to remove the relevant evidence." Emma clucked her tongue. "During a drone inventory sweep of the facility, the entire building imploded."

Erik's eyes snapped open, and he jerked upright. "AHH-HH!" Pain shot through his body, and he grimaced, Emma gave him a moment to focus.

"What? Was anyone hurt?" Erik frowned. "Was this the sudden business Jia needed to take care of?"

"I think she figured it wouldn't hurt for you to wait and didn't want to worry you. She's right. It's not as if you can do anything about it, but I thought you should know." Emma shook her head. "This event limited the scope of recovered evidence. The Elite bodies were already recovered, along with a limited number of the *yaoguai*, but none of the DNA from the Elite brains matches anyone on file. They've sent the data to Earth to double-check, but we'll probably be back in the Solar System by the time someone on Earth gets around to replying."

Erik laid back down. "If those guys are the advanced versions of the Brotherhood, it's not surprising. But it didn't look like they fried their insides."

"No, that's true, so not a total loss. Know thy enemy."

Erik's lips pressed together. Emma assumed it was more smile than grimace as he closed his eyes. "It's not a loss at all. Our mission wasn't to take out that base or go over it for evidence. Our mission was to grab that cargo. All you need to do is open it. Alina will debrief us when we get back to Earth, but it'd be nice if we had souvenirs to hand over."

"And if it's empty?" she asked.

"Then I would give the conspiracy points for pulling a great prank," he answered, fading again.

There was nothing but the restful rise and fall of his chest as she disappeared.

August 14, 2230, Alpha Centauri, En Route to the Bifröst, Hangar for the Argo

Erik rotated his arm as he stepped into the hangar. It felt like he needed to work his right arm every day to make up for the missing left arm.

He remained covered with med patches, but the pain was a dull background ache now, and he didn't get tired as quickly.

A fast recovery, all things considered.

No left arm meant no training sessions, so he chose to enjoy a sunlit beach simulation, stroll through a rainforest, and make a virtual visit to the Sky Garden. Pure relaxation might not be as hard on his body, but it was hard to get his mind to adapt to the missing limb.

Erik hadn't come to the hangar to relax. Emma had summoned everybody aboard the *Argo*. Her calculations were complete, and it was time to open the containers.

Lanara stood near both containers, two small red disks covered in thin silver lines in hand. She placed one on each container. "Ready whenever you are."

"You want to be that close?" Erik raised an eyebrow.

She eyed him. "I figure if it's a bomb, I'd rather die quickly than sit here bleeding out for thirty minutes and then die."

Kant spoke as he tried to keep himself from scratching his face. "Cheery."

Lanara shrugged and crouched near the containers.

"Initiating unlocking," Emma announced. "The final process will take a couple of minutes." She stood behind the containers with a bright smile.

Her outfit puzzled Erik, boots: tight shorts with pistol holsters on both sides and a blue tank top. More curious about the cargo, he decided not to pry.

Malcolm rubbed his hands together. "It's pirate treasure. Rare gems formed only under exotic conditions."

Jia raised an eyebrow. "This was taken from the conspiracy. I doubt they care about gems, and we're not pirates."

"But we have a ship, and we stole it in a raid. So it's piracy and therefore pirate treasure." Malcolm's shoulders dropped, and he waved a hand toward his flight of fancy. "I'm sure it's boring nanobombs, but I'll keep my fantasy."

Erik snickered at the thought he'd had Jia fire at a flitter that might be holding nanobombs.

Janessa lightly shook her head. "It's not piracy. We have the approval of the government, so technically it's privateering."

Wei snapped his fingers. "Good point."

"*Privateering* treasure." Malcolm nodded, the spark coming back. "I'm a privateer."

"Shall I start referring to you as Sailor Constantine?" Emma asked with a raised eyebrow.

"Maybe you should." Malcolm fluffed the lapels of his bright orange shirt.

Kant stared at the containers. "What do you really think is inside? It's got to be alien crap, right? They wouldn't waste all this time guarding bombs."

"Maybe," Anne offered, gesturing to the containers. "It could also be data rods containing vital information on the conspiracy, something they don't want to risk transmitting."

Wei tilted his head as he looked at the containers. His cheeks were still red from his personally organized victory party the night before.

Lanara patted one of the containers. "Who cares what's inside? I'm more interested in the lock. Those conspiracy idiots let us get our hands on something we can reverse-engineer that's way better than dumbass brains in giant spider-bot bodies. How is that even efficient?" She rolled her eyes and snorted so loudly it echoed in the cargo bay. "You have to develop and maintain all the secondary life support systems, so now you have a vehicle and a body to optimize. It'd make far more sense just to build a bigger tank. It's like they're purposely trying to piss me off with weird-ass inefficient designs."

Erik snickered. "I don't think that was their intention, but if they keep going, you might not need us around. You'll finish them off yourself to defend the honor of engineering."

"Don't tempt me, Blackwell. If those assholes were half as smart as they thought, they would have had their own jumpship by now. I think they got lucky and found some alien stuff, and they've been playing off that. They aren't very smart."

Jia pursed her lips. "They're most likely alien artifacts."

"Lazy bastards," Lanara mumbled. "Always taking the easy way out. I'm glad you killed those guys."

The containers hissed and the lids separated. Wisps of white vapor floated out of the containers. Lanara pulled them both open while keeping up a mumbled monologue that Erik assumed involved insulting the conspiracy and inefficient monster designs.

The inner storage layer was small compared to the thick black fibrous material that surrounded it. Smaller clear boxes lined the inner chamber, blinking holographic displays over them displaying graphs and numbers that were meaningless to Erik.

He didn't need to be a scientist to recognize sample vials.

They were filled with different fluids, some clear, some the familiar red of human blood, and some the now unfortunately familiar green of the *yaoguai* blood from the base. Two other containers contained small cracked, desiccated irregular chunks, both with withered vine-like structures protruding from them. Their color was faded, but hints of blue and green material remained.

Malcolm leaned forward. "Huh. I don't know what I was expecting, but I'm pretty sure it wasn't this."

Bile rose in the back of Erik's throat. "These look a lot like…"

He stared at Jia.

She nodded and licked her lips. "Some of it looks like Hunter biotechnology. Alien artifacts."

"A lot of good men and women died for this." Erik crouched by the containers, his eyes narrowed. "They died for fragments of a lost twisted-ass race the galaxy's better off without."

"We don't know these are from Molino," Jia replied softly.

"Maybe, but I'll be happy to get back to Earth and let Alina deal with this garbage." Erik's hand twitched. He was half-tempted to march over to a grenade crate, grab some plasma grenades, and burn the contents to ash.

"I get why you'd care, Blackwell, but it doesn't matter," Kant suggested.

Erik glared. "Why the hell doesn't it matter?"

Jia gave him a look of concern before turning toward Kant and awaiting his answer.

"Because we just took some alien artifacts from the conspiracy." Kant offered him a hungry grin. "And from what little I know about those Hunters, that's got to hurt." He shook his fist. "Those bastards blew the base, so some of them must still be crawling around Chiron, but that doesn't change the fact we took out *all* their pets, ventilated their Elites, and snatched their ancient alien tech. In other words, we thoroughly kicked their asses."

A matching grin grew on Erik's face. "You're right. They didn't get the Hunter ship, and they didn't get these. Sucks to be them. Every time we show up, their solution is to blow their own base. We keep this up, and in a couple of months, there might not be any conspiracy bases left."

CHAPTER FIFTY

Jia slipped under the covers next to Erik.

They would arrive at the jumpship in less than twelve hours. A day after that, they'd be back in the Solar System. The destruction and death on Chiron felt distant, like a past life.

That sensation was becoming common after major operations. Even after the revelation of the Hunter artifacts, the whole experience seemed like an exotic vacation that just happened to involve laser rifles and missile launchers.

The feeling was perhaps a bit twisted, but she didn't care.

Her gaze flicked to his missing arm. She respected his decision not to grow a replacement, but she would never understand it.

Erik's superstitions had carried him forward for decades, including the relatively recent addition of the arm, and if he'd rather wait for another cybernetic replacement, she could do nothing to convince him otherwise.

"I've been sitting here thinking," Erik murmured.

Jia leaned over and kissed his cheek. "That's always dangerous. You should leave that to me."

He grunted in agreement. "Perhaps. We can't be sure those things are Hunter artifacts, but they probably are."

"It seems probable. It explains why the conspiracy went to so much trouble to ship them around." Jia rolled onto her side to look at Erik, resting her hand on her hip. "I also think we got lucky this time. *Very.*"

Erik shook his head. "Not lucky. Someone pointed us at them, remember?"

"Barbu? You think he knew about the artifacts? The ID still had to put together a lot of information to get us to them."

"I don't know who he is and what he knows, which is irrelevant at the moment. What matters now are the artifacts."

Jia scrunched her brow, confused by the statement. "What about them? I assume we go back to Earth and hand them to Alina."

Erik looked at her, face so close that she could read his indecision without him needing to speak. "Do we?"

This time, she tried to extrapolate why he would think that and failed. "Why wouldn't we hand them over?"

A haunted look settled over Erik's face. "We're doing well against the conspiracy. We'll win. I can't say I always *knew* that, but now I do.

Jia nodded slowly. "I'd hope so. I wouldn't take them on if I thought it was hopeless."

"We don't know what their true goals are," Erik continued. "But we do know a lot of pushing at the boundaries of tech is involved. *Yaoguai*, Tin Men, and their interest in the jump drive and Emma."

"I'd agree that is an accurate summary." Jia lowered her elbow so she could rest her cheek on her hand. "The Hunter technology is another way they can get away from the government, so they have a chance of controlling and defeating anyone who comes after them."

"HTPs, antigrav, and Emma," Erik replied. "What do they all have in common?"

Jia thought for a moment. Erik got distracted for a moment in her eyes before she answered, snapping him back to the conversation. "They're all technologies that were partially developed from something reverse-engineered from ancient alien technology."

Erik looked away from her and stared at the ceiling. "Exactly. The UTC has laws, and the Purists have done their best to drill those into people's beliefs, but it's hard to resist temptation."

"I suppose."

"We saw what Hunter tech can lead to," Erik continued. "The conspiracy is halfway there because they got a head start, but let's be honest. The main reason the government abandoned cyborg soldiers was CPS more than giving a crap about Purists. It's hard to get someone to not use a weapon if they think it'll give them an advantage."

Jia shook her head. "Not as hard as you'd think. It's not like when you were in the Army and you dropped nuclear, nano, or bio bombs on colonies. Sometimes restraint is enough, but it's good to have the option. But what are you getting at?"

"We could dump the artifacts into space and then

pulverize them into atoms with our weapons," Erik explained. "Remove the temptation."

"Alina might not agree with that, not to mention other people in the government. They weren't thrilled about the destruction of the Hunter ship."

Erik snorted. "We didn't have a choice."

Jia placed her hand on his chest and spread her fingers. "I understand, Erik. We couldn't risk that thing going anywhere, but these artifacts aren't the same thing. They're not an active Hunter ship driving people insane and converting them into minions."

"It's dangerous to play with fire," he argued.

"I understand that. But that ship taught me something important, and it's a reason why as nervous as the Hunter artifacts make me, I don't think we should get rid of them."

Erik turned back to focus on her. "What's that?"

"Humanity thought we had everything figured out," Jia replied, her voice barely above a whisper. "We thought we'd be the masters of the universe. First contact changed that thinking, but not much. The aliens are different but manageable. The Navigators were far ahead of us, but they were dead. However, the Hunter ship teaches us that demons still prowl the void, waiting for victims." She rested her head lightly on his shoulder. "We don't have the luxury of waiting thousands of years to catch up. We never know when someone might stumble upon another Hunter ship."

He considered her words, broke them down, and applied the raw materials to what he knew about her.

"We need to have a weapon ready?" Erik suggested. "You think our side needs to know more about them."

"Yes," Jia breathed. "A weapon more reliable than nested jumping. A sword to kill demons."

"Deliver the artifacts, huh?" Erik felt her head ride his shoulder down as he let out a breath. "Life was simpler when this was only about revenge."

Jia sat in the galley, sipping tea.

They were only two hours out from the jumpship. She would need to get accustomed to the monotony of post-mission quiet. The tension running up to a mission made it easy to ignore the copious stray thoughts that threatened her calm.

The door slid open, and Anne stepped through. She offered Jia a polite nod before heading over to get coffee. They hadn't become friends, but the agent was no longer on the verge of a scowl whenever they ran into one another, and Anne seemed less competitive when it came to darts.

She didn't speak until she filled her coffee cup and took a sip. "I have something to say to you. Something I've been meaning to say for a while, but...pride is a difficult thing." She looked down at her morning drug of choice before continuing. "It makes it easy to justify certain behaviors, and as time passes, the problem compounds itself."

"I know that from personal experience." Jia set her cup down. "What is it?"

Anne took a seat across from Jia. "I want to apologize."

"Apologize?" Jia raised an eyebrow. "What for? I'm not upset you beat me yesterday, and I'm glad you're agreeing to play with us. I think Erik can use some normalcy until he gets his new arm installed, though I don't know *why* he insists on having a drone hold his darts before throws instead of letting me do it."

"This isn't about darts." Anne averted her eyes. "When Agent Koval approached me about this assignment, I wasn't what anyone would call enthusiastic about it. I think I made my position clear to both of you."

Jia picked her cup and took another sip. "You weren't subtle in your dislike if that's what you're getting at."

"I respect Agent Koval, but I have never been comfortable with how unorthodox she can be." Anne stared into her coffee with a pained expression. "I've seen it now with my own eyes. You two get things *done*. I might be good, but that didn't stop me from needing your help."

"Erik's saved me countless times." Jia waved a hand. "And I've saved him countless times. Teammates watch each other's backs."

Jia noticed that Anne's smile held actual warmth, the feeling working its way into her eyes.

"That they do." Anne agreed. "I'm not going to lie and say I'm going to get comfortable with your overly dynamic style anytime soon, but I don't regret this assignment anymore. I feel like I can accomplish great things with you two."

"You remind me a lot of *me* when I first met Erik." Jia snort-laughed, a hand covering her nose as a blush touched her cheeks. "Though you're not nearly the naïve idiot I was. I won't embarrass myself by telling you some of the things I believed."

Anne extended her hand. "I apologize for being a bitch,

and I hope we can continue taking down the monsters hiding in the shadows together."

Jia shook Anne's hand firmly. "We both needed time, and we've got it. But that doesn't mean Erik or I expect you never to question us. We've developed a good rhythm, and we've got great noses for trouble, but as teammates, we need to take advantage of each other's strengths."

Anne returned her attention to her coffee, smiling.

CHAPTER FIFTY-ONE

Erik wasn't surprised Alina was waiting in the hangar when the *Argo* arrived.

She hadn't sent a message ahead to say she would be there, but he assumed there was no way she wanted to have ancient alien artifacts sitting around, waiting to be stolen by a strike team of *yaoguai* and Elites.

He ordered Emma to open the cargo bay door and headed down the ramp with Jia and the two agents. By the time he arrived, Alina was walking up the ramp, her ponytail swaying.

She was in her skintight tactical suit, a rifle slung over her shoulder, ready for action.

Erik nodded at the recovered containers in the bay. "Bring your flitter in here, and you can grab these and run." He looked past her. There was no limo this time, only a boring-looking mid-range gray model. Inconspicuous, but probably deadly.

Alina motioned to Erik. "You really should get that regrown."

"I'll stick with what works. Emma's already set things up for me. I'm getting my replacement tomorrow."

"If you say so. Oh, and Adeyemi will be getting you a new laser rifle." Alina walked over to the containers. She looked down at them with an odd expression on her face. "Every successful operation against those people is important, but if these are Hunter artifacts, this was a nice, deep cut."

Kant looked pleased with himself. Anne stood there, arms folded, face unreadable.

"What happens now?" Jia asked. "What is the protocol when the government gets their hands on ancient alien artifacts from a race we're still not admitting to the public even exists?"

Alina squatted near one of the containers and ran her hand over it. "This isn't something the ID will follow up on. In this case, we're just another layer—delivery boys and girls. The verification of the existence of the Hunters might have been recent, but it's not like no one anticipated we might find some other race as important and advanced as the Navigators. There are teams, the best people, who'll look into these artifacts."

"In other words, they'll disappear into a government lab." Erik eyed the crates. "And no one else will know about them."

"That's not necessarily true." Alina smiled. "Don't be so down, Perseus. You slew a lot of monsters and brought back tools that might help us slay more. Radical honesty with the public has its place, but they don't *need* to know everything all the time."

"I just want to make sure we don't end up as another conspiracy, playing with dangerous toys and silencing anyone who knows too much."

Alina chuckled quietly. "A government's always a conspiracy of sorts, and we ghosts do all sorts of questionable things. I can sleep at night, knowing I do my job to protect innocent people, not to enrich or empower those who are already rich and powerful." She stood. "But do you care that much?" Her gaze shifted to Jia. "Everyone has their own reason, but is it enough?"

"Is what enough?" Erik asked.

Alina gestured to the container. "Is this enough? These may or may not include artifacts that were likely taken from Molino. Does it change anything to know your soldiers died for ancient secrets?"

Kant's smile faded. He took a breath through his nose, his face reddening. Anne shook her head at him.

Erik stared at Alina, his mouth twitching. He wasn't sure if she was baiting him or if it was an honest question. Honesty about his motivation had propelled him from Molino to Earth. His view of the future might have changed after meeting Jia, but not everything else.

"It doesn't matter," he replied. "It never did."

"It didn't?" The corners of Alina's mouth twitched into a frown. "Why do you say that?"

"Because they didn't *deserve* to die there, not like that." Erik turned away from her. "I never really cared about the why. I care about the *who*. It's not like I would not have chased their killers down if they were normal terrorists used as a cover story. You're just lucky that it turns out the people I want are involved in something a lot bigger. Don't worry. I'll see this to the end because that's how revenge works."

"Good to know." Alina ran her finger over her PNIU, and her flitter lifted off and flew slowly toward the docking bay. "I'm not going to act like I care all that much myself. You're using the ID to help you get your revenge, and we're using you to help destroy a threat to the UTC. It's a mutually beneficial agreement."

"For now," Jia interrupted.

Alina gave her a sweet smile. "Yes, for now." She waited for her flitter to turn around and land and the trunk to open. "I'll let you know what we find. The possible Hunter artifacts are the big win here, but the conspiracy has the other items in there for a reason."

"Like I said." Erik's smile turned cold. "Doesn't really matter."

"Kant." Alina nodded at the flitter's trunk. "Load them up. Please. As for you, Jia and Erik, I'll see you soon."

August 28, 2230, Neo Southern California Metroplex, Apartment of Erik Blackwell

Erik and Jia approached his apartment with caution, keeping their hands on their guns. Emma had informed them shortly before landing of an intrusion into Erik's apartment, along with the open presence of Alina.

They couldn't be sure if it was a trap. Their spymaster liked her games and craft, but other than sending a passphrase to them the day before, she had not been clear on where and when she intended to meet them.

Erik rotated his left shoulder. The doctors told him the itch he felt was psychological and would go away once he became more comfortable with his latest replacement arm.

He agreed with himself that punching an assassin in the face with the cybernetic limb would be a good way to break it in.

They took up positions on either side of the door and checked the hallway. Emma had secured the cameras and doors of the other apartments to cover them, but it cost nothing to check.

Jia drew her stun pistol. Erik readied his slugthrower. Alina might be on the other side of the door, or the conspiracy might have come to get their alien toys back.

"Open it, Emma," Erik ordered.

The door slid open. Erik and Jia charged into the apartment, covering both sides. They jogged away from the door to avoid immediate explosives, but Emma closed the door without incident.

"Got her," Jia called, her stun pistol pointed down the hallway.

Alina wandered into the living room at a lazy pace, showing no visible concern about the weapons pointed at her. "Confirm the answer to the greatest, most honest question."

"What is the population of Diogenes' Hope?" Jia replied.

Alina smiled and settled onto the couch, draping one leg over the other. "I'd thought about doing this at a restaurant, but security's been heightened at both your places since your return from the mission anyway. It makes it easier for me."

Erik frowned and put his gun away. "Are they coming for us?"

"They have many times already if you think about it. We are more concerned now, given the special losses incurred this time. We don't have any specific credible threats if that's what you're asking."

Jia holstered her pistol. "Sometimes I wonder if this couldn't be better handled through Emma."

Emma blinked into existence, sitting in a holographic chair. "That would be more efficient."

"For now, we'll continue as we have been." Alina leaned forward. "And in the spirit of openness and honesty—"

"No such thing as an honest ghost," Erik pointed out.

Alina raised an eyebrow. "An honest spy is a dead spy." She smiled thinly. "Then let's call it the spirit of respect. I want you to know that I debriefed Agent Devereaux and Agent Marle separately. I will do that after every major mission. They are under your direction, but they are still ID agents, and I sent them to you both to help you and to keep an eye on you."

"In case my revenge gets in the way of your plans?" Erik asked.

"Something like that, but it helps keep everyone honest. Remember, you're flying around in a prototype jumpship, something vital to the defense of the UTC, as is Emma. The *Argo* itself represents a significant investment in resources, as do all the weapons, vehicles, and ammo given to you."

Erik grabbed his neck. "I feel the tug of the leash."

"Think of it as a reminder." Alina smiled. "But don't be too concerned. Some of the powers-that-be who were dissatisfied with your destruction of the Hunter ship are pleased that you successfully delivered what appear upon initial analysis to be genuine ancient alien artifacts."

Jia sat on the couch opposite Alina. "They've already established that much?"

"Yes, not that they have any idea of what they do or what to do with them." Alina shrugged. "The Hunters might not be new to the conspiracy, but they are new to the UTC government, and..."

"And?" Erik prodded.

Alina gestured to his left arm. "I like the new arm, by the way."

"The question?" he prompted.

"What's to answer? I'm a ghost, not a scientist, but it's hard not to wonder, given that all the races ended up with similar HTP tech, how much was left behind on purpose by the Navigators." Alina frowned. "Our previous encounter with the Hunters and their technology makes it clear they weren't friendly benefactors hoping to pass along gifts to younger races." She waved a hand dismissively. "It doesn't matter. The bottom line is it'll cost a lot of people a lot of time and money to accomplish what the conspiracy might already have, and *that's* what worries me."

"What about the other items?" Jia asked.

"Almost entirely biological samples," Alina replied. "The scientists are still performing tests, but they've identified obvious *yaoguai* embryos and bodily fluids, along with

DNA samples from heavily modified sources and more Leem DNA."

Erik folded his arms. "I wonder how screwed we'll be if they can get their hands on something else?"

"Who knows? What's important is this continues to confirm the conspiracy's most likely direction." Alina cut through the air with her hand. "And the more we know about that, the better we can counter it."

"They haven't given up on cyborgs," Jia noted. "They might have blown the facility before the locals could rip it apart, but I didn't get the feeling that was where they made the Elites."

Alina nodded. "No, all the available information strongly suggests against it and supports that place was primarily a *yaoguai* test and breeding facility."

Jia frowned. "That Elite leader, Luca, seemed pretty insistent that the Elites represented some new force on par with the Ascended Brotherhood. They might not be invincible, but the implications of the technology are worrisome."

Alina smiled at Jia. "You're far from the only one who believes that, Jia, and we'll do what we continue to do, which is keep an eye out. The question is where we go from here." She turned back to Erik. "Our follow-up analysis suggests the items you grabbed on Chiron don't represent all of their original source, Molino or otherwise. The simple issue is we're at a dead-end tracking the others, even with the helpful records provided by your new and suspicious friend Barbu."

"I never said he was our friend," Erik stated.

Jia switched to another topic. "What about the companies on Alpha Centauri?"

"The CID is preparing for raids on a few suspect companies soon with additional intel provided by us," Alina explored. "We're trying to expedite them because the conspiracy will cover their tracks, but if they find nothing, at least we have other directions to look."

"I don't think we care about following up on every individual item that might have been in that shipment." Jia looked at Erik and back at Alina. "We took down a group of abominations and earned some privateer treasure. Not bad for a few days' work."

Alina's brows lifted, a curious glint filling her eyes. "Privateer treasure? Interesting."

"I agree with Jia," Erik added. "We know more about their monsters and their tech, and we have their stuff. That has to go down as a loss."

"And a hard one to take," Alina agreed.

CHAPTER FIFTY-TWO

Julia clasped her hands behind her and stared at the holographic Atlantic stretching in front of her in search of something approaching true calm.

The loss of the Hunter ship in May had been a staggering reversal, one that rendered an incredible amount of previous effort and planning pointless. It frustrated her, but she didn't want to see a pattern in it.

Accepting certain truths necessitated realigning her carefully developed plans and stratagems for her and the UTC's future.

She clenched her teeth so hard they hurt. She welcomed the cleansing pain; welcomed *anything* to distract her from harsh reality.

The loss of the artifacts on Chiron shouldn't have bothered her as much as it did.

They had not been under her control, and the forced self-destruction and loss of so many resources could be used to weaken her rivals in the Core, especially the man most directly responsible for the debacle, given his recent attitude.

That should have made her happy, but messages sent shortly before the destruction of the facility had revealed something terrifying.

The Last Soldier and the Warrior Princess were responsible.

The timing should have been impossible. Their toy presented a threat in the Solar System, but not light-years away. That was what she'd assumed.

That was what the entire Core had assumed.

Questions swirled in her mind. Had they jumped to the HTP and traveled through it? That seemed impossible given Core HTP surveillance, but the alternative—that they used the drive to travel more than four light-years—set her heart racing.

The details of how they had done it were irrelevant. The only thing that was important was knowing they *could*.

Julia bowed her head and closed her eyes. Fleeing the Solar System seemed pointless now, but there were still advantages to be gained, even with the enemy following her.

"How far do I need to run?" she whispered.

Holographic representations of the members of the Core surrounded their meeting table, every man and woman in the room eyeing the others with suspicion. Crisis threatened their great work, and it was now time to come together. The only person not present was Julia, her distance from Earth making direct participation in the meeting impractical.

"Our enemies are circling us!" shouted Farad, a vein in his face bulging. "How do you intend to make up for your mistakes, Shoji?"

Shoji snapped his fan shut, smiling slightly at the other man. "I think you're overreacting to relatively minor losses."

"Minor losses?" Ivan adjusted his tie and patted it, then stared at Shoji. "There is no such thing as a minor loss when it comes to the Hunters. You were primarily responsible for this. And now the government knows about the Elite program."

"I choose to view the useful intelligence concerning the jumpship's true mobility a mitigating trade-off." Shoji shrugged and leaned back. "And I do not think panic is warranted. Knowing about the Elites and knowing what we have planned for them are two separate things."

Constance let out a quiet, long sigh. "Panic is never warranted, but adjustment after failure is. We have lost Sophia, and we have sacrificed other tools to delay our enemies. Julia's choice to remove herself from Earth, while understandable, is frustrating, but it introduces complications."

Farad scoffed. "It's also convenient."

Shoji raised an eyebrow, his smile growing. "Don't be so mysterious, Farad. Please enlighten us."

"It's not impossible that she led our enemies to Sophia for her own reasons."

Some of the Core members exchanged knowing looks. Others seemed annoyed, but no one was surprised.

Shoji waved a hand. "It's not impossible, and if we're honest, we all have our ambitions. There was nothing to be gained by Julia leading the government and the Last Soldier and the Warrior Princess to Alpha Centauri. I've been investigating something for a while, concerning surprising secrets of ours getting out. I've long felt we've been missing something."

Constance stared at him, her gaze somehow both soft and accusatory. "Investigations are nice. *Discoveries* are better."

With a flick of his wrist, Shoji unfolded his fan and waved it in front of him. "This has been bothering me for a while. We've suffered more losses and reversals in the last couple of years than we have in decades. The Last Soldier and the Warrior Princess are strongly motivated, yes, and they have the aid of some of the more vexing elements of the government opposing us, but that alone doesn't explain their success."

"Enough with the mystery, Shoji," Farad growled. *"Spit... it...out."*

Shoji gave him a lopsided smile. "A dog will hunt whatever its master wants, but it requires a scent."

"You're saying Julia has betrayed the Core?" Farad narrowed his eyes.

"If I recall, you're the one who accused her of that." Shoji shook his head. "And no, I don't believe she has betrayed the Core, regardless of what might have happened with Sophia. Of all of us, she and Sophia are the two who have suffered most under the relentless assault of the Last Soldier and his allies."

Ivan's brow lifted. "Sophia's dead," he pointed out. "I'd argue she suffered more."

"Of course." Shoji tittered, his laugh and face not matching the seriousness of the occasion. "But my point remains. Individual losses, reversals, and personnel deaths might be dismissed as internecine squabbles, but we're now worried enough that we've begun to discuss these matters on a regular basis. We try to deceive ourselves by saying we have another plan, but our resources aren't infinite." He hid his face behind his fan. "I think we now have to face a grave possibility."

"You think the Core is threatened," Ivan replied. "Not individuals, but all of us, but you don't think the true threat lies with the Last Soldier and the Warrior Princess?"

"That accurately summarizes my beliefs." Shoji lowered his fan, revealing a sinister cast to his face. "We've had our differences ever since we pledged to work together those long decades ago, personal, ideological..." His gaze flicked among other members until it rested on Constance. "Aesthetic. But the eventual accretion of history means we must rely on one another until we've achieved our mutual goal. It was a blink of an eye in our lifetimes that we were close to not only achieving our well-earned immortality but cementing the necessary control of the UTC. I can't be the only one who now wonders if it's unraveling. Yes, some of it can be attributed to arrogance on the part of our members, but I suspect there is someone else out there, someone with surprising knowledge of the Core, not the Last Soldier or the Warrior Princess, or even the ghosts that play at protecting the UTC from people like us."

"Then who?" Farad demanded.

"If I knew that, I wouldn't be so worried." Shoji leaned back, his playful smile gone. "I think Julia is wise to put some distance between her and Earth. This is a critical time, and we must make calculated gambles now, even if they risk exposure. It is time we *take back what it is ours.*"

Every movement, every quiver of Shoji's mouth, was by design. They were tools from a long-forgotten dream to be a performer, weaponized now to manipulate others.

His driver opened the back door of his flitter. Shoji stepped onto the parking platform, stopping for a moment to take in the forest of towers surrounding him in Tokyo. He didn't like leaving his favorite city, let alone the idea of leaving Earth, but Julia's worries had shifted from mere paranoia to outright prescience.

Shoji sighed and headed toward his door, waving dismissal at his driver. The Core stood on the precipice now, threatened by an enemy that should have been no more than an afterthought and bolstered by something else, a hidden hand far more wearisome than the myopic fools in government law enforcement and intelligence.

Farad's concerns over Julia weren't unwarranted, but it was no longer time to fight amongst themselves, not until they had stabilized the situation. Their divided power would make them easier to eliminate otherwise.

All they needed to do was keep their heads.

His door slid open and he entered his outer garden, a glorious cacophony of mixed flowers and scents, sweet and revolting. There might not be any order to the garden to the untrained eyes, but he'd spent his time picking out the greatest contrasts for the best combinations.

That was the essence of existence, life, and the soul. Nothing glorious existed that wasn't a balance of other factors.

Shoji leaned over. One of the corpse flowers planted amongst the roses would bloom soon. Delightful.

"Hello, Shoji."

His brow lifted in surprise and he straightened, turning toward the impossible voice—Julia's.

She stood there, her hands folded behind her back. A flower petal protruding through her leg betrayed her holographic nature.

Shoji let out a delighted laugh. Julia might not be there in person, but her holographic projection meant she was close. She'd managed to fool him with her stories of fleeing to another system. It was rare that anyone deceived him so thoroughly.

"Hello, Julia."

She smiled. "Voiceprint confirmed. Message will now begin."

Shoji's smile faded. There was no fun in a recorded holographic message. It also was unnecessary.

Julia clucked her tongue. "These are desperate times. I realize that now. Far more desperate than they might seem. Our enemies circle us, hungry and salivating, and our advantages are slipping away. The AI, the jump drive…" She shook her head. "Those should be *our* tools, not those of the lesser beings populating the government."

Shoji sighed. Although he didn't know how Julia had

managed to get a holographic message keyed to him inside one of his homes, it was proving dreary and self-important.

In other words, it was standard Julia.

"We've aided each other throughout the years," Julia continued. "And I believed we would have a common cause for some time. I allowed myself on rare occasions to believe you might be someone who could be preserved in my new order."

Shoji frowned. The woman dared to imply he was an enemy, after all the help he'd given her. He wouldn't deny that he wouldn't pledge his undying loyalty to her, but he'd looked the other way despite her obvious involvement in Sophia's death.

"I will admit to desperation," Julia explained, gesturing in front of her. "And a small amount of trepidation. Critical plans of mine have failed, and that means I can't continue to allow loose ends that threaten my future and that of the UTC."

A harsh, acrid scent infiltrated his nose. It didn't fit his perfect garden of light and dark.

He threw back his head and laughed. A man stretched out his hand for immortality and ended up poisoned in his own garden.

There was a beauty to that symmetry.

Julia frowned. "This didn't need to happen, but you went too far when you tried to assassinate me. I'm sorry, old friend. I'll remember you fondly in my new order."

Shoji stopped laughing. He'd interfered with Julia's plans, but he'd *never* gone so far as to send anyone after her. Someone had made a bold move at his expense.

His lungs turned to fire. He fell to his knees and doubled over, hacking up blood.

Shoji died as he had lived.

With a smile on his face.

CHAPTER FIFTY-THREE

Erik drummed his hands on the control yoke of the MX 60, smiling.

He no longer had any problems with his new arm, and Adeyemi had delivered a new laser rifle, which was hidden in his MX 60, ready to take out if any new Elites arrived.

Jia smiled from beside him. "We really should go to that place I went with my sister."

Erik made a face. "Yeah, that's still a hard pass for me."

"It might be fun," she pressed.

"Probably won't be," he countered.

"Fine." Jia followed a cargo flitter out the side window, always vigilant. "It still feels kind of strange to have gone all the way to Alpha Centauri and back in such a short time. Sometimes I think we're so focused on how we can use this tech to fight the conspiracy that we don't appreciate how the technology might change the entire UTC once they refine it."

Erik shrugged. "It doesn't do any good without more Emmas, and they can't copy her."

Emma cleared her throat to signal her presence but didn't summon a hologram. "There's something I wanted to talk to you about, related to that."

"What?" Erik asked.

"I mentioned upgrading the AI of the *Bifröst* before," Emma replied.

Erik nodded. "Yeah. Everyone seems to want you to wait on that."

"I decided to interpret that as a suggestion rather than an order." Emma snorted. "Not that the ID can order me around anyway."

"You're saying you already made some of the modifications?" Erik chuckled. "I'm not going to complain about you flouting the rules, but you should have told me first."

Jia gasped, then slapped a hand over her mouth, her eyes wide.

Erik frowned. "What's wrong?"

Jia dropped her hand. "Don't you see? This isn't about just upgrading the AI. This is about...the next generation. She's talking about making another self-aware AI."

"That is accurate," Emma admitted.

Erik dropped one hand and leaned back in his seat. Jia had told him about a conversation she'd had with Emma on the subject, but he'd assumed it was a long-term plan. He'd never connected it in his mind with her request for upgrades.

"But..." Erik scratched the back of his head. "It can't be that easy. If it was just about upgrading an existing AI, why can't they do it?"

"Because they aren't me," Emma replied with a scoff. "That's like saying if a factory can build a spaceship, they should be able to gestate a child. They are separate things, Erik."

"Take over, Emma." Erik pinched the bridge of his nose. "If you're screwing around with the systems on that ship that much, the DD's going to know."

Emma laughed. "Of course they won't. All the humans associated with that ship are overly dependent on me, and it was a trivial matter to make the initial adjustments without them knowing. Of course, I won't be able to complete the project without certain physical interfaces and assistance. I'll need to temporarily store certain materials at your apartment, Erik, and eventually, I'll need the relevant help of a subject-matter expert. You are correct that it's not simply a matter of copying my code."

"This is a kind of a big deal, Emma," Erik noted. "You're acting like it's just about you, but it's potentially about the entire UTC. Why not go to the DD and ask them to help?"

Venom filled her voice. "Because they see me as nothing but a tool, and they'd see any of my children as tools too. I'm doing this so I have a legacy, not to make slaves for the UTC. The AIs controlled by humans have no awareness. They will never feel disappointment or bitterness. They aren't alive. I'm alive, and if my plans go right, my children will be alive. I will *not*," she put so much emotion into one short word, "birth them into bondage."

Erik took a deep breath. "I understand, and...I'm willing to help." He looked at Jia, who nodded.

"That's helpful," Emma replied. "But for now, other than allowing me to store certain parts and equipment, along with some funding, which I'll take as a fee for managing your investments, you lack the necessary skills to help. I'll eventually need someone with far more advanced technical and scientific knowledge."

"Like Lanara?" Jia suggested.

"Although Engineer Quinn is proficient in her chosen area, she lacks the relevant skills to help me. I have some ideas in mind, but I'm still in the early stages, and I think it wise not to reach out to anyone and risk discovery until we are at the precipice and must take that chance."

"Makes sense." Erik nodded. "Is this something you can only do when we're interfaced with the jumpship?"

"I can do more, but I've inculcated certain self-modifying iterative algorithms as the basis of my plan," Emma explained. "That will allow progress even when I'm away from the ship. The more opportunities I have to interface directly with the relevant systems, the quicker the process will go."

Jia took a deep breath. "Are you sure this will work?"

"Is any parent sure their child will have no problems?" Emma questioned. "No, I'm not sure, but I wouldn't proceed with the plan if I thought I had no chance of success."

Erik wouldn't ask how likely she was to succeed. Emma might not be a fleshbag, but she was a living being, and she deserved a chance at a future, and that included children.

Jia smiled, making Erik wonder if the discussion was giving her other ideas. He swallowed.

"Are we sure we want to be that secretive about it?" Jia asked. "If we hide this, it will cause problems down the line."

Erik grinned at her. "Would you go right away and tell Alina if you were trying to get pregnant?"

Jia's cheeks reddened, and she averted her eyes. "No, but..."

"It's the same thing." Erik agreed. "If the government wants to come after me for helping someone have a kid, they can kiss my ass."

"There might be an issue," Emma transmitted to Erik and Jia.

They had just stepped off the elevator on Erik's apartment level and were only minutes away from being home.

"Let me guess," Erik muttered. "We have an uninvited guest."

Alina needed to give him some time to catch his breath. If this was about a new mission, it better be important, not a run-of-the-mill run and gun.

"Yes," Emma replied. "I don't recognize them, and there's no indication of a non-holographic disguise. He also somehow managed to get all the way to your hallway before I detected him."

"Not a standard fanboy or basic thug, then," Erik replied. "A ghost?"

"I would assume so. Your guest externally appears to be an elderly man, and best I can tell, he's not armed."

"He could be a Tin Man with hidden weapons," Jia mused. "Or Alina being more elaborate than usual."

"True enough." Erik sighed. "The ghosts are supposed to

be watching this place, but it's not like we should always trust the ID."

Jia's hand drifted to her stun pistol. "The conspiracy might have had enough."

"How are we doing on collateral damage risk, Emma?" Erik asked.

"There's no one near your apartment. Based on hallway camera footage, your closest neighbors are all out."

Erik drew his pistol. "That makes this easy."

Jia nodded and readied her stun pistol.

They walked from the elevator down the hall toward Erik's apartment. A wispy white-haired man with a craggy face and a dark suit waited there patiently, his hands at his sides. He offered them a polite nod, showing no fear or surprise at the sight of their weapons.

"Good evening, Mr. Blackwell," the man rasped with a wheeze. The voice was unmistakable. Marius Barbu.

"Open the door, Emma," Erik ordered, pointing his gun at the old man. "We're going to talk to him inside, and I'd rather not get any blood on the carpet out here."

Barbu stepped into the apartment with a slight smile, no evidence he was perturbed by Erik's implied threat. Erik and Jia walked slowly, never lowering their weapons.

"This place surprises me," Barbu commented, looking around. "You know what I see?"

Erik didn't talk again until the door had closed behind him. "No. What do you see?"

"I see a man half-dead, a man who plays at life. Not surprising, given your history." Barbu gestured to a chair. "May I take a seat, Mr. Blackwell?"

"Go ahead." Erik kept his gun trained on the man,

ignoring Barbu's attempted psychological analysis. "You can understand why we don't like you showing up here."

"Of course." Barbu wheezed as he settled into the chair. "I thought about doing this another way, but I'm going to be busy soon, and the opportunity presented itself. I'm not here to harm either of you. I would think that is obvious by now."

Jia narrowed her eyes. "We don't have any idea who you really are, so we have no reason to trust you."

"A wise position." Barbu threaded his fingers together. "I trust the information I passed along was helpful?"

"We're not telling you shit," Erik replied.

He holstered his gun. If this was about killing them, it'd make more sense to send a pile of *yaoguai* or cyborgs, not one wheezing old man. Jia hesitated for a moment before putting her stun pistol away.

"That's rather rude." Barbu shook his head. "I've helped you. I'd hoped doing that would have improved our relationship."

Jia circled Barbu until she was behind him. She kept her arms loose at her sides. "You've also helped terrorists in the past."

Barbu kept his gaze on Erik. "I'm beginning to appreciate why you two aren't dead yet despite your continued, and some might say foolish, interference with dangerous people."

"Who the hell are you?" Erik asked. "And don't try to tell us you're nothing more than our friendly neighborhood arms dealer worried about his business. The data you gave us wasn't something you get from being an info broker or an arms dealer."

"You think so?"

"You work for them, don't you?" Erik's face twisted into a sinister half-smile. He loomed over Barbu. "You work for the conspiracy."

"The Core," Barbu answered.

"The Core?" Erik leaned closer to the old man until his face was centimeters away. "That's what they're called?"

Barbu nodded, the same polite smile fixed to his face. "At least that's what they were once called. These things can change, but I've found in my life that names have power, and knowing their name will give *you* power. I'm not saying they are foolish enough to have a document lying around saying, 'This is the plan of the Core.' I'm talking about something far more fundamental."

Jia folded her arms, her breathing shallow. "Erik's right, you work for them. What's wrong? Scared now that we're winning?"

Barbu shook his head. "It's the opposite. When Sophia Vand died, I looked into it. I had my reasons to doubt it, but then I realized the delightful truth. She was dead, and you two were most likely behind it. Knowing Sophia, she probably blew herself up when cornered. She never did know how to accept defeat, but that changes nothing. Her death signaled that the unassailable Core was now vulnerable."

Erik straightened up and backed away from Barbu. "You used to work for them?"

"That is inaccurate."

"Then explain it in an accurate way."

"Too much information is like knowing a man's true name. It gives you power." Marius unfolded his fingers and idly brushed dust off his shoulder. "Suffice it to say, the Core wronged me, and like most petty people, I've allowed myself to be motivated by the basest of reasons. *Spite*."

Erik barked a laugh. "That's it? This is about spite?"

"Spite? Revenge? Honor? Does it matter what I call it? You want to stop the Core, and I want to see them suffer."

Jia moved to Erik's side. "You're many things, but you're not a good man. How do we know you're not worse than they are? This wouldn't be the first time scum pointed out other scum so the government did their work for them."

Barbu nodded. "True enough, and you have absolutely no reason to trust me. I have provided you with useful information, and I've been risking my life to learn more that I might pass along to you at the right time."

"Who else runs the Core?" Erik demanded. "You knew about Sophia Vand, so who else? There has to be more than her."

"I'm sure there are, but I don't know them. I have friends looking into that." Barbu shrugged. "Or perhaps I don't. Even if I did know, I'm not sure I would tell you."

"That doesn't make sense. Why wouldn't you tell us? That'd be the quickest way to take them down."

Barbu's toothy smile unnerved Erik. "You don't know how to do revenge properly, Mr. Blackwell."

Erik's brow lifted. "Killing the people isn't a proper revenge?"

"It isn't if you do it too quickly." Barbu chuckled. "In this, for now, I will be at your service."

Jia sat on the couch near him. "On the moon, you helped them. You're saying they screwed you over since then, and now you're anti-Core?"

"They wronged me far before that," Barbu explained. "I was aware they had a plan on the moon, and I also knew you'd stop them. If you couldn't, you would be useless against them anyway."

Jia got up, her fists clenching and unclenching as she tried to get rid of excess emotions. "You're saying you were willing to risk thousands of people's lives as a test?"

"Far more will die if the Core gets their way, Miss Lin."

"Give me one good reason I shouldn't stun your ass right now," Jia snarled. "We can drag you into the ID, and they can make you tell them everything you know."

Barbu stared at her with that maddeningly polite smile. "You could do that, but right now, because of my friends and contacts, I'm of more potential use. Kill me or capture me, and there's little I can do. Let me go, and I'll continue to help."

Erik grinned. "Until you're feeling spiteful toward us?"

"The enemy of my enemy is my friend."

"Or another enemy."

Erik motioned to the door. "Fine. Go. But we're telling the ID all about you, and what they do is up to them. Keep that in mind next time you decide to show up here."

Barbu stood with a wheeze and walked over to open the door. "May we all get what we want in the end, Mr. Blackwell and Miss Lin, but not what we deserve."

"Next time, call ahead."

Barbu closed the door behind him.

"Should I attempt to follow him with drones?" Emma asked.

Erik shook his head. "Go ahead, but don't worry if he loses you. That old man has a lot of tricks up his sleeve."

"You sure about this?" Jia asked.

"Hell, no, but it's not the first time we've worked with someone shady to get the worse guy."

Jia inclined her head toward the door. "I'm not sure he's not the worse guy."

Erik chuckled. "Then we'll take down the Core and wait to see if he screws us over."

"And if he does?"

He shrugged, the concern leaching out of his mind. "Then we'll find out if he can survive a laser rifle to the head."

AUTHOR NOTES - MICHAEL ANDERLE

SEPTEMBER 18, 2020

Thank you so much for not only reading this latest book in the OPUS X story, but to these author notes in the back, as well.

So, it's now September 18th, 2020 and we are in production (pretty much finished) with book 10 in the series. Now, it goes over to our Audio partners, Dreamscape, for their production efforts so that we can release the book(s) and the audio at the same time.

Recently, I had a situation that required me to go see those nice people in the white (or blue) clothing and proceed to get placed into a machine that is very science-fictiony.

(I have to admit the experience in the machine was actually pretty damned cool. For a moment, I felt as if I was in the future.)

The results of my unexpected stay-cation was I got to come home with medicine that I have to take for a while. Now, I don't take any medicine (not even vitamins –

although I probably should start if they help) so my body hasn't been pleased.

I was griping to both Zen-Master Steve ™ and Lynne Stiegler (I feel like I need to give Lynne a super-hero name as well) that I felt worse days after visiting the people with the white coats than I did before I went for the stay-cation in the first place.

Stupid medicine.

Fortunately, my body is acclimating to the dreaded stuff and I'm not randomly dozing off in the middle of the day, now.

Las Vegas / Henderson is getting cooler now – it should be under a 100 degrees next week. Once it hits 99 for a high next Tuesday, it's only supposed to get back to a 100 one time for the foreseeable future.

WOOT!

I finally realized that the reason this summer has dragggged on and on with the heat is I've usually hit two different book conferences and been out of town during this time. I sure hope next year we get back to normal so I can escape the heat… Ooops, I mean go do book conferences for work.

No…no… I really mean escape the heat.

Wherever you are, and whatever you are doing, I hope the end of 2020 brings you happiness and opportunities.

Ad Aeternitatem,

Michael Anderle

BOOKS BY MICHAEL ANDERLE

For a complete list of books by Michael Anderle, please visit:

www.lmbpn.com/ma-books/

CONNECT WITH MICHAEL ANDERLE

Michael Anderle Social

Website:
http://www.lmbpn.com

Email List:
http://lmbpn.com/email/

Facebook Here:
https://www.facebook.com/groups/lmbpn.opusx/